BRACE
FOR
IMPACT

Books by
ANTHONY J. TATA

The Zara Sheridan Thrillers

Brace for Impact

The Captain Jake Mahegan Series

Foreign and Domestic
Three Minutes to Midnight
Besieged
Direct Fire
Dark Winter
Double Crossfire

The Garrett Sinclair Series

Chasing the Lion
Total Empire
The Phalanx Code

The Reaper Series (with Nicholas Irving)

Reaper: Ghost Target
Reaper: Threat Zero
Reaper: Drone Strike

The Threat Series

Sudden Threat
Rogue Threat
Hidden Threat
Mortal Threat

BRACE FOR IMPACT

ANTHONY J. TATA

KENSINGTON
PUBLISHING CORP.

kensingtonbooks.com

KENSINGTON BOOKS are published by

Kensington Publishing Corp.
900 Third Avenue
New York, NY 10022

All Kensington titles, imprints, and distributed lines are available at special quantity discounts for bulk purchases for sales promotion, premiums, fundraising, educational, or institutional use. Special book excerpts or customized printings can also be created to fit specific needs. For details, write or phone the office of the Kensington Special Sales Manager: Attn. Special Sales Department, Kensington Publishing Corp., 900 Third Avenue, New York, NY 10022. Phone: 1-800-221-2647.

Library of Congress Card Catalogue Number: 2025939715

KENSINGTON and the K with book logo Reg. U.S. Pat. & TM Off.

ISBN: 978-1-4967-5555-1
First Kensington Hardcover Edition: December 2025

ISBN: 978-1-4967-5559-9 (e-book)

10 9 8 7 6 5 4 3 2 1

Printed in the United States of America

The authorized representative in the EU for product safety and compliance
is eucomply OU, Parnu mnt 139b-14, Apt 123
Tallinn, Berlin 11317, hello@eucompliancepartner.com

In memory of Gary Austin, my best friend in life, and of Scott Miller, the Trident Media Group literary agent who took a chance on me and became my friend and mentor. Both left us this year well before their time. Rest in peace.

In the town they tell the story of the great pearl—how it was found and how it was lost again. They say that it was cursed and they know how it destroyed Kino and his family.
—John Steinbeck, *The Pearl*

PROLOGUE

MASTER SERGEANT ZARA SHERIDAN, US ARMY, MILITARY POLICE CORPS ROCK BATTALION

Kabul International Airport (KIA)
August 24, 2021

CHAOS UNFOLDED IN THE VALLEY BELOW HER UNIT'S SERIES OF checkpoints protecting the high-speed access roads into Kabul International Airport (KIA). Random gunfire and swarming mobs swirled around the US Air Force airplanes taking off at irregular but frequent intervals.

"Looks like something out of *World War Z*," Zara muttered under her breath as she watched the mobs swarm every fence line and gate of the relatively defenseless airport.

"Got that right, Sergeant Major," Zara's driver, Sergeant Laney Thibodeaux said. Thibodeaux was from Slidell, Louisiana, and had been Zara's driver for the yearlong deployment to Afghanistan.

"I'm not the sergeant major," Zara corrected.

"We know that, but damn sure ain't nobody else doing that job." Zara smiled. The actual command sergeant major had rede-

ployed early because of an illness and left her to serve as the senior enlisted advisor to the commander. Lieutenant Colonel
Aubrey Clementine was at the airport talking to the commander
of the 82nd Airborne Division about the mounting terrorist
threat to the operations at Kabul International Airport.

The staccato ping of machine-gun fire echoed throughout the
valley. It was impossible to determine friendly fire from that of an
adversary during this pell-mell rush to leave the country. As the
senior noncommissioned officer in charge of the 15th Military
Police Battalion, Zara had a responsibility to inspect the readi-
ness of her troops at multiple checkpoints throughout the Kabul
region. Her command vehicle had two radios stacked atop one
another. One was for communicating with her battalion commander and the other was for communicating with her subordinates. Two separate radios helped keep the chaos of small unit
tactics off the higher command channels, allowing for the pas-
sage of uninterrupted communications for situation updates and
spot reports.

A C-17 Globemaster airplane climbed into the sky above them
after taking off from KIA, no doubt filled with hundreds of Afghans who preferred anywhere in America to wherever they were
from in Afghanistan. The cargo plane banked high and to the
west as it crested one of the endless jagged mountain ranges that
defined this land.

"I hate airplanes," Zara said.

"Only way home," Thibodeaux reminded her.

"Put me on a boat," Zara chuckled.

"Scared?"

"Nah. Nothing much scares me, Tibs. I'm a North Carolina
girl. I grew up playing volleyball and riding around the state. Any
place worth going to you can get to in the car. That's my feeling."
After a pause, she smiled and said, "But yeah, it bothers me some
that everything's got to work right for it to fly. Nothing's ever one
hundred percent."

"Heard that, boss. But if we didn't have planes, we couldn't
have gotten to Afghanistan," Thibodeaux said.

"Exactly my point, Tibs. Exactly my point."

Their banter was interrupted by a call from the battalion commander.

"Rock 7, this is Rock 6," Clementine said over the radio.

Zara and Thibodeaux exchanged questioning glances.

"What's big boss want now?" Thibodeaux smirked.

Zara shrugged. She generally liked Clementine, who seemed to genuinely care about his troops and the mission. As the acting sergeant major, Zara carried the "7" suffix on her call sign while the commander was always referred to as "6." Rock was the unit motto dating back to World War II, where the military police unit held their outpost under intense assault from the Germans during a small-scale but fierce fight during Operation Overlord.

"Rock 6, this is Rock 7," Zara replied.

"Yeah, roger, Rock 7, this is Rock 6. I need you to gather up checkpoints three and four and meet me at Abbey Gate. It's about to get out of control."

"Roger that," Zara replied. She did a quick calculation in her mind. If she moved those two checkpoints, the entire highway to the north would be wide open for counterattack. She was sure that Clementine had considered that but needed to confirm.

"To be clear, Rock 6, that directive leaves Route Panda wide open," Zara said.

"Yes, roger that. Instructions are to move now. Situation is developing fast."

"Wilco. Moving now," Zara replied. The situation must have been dire for the commander to unplug a major roadblock guarding against counterattacking enemy forces. Likewise, the term "moving now" always meant something other than the directed unit was presently moving. Instructions had to be delivered, routes calculated, tactical measures assessed, and a host of other preparatory activities. Of all the contingencies they had planned for, moving to Abbey Gate had not been one of them. The airborne guys had been clear that they had control and wanted no competing interests or underlaps in communication.

Zara quickly barked her order to those two checkpoint commanders, who complied and began moving expeditiously to fall in behind Zara's vehicle.

"Follow me," she said into her radio handset.

Thibodeaux maneuvered the up-armored command Hummer through a series of switchbacks that put them on the valley floor headed toward the narrow alleys of Kabul that led to the eastern access point to KIA. She had six vehicles behind her and still didn't know her mission.

"Rock 6 this is Rock 7. Approaching destination. State mission and comms net I should be talking on," she said.

After a moment, Clementine replied.

"Mission is to kill or capture a suicide bomber. Intel reports that human intelligence indicates a suicide bomber is headed to one of the gates. We've shut down the other, but State Department won't let us close Abbey. Marines and paratroopers are at the gate, but there are thousands of Afghans pushing up against the checkpoint."

"Comms channel to talk to the gate so we don't shoot each other?" Zara repeated.

"Relay through me," Clementine said.

With the handset off and away from her mouth, she said to Thibodeaux, "That never works." Then with the handset on and to her mouth, she said, "Roger. My best advice is to close the gate, Rock 6. Let's get control of the situation," Zara said.

"That's what I advised, but the Pentagon wants the numbers. The more evacuees the better."

Thibodeaux turned the corner, and they were upon a large mob of Afghans pushing against one another for at least a half mile. The crowd reminded her of a rock concert mosh pit. Someone was probably getting trampled to death right now.

"We are at the backside of the crowd pushing on Abbey," Zara reported to Clementine. "Convey to the gate commander."

"Wilco. Get your vehicles all the way to the checkpoint to use as standoff," Clementine ordered. "Checkpoint commander knows you're inbound."

Thibodeaux and Zara exchanged knowing looks.

"We the buffer for the bomber?" Thibodeaux asked rhetorically.

"Mission over men," Zara muttered.

"That ain't like you, boss," Thibodeaux said.

"I wasn't talking about myself," she replied. "Push through this chaos and let's get there. Sometimes the mission is to protect the men."

Of course, she was referring to the "men" in the general sense, meaning all her troops. Zara didn't get wrapped around the axle of political correctness. She was a senior noncommissioned officer in the United States Army, and from her point of view, that alone meant progress was being made. The debate about accomplishing the mission or protecting the "men" dated as far back as her army training and was usually couched in terms of the commander having to decide in the face of formidable odds. If the mission was to take a heavily defended and fortified enemy position, was it worth the cost in lives lost to own the terrain at the end of the battle?

The answer was never clear, and too often she saw senior officers making bad decisions. She even sometimes wondered, was war ever worth it? She could do her duty, love her country, and still question the efficacy of war, especially when measured against the country's string of strategic failures following the costly but ultimately victorious World War II.

Thibodeaux started weaving the command vehicle through the dense crowd, angry and scared faces barking at them. She hit the police siren and light rack, causing a few to scatter, but the wall of people shrugged off the hulking command vehicle and the column of Hummers behind it. A few brave souls jumped on the hood until Thibodeaux slammed on the brakes, causing them to slide off.

Standing in the turret of the vehicle was Private First Class Jimmy Allen, from Long Island. He barked into the internal vehicle communications set, "Suspect one o'clock, moving fast."

"Do you have a shot?" Zara asked.

"Not without killing a bunch of people, and I could be wrong, but he looks right. I could do some warning shots high up."

Zara looked at the map. They were moving east to west directly toward the airport. Any stray rifle fire could hit US aircraft or personnel.

"Negative," Zara said. "Describe the suspect. I'll report to higher."

"Looks like every other person in the crowd. His robe blew open and I saw the suicide belt. It's him. Bearded dude, all the usual clothing. But a dark brown pakol with diamond-shaped embroidery. That's different. The diamond shapes. I know I saw a suicide vest. Maybe fifty meters to our front."

The checkpoint with the soldiers and marines was maybe one hundred meters away, and there were perhaps five thousand people in that expanse. The pakol was a trademark headwear of the Pashtun tribe, later adopted by the Northern Alliance and Ahmad Shah Massoud. It wasn't an indicator of friend or foe, but Allen was using it as a marker to track the suicide bomber.

"Rock 6, this is Rock 7, we've got eyes on the bomber. Male wearing white robe fifty meters from the checkpoint. Dark brown pakol on his head. Some kind of diamond-shaped pattern on the pakol. Close the checkpoint now! Tell the security team there to back up. I've seen this in Iraq. Close it!"

"We don't have permission!"

"Then beg forgiveness and do it anyway!" Zara shouted. She was bordering on insubordination but didn't want any American soldiers to die. Clementine had never deployed to combat and was inexperienced. Zara had served in Iraq, Syria, and Afghanistan. She'd seen more war than she ever cared to admit.

"Wait. They say a sniper has him. Sniper is taking the shot," Clementine said.

"He better hurry," Zara barked.

"Waiting on permission," Clementine replied.

"Get the Black Hornet up, Allen," Zara directed.

The Black Hornet was the smallest military reconnaissance drone. Allen lifted the device in the palm of his hand and let it fly. Zara looked in the display screen next to her command radios. The Black Hornet buzzed through the crowd and hovered directly over the suspected suicide bomber.

"Thermal," Zara said, directing Allen to switch from daylight to thermal camera.

The thermal showed rows of explosives wrapped around the man, who was now jogging toward Abbey Gate, perhaps spooked by the drone if he saw it or eager to accomplish his mission.

In her periphery, Zara noticed a group of Taliban soldiers with their black henna beards and dark eyeliner guarding perpendicular alleys into the main road to Abbey Gate. They stared at the column of American vehicles moving slowly through the throng.

"Allen, provide me overwatch. I'm going after this guy on foot."

"Roger that," Allen said.

"Sergeant Major, NFW!" Thibodeaux said.

"Only way," Zara said.

She said into the battalion communications channel, "Bentley, meet me at my vehicle now."

Carson Bentley was a former college linebacker from Georgia and was riding in the vehicle behind Zara's. The biggest man in the battalion, Bentley would be a good wedge breaker to help her chase down the suspect. She grabbed her M4 carbine from its muzzle down position next to her seat and patted her holster, registering the presence of her 9mm Beretta pistol. "I'm up on our internal comms."

She pushed out of the vehicle, having to knock down three men thrusting forward through the logjam. Bentley was right there, doing what he knew his boss wanted him to do. He was shoving through the crowd, opening a hole. She used her height and heft to push through the crowd that tried to fill in his wake. She grabbed onto his load-bearing vest to prevent separation in the melee.

"I'm following you, Bentley. Brown pakol with diamond-shaped brim. The guy is to your ten o'clock maybe twenty meters away. Possible suicide vest. Black Hornet confirmed."

"Roger that."

To her gunner over the internal communications, she said, "Vector us, Allen. You can see above the crowd."

8 ANTHONY J. TATA

"You guys are closing in on him. Thirty meters. He's got that brown pakol on. That's the only thing different."

The shouts in the street were deafening. Thibodeaux was beeping the vehicle's horn, the lights were spinning, and the sirens were blaring. Still, the throng was a single living organism moving in a solid mass toward the gate.

There, Zara thought. At six feet tall, she towered over most Afghans. She thought she saw the brown pakol and the distant stare that all suicide bombers seemed to carry.

"There, to the left, Bentley!"

"Got him," Bentley said. He was sawing his way through the crowd. They were closing in. The smell of body odor, piss, and feces was overwhelming.

Allen reported, "Ten meters, Sergeant. But he's closing on the gate. He's running now!"

Zara let go of Bentley and pushed through the crowd. She saw the soldiers and marines processing Afghans at the gate. Saw the brown-hatted man moving swiftly.

Why haven't they shut the gate, damn it!

"You're close," Allen said. "Be care—"

That an individual could carry enough explosives to kill and maim hundreds of people had always been a mystery to Zara. She felt the blast immediately. Saw the orange and black fire lick forward, away from her, spitting nails and ball bearings at her comrades in arms. Still, the wall of Afghans between her and the bomber fell like a musket line hit by cannon fire. She and Bentley were knocked backward into the wall of an adobe building lining the street.

Her head hit the dirt street, and she smelled the blood and spent gunpowder. Her mind wafted, desperately trying to stay present in the moment, but the task was too difficult. She caught a glimpse of Bentley, blood streaming from his head.

And then she went blank there amid the chaos.

CHAPTER ONE

LUCAS SHERIDAN

Swan Quarter, North Carolina
Present Day

THE SEARING HEAT FROM THE EXPLOSION IN THE SKY CAUSED fourteen-year-old Lucas Sheridan's skin to prickle.

The military jet pinwheeled from the clouds and ripped through the woods and swamp to his front. It tumbled and screeched and burned until there was no noise at all, as if the marsh had swallowed it whole. Not even the gators and bears that populated this path through North Carolina's Inner Banks stirred, perhaps stunned by the manmade contraption that plummeted into their habitat.

Lucas's first instinct was to haul ass in the opposite direction, but his mom had always told him, "You may be a little man, but you can make a big difference." In truth, a growth spurt sent Lucas to a rangy five foot nine already and he was no longer his mother's "little man," even if she still called him that. He lifted weights and ran sprints every day to become better at his beloved baseball and felt he was becoming a prime athlete.

Now, he wondered if someone was injured and might need help. Surely there was a pilot in the airplane, if not two. He didn't know. He balanced his Louisville Slugger over his shoulder with the backstrap of his Rawlings infielder glove cinched tight on the fat end of the thirty-two-inch bat. Then he feverishly pedaled down the trail, managing the chattering handlebars of his Reaper mountain bike with one hand. The erupting fireball maybe two hundred yards away caused him to skid to a stop and open his mouth in a giant O.

"Oh, my God," he whispered to himself. Flames licked at the sky and settled into a burning pile of black smoke. An aftershock of heat rushed past him like a sonic boom.

Urged on by his retired army sergeant mom's altruism, Lucas doubled his effort to get to the crash site. On a normal day, with both his parents working and barely speaking, Lucas enjoyed riding his bike through the game reserve and exploring for snakes and shark teeth, both of which he found in abundance.

But today was different. There was no joy in watching the wreckage burn and wondering if someone might be inside the debris field.

The heat from the fire licked at his face as he bore through the wafting smoke. An acrid stink filled his nostrils when he laid his bike in the tall grass next to a large hunk of smoking metal. He took a few steps, stumbled, dropped his bat, hit his head, and rolled to the ground. He felt like he did that time he collided with that fat catcher from Swan Quarter when he was trying to leg out an inside-the-park home run.

A secondary explosion maybe a football field to his front made him crab walk back until he was pressed into something made of glass. He'd been to enough air shows at Cherry Point Marine Corps Air Station across the Pamlico and Neuse Rivers to know he was staring at the mangled remains of a pilot's cockpit in some kind of fighter jet. A seat belt and headrest were next to the split open metal of what he would call a dashboard. It was dotted with buttons and small globes that probably covered lights. Before taking the Swan Quarter Ferry maintenance chief job, his dad had been the head of maintenance at Fort Bragg and had taught him all about indicator lights that would switch on when the operator was supposed to take some kind of action.

Hanging from the cracked dashboard were some wires with a small orange rectangle on each end. Lucas studied these and saw "Classified" printed in black letters on the side of each rectangle. "Code Word" was displayed on the opposite side of the devices. He held the two pieces in each hand and saw that they fit together if properly mated. Beneath the "Code Word" markings was the word "TYRANT."

Lucas knew a little bit about classified material. One day when in his mom's military police office at Fort Bragg, he had asked, "What's that, Moms?" as he pointed at a document folder that said "Secret."

"Just an empty classified folder," his mom said, holding up the manila folder. "If there was something in here," she joked, "I'd have to turn you over to my MPs. They'd lock you up real tight." After a moment, she smiled, rubbed her chin, and said, "Now that sounds like a good idea." Even though Lucas knew his army master sergeant mom was kidding, the thought of the military police and classified documents scared him at the time.

Now he was staring at the classified equipment that was on a fighter jet, and he knew his parents, especially his mom, would want him to try and do the right thing. They had always told him about the importance of protecting government secrets, because "if the bad guys get them, bad things happen to soldiers like us in war."

He looked up at the hazy, late afternoon sky, smoke floating like a lingering ghost, and wondered what happened to the pilot. He hadn't seen any parachute when he had noticed the plane whistling to the ground. And thank God, he didn't see a dead body in the mangled cockpit seat to his front. That would freak him out. He searched a small circle around the husk of the cockpit and couldn't find any sign of life—or death—in his immediate vicinity. He figured it wouldn't be long before scavengers came to loot the airplane and they might not have the same sense of nobility when it came to protecting secret government information.

He decided to secure the small rectangular housings marked "Classified/Code Word." Each was the size of his thumb, like a flash drive. He detached the first one and then the next by pressing on the orange rubberized material covering the storage drives. Each detached easy enough, as they were seated in a coupling designed to allow for removal. At Fort Bragg, Lucas's father had let him watch diagnostics tests on vehicle engines by plugging a similar-looking gadget into a receiver in the vehicle electrical system. He didn't remember any of them being classified, but that would make sense because his father had a top secret clearance and of course he didn't.

His baseball pants had a hole in the back pocket from too many butt slides. His coach was working with him on the headfirst technique, but his mom didn't want him diving into another player's legs for fear of Lucas breaking his neck. He held the two sections in the palm of his hand and wondered how best to protect them. Looking at his bat and glove, he had an idea. He loved baseball so much that he slept with his glove next to him and even took it to school. There was no separating Lucas and his glove.

He rammed one device into the slot for his index finger and one into the slot for his pinky, those two being the least used of the five finger holes in his glove and therefore the tightest fits.

As he was making sure the devices were snug, a buzzing noise caught his ear. From living at Fort Bragg, he knew the sound of a helicopter when he heard it. He scampered into the wood line as the helicopter passed over him and swooped around again, landing about two hundred yards away. He could name most of the army helicopters like the Blackhawk, Chinook, and Apache. He liked them mostly because of the Native American names and he enjoyed reading history, especially about the indigenous people of North Carolina like the Lumbee and Croatan Indians. His "Moms" was part Croatan, descending from the earliest known Native American tribes in what became North Carolina. This helicopter wasn't anything he recognized, though. It was painted tan and had a circular ducted fan at the back. He had seen those in movies but not on any military base. On the side, he saw what looked like a giant painted snake's mouth with the fangs prominently displayed. He recognized the logo as that of a local private military contractor called Copperhead, Incorporated.

Two men jumped out of the side cargo doors. They held rifles attached to tactical vests by three-point slings as they scouted the area, looking left and right, before giving a thumbs-up sign to another person, who jumped out. He was tall and thick, having to duck beneath the whipping blades of the chopper. The three men walked to what he guessed was the main wreckage of the jet and began poking around as if they were looking for something.

Maybe they were a team sent to retrieve any classified materials before scavengers could pick the site clean?

As Lucas was thinking this, he heard another helicopter buzz low and saw that it was the kind he recognized, a Blackhawk, but painted with US Coast Guard white-and-red paint, which meant it was probably out of nearby Elizabeth City's coast guard base. As it began to hover, the men on the ground aimed their rifles at the chopper and began firing.

Why would they be doing this? Lucas wondered. And then he realized *they* were the scavengers, not the good guys.

The coast guard helicopter banked away, its right engine bursting into flames and leaving a smoking trail on its egress. Lucas decided then to run the other way. He carefully lifted his bike from the tall grass, crouching low as he pushed it back toward the trail he took home every day. The smoking helicopter flew directly over him, causing the men on the ground to look in his direction. He tried to blend into the tall grass and trees, but he thought one of them might have seen him as he pedaled away on the trail. While he knew he could outrace them on his bike, he also knew he couldn't outrun a rifle bullet.

Still, he dodged and darted his way through the brush. Shots whistled overhead, snapping tree branches. He didn't know if they were shooting at him or the distressed chopper. Returning to the main trail he had left before finding the jet wreckage, he pedaled as fast as he could, as if he were stealing second base a million times over.

A buzzing noise seemed to be following him, but sometimes the Inner Banks did that. It buzzed. Buzzed with insects, reptiles, birds, and mammals all sounding off in an electric symphony.

Still, Lucas kept looking over his shoulder and couldn't see anything. Maybe his ears were just ringing from the explosions and gunshots? Racing into his driveway after what seemed like a lifetime but was only twenty minutes max, he saw his mom standing outside her car next to a suitcase as she argued with his father.

Unaware that Lucas had approached from the trail in the backyard, they were shouting at each other. Lonnie Sheridan, his father, was a physically imposing man, over six and a half feet tall, broad-shouldered, and physically fit. He had played football at Morehead State, joined the army after 9/11, and met his mother, who was graduating from Fayetteville State University. They both rose through the ranks and retired as master sergeants at twenty years, vowing to slow down the pace and provide a more wholesome life for Lucas in Eastern North Carolina, where his mother was born and raised.

"I can't do this anymore, Zara. I'm done!" his father said, who was halfway in his Ford F-150 pickup truck with one booted foot on the ground and the other in the well of the driver's compartment. He was wearing his standard-issue NCDOT Ferry uniform of short sleeve khaki shirt and blue jeans. "We were supposed to retire, for Christ's sake! And now you're off traveling the world . . . without me! At least I'm local!"

"I have to go do this job!" his mother said. "I'm doing the best I can!"

"Well, I have to go do mine. There's a ferry accident in the middle of the river."

"Fine. Lucas can take care of himself until you get home," she said.

His mom checked her watch with a worried glance. He typically would have already been home from baseball practice.

"I have no idea what time that will be. Why did you have to take this job that takes you away from home?"

"That's not fair," she said in a hoarse voice.

"It's more than fair. We agreed on retirement. We agreed on putting family first. And now this . . . this air marshal gig? I thought you were just taking some admin job with Sharpstone or Copperhead!"

"You know I'm no admin, goddamn it! No more than you are!"

His parents had been fighting a lot lately, even sleeping in separate bedrooms frequently. He loved them both with all his heart. They had been through so much together. From the time he was three until he was seven years old, one of them had been constantly deployed to combat in Afghanistan, Iraq, or Syria. The stress had been high, but they had made it to the twenty-year military retirement mark. The problem was, he guessed, that neither was truly retired. With the economy in trouble, they both held steady jobs to make ends meet and provide a standard of living they thought Lucas deserved. He wished there was something he could do to help the situation and blamed himself. Maybe if it weren't for him, they might have stayed in the army and made command sergeant major or general or whatever rank was best for them.

As it was, he mostly kept to himself, made sure he didn't place too many demands on his parents, and tried to help where he could. He understood they loved him, but he hated watching them fight. His only two real requests were for some computer equipment and the chance to keep playing baseball. That seemed totally reasonable.

He watched his father storm off in his truck, the tires spitting gravel as he sped to Swan Quarter Ferry landing to manage whatever accident had occurred.

His mother stood there, watching him drive away, and put her face in her hands, sobbing. Her phone rang and she wiped at her eyes, took a deep breath, and stood up straight before answering.

His mom, retired Master Sergeant Zara Sheridan, was a tall, fit woman, having played volleyball at Fayetteville State University before meeting Lucas's dad at Fort Bragg, where she joined the army, after which they were married. She was the daughter of the highly respected former 82nd Airborne Division Command Sergeant Major Lincoln White, who had conducted combat jumps into Grenada, Iraq, and Afghanistan. Lucas's grandparents lived in Edenton, North Carolina, about an hour away from Swan Quarter.

"I'm leaving now," Zara said into the phone, her voice finding its footing. She lifted her suitcase into the hatch of their Toyota 4Runner. "Taiwan? First flight? Yes. Okay, that's what I understood from the first call. Got it."

"Moms! Moms!" Lucas shouted.

Zara turned and saw her son and held up a finger, as if to say, "Just a second." Her furrowed brow and rushed movements told Lucas he might not have much time.

"Moms! Moms!" Lucas shouted again, tugging at her blazer.

"Raleigh is three hours away, and if I leave right now, I'll make the flight," she said. After a pause: "Understand. They'll hold it for me if necessary."

Keeping the phone held to her ear, Zara shrugged off her blazer, tossed it into the passenger seat, and stepped into the driver's seat of the Toyota.

"Roger, I'm on my way," she said.

Lucas scrambled to the driver's side of the truck. "Moms! I really need to talk to you! An airplane crashed and a helicopter was shot at and there's bad guys with rifles!"

"No. No. It's my son. He's always excited about everything. Probably some video game he's reached a new level on," Zara said. She started the engine and began to close the door when she saw Lucas still standing there. She shook her head and formed "sorry" with her lips and then said to her boss, on the other end of the phone, "Can you send me any intel so I can study up on the plane? I've never been to Taipei."

Frustrated, Lucas spotted his mom's blazer in the passenger seat and had an idea. He ran around to the passenger side of the SUV, dropped his bat, snagged his glove, fished out one of the classified devices, and slipped it into the pocket of her blazer. That would make his mom talk to him, which usually wasn't an issue. As he was digging for the second piece, it was stuck way too far down the index finger slot of his glove for him to retrieve in a timely fashion.

"Lucas, dear, my blazer, son. I'm late for the airport and I've got an intel briefing happening in two minutes about this flight. I'll call your dad, and we can talk once I'm settled, but Mama's gotta go to work. Love you," she said. She ran around the vehicle and gave him a quick hug.

Lucas tossed his mom's coat in the seat of the vehicle, hugged her back, and muttered, "Love you, too."

As his mom's SUV pulled away, the buzzing noise returned, and Lucas thought he saw a drone banking away behind the tree line.

But maybe not, because that would be weird.

CHAPTER TWO

ZARA SHERIDAN

*D*URING THE DRIVE, ZARA FELT THE CRUSHING WEIGHT OF HER MARital discord with Lonnie coupled with her failure at Abbey Gate, which continued to gnaw at her psyche.

Could she have done more? Acted more quickly? Taken a shot in the crowd? Even if she had wounded a few innocents, it would have been better than the resulting thirteen dead US military personnel and dozens of others with grievous wounds. Hundreds of Afghans attempting to reach the gate were brutally slaughtered, too.

Her wounds, minor compared to others, were a constant reminder of her failure. Two scars ran along her left jawline, offset like a single lightning bolt. She would absently run her hand along the slightly raised welts when deep in thought. As if the wounds had opened a portal to an inner sanctum of truth and understanding, helping her realize her priorities.

She'd suffered traumatic brain injury, as well, but seemed to have shaken that off, or so she had convinced her doctors. On a pragmatic level, she understood that the Abbey Gate bombing was not her fault, but the soldier in her felt the pain of every killed and wounded soldier and marine.

The fighting with Lonnie was related, for sure. She'd retired from the army shortly after the action in Afghanistan, forcing his hand to do the same. The resentment was palpable, and she wondered if they would stay together. Add to that the sorrow she felt about leaving Lucas or, for that matter, not even listening to what her son had wanted to tell her, and she had a hat trick of guilt consuming her.

But she convinced herself that she'd been so bewildered from the fight with Lonnie, and in a such a rush to get to Raleigh-Durham Airport, she could excuse her treatment of Lucas.

"What are you talking about?" she whispered to herself. "There's no excuse for ignoring your son." She pounded the steering wheel, caught between the triple vector of Lonnie's anger, job pressure, and simply loving her kid.

She knew that loving your kid always came first. So, why didn't it? Why did adult matters seem to pass like a dark cloud over even the smallest moments? Had she even kissed Lucas on the cheek before leaving? She didn't think so. Not that at fourteen years old he wouldn't have turned away, but still.

The jumble of confused thoughts and emotions translated into a choppy synchronization of her last-minute tasking to co-marshal the maiden voyage of TransPac Airlines from the Research Triangle region of North Carolina to the tech heavy city of Taipei, Taiwan. Family and work were always a challenge for any parent, but she had vowed to spend more time with Lucas when she retired from the army. Mostly, she had been successful, but this new gig as a US federal air marshal seemed both exciting and challenging. Truthfully, she had missed the rush of combat and mission focus from her army days.

But she had missed so many birthdays and baseball games from Lucas's childhood, and her teenager would be in college before she knew it.

Nonetheless, during the three-hour drive, she had a long conversation with Lindy Van Horn, the operations chief of the Charlotte, North Carolina, Federal Air Marshal Service office. Lindy had walked her through the passenger list, the crew, and the fact that she was replacing long-serving Air Marshal Arnold Winston, who had been diagnosed with the flu an hour before she got the call. She would be the deputy in charge behind another tenured Federal Air Marshal, Lloyd Bucknell.

She didn't know Bucknell, and Lindy had only said, "He's steady. Punches the clock. No emotion. Gets the job done."

Unremarkable, she thought, which was good.

Zara made it to Raleigh-Durham Airport in time to park in premium, hoping it would be reimbursed by the stingy government. She hooked a left in the main terminal and then snaked her way through the throngs of people to the private marshal's security screening area, which was near the often-vacant offices at the far end of the terminal.

Her heart froze when the door was locked. Was she too late? She glanced over her shoulder at the lengthy line of passengers at the main security checkpoint nearly half a football field away. She could cut to the front of the line, but that would identify her as a marshal to any potential passengers on her flight, and novice TSA agents sometimes didn't know what to make of her pistol and ammunition. She preferred to remain as anonymous as possible. As a mixed-race woman, the most frequent take she received were comments about her beauty, not the fact that she was six feet tall. But still, she stood out if someone caused a scene.

The door flew open and a large balding man in a Transportation Security Administration hat was smiling at her. Bold yellow letters that read "TSA" screamed from the blue hat.

"Was just about to close. You're Sheridan, with the marshals?" he asked.

"That's me," she replied.

"Bucknell was looking for you, but he got tired of waiting and already boarded."

She stepped into the room, which was outfitted with a millimeter wave scanner, the type where a passenger steps into and lifts her arms, and a computed tomography scanner for luggage and bags. The TSA agent closed and locked the door.

It wasn't the scanner and X-ray that caught her attention, though. His eyes were more intrusive and assessing than any equipment could ever be.

"Like what you see?" she snapped.

He looked toward the back door that led to the air side terminal, his tongue running along his bottom lip as he did so.

"Let's get you going," he said. "Name's Clark."

Clark had broad shoulders, a shaved head, and tattoo sleeves up both arms. Though he wore a TSA hat, he had a black polo shirt on. On the upper left breast was the logo "Copperhead Security." The stem of the two *P*s were snake fangs protruding from a muted outline of a copperhead snake's open mouth ready to strike. She knew Copperhead but had never seen this individual. Their headquarters was in northeastern North Carolina not far from Swan Quarter. They had a lingering notorious reputation from the wars of the last two and a half decades.

"Roger that," she said.

She placed her bag, pistol, ammo, and blazer on the conveyor belt for the CT X-ray.

"What's this?" Clark asked, lifting her blazer.

"A blazer," she snapped. "I'm in a rush here."

"Darling, I'm talking about the classified flash drive in your pocket."

Zara wrinkled her brow and said, "No idea what you're talking about." After a pause, she added, "Clark."

He held up an orange device the size of his thumb.

"Can't be carrying classified material unsecured," he said, holding it so she could see. "Says 'Classified/Code Word' right here."

Thinking quickly, she said, "Yes, it's secured in my coat pocket."

"Has to be in a briefcase. This is loose. I can't let it on," he replied, tensing up.

"It's mine," she replied.

"You didn't even know it was there," he replied.

She couldn't really argue with Clark's point as her mind spun to how it got there. Her husband? Then it hit her. Lucas had grabbed her blazer. He was trying to tell her something. Had he put the classified device in her coat pocket?

"I did. I was going to stow it in my bag," she said, reaching for it.

He pulled his hand away.

"Best I can do is lock this up for you and you can get it when you return," he said. "It's my call what gets on the plane. This is suspicious, and you didn't know it was there. A terrorist could have put it in your pocket."

She smiled lightly at the prospect of Lucas being a "terrorist."

"Something funny, Marshal?"

"Nothing. I'm just in a rush. You're going to let me take my Sig but not my flash drive?" Her Sig was her Sig Sauer P229 pistol, one of the four standard carry options for federal air marshals.

"Your Sig and ammo are authorized on the manifest. I'm going to secure this flash drive in that bank of lockers over there, give you the key, and you can get it when you return."

No harm in that, she thought. In a sense, he was right. She had no idea what the device was or how it got into her pocket. Zara couldn't argue with his logic. She watched him open a small locker that looked more like a safe deposit box and place the item inside. He closed the door, turned the key, and then handed it to her.

"Place it on a key ring. There's a master, but I'll have to charge you a hundred bucks to make a new one, darling."

"Seriously, you're a pain in the ass," she said. "And I'm not your darling."

He puffed up and smiled.

"You could be though," he said, winking. "We'd have fun."

She held up her wedding band on her left hand. He shrugged. "Never bothered me much."

"Right," she said. "I figured."

She shook her head, then gathered her blazer, pistol, and luggage, put it all back together, then merged from the private screening area into the general population air side. She was beelining through the general boarding area when she checked her phone, which had a litany of texts from Lucas, most of which read:

Mom! Check your pocket. That thing is important!!!

Zara texted back: What is it?

Lucas: Jet crashed. It's classified.

She stared at her phone. Looked at the key in her pocket and glanced back at the door she had just walked through. She walked quickly back to the private screening room and knocked on the secured door.

Clark opened it, smiled, and said, "I knew you'd be back, darling."

"I think I left something in the X-ray," she said with a smile, playing along as much as she could stomach.

He let her back in and then locked the door behind her. He walked over and checked the locked entrance. It was just the two of them.

"I get it all the time," Clark said. "Female marshals are just attracted to me."

She cringed, but smiled and said, "I can see that."

He was a big man, maybe 225 pounds and five foot eleven. Stocky, layers of muscle, but soft around the edges with some fat. Zara maintained a strenuous training regimen and practiced Krav Maga three days a week.

Clark stepped toward her, evidently wishing to seize the moment before it passed. Zara relaxed and welcomed him, understanding there were cameras that would review every moment. She pressed the record button of her iPhone for backup.

"I just need what you took from me," she said.

"Oh, I'm going to take what I want," he replied, lifting his hand toward her face.

"No. Please don't," she said loud enough for the iPhone.

He smiled. "You mean, 'Don't.' 'Stop.' 'Don't stop'?"

"No, I mean, please don't touch me."

As he stepped into her, she rifled her elbow into his larynx and her knee into his groin, something the cameras would show as a completely self-defensive move. As he doubled over from the pain, she laced her fingers over his head and brought her knee into his face, smashing his nose. She danced sideways to avoid as much of the blood as possible, but there was still some spatter on her black pants leg.

A solid blow to the back of his head knocked him unconscious. She lifted and dragged his dead weight to a chair and arranged his body so that he was sitting with his arms folded over a table and his forehead was nestled on his forearms. She took a step back, cocked her head, and said, "Sleeping."

Zara used the key to open the locker, grabbed the device Lucas had put in her pocket, and then debated internally whether she wanted her defensive actions on video or whether it would be best to delete it altogether. She sat at the video CCTV device, saw that she *couldn't* delete the video, and muttered, "That settles that." She quickly left through the private screening area to the air side again and hustled to her gate. On the way, she glanced at the flash drive and wondered what the word TYRANT might mean. Was it a classified code word defense program? If so, she was holding something extremely sensitive and valuable.

Boarding the plane, she stowed her bag above business-class aisle pod 11B and stepped aside, nudging the Sig Sauer 9mm pistol beneath her blazer. Her row was the last in business class, separated from economy by a galley. As she turned around, she accidentally clipped the shoulder of a broad-shouldered Asian man dressed in a gray suit with a white shirt and coral Hermes tie.

"Excuse me," she said.

The man didn't budge.

"My apologies," the man said. His English was inflected with a heavy Chinese or Taiwanese accent.

"No problem," Zara said.

They locked eyes. His were flat gray, like his suit. He was tall, strong, and crisply outfitted in an Italian ensemble with lapel stitching. He carried a two-thousand-dollar leather Von Baer briefcase. She stepped to the side and watched him walk toward the first-class cabin. He disappeared toward the nose of the airplane and then reappeared on the opposite side of the aircraft. He stowed a bag in the overhead bin and settled into his luxury seat.

She found herself judging him and checked herself. On second thought, judging had been part of her job in combat and perhaps it was here, too. It was her job to question the intentions of every single passenger, she reminded herself.

There were no good guys. Only neutral or bad.

On leave of absence from Sharpstone Global Security, Zara was filling a void in the Federal Air Marshal Service. With the world on fire in Europe, the Middle East, and the Pacific Rim, President Kim Campbell had ordered the Transportation Security Administration to rapidly recruit, train, and deploy former military personnel as air marshals and employ them in a higher percentage of domestic and international flights. Zara's combat skills and experience were what the TSA needed. She breezed through the training and even learned some new tricks such as tubular tactics, as the air marshal pros called them. While determining friend or foe was never a sure thing when on the battlefield, it was infinitely harder on a planeload—the tube—of three hundred passengers. And if all else failed, in Afghanistan or Iraq, you could typically figure it out once they started shooting at you.

But on an airplane, that would be too late.

She walked to the cockpit to introduce herself to the pilots, attempting to be as inconspicuous as possible. A tall man in first class caught her glance and stood, cutting her off in the stew galley.

"Sheridan?" the tall man asked. He was dressed in a navy blue suit with thin gray pinstripes. He was at least six four, as Zara in her practical pumps stood at six two. He had thinning hair that was combed in wisps across his balding pate. He didn't appear particularly muscular, but was perhaps wiry, Zara assessed. He looked like any businessman flying first class to anywhere in the world. Other than his height, he was nondescript.

"Bucknell?" she replied.

"Glad you made it. Damn shame about Winston coming down with the flu, but he's going to be okay."

"Roger that."

"Let's get moving," Bucknell said. He rapped on the cockpit door, which was partially open.

"Captain Prescott and copilot Monroe? This is the backup. Sheridan. She's in business. I'm in first."

The two pilots were busy doing preflight, spinning dials, running through checklists, and chatting through the headset mouthpieces.

Prescott had shaved his head with a still visible hairline that suggested balding. He had one earpiece covering his left ear and the other perched on his temple so he could hear Monroe. He had a warm smile and greeted Zara with a "Hey, Marshal. Just another milk run, right?"

"That's the plan," she said.

"Marshal, great to meet you. Understand this is your maiden voyage?" Monroe said. Monroe had a shock of graying blond hair. He seemed older than Prescott, but Lindy Van Horn had told her that Monroe recently retired as a colonel from the US Air Force working in the Next Generation Air Dominance fighter program. Prescott, she had told her, was a former naval aviator.

"I told them this was your first flight when Winston went down with the flu and we got you as a replacement," Bucknell said.

"Gotta start somewhere," Zara said. "Understand this is a joint operation. Navy, air force, and army."

"Yep. We checked you out. Lucky us," Prescott said. "Silver star in Afghanistan? I think we'll be safe."

Zara didn't like talking about the combat that had resulted in her being awarded a silver star, which was for conspicuous gallantry on the battlefield, right behind the medal of honor and distinguished service cross. She felt like an utter failure for not having stopped the suicide bomber at Abbey Gate.

"Well, you hang around long enough and you get some awards," she said, deflecting the compliment.

"Maybe the other ones, but not the silver star," Monroe said.

"Anywho," Bucknell interrupted. "We need to get situated."

Bucknell's interruption put a hard break in Zara's rapport building with the pilots. She couldn't quite put her finger on it, but it bothered her. She considered it very similar to military officers or senior noncommissioned officers who wanted to control the situation and didn't trust their subordinates enough to grow and learn.

"Great to meet you guys. Hope we don't talk until Taipei," Zara said.

"Indeed," Prescott replied. They both turned around and went about their preflight business.

As they stepped out of the entry to the cockpit, Bucknell said, "This is Marcus and Amanda, the cabin chief and his number two."

Standing before her was a tall black man who wore John Lennon glasses. He was older and spoke with an Eastern North Carolina accent.

"Nice to meet you, Ms. Sheridan."

"Likewise, Marcus. And please call me Zara."

"Zara," Amanda said. Amanda was a sturdy woman who appeared to have an ancestry of European and Asian mix.

"I'm in first class and Zara is in business."

"Understand," Marcus said. "Let us get everyone boarded and then maybe we can chat. We've done the preflight brief with the team, but we understand why you were running late as a last-minute replacement. We're at full crew right now, but once we take off, we'll be taking shifts. And we've got an extra pilot above."

Marcus's eyes flitted upward when he said, "Above." Zara knew there was a pilot crew rest area above the first-class cabin on the Boeing 777-300ER. Likewise, above the business class was a small cabin where crew could rest. Both compartments had beds and chairs that the pilots and crew could use to rest before starting the next shift.

"Sounds good," Zara said, then looked at Bucknell.

"Yes. Please go about your business. Marshal Sheridan and I will go over a few notes."

They moved to the far end of the galley where the service truck had just finished loading the provisions for the flight and closed the starboard door.

"I'm assuming you know the plane. I reviewed your tactical assessments from HQ. Impressive. If we get into any kind of situation, you come to the front and cover the port side. I'm on the starboard side over here. I've reviewed the manifest. Nothing really stands out. I got notice from Lindy Van Horn that she prepped you during your drive to Raleigh. We've got VPN communications inside the aircraft. Should be on your tablet and phone." He paused, the last sentence a question.

"Roger," Zara said. She pulled out her iPad tablet and opened the screen, sending a "Test" text to Bucknell. His phone didn't make a sound, but the text was there when he showed it to her, holding the screen face out.

"We're up on comms. Any questions?"

"Besides us, are there any weapon carriers onboard?" Zara asked. It was common practice for all people authorized to have weapons onboard an aircraft to know who else has a weapon. Zara had images of memes of several characters dressed like the cartoon character Spiderman, all pointing a weapon at one another, and each labeled as FBI, CIA, DIA, DHS, etc. The point being that to avoid friendly fire, it was best to have situational awareness of all weapons on board.

"Just you and me," Bucknell said. Then he added with a smile, "That I know of."

A rare joke from the straitlaced career air marshal?

"I've got a Sig 229. You?"

He replied, "Same. 229."

Standard-issue pistols for the federal air marshals were Sig Sauer or Glock, depending upon the marshal's preference.

"Sounds good."

"They are about finished with boarding, so let's get to our seats."

"Roger that," Zara said. She filed in with the flow of passengers trickling in and found her seat in business class.

"Something to drink?" the flight attendant asked her. She was midthirties, thin, and had a serious demeanor as she stared at the bulge in her blazer.

"No, thank you, *Priscilla*," she said, reading the attendant's name tag.

She nodded, paused, and said, "Hopefully no need for you today."

"Just another milk run," she mused.

Priscilla offered a tight smile and whirled as a few passengers dodged her in the aisle. Zara looked at her satellite-enabled and encrypted phone with enhanced Federal Air Marshal Communications Service, FAMSCOM, which had video, voice, and texting features. It was the device she had just tested with Bucknell. She typed and sent the message:

> Passengers boarding. Link up with Bucknell and pilots complete.

Lindy Van Horn in the Charlotte office responded.

> Roger.

The message indicator began bubbling as Zara held the tablet.

> Hyperion X crash in Hyde County, North Carolina. Pilot ejected. FYI.

Hyde County was her home in North Carolina's Inner Banks. She did a quick Google search on her phone and learned that the Hyperion X was the frontrunner to replace the F-35 fighter jet, one of the most expensive pieces of military equipment in the budget.

Was this what Lucas was talking about?

> Location? she typed.

> Swan Quarter swampy area. Coast guard reports shots fired when searching.

Shots fired? Zara thought of Lucas and touched the breast pocket of her coat that held the device she had retrieved from "Clark." Had Lucas been shot at? Was he in danger?

Zara, tired of the texting, called Lindy as the passengers continued filling first- and business-class seats.

"Talk to me," she said.

"All we know right now, Zara."

"Is the cipher secure?" She retrieved the orange device and stared at it.

"Don't think the plane is secure," she said. "So that would be a no."

Zara thought for a minute about the rubberized flash drive she had in her blazer pocket.

"Does the term 'TYRANT' mean anything to you?"

Static masked the conversation for a moment, and then Van Horn said, "No."

"Okay, well, you might ought to get a team up there," Zara said.

"Already on it. We're calling in Sharpstone to help. They have a fixed wing spooling up at Moore County Airport. Van Dreeves, Hobart, and Mahegan will be the go team . . . if there is a go team. Rumors that Copperhead took some shots at the coast guard coming in to secure the site."

Zara remained silent. She was jealous. Her brief stint with Garrett Sinclair's global security company, Sharpstone, replicated the type of adrenaline rush she had become accustomed to in combat. Zara's father had been Sinclair's command sergeant major at one time, hence the connection. When Zara decided to retire and slow down the pace to spend more time with Lucas, Sharpstone was looking for an operations chief that required limited to no travel. Van Dreeves was a friend and talented operator, as were Joe Hobart and Jake Mahegan. Hobart, Van Dreeves, and Mahegan all served in special mission units together and had been pulled into Sharpstone. Embedded in Sharpstone was a subunit called Dagger, which was a presidential response team. There was some speculation now that they were all out of the service that President Campbell had maintained her retired friend General Garrett Sinclair's services in a private capacity.

The job had been a perfect fit until Sinclair's friend in the Department of Justice contacted Sinclair asking who his best shooter might be. The Federal Air Marshal Service had already contracted with Sharpstone to conduct passenger background checks, provide security when manpower was lacking, and to conduct special tasks not related to being on the airplane, which was the exclusive preserve of the Federal Air Marshal Service.

Indeed, Zara was the best pistol marksman on the team. Hobart was the best sniper with a long gun, but Zara had the steadiest hand with the Glock or Sig. Sinclair promised Zara a position when she was done with her air marshal service if she would help the Department of Justice this once.

A loyal soldier, especially to Sinclair, Zara discussed with her father and then agreed to the transition a few months ago. She completed training and here she was.

"Keep 'em safe up there in the friendly skies," Van Horn said. "I'll update you if Sharpstone gets anything. Their contract requires them to keep us in the loop."

"Aware and roger that," Zara said.

She debated telling Lindy about the classified device that Lucas had placed in her pocket, but instead returned her attention to the task at hand. Of the boarding passengers, a tall black man in a blue sport coat, khakis, button-down shirt, and running shoes hurried past her, one of the last to board. He fumbled his way into the middle seat two rows back in business. A few more stragglers hurried onto the plane just before the flight attendant announced that the doors were closing and to shut down all electronics. Zara, of course, was exempt from that directive.

She studied the last few men boarding. So far, the bulk of the passengers had been garden variety citizens. Moms, dads, babies, college kids, black, white, Hispanic, Asian. Some were wearing suits, hoodies, tracksuits, Gucci loafers, running shoes, and flip-flops. The usual.

Until three men looking like they had stepped from a military recruiting poster were the last to board. Tall, fit, muscled, military haircuts, cargo pants, poly pro shirts, Revision sunglasses, and duffel bags. Each had a middle seat, one in first class, the next in business class across from Zara, and the last in economy. Middle seats typically meant a late ticket purchase.

The men stowed their bags, studied the other passengers, much the way Zara was studying them.

The man in first class then stared into the rear of the business section over his left shoulder. At first Zara thought he was checking in with his coach class pal who had boarded with him. But when Zara turned and looked, both men were staring at the late arriving black man as he placed his briefcase under the seat in front of him and shrugged off his blue sport coat.

Zara made a mental note but didn't get overly concerned. As the pilot taxied the airplane for takeoff, her mind immediately went to Lucas and the jet crash near Swan Quarter. She wondered if the flash drive Lucas had recovered was somehow related.

The pilot then came across the intercom and said, "Folks, we want to welcome you to the inaugural Raleigh-Durham to Taipei, Taiwan, nonstop flight. TransPac Airlines is strengthening the economic ties between the countries, as well as the cultural bonds.

With the Research Triangle Park here in North Carolina and Taipei Semiconductor, the world's largest maker of artificial intelligence chips, we are forging into a new era of technology for both countries. Thank you for joining us today on our brand-new Boeing 777-Extended Range. We have a fabulous crew onboard, and we look forward to serving you. We will be flying west, into the sun, and we imagine many of you will be sleeping during the initial several hours of the flight. Our flight attendants will promptly do meal service and then shut the cabin lights. Now, sit or lie back, relax, and enjoy the flight."

The message was repeated in Mandarin and then the aircraft began taxiing for takeoff.

CHAPTER THREE

LUCAS SHERIDAN

*L*UCAS RAN INTO HIS BACKYARD CHASING THE BUZZING SOUND, BUT never could see what was causing the high-pitched thrum. Bees? Distant airplanes? Helicopters landing at the crash site?

Or a drone that followed him home?

The house he had moved to three years ago after both of his parents retired from the army was a white two-story Cape Cod with a basement, which wasn't common in Eastern North Carolina where the water table was so high. The previous owners had found a hill, though, and dug into it, creating a nice view of the surrounding forests over two acres of manicured lawn and mature, towering oak and maple trees. A gravel driveway cut off Main Street about a mile outside "downtown" Swan Quarter and did a horseshoe through Lucas's front yard. It was maybe ten feet to the three front steps with bullnose brick that led up to the covered porch with painted gray flat boards. Two rocking chairs and a red cedar wooden swing provided ample seating to watch the sun rise or set, as the house faced south toward the Pamlico River.

Standing in his backyard, Lucas studied the distant tree line, searching for answers as he whipped out the cell phone his parents let him use for emergencies. If finding classified information in a plane crash less than two miles from his home wasn't an emergency, then what was? His parents were strict about keeping

Lucas focused on sports and social interaction but acknowledged that having a phone was important in today's hyperconnected world. Though they still forbade Lucas from having accounts on any social media applications such as Instagram, Facebook, X, and Snapchat. Lucas was fine with that because he was busy enough playing baseball, studying, and developing mad computer science skills. Taking Coursera's Full Stack Web Developer training online and earning his IBM Full Stack Software Developer professional certificate was his bargain with his parents. No apps on the phone, but his mom allowed him to take classes that might make him a computer genius. Seemed like a fair trade to Lucas.

"Mia," he whispered into the phone. "You've got to get over here, ASAP. It's an emergency."

"Wait. What?" his friend Mia responded. "An *emergencié*," she said in a fake French accent with a hint of Eastern North Carolina dialect.

Mia Barlowe lived a mile on the opposite side of Swan Quarter from Lucas, but they had become best friends through their private math tutor. The Hyde County public schools didn't have classes sufficiently advanced for either Lucas or Mia, and both sets of parents had placed their children in Sandy Acton's advanced placement private tutoring class, which she ran out of her old Victorian home in the middle of town. Among all the normal advanced mathematics classes such as differential equations, probability and statistics, and advanced geometry, she taught programming, coding, and computer science, the primary interests of both Lucas and Mia, who had also earned her full stack developer certificate through the IBM program. Sometimes Mia and Lucas would teach Ms. Acton how to write code and develop software.

"Seriously, just come now. Take your bike," he pleaded.

"You're acting awfully strange, Lukie Dukie, but okay."

Less than five minutes later, Mia fishtailed her mountain bike into the gravel lot, rocks spitting everywhere, and said, "I love doing that."

Like Lucas, Mia was fourteen and just finishing up eighth

grade and her last year of middle school. She was lanky and athletic with sinewy arms poking from her Taylor Swift "Tortured
Poets" T-shirt. She wore cutoff jeans with tattered hems and Nike
running shoes with no socks. Her brown hair was pulled back in a
ponytail that ended between her shoulder blades.

"Mia, you've got to help me," Lucas said, clasping her hand
and pulling her inside. They raced downstairs into the basement
where Lucas had a powerful Apple Mac gaming studio with M4
Ultra Mac Studio microprocessors capable of thirty-eight trillion
operations per second.

"You're scaring me, Smalls," Mia said, referencing one of their
favorite old-time movies, *The Sandlot.*

Lucas looked Mia in the eyes and retrieved the flash drive from
his baseball mitt.

"You know the plane crash in the swamp just now?"

"You mean like an hour ago. Uh, *yeah?*" she replied, inflecting
her lilt in a higher octave to emphasize the obvious. "It's only like
the biggest news story in the hemisphere."

Lucas smiled. They had nicknamed their little corner of the
world, "the hemisphere," because it was just the opposite: small,
remote, and typically unnewsworthy.

"You mean other than this crazy presidential race," Lucas said.
"All I ever see on TV anymore is President Campbell running for
reelection."

"Tell me about it. What's up with the crash, though?" Mia
asked.

"I was there," Lucas said.

"What do you mean, you were there? You're not burned up or
anything. This is just hitting X," she said. Mia's father was the
sheriff of Hyde County and allowed Mia to have X, formerly Twit-
ter, with parental controls such as no direct messages and all sex-
ual content blocked. Sheriff Barlowe did believe that news broke
so fast that X was the best way to learn what was happening even
though sometimes, like combat, the first report might be wrong.

"It happened maybe, I don't know, a half a mile in front of me.
I was coming back from baseball practice."

Mia stared at him a long time. "And?"

"I went into the crash looking to see if anyone needed help and found this. It's classified."

Lucas held up the orange rubberized flash drive.

Mia snatched it from his hand and studied the plug-in device that said "Classified" on one side and "Code Word" on the other with bold letters "TYRANT" at the bottom. While staring at the flash drive, she asked, "*Was* anyone hurt?"

"I couldn't find the pilot before I had to get out of there," Lucas said. "Some guys started shooting at me."

Mia looked up at Lucas's eyes.

"Shooting at you?" She held the back of her hand to Lucas's forehead. "Are you feverish? On any medications?"

He gently removed her hand and said, "Mia. Stop. I'm being serious. No, I'm not delusional."

She regarded him for a moment.

"Okay, then. What is it?" Mia held it up to the high, rectangular window between where the crawl space met the basement cinder-blocks. The basement was half the size of the house with three one-by-two-foot windows just above ground level. Lucas called them periscope windows because he figured it was like being in a submarine where you could see along the surface of the ocean. Same concept, but with land.

"It came from the cockpit. It's classified."

"Classified?" she asked.

"It's got secret information on it. That's all I know." Lucas shrugged. "Government secrets."

"Should we turn it in?" Mia asked.

Lucas smiled. It was always "we" with Mia. They were best friends.

"It might be dangerous. Some bad guys saw me and started chasing me," Lucas said. "I'm not sure what to do. My dad's working late at the ferry. Plus, he'll just think I'm crazy. My mom didn't have time to listen to me. She was headed out on an air marshal job. I gave her the other half."

"Other half?"

"Yeah. There were two sides to it. Like a receptacle."

She held up the device again and studied it. She lifted a flash drive from the many scattered on Lucas's gaming console and compared the two.

"You got the main part," Mia said. "The other half was probably what connected it to the airplane."

"Maybe that's why those guys started chasing me."

Mia's eyes flitted up to the windows, perhaps looking for boots striding past.

"You got the fastest mountain bike out there, Lukie Dukie." Mia grinned.

"Yeah, but I think they followed me with a drone. I heard it," Lucas said.

The drone comment seemed to change Mia's attitude from her typical surface skimming, happy-go-lucky, glass-is-half-full optimism to serious. Her eyes grew wide. Perhaps the volume of information she was digesting had finally reached critical mass.

"Oh, my God. Is it still out there?"

"Only one way to tell," Lucas said.

He walked to his computer station and switched on the powerful device. The thirty-six-inch monitor showed a series of images from his backyard. Mia and Lucas had installed a network of cameras one day after someone had stolen his mother's jewelry and maybe a few other things his parents hadn't mentioned. It had caused a big fight between his mother and father, though, and because the fighting had become more frequent, Lucas had enlisted Mia's help to rig the property with security cameras. He had gotten permission from his mother to do so and used her Amazon credit card for all the parts.

"There," Mia said, leaning over his shoulder.

"Looks like a bird, doesn't it?"

"Not there—*there*," she said, using a slender finger to trace the movement of an inanimate object flying along the backyard.

Lucas's fingers flew across the keyboard, sending commands to the high-resolution camera nearest the drone to zoom and screenshot.

The drone was a black quad copter.

"Skydio X10," Mia said. "One of the most advanced drones on the market."

"On the market is the key term," Lucas said. He bit down on his lower lip, something he did when he concentrated. His fingers continued their sprint across the letters and numbers.

"It's got 5G and is not on waypoints," Lucas said.

Lucas was referring to the fact that the drone was using the local wireless network as opposed to satellite to navigate and it was not following a preloaded set of coordinates. Rather, whoever was controlling the drone was doing so from a terminal and had followed him home using the camera. He had no doubt that it was taking pictures and recording the location of their house and the path he had followed to get here.

"Hackable?" Mia replied.

"Most definitely."

"Crash it?"

Lucas stopped and looked at her. "No. I'm going to follow it back so we can spy on them with my drone."

Then his phone pinged with a text from his mother.

CHAPTER FOUR

ZARA

"Y OU KNOW MARS IS CONJUNCT PLUTO. I'VE GOT A BAD FEELING about this flight."

Zara looked up from her tablet where she was reading the slow updates on the Hyperion crash.

"Excuse me?"

"Hi, I'm Carrie Starlight, the world's most interesting astrologer."

Zara smiled tightly. With so many pressing matters on her mind, the last thing she needed was a "chatty Cathy" distracting her. But the training manual for federal air marshals had a whole chapter on blending in and being seen but unseen.

"What makes you so interesting?" Zara obliged.

The woman was midthirties if she had to guess. Long blond hair, minimal makeup, freckles bridging her nose, and a slender yet muscular body. She wore a short-sleeve top but held a long sleeve hoodie in her lap. Her backpack was stowed near the foot of her business-class pod, and it had a logo with several stars diminishing into the blackness with the words "Starlight Astrology" beneath.

"I was actually a nurse practitioner who used to do astrology for kicks. I read the stars and made predictions about the Brangelina breakup to the exact date. The horrible Hamas invasion on October 7 a couple years ago. The presidential elections. Et cetera, et cetera. So, now I have people from all over the world asking me to do readings. I quit my nurse job, which I loved, by the way, and started my own business, which is taking off in a big way since I predicted the latest presidential victory by the exact margin of electoral votes. Do I seem nervous? I *am* nervous, aren't I?"

Zara couldn't help but smile. She *did* seem nervous.

"Everything's going to be fine. Congrats on your business," Zara said.

"It's just that I looked at the charts for travel and the Taiwan part of the world. The most powerful family there is paying me big bucks to do a reading for their daughter who is marrying some politician. They're flying me over. Wanted it in-person. And you know Mars is conjunct Venus, which means conflict or war. So, I'm just nervous about that."

Not a big believer in the zodiac, Zara smiled politely and said, "I'm sure it will all be okay."

"But Mars is war and Venus is, well, love. I'd love to do your chart. Give me something to do. You have children? I could do theirs?"

"What the heck?" she said, and gave Carrie Starlight Lucas's birthday. "Let me know what's in store for him."

Zara then stood from her seat after the airplane leveled out at cruising altitude. She walked through the business-class section to the galley separating it from economy, stepped inside the restroom, did her business, and checked her phone, which was satellite-enabled.

She texted Lucas using the fully functional airplane Wi-Fi:

Thank you for the gift. It's our little secret and I look forward to receiving the rest of it in a couple of days. Love, Mom.

She stepped out of the lavatory and found the flight attendants hard at work preparing drinks and snacks for the passengers. Snaking her way through the busy staff, she walked through business class on the starboard—or right-hand—side of the airplane all the way through first class and into the forward flight attendant station.

There she saw Marcus, whom she had met briefly earlier. He was a tall, fit African American man in a steward's uniform studying a piece of paper on a clipboard. He had readers halfway down his nose and was intently focused on the documents in his fingers. She let him concentrate until he noticed her in his periphery, looked up, and smiled.

"Ah, Ms. Sheridan. I didn't get to properly introduce myself earlier. Marcus Jones." He held out a firm hand, which she shook.

"Marcus Jones, pleasure to properly meet you. I'm in 11B, FYI."

He looked back at the paper, smiled, and said, "I know where you are. Glad to have you along, Ms. Sheridan. Maiden voyage and all. Sorry to hear about Marshal Winston and his flu diagnosis."

"Please call me Zara. And yes, tough news about Winston, but I'm glad to be here, and now that I think of it, I wouldn't mind getting a few names from you. I walked the aisles, and I've got some curious activity in a few seats."

"Did you talk to Bucknell?"

"Not yet. I'm a newbie and he'll think I'm just nervous."

"Are you?"

"Do I look nervous?"

"You look like you could kick some serious ass, so that would be a no. Seat numbers?"

She provided them, and he wrote down five names on a sheet of paper.

"Here. How are they acting curious?"

"Most likely nothing. Nervous flyers probably."

That wasn't exactly the truth, but she didn't want to raise any alarms.

"Right," he said, unconvinced.

"I'll let you know if there's anything to be concerned about."

He studied her for a moment. Creases furrowed on his brow.

"You do that," he said without smiling. Then after a minute, "Eastern North Carolina?"

Zara smiled. "The accent?"

"Well, that and the name," he said. "I grew up in Grifton and I remember some Sheridans in Ayden."

"You're kidding," Zara said. "That's my family. We're from Ayden right next to Greenville. Live in Swan Quarter now, though."

"Girl, I know where Greenville is. You're not the one that got in all that trouble with the mayor's daughter, Annie Taft, that one time, are you?"

"You'd have to be more specific than that," Zara quipped. It was true that growing up, she and Taft hung out together, played some soccer and softball, and maybe even ran the streets at night, feeling an unwarranted protective bubble around them believing incorrectly that Mayor Taft would bail them out if their hijinks ventured into lawbreaking.

"That's what I thought. Annie Taft was a fighter, and if you're anything like her, we're going to be just fine on this flight."

Feeling the connection, Zara asked, "Would it be possible to get a list of the crew? As you know, I was late getting here because of an absence and didn't have a chance to print out all the manifests."

Marcus stared at her over the brim of his wire-frame glasses, and after a pause, nodded.

"Sure." He reached into the clipboard and handed her a two-page list of the thirteen flight attendants and two pilots.

"Here you go. Fifteen of us plus a spare pilot up above."

"Roger that."

As she was gathering the papers, a stocky Asian woman with her hair pulled back into a tight bun approached. She was wearing the standard TransPac Airlines flight attendant's outfit: dark blue dress, blue stockings, black pumps, and gold name tag that read "Amanda."

"Zara, you also briefly met Amanda, my number two on the plane. Be careful, she's a hard-ass," Marcus said.

Zara and Amanda locked eyes when Amanda said in a low voice, "Marshal?"

Zara nodded, noticed the slight Mandarin inflection in her voice, and said, "Nothing but a milk run, right?"

"Well, a first flight milk run," Amanda said. "But yes."

"And into Taipei, no less," Marcus added.

"I detect some nervousness up here," Zara said, smiling.

"It's just a normal flight as far as we're concerned. We were expecting more security, though," Amanda said.

"Two marshals is pretty standard," Zara said. "Plus, we're understaffed, and I doubt there's any desire to draw extra attention to the flight."

"It's not like we're flying into a war zone," Amanda said.

"Been there, done that," Zara replied.

"As a marshal?" Amanda asked. Marcus was also listening intently.

"No, as a soldier. Afghanistan withdrawal shit show and a couple tours prior to that. Syria, and so on."

Amanda nodded. "Intelligence?"

Zara had already given away too much information attempting to bond with the crew.

"Something like that." She smiled.

"Like she's going to say if she was," Marcus chimed in.

The truth was that as a military police master sergeant she had to integrate intelligence briefings into her daily operations. Many people believed that being in the intelligence community was an end to itself, but Zara understood the IC existed to inform the decision-making of operational commanders.

Or at least that was its design. Of late, it seemed to her as if all intelligence agencies had become what she called "self-licking ice cream cones." Meaning no one else got to eat it or enjoy it. The IC agencies were out there collecting information of their own design as opposed to that driven by commanders and their operational needs. She included the marshal's service and even the whole of federal government in her assessment of this drift of purpose of the IC.

"Let's just say that we all need good information to make good decisions," Zara said.

"What do you soldiers say?" Marcus asked. "Mission versus men? Think I saw that in a magazine somewhere."

"That is the age-old dilemma," Zara replied.

"Where do you come down on it?" Amanda asked. She was fixing a cup of coffee for herself while two other stewards busied with serving first-class passengers.

Zara smiled. "I always try to do both: protect the team and accomplish the mission."

"But what makes it a dilemma is that you might have to pick," Amanda replied.

"Let's hope it doesn't come to that," Zara said.

"It's always the mission," Amanda replied. "I mean, that's what I've read and seen in the war movies."

Zara shrugged and said, "Every situation is different, but ultimately, is there anything more important than family, our friends, even the people we're charged with protecting? I think not." She swept her hand across the rows of seats. "These people."

But what she was really thinking about was Lucas, and her husband. She had blocked much of the angst she and Lonnie were feeling. The verbal altercations. Sleeping in separate bedrooms. Putting on the good face for Lucas. Knowing Lucas knew, but they were both too ashamed to sit him down and talk to him. Maybe they should trust him more. Divorce was a tough thing, but that's where things seemed to be headed.

She turned and walked back to her seat, powered up her computer, and turned on her blackout screen so that only she could read the text from a perfect ninety-degree coincident angle. She powered up her encrypted FedAir application and clicked on the people search database.

As she cross-referenced the FedAir database with the paper manifest Marcus had provided, she identified the three late arrivers as Joshua Hembrick, Terrance Rogers, and Juan Rodriguez. One white, one black, one Hispanic. All had close-cropped hair, were physically fit, and were carrying similar duffel bags that looked a lot like go bags. Hembrick and Rogers were early thirties while

Rodriguez was twenty-nine years old. Hembrick was in first class, and she presumed him to be the alpha of the three.

They were all members of Copperhead Security Services based out of Edenton, North Carolina, which was the same company that employed Clark, the contract screening agent she had . . . *confronted.*

Interesting.

All three had military backgrounds. Hembrick had been an Army Green Beret communications specialist. Rogers was a former navy P-8 pilot, which she found to be an odd mix with Hembrick, and Rodriguez a former marine infantryman. Zara knew that marines would tell you that there was no such thing as a "former marine." Once a marine, always a marine. All three had served in Afghanistan and Syria while serving on active duty and had transitioned to more lucrative careers in private security.

Next on the list was General John Wang, deputy commander of the Taiwanese Air Force. The background information on him indicated that he had been in the Raleigh-Durham area meeting with technology executives regarding artificial intelligence initiatives related to drones. He also was interested in the progress of the Hyperion X fighter jet program because the Taiwanese Air Force had received four experimental versions off the assembly line. Van Horn included a footnote that he often traveled with security given his rank and profile.

Next was Johnnie Wilson, an aerospace engineer for Blackwood Aviation, which was building the new Hyperion X fighter jet.

Like the one that just crashed.

Zara looked up from her computer and processed what she had just read, then did a search on the Hyperion X fighter jet. She learned that it was the replacement for the F-35, which was the most capable jet in the world. No Russian or Chinese fighter aircraft came close to matching its capabilities, the report indicated. The Hyperion X was an experimental jet that had been tested in Hawaii, Guam, and Wake Island. It was produced in the military-industrial complex of Hampton Roads, Virginia, with of course, parts from each of the fifty states in the nation to keep all the senators and congresspeople happy with jobs in their districts.

The key difference between the F-35, which had begun production twenty years ago, and the Hyperion X was that the latter had full Combat Artificial Intelligence Technology Integration, or CAITI, an acronym that had the test pilots calling the aircraft "Katy."

She looked at the half a flash drive on her tray table, then stared at her list of names that included three private military contractors, an engineer for the Hyperion X, and a Taiwanese Air Force general.

The display on her monitor showed the plane reaching cruising altitude of thirty-five thousand feet and angling toward Michigan and presumably toward the North Pole to take advantage of the curvature of the earth, making the flight much shorter than a straight line distance.

She tapped her lips with her right index finger, thinking. Three security guys. A Taiwanese general. A Hyperion X engineer . . . and the top-secret flash drive that Lucas found, potentially worth billions or more if it contained the encryption and cyberattack algorithm for the Hyperion X.

She typed a note to the operations manager, Lindy Van Horn in the Charlotte office.

Interesting mix of ppl. Run these names first but then the entire manifest plus the crew.

Her tablet screen began bubbling with Van Horn's response.

Can't do entire manifest. Profiling not allowed. Can do the names you sent.

Zara shook her head. *Profiling?* She was just trying to keep the passengers safe by being proactive. She had a potentially lethal combination of people on the plane. *Too many variables,* she thought. What was that saying about unknown unknowns? Without vetting all the passengers, she could be missing critical information. Were there other passengers that might pose risks?

She stood and looked across the business-class cabin, then

strode forward into first class. She locked eyes with the sturdy Asian man who had bumped into her. The man's finely tailored suit was offset by a long scar on his face and black, soulless eyes. A dead-eye businessman or ruthless terrorist? Was the bump coincidence or intentional?

After her combat experiences, she took nothing for granted.

CHAPTER FIVE

XIAO CHEN

XIAO CHEN STOOD FROM HIS FIRST-CLASS SEAT DIRECTLY BEHIND the man named Bucknell, who he knew to be a federal air marshal.

He smoothed the lapels of his uncomfortable Zegna suit as he stepped into the forward lavatory of the TransPac 777-300 Extended Range airplane. It was churning through the night sky at thirty-five thousand feet above ground level over Montana on its path to Taipei, Taiwan. He knew Marshal Bucknell was seated directly in front of him but had yet to locate Marshal Winston. Typically, the air marshals were seated toward the front, and his source had told him yesterday that the two marshals for this flight were Bucknell and Winston, both seasoned veterans.

He removed a monitor from his pocket that told him the Wi-Fi jammer he had smuggled onboard in his briefcase was awaiting his signal. He would turn it on when the moment was right, but not yet.

He ran through his checklist, the most important of which was the poisoning of the head pilot, Logan (call sign "Titan") Prescott, who had now gone to the lavatory for the third time. It was evident his ground team had been effective in lacing Prescott's preflight dinner with a toxic brew of GoLYTELY, MiraLAX, and NuLYTELY, the common mix of pre-colonoscopy drugs.

He timed the black man and Asian woman each time they moved the beverage cart to block the lavatory and how that was synchronized with Prescott increasingly tumbling out of the cockpit to make it to the lavatory before having an accident.

Chen was counting on the fourth time soon, maybe fifteen to thirty minutes, which was why Chen carried his ceramic knife with him.

A street urchin from Shanghai and the spawn of a long-dishonored family, Xiao Chen was intent on restoring honor to his surname. Xiao, the grandson of a failed Gǎnsǐduì warrior, had been born amid the chaos of a city in transition, and his early years had been marked by ridicule and adversity. As a child, he had navigated the shadows of Shanghai's neon-lit streets, listening to the whispers of influence throughout the shadowy underworld of Chinese power.

Raised by his mother in the ancient, rat-infested alleys near the port, he learned the art of survival, honing his instincts amid the clamor of a bustling metropolis teeming with secrets and deceit. It was whispered among the criminal elite that Xiao Chen had once been a promising student, his brilliance matched only by his ambition, despite the squalor from which he sprang. After winning a card game of Dou Dizhu in the musty confines of a restaurant kitchen, his "friend" Lang Wu snatched the coins away and ran, telling their entire network about Xiao Chen's grandfather's failures in combat. The turncoat Wu was the first to die as Xiao's life made a hard turn toward violence.

Mocked by his erstwhile friends, he became driven by a thirst for vengeance that consumed him. Tall, broad, and strong, Xiao Chen descended into the depths of the criminal underworld, forging alliances with the darkest elements of society that held no concern for his family's soiled lineage. His rise was swift and merciless, his name becoming synonymous with fear and retribution. As the years passed, Xiao Chen's legend grew, his influence spreading like a creeping shadow across the cityscape.

Behind the gelled hair and mask of civility and sophistication lurked a mind as sharp as a blade, a strategist who played the

game of power with a cold and calculating precision. But the ruth-
lessness was often a tactic to keep the ghosts of the past at bay.
Horrible memories clawed at the edges of his consciousness,
threatening to unravel the carefully constructed façade he presented to the world.

In rare quiet moments of solitude, Xiao Chen wrestled with
demons that few could comprehend, grappling with the weight of
his choices and the toll they had taken on his soul. His mission
today would prove once and for all that the Chen family was a
loyal partner to the Chinese Communist Party despite his grandfather's connections to Chiang Kai-shek.

General Zang Chen, Xiao's grandfather, had forsaken his suicide
mission to kill Chiang Kai-shek at Chengdu Shuangliu International Airport and joined the exodus to Taiwan, forever relegat-
ing his bloodline to cross-purposes with the Chinese Communist
Party. Mao had begun ruthlessly exterminating the families of any
of those who exfiltrated to Taiwan. Only Xiao's crafty grand-
mother had managed to keep herself and her daughter—later to
be Chen's mother—alive.

Even after his mother had married and then given birth to
Xiao Chen, the CCP's Silent Fang assassination squads had mur-
dered his father in front of them, telling his mother of Xiao,
"When he is of age, he will meet the same fate."

They had moved several times, until he was a young teenager
who finally hit the streets and embarked on his shadowy criminal
career—until a year ago, when he was visited by an operative
called Night Viper. The Night Viper knew of his family's infamous
legacy and gave Xiao Chen an opportunity to right the wrongs of
his grandfather, who had the last best opportunity to kill Chiang
Kai-shek and demoralize the resistance of his followers. Instead of
being a thorn in the side of China today, Taiwan would be an in-
tegral part of the mainland and its government.

The Night Viper was giving Xiao Chen a second chance.

Now, he opened the screen of his satellite-enabled and encrypted smartphone, typed in a series of passcodes, and opened
the secure messaging application he had installed. He typed in
Chinese:

Yue Liang Dao Ying Zai He Li.

Those words, when translated to English, meant "The Moon Reflects in the River." The most notable work of Chinese poet Zhang Ruoxu was "Spring River in the Flower Moon Night." His handler had given him this phrase to use to avoid alarm. It was his code to signal that the mission was a "go" and that his network of Gǎnsǐduì suicide operatives was to put his plan in motion, the plan that would salvage his family's honor and restore its legacy.

The logistics involved were globe-spanning and he needed a confirmation from each node that they were prepared. Some would take seconds to respond, others would require more time. He was patient, though, watching his team respond in the group text chat.

But today he was not Xiao Chen. His passport was that of Charles Lei, a Taiwanese American hotelier and software businessman from Los Angeles. Two days ago, Xiao had made sure Mr. Lei wasn't available to use his passport. Xiao then purchased the correct clothes and undertook the appropriate grooming standards to pass muster. He made sure to connect to Raleigh-Durham Airport through a small airport in California where eye scanners and facial recognition were not yet implemented. Once air side, he was good to go.

As he flushed the toilet, the loud swooshing sound sucking the water away, he thought about how his life and that of his family had been stolen from him, sucked away by the powers that be.

Xiao Chen/Charles Lei would not make that mistake today.

With most of his team having confirmed their positioning, and an impatient passenger knocking on the lavatory door, he slid the latch, stepped into the starboard aisle, and returned to his seat.

As he entered his first-class pod, his phone buzzed. The last team reported that they were ready. He removed a small bottle of cyanide from his briefcase, watching as Bucknell stood and walked to the lavatory.

He'd heard Bucknell order a Coca-Cola, and there it was, half drained and resting on the tray table, condensation pooling around its base and soaking into the napkin.

Overconfident fool, thought Xiao, but he did not allow himself to lose focus. He would not fall victim to the same unforced errors as Bucknell.

Xiao's heart pounded, but his face remained a picture of calm. He knew there were two air marshals onboard, but if he could eliminate one, he could succeed. Xiao looked at the small, inconspicuous vial in his steady hand. It contained a fast-acting sodium cyanide solution, meticulously crafted for this very moment. The crystals looked like large chunks of salt yet were deadly when one gram or more was dissolved in any liquid.

Xiao's mind raced through the sequence—acts rehearsed so many times they were muscle memory. He had exactly three minutes. He took a deep breath, steadying his nerves, and stood up, adopting the pretense of a passenger stretching his legs. With measured steps, he approached the air marshal's pod, glancing quickly around to ensure no wandering eyes.

The flight attendant, busy at the galley, didn't notice as Xiao discreetly unscrewed the vial's cap. With a swift and practiced motion, he emptied two grams of sodium cyanide into the marshal's drink. The crystals dissolved without a trace, leaving the cola as inviting as before. Xiao returned to his pod, heart racing, but his face betraying nothing.

The air marshal returned shortly, a confident stride in his step. Xiao watched from the corner of his eye as the marshal settled back into his seat and reached for his drink. Each second stretched longer, the anticipation building like a crescendo in a symphony of dread.

The marshal's hand paused inches from the glass as he turned to speak with the passenger in the pod beside his, then lifted the glass to his lips. Xiao's fists clenched as the glass tilted, the dark liquid sliding towards the marshal's mouth.

Just as the marshal took a sip, the airplane hit a pocket of turbulence. The sudden jolt caused the glass to slip, but Bucknell's quick reflexes caught it. He held the glass up high, using his body as a shock absorber as the plane bumped through a pocket of unstable air. Once the flight smoothed out, Bucknell downed the entire drink, as if he wanted to finish it before the next bout of turbulence. The liquid disappeared in a single gulp. Xiao exhaled slowly, the tension easing from his shoulders.

Now, he thought, scanning the faces in the cabin again. *Now to execute my part of the plan.* He waited for Prescott to need the restroom one final time. He watched the door and the two first-class stewards. He watched their eye movements. Their gestures. Would Prescott call before needing the restroom or would he race out without warning?

The clock was ticking, but Xiao remained composed. He knew the game had only just begun.

And that the Night Viper was on this flight.

He watched the cockpit door, rehearsing his three-step maneuver in his mind, and texted: Stand by.

CHAPTER SIX

ZARA SHERIDAN

AS SOME ROUGH AIR HIT THE AIRPLANE, ZARA WAITED IMPATIENTLY for Lindy Van Horn to run deep background checks on the names she had forwarded.

The plane rocked through some light turbulence and settled. Flight attendants went about their business. The young astrologer to her left had extended her seat into full recline and rapidly brought it back up only to recline again, before ratcheting it back up and pulling down her tray table. She hefted a MacBook on it and then pulled out an astrology book and started switching between the two.

Nervous flyer, Zara thought.

She texted Lucas but didn't hear anything back, then reluctantly texted her husband, who responded that he was still working late at the Swan Quarter Ferry. A Jet Ski had sideswiped the Swan Quarter Ferry, and Lonnie and his team were doing accident reports.

Because the marriage had been especially rocky lately, she searched for news of the incident and scrolled around, wondering if Lonnie's affair had reignited. She waded through dozens of stories about President Kim Campbell's reelection until she found a video on X that was taken by a passenger on the ferry. Some inebriated teenagers were goofing around and accidently banged into the ferry. It didn't appear that anyone was injured, but she understood that investigations and paperwork had to be done. She sighed with relief and checked herself for doubting Lonnie. Fortified by the confirmation of Lonnie's veracity, she held onto the thin thread of hope that her marriage would survive.

Refocusing on her mission, she remembered that Lucas had installed new software on her phone. In his daily Internet dumpster diving, as he called it, he had discovered PureCipher, an artificial intelligence software that could discern deepfake videos from their authentic counterparts through algorithms that detected heartbeat, veins pulsing, oxygen levels, and other biometric indicators. Always wanting to help his mother, Lucas had paired a plain-looking pair of glasses to the software he had installed on her phone.

"Moms, all you need to do is punch one of these buttons to show what you're looking for, put your phone in a pocket or something, the camera facing out like you're taking a picture, put these glasses on, connect them to your Bluetooth, and walk around the airplane. If the camera sees what you're looking for, a red box will pop up around it, like this."

They had been in the basement where Lucas maintained his digital command post, or DCP, as he jokingly called it. Zara didn't know if he was a savant or not, but she gave him plenty of leeway in his creative programming that he did. He had selected "baseball equipment" from the drop-down menu he had created within the PureCipher software. When Zara put the glasses on and looked around the basement, every time she saw a bat, glove, or ball, a red box popped up and framed the piece of equipment.

"Cool," she had said. "I'll give it a shot."

Lucas had beamed, knowing he was helping his mother do her important new job as an air marshal.

With still no response from Lindy Van Horn in the Charlotte field office, Zara decided to give Lucas's creation a test drive. Zara smiled as she opened her phone and pressed on the app icon with her forefinger. Lucas had reconfigured the app to be two crossed baseball bats with an open brown glove and white ball with red stitches in the pocket of the glove. Lucas with his baseball and computers. Honestly, she was so proud of him for being a well-balanced, polite, and creative young man. Why hadn't she stopped long enough to give him a hug before she left for this trip? He'd had something important to tell her and she hadn't given him the opportunity to talk, much less hug her. A bolt of guilt coursed through her, motivating her to use his app and then tell him all about it.

When the app opened, she saw the "Pair" function, which she pressed after sliding the nonprescription glasses on her nose. In the glasses' lens, a heads-up display appeared in light blue colors. The selection menu on the phone display was now also projecting via Bluetooth to her glasses. She reviewed the list of choices that Lucas had built into the app for her to choose from:

Target Descriptor:

Man
Woman
Glasses
Shirt (red, blue, white, green, yellow)
Shaved head
Medium length hair
Long hair
Scars
Fat
Skinny
Medium
Tall
Short
Medium

Behavior Descriptor:

Nervous
Sweating

Angry
Sad
Happy
Violent
Kind
Emotional
Passive

The list continued, but she noticed some were about physical appearance and others were behavioral. That her fourteen-year-old son would understand these nuances made her even more proud of Lucas. She selected "Nervous" and "Violent," realizing that many airline passengers were most likely nervous but that a combination of the two might prove useful. She still wasn't clear how Lucas or PureCipher had written an algorithm that could detect violent intentions, but Lucas had explained that it combined diagnostic software with an ability to measure heart rate, facial expression, muscle tightness, brain waves, and a host of other biometric data. Lucas had explained to her that he wrote programs that mimicked the properties of photoplethysmography (PPG) and magnetoencephalography (MEG), which were methods to measure heart rate and brain waves without human contact. Frankly, she was baffled by his intellect.

The artificial intelligence then combined the nanosecond reading with the preloaded criminal database to determine if the selected target was a registered felon or on any of the international watch lists that were publicly available.

With the application activated, she looked at herself using the selfie camera function of the phone, like a mirror. The glasses were medium rimmed with clear glass. They looked perfectly normal against her olive skin. She reversed the camera function and kept the app running, putting the phone in her blazer pocket. She looked at Carrie Starlight next to her, who seemed to finally calm down and sink into her work. The heads-up display showed a normal heart rate of seventy-two beats per minute with a 96 percent blood oxygen level with an indication of nervousness but no violent intentions. She stood and entered the aisle, turning toward the rear of the airplane.

She picked out the seating assignments of her known suspicious actors: Hembrick in first class on the starboard side, Rogers in business, and Rodriguez in the economy middle set of seats and port side, respectively. The software popped up with a red rectangle on Rogers's face when she looked at him through the glasses. Orange letters flashed:

Nervous. Violent.

She kept walking, looked at Rodriguez, who was sleeping. No indication of either behavior. In her periphery, she noticed Rogers's eyes tracking her, his head swiveling slightly, perhaps marking her as an adversary or even an air marshal. Or maybe it was the fancy new glasses. She was an attractive woman, and when she tried on the glasses, Lucas had beamed, "Moms, they make you even more beautiful!" She couldn't discount that a man might be simply ogling her.

As she scanned other passengers, the glasses indicated nervousness in several cases, but no violent intent to match the nerves. As she was approaching the forward set of lavatories, the well-dressed Chinese or Taiwanese man who had bumped into her stood from his seat and adjusted something in the overhead bin, all the while looking over his shoulder. The red square appeared and framed his face in her heads-up display.

Violent.

Not nervous? she wondered.

When he looked her in the eyes, though, *her* nerves buzzed. He had flat gray eyes to match his tailored custom suit. A *Zegna* label was stitched on the inseam, observable when the suit jacket fluttered open as he reached into the overhead bin. His pale yellow tie had repeated blue *H*s fashioned into movie theater seats, a signature of Hermes. The white shirt looked crisp and fresh with a spread collar, indicating some kind of fashion taste. A scar ran across his left cheek, the sun having turned it white, not unlike her Abbey Gate shrapnel scars. Her intuition rang with a warning, but she wasn't sure why. Something about the suit and the man. *Did they go together?* she wondered. The violent alert didn't trigger Lucas's artificial intelligence database, however. What was it that triggered the "Violent" alert? His eyes? The scar? Something about his demeanor? His profile didn't match any in Lucas's database or her classified TSA database, leaving her thin gruel. She would have to watch him more closely and do some research.

The man politely stepped aside, allowing her to pass. She kept her eyes on the Asian man as she stepped past Bucknell's seat, which was fully reclined. Evidently, he had fallen asleep with a Robert Crais detective novel on his chest. Never focusing the glasses on Bucknell's face, she noticed Bucknell had covered himself in his blankets and reclined his seat fully. She noticed, though, that he didn't remove his shoes or his coat, which seemed odd. She finished her lap of the airplane and approached Marcus in the forward galley.

"Who do we have in seat 4G?"

"Nice glasses," Marcus said. "Stylish."

"Thank you," she replied, self-consciously adjusting them. He lifted his manifest and said, "Charles Lei. His passport shows a Los Angeles address. Brentwood, to be specific."

"Brentwood? Like OJ?"

Marcus looked at her through his wire-rim spectacles, and the crow's-feet around his eyes hinted at amusement. "Yes, I believe Orenthal lived in Brentwood. What's the issue with Mr. Lei?"

"Not sure," she said. "Just made my spidey senses go off."

"The scar and the three-thousand-dollar suit?" he asked.

"You noticed?"

"I try not to miss a beat. I am in charge, after all."

"Well, that's mostly it. His look seems juxtaposed to the clothing."

"He could be going to see a long-lost friend. Maybe he's getting married. Perhaps he manages a hedge fund. Or maybe he just likes fine clothes."

"But you don't believe any of that," she said.

"Perhaps not, but I try not to judge."

"My *job* is to judge and make the tough calls."

"What's your call here?"

"I'm going to do some digging and I'll let you know."

She returned to her seat and looked at her phone. Her heart stopped when she opened her tablet and saw Chinese symbols: 月亮倒映在河里.

What the hell? Zara wondered.

CHAPTER SEVEN

LUCAS SHERIDAN

*L*UCAS SAID, "GOT IT."

He spun around in his chair and showed Mia the display monitor.

"That's their drone feed?"

"Yes, I've hacked the camera. It's low on battery. See the indicator there," he said, pointing at the red 14 percent marker that looked like a D cell battery in the upper right-hand corner of the display.

"They have to go back and recharge," she said.

"And we are following them."

"When does your dad get back?" Mia asked.

"He's working late at the ferry. Something happened with some Jet Skis. He's filing paperwork."

"I think I should call my dad," Mia said. "This plane crash and drone stalker stuff is serious."

"Let's see where this drone goes first before we get any fam involved."

They watched as the camera showed the main road leading into Swan Quarter from the east, which was the same path Lucas had taken after the Hyperion X crash. It cut across some swampy land until it reconnected with the road, the battery showing 9 percent now. The drone banked to the north and then landed at a trailer on the banks of Lake Mattamuskeet, which was just north of Swanquarter National Wildlife Refuge.

"There," Mia said. Two men approached the drone, lifted it, and then the camera shut off. "I know where that is. It's right by Granny's Farmhouse, the restaurant."

"Yeah, we go there some," Lucas said. He was thinking, though. Should they call the police or just monitor the situation? Would he be able to get back into the drone when it was fully charged and headed their way?

"Way I see it," Lucas said, "we've got some options. Let this thing go. Call the cops. Call your dad."

"My dad is a cop," Mia said.

Mia's father was not just any cop. He was the Hyde County sheriff, and the airplane crash was probably something he was already working. Sheriff Barlowe had been his mom's first boss out of the military until Sharpstone doubled her salary and she followed the money.

"I know. That's what I meant. He could help us, maybe."

"Say the word. I can have him check out the trailer or send someone," she said.

"Facts. Let's let him know what's going on," Lucas said.

"What *is* going on?"

Lucas shrugged and said, "You know as much as I do. If you can get through to him, it might be a good idea."

Mia pulled her phone out of the hip pocket of her cutoff jeans and pressed speed dial. Her father answered immediately.

"Mia, not much time right now. What's happening, darling?"

"Daddy, Lucas found something at the plane crash and brought it home. Some men followed him with a drone. Then he called me, and I came over. And that's when we followed the drone back to a trailer on the lake."

"Where are you? I'm at the crash site."

"We're in Lucas's basement," she said.

"Then how did you follow the drone? I'm confused . . . and running out of time."

"Lucas did some computer stuff and hacked into the camera," she said.

Lucas was waving his arms to ward off the word "hack," but it was too late. He shook his head and put his face in his hands.

After a long pause, her father asked, "Where did this drone go?"

"I'll drop you a pin, Daddy. I know you're busy. You might want to have a deputy check out these guys. Lucas says they shot at the coast guard."

"Hey, Randall," her father said in a distant voice. "The chopper with the hard landing. Any bullet holes in it?"

Mia took the location that Lucas had shared with her and then dropped a pin on her iPhone into a text for her father. Randall mumbled something unintelligible for either Mia or Lucas to overhear when her father came back and said, "I'll check it out. We've got a mess on our hands. Still can't find the pilot. He's pinging in the middle of the swamp, the navy says."

"All right, Daddy, love you."

"Love you, too, darling. Stay safe."

Lucas knew that Mia's mother had passed away from breast cancer two years ago and that it was just her and her father now. Sheriff Barlowe worked long hours and trusted Mia to take care of herself much of the time, with the tutoring from Sandy Acton serving as a quasi-latchkey daycare. Typically, Mia would have dinner ready for her father just as her mother used to do, though Lucas knew she was worried that she hadn't mastered many of the dishes in her mom's worn recipe book.

"Your dad is working late, and my dad is working late, and my Moms is on an airplane somewhere over Canada by now," Lucas said.

"So, it's just the two of us," Mia said intently as she brushed a loose tendril of brown hair behind her ear.

"I like those odds," Lucas said.

Mia giggled and said, "What are you, Arnold Schwarzenegger or something? I'll be baaack." She used an inflected Austrian accent when imitating the famous weight lifter.

"No, but we may have a problem," Lucas said, pointing at the display monitor that was capturing the local camera feed that Lucas and Mia had established.

A pickup truck rolled slowly past Lucas's gravel driveway. It was painted desert tan and looked well-worn with dents and scrapes. Two men occupied the front seats. They wore ball caps, sunglasses, and black long-sleeve shirts. A black-and-tan diamond-shaped logo was covered with dust on the driver's door. He couldn't make out the writing, but he saw the openmouthed fangs of a snake in the middle of the word.

"Screenshot that," Mia said.

Lucas clicked a button and took several screenshots.

"They're cruising us," Lucas said.

Sure enough, the truck returned a couple minutes later, the men attempting to appear nonchalant as they conducted reconnaissance of Lucas's home.

"Probably trying to determine if any adults are here," Mia said.

"Shotgun's in the corner. Shells are next to it," Lucas said. He got up and grabbed the ten-year-old Remington 11-87 shotgun and a green box of twelve-gauge bird shot. His father had wrapped the gun in a saw grass camouflage for duck hunting. He checked the chamber and then loaded one shell in the chamber and two shells, the max load, into the tube using the trigger guard as a guide like his dad had taught him. Lucas aimed the shotgun at the window, practicing, squinting with one eye, and then laid the shotgun beneath the table of his command post.

"I'm not shooting anyone," Mia protested.

"Me neither, but it'll scare them. I've done some bird hunting and gone after some deer. I know how to handle it."

"Let's hope it doesn't come to that," Mia said.

He snapped several more screenshots.

"Copperhead Security Services," Mia said. She had expanded one of the photos and zoomed in so that she could read the letters. She was operating on Lucas's other computer terminal station now and was expanding the facial images.

"Hard to tell with the hats, beards, and glasses," Lucas said. "Which I'm sure is the purpose."

"Yeah, these guys are based up near Edenton and even in Chesapeake, Virginia. Totally sus," Mia said.

The truck pulled into the driveway and stopped in front of Lucas's front steps. They heard two doors slam and two sets of footprints scrape up the bullnose bricks and the wooden porch until the doorbell rang.

Lucas held his finger up to his lips, indicating silence. He typed on the computer:

Let's hide under the table.

They moved quietly until they were both huddled beneath Lucas's large command post next to the overheating computer towers. Lucas slowly moved the shotgun until he was cradling it with his shooting hand resting on the cold metal of the trigger assembly. The doorbell rang again, and they could hear deep voices talking on the porch.

Lucas's parents had placed a US Army veteran logo on the window, and they flew the American flag every day. Would either of those facts count with these Copperhead guys? Why would it, if they shot at the coast guard helicopter? What was little ol' Lucas and his parents' military service compared to whatever their motivations were? If they had bad intentions, it didn't seem like much would stop them.

Mia's eyes got large as the front door opened with a slow squeak that Lucas knew all too well. Floorboards creaked above them.

Copperhead was coming for them.

CHAPTER EIGHT

ZARA SHERIDAN

Zara continued to stare at the symbols: 月亮倒映在河里

She clicked on Google translate and cut and pasted the symbols into Mandarin to English just as Lindy Van Horn in Charlotte texted.

We just intercepted a text message on your aircraft: "The moon reflects in the river." We think it's a code.

I got it, too. Where did this come from? Why do you think it is a code? What does it mean?

Intercept from within the plane from a burner phone. NSA is pulling down all the comms.

Can they say whose phone it came from?

It's a burner. Could be any one of the passengers. Came from the Wi-Fi on your plane.

Satellite can track that?

According to the NSA, yes.

On it.

A chill shot up Zara's spine. A coded message from within the plane? It was like a horror flick where the killer calls from within the house.

Zara shook off this unsettling notion and went with her instincts to follow up on her conversation with Marcus about the man in 4G. She quickly researched Charles Lei on the Internet. While there may have been several Charles Leis in the greater Los Angeles area, only one was found dead, washed ashore in Stone Canyon Reservoir north of Beverly Hills, according to a series of articles. When she cross-referenced the federal database to which she had access with the passport photo "Charles Lei" used to board the flight to Taipei, they were identical pictures.

"How could that be?" Zara whispered. Obviously, she knew the answer. The man she had encountered was someone else, a murderer at a minimum, and most likely an imposter using Charles Lei's identity. She found the TSA tape from the Burbank security line and isolated Charles Lei's image as he was walking through the metal detector. She expanded the photograph, blowing it up as much as possible until she began to lose granularity.

The likeness between the two men's pictures was passable to the casual observer, but any serious inspection revealed the actual Charles Lei did not have a scar on his face, their eyes were different shapes, and the imposter's hair was thicker with a slight widow's peak. She read a few online articles about the real Charles Lei. Two kids bass fishing from the bank found him in the shallows and called the police, where it was identified that he had a knife wound on the left side of his neck with a severed carotid artery.

She texted Lindy Van Horn in the Charlotte command post:

Contact LAPD re Charles Lei murder. May be an imposter onboard. Run facial recognition.

Roger that. Other list inbound in a sec. Everyone freaking out here.

Enough to land the plane?

No one wants to land the plane. Inaugural flight and all. One of the analysts said there's a famous Chinese poet who wrote that line so they're digging through that.

Okay, thanks. Get me intel.

First list inbound now.

Zara opened the report Lindy sent when it arrived in her inbox:

FAM Intel Response to Query from FAM Sheridan:

Copperhead Security Services: Copperhead is a global private military contractor that focuses on US and NATO government requests for proposal. Lately they have broadened their defense business unit to include homeland security and in particular, the Transportation Security Administration. Two years ago, they won a five year $100m contract to provide training and personnel to the Department of Homeland Security for all TSA agents in the United States. They conduct the training primarily at their headquarters in Chesapeake, Virginia, and Edenton, North Carolina. Last year, they lost the air marshal contract to retired army general Garrett Sinclair's Sharpstone Global Security (SGS). The three individuals mentioned, Joshua Hembrick, Terrance Rogers, and Juan Rodriguez, are operators for Copperhead with recent experience in Poland training Ukrainian special forces for sabotage missions in Russia. Importantly, Hembrick speaks Mandarin Chinese, having been trained at the US Army's language school in Monterey, California. During his military career, he was assigned to the 1st Special Forces Group in Okinawa and conducted operations throughout the Pacific Rim. His military career was marked with decorations and awards indicative of a good soldier who performed his duties well. He will most likely be the leader of the three men, whatever their purpose on the flight. To that point, it is suspected that the Taiwanese military has a need for special forces training similar to what Hembrick and his team did in Poland for Ukraine. Classified conversations between the Taiwanese Economic and Cultural Representative Office (TECRO) and the US Department of Defense hint at discussions around sabotage missions in China. But the need for plausible deniability outweighs the ability to confirm these suspicions. Given Copperhead's rapid growth, our analysis is that these men are on a mission to seek new business in Taiwan and do not pose a threat to the flight.

Rogers is a retired navy commander who flew P-8 submarine hunter aircraft and UH-60 series helicopters. A rare pilot who flies both fixed wing and rotary wing aircraft, Rogers was flying Copperhead ammunition resupply missions from Romania into Western Ukrainian airfields.

Rodriguez is viewed primarily as muscle having served as a marine force recon sniper and general infantryman. He may be performing security functions for Hembrick and Rogers, who have the technical skills to assist in training the Taiwanese military.

Regarding General John Wang, the deputy commander of the Taiwanese Air Force, his recent clandestine visit to the United States centered on discussions around the new Hyperion X aircraft and Blackwood Aviation's development of this Next Generation aircraft. Taiwan has recently received delivery of four Hyperion X aircraft, albeit with diminished capabilities. With Q-level classification of the software and hardware components, we cannot in this medium refer to the sensitivities or capabilities. Suffice it to say that Wang was unhappy that his new aircraft were delivered absent many of the aircraft's most advanced capabilities. It is in the public domain that these aircraft have the satellite networking capabilities to hack the flight controls of opposing aircraft and, at a minimum, disrupt their ability to fire weapons accurately. We do not perceive Wang to be a threat to the flight, despite his present unhappiness with the US government. He typically travels with his aide-de-camp, Major Li Van, whom we are still researching. There is very little information on the Taiwanese major other than he was raised in Taipei by a single mother. We are continuing to research.

Regarding Johnnie Wilson, an aerospace engineer with Blackwood Aviation, he is a graduate of Saint Augustine's University in Raleigh, North Carolina, with a master of science degree in computer and software engineering from North Carolina State University. He obtained a PhD in aerospace engineering from Embry-Riddle and has worked his way up the Blackwood corporate ladder from systems design engineer to executive vice president for international defense systems. He is the lead for all Blackwood corporate engagements with foreign nations. We view his visit to Taiwan as a business development trip that may also include some advisory work. That General Wang and Mr. Wilson are on the same flight is a coincidence in as much as TransPac Flight 1001 is the first and only direct flight from the Research Triangle Park of Raleigh-Durham, North Carolina, to Taipei, Taiwan. We do not view Mr. Wilson as a threat to flight 1001.

Not requested, but providing as context, is the fact that copilot Richard Monroe maintains an active Q-level security clearance and consults with the Pentagon on classified aircraft programs. Monroe is a former A-10 ground attack pilot with over five hundred hours of combat time in Iraq, Afghanistan, and Syria.

In summary, we view Copperhead and Blackwood as engaging in business development and General Wang as a simple return trip to his home.

End of Message

Zara looked up from her tablet and processed what she just read. The intelligence report prior to the poetic "the moon reflects in the river" message intercept indicated no threat. Just business as usual. A milk run. But now? After the message?

What about Charles Lei? The Hyperion X crash? Was she overthinking things or was she onto something important? She quickly typed a message:

Thanks. Need info on Charles Lei stat. Also, anything new on Hyperion crash.

Lindy responded with a thumbs-up emoji.

Zara turned her attention to the crew sheet that Marcus Jones had given her. Grok Ai had backgrounds on each of the pilots and flight attendants.

The captain, or pilot in command as Zara thought of him, was Logan "Titan" Prescott, a Naval Academy graduate who flew F-35s in the navy before retiring and flying jumbo jets for start-up airline TransPac. Prescott's first officer, or copilot, was retired Air Force Colonel Richard "Hawk" Monroe, a former Air Force A-10 attack aircraft pilot who, after retirement, had transitioned to NetJets and switched airlines from Southwest to American and now to TransPac. Both men were married with two children. Prescott had relocated to the Raleigh-Durham area, TransPac's US-based headquarters, while Monroe commuted from the DC metro area with his home being in Frederick, Maryland. The intel report mentioned that Monroe maintained a security clearance and consulted with the government when he wasn't flying. What was that about? Wasn't military retired pay and an airline pilot's pay enough to live comfortably?

Regardless, the pilot backgrounds gave Zara some reassurance because they were combat veterans, like her. Most military men and women shared a common bond derived from the oath of office, demanding training, frequent deployments, and rigors of combat. Typically, those who served had like experiences whether from the comfort of a cockpit or the confines of a foxhole. They served for a purpose greater than themselves, and even if the pilots were in the officer's club by 5 P.M., Zara thought, they had saved her rear end more than once in Afghanistan, Iraq, and Syria.

She quit reminiscing about combat and continued to study the manifest.

During Zara's drive to Raleigh, Lindy Van Horn had provided background that TransPac Airlines was a private joint venture between Clouded Leopard Private Equity in Taipei and White Glacier Private Equity in Raleigh, North Carolina. Part of the agreement between Taipei and Raleigh-Durham airports was that each airline would have mixed crews on the flights. The US Federal Aviation Administration and Taiwan's Civil Aeronautics Administration had approved the airline and the flights as a path toward normalizing relations with Taiwan. It was a bold political step toward an island and a people that the Chinese Communist Party had coerced the world to never acknowledge.

Zara looked up "Clouded Leopard Private Equity based in Taipei" and learned that it carried nearly two billion dollars in assets under management and was named after the extinct Taiwanese leopard, also known previously as the Formosan leopard. The fund was managed by Phu-Shen, a revered and feared woman who had outmaneuvered many ruthless competitors in a male-dominated society and field. White Glacier was run by former secretary of defense and retired four-star air force general Michael "Stanley" Stanhope. What else was new? Powerful people invested money in big operations to make more money.

Nothing new here, Zara thought. Big money. Big plays.

But all the background *was* interesting to Zara and helped fill in some gaps as she considered holistic threats and motivations for derailing the flight in any way. Phu-Shen and Stanhope had a financial stake in the airline's success. Copperhead Security was trying to grow its business. Blackwood Aviation was being paid to train the Taiwanese Air Force on the Hyperion X Next Generation fighter aircraft, which explained Johnnie Wilson's mission for Blackwood. General Wang had a vested interest in the enhanced security of his native land, Taiwan.

On the surface, everything seemed okay, but who knew if, below the surface, there were secondary deals cut by the Chinese Communist Party to disrupt the flight that very clearly challenged China's claim to Taiwan?

Then it struck Zara.

This flight was an international incident simply by existing. China could not let this flight be successful. Otherwise, its territorial claims to Taiwan would further erode. Other nations might follow.

She looked over her shoulder and thought about "Charles Lei," or whoever it was.

Was he a Chinese government operative with a mission to ensure the flight failed by any means possible?

Was he the source of the "Moon in the River" coded message? For that matter, was it even a coded message?

CHAPTER NINE

LUCAS SHERIDAN

*L*UCAS LOOKED AT MIA, WHOSE PUPILS WERE PRACTICALLY BULGING from their sockets like spring-loaded cartoon eyes.

Judging by the squeaking floorboards above them, the Copperhead Security men were in the house.

"I'm going to go up there with this shotgun," Lucas whispered.

Mia shook her head and mouthed, "No."

Lucas considered Mia his best friend and typically listened to her advice. A teammate in all endeavors in life thus far. But he was feeling a newfound machismo. These men were violating his *home*. They had no right to be inside without an invitation.

Lucas slid out from beneath the table, lifting the shotgun to port arms as he stood. Mia came out with him and stood shoulder to shoulder with him. Her gesture gave him more courage.

They moved silently, like apparitions, up the wooden staircase from the concrete floor of the basement. The door at the top of the stairs fed into the kitchen. Lucas could see the chairs and kitchen table. The last vestiges of sunlight poked through the dense forests surrounding Lucas's home, soon to give way to total darkness. There was a lone light on upstairs in the kitchen to Lucas's right.

Mia's hand landed like a butterfly on his shoulder, reassuring him. She motioned with both her hands, making a cocking motion. She wanted him to warn them off with the unmistakable sound of loading a shell into the chamber of the shotgun. He thought it was a good idea.

"Nobody's home. The kid must have it. You search upstairs and I'll look around down here," one of the men said.

"Roger that," the other replied.

Their voices were deep and hoarse. He could smell their sweat just around the corner of the kitchen as he stood on the top step. Mia had her hand on his back.

He racked the shotgun by pulling the charging handle to the rear. A shell ejected since he had already loaded it. It spiraled up into the air and bounced off the wall of the stairwell right into Mia's outstretched hands, like a line drive off the centerfield wall.

"What the fuck!" the second man shouted before he had ascended the steps to the second story.

"Gun!" the first man shouted.

The charging handle of a pistol slid back. Lucas waited for silence, then clicked off his safety. The metallic sound pinged loudly through the kitchen.

"Back up, Will. That's a shotgun," the second voice said.

Feet shuffled along the floor. Lucas looked in the glass frame of a family picture in the kitchen. In the reflection he could faintly see the two men backing slowly, pistols drawn and sweeping back and forth. Mia's hand rested on his back, now clutching his shirt, her nubby fingernails digging into his back. The two men stood at the door for a long moment. Lucas was worried they had changed their mind about retreating, but he held steady. Kept his gaze on the window. Perhaps if he could see them, they could see him. It made sense, but he wasn't sure they were focused on any one spot. They were searching for a threat. A long moment of silence was followed by the sound of the hinges on the front door squeaking.

Finally, the men retreated down the steps, the truck started, gravel crunched, and the diesel engine roared into the distance.

Lucas was up the steps with the shotgun held to his shoulder like a soldier might do as he cleared the remainder of the house. He put his back to the door and watched as the Copperhead truck's headlights swept across the house and turned north.

"Check to see if anything is missing," he said to Mia.

She didn't reply but followed his wish and moved in the opposite direction toward the living room where the men had stopped. Lucas went up the steps and entered each of the bedrooms. Nothing. When he came back down, Mia was on her knees picking at something on the floor.

"Like a business card or something," she said. She lifted the small piece of laminated paper with some words and numbers on it.

Lucas held his finger to his mouth and knelt next to Mia. He pulled out his phone and typed:

Might be a listening device or GPS marker.

Mia nodded, holding it in her outstretched hand. Lucas took the card and put it in his pocket. They returned to the basement, where Lucas retrieved a Faraday sleeve, which was made with metalized materials that disrupted electronic communications and intercept or connection attempts. He placed the card inside the device, which was the size of an envelope, and sealed its opening.

Turning to Mia, he said, "There's a reason they left that. GPS or voice intercept are the most likely."

"A drone follows you home. Two guys show up with guns. They leave behind an intercept device of some sort," Mia said. She looked at the rubberized orange flash drive. "I'm thinking that this is something very valuable to a lot more than just a couple of PMCs," she said, using the localized slang for the abundant private military contractors that roamed northeastern North Carolina.

"It's like that book Ms. Acton had us read in AP English," Lucas said. *"The Pearl."*

Mia considered his comment and nodded. "Like Kino and all the bad luck it brings?"

"Exactly," Lucas said.

Lucas was having misgivings about having found something seemingly so valuable. Ms. Acton had had her advanced placement students read *The Pearl* and write a one-page summary of the lessons learned. Lucas had written a paper he called "Envy and Its Destructive Nature." In the classic, John Steinbeck tells the story of a small, struggling Mexican fishing village where a young diver named Kino finds a giant pearl in an oyster. When the village learns of Kino's discovery, many suddenly befriend him and his wife, Juana. Some even attempt to steal the pearl and inflict harm on Kino, his wife, and infant son. Ultimately, Kino tosses the pearl deep in the ocean after seeing firsthand the destructive nature of greed. In his paper, he also explored the concept of moral integrity, doing the right thing, over the ruthless pursuit of wealth. These were heady, nascent concepts for a fourteen-year-old, but he enjoyed learning.

"Even though it's not like a gazillion-dollar pearl, someone obviously wants it badly. Is it valuable in a monetary sense, you think?" Mia asked.

"Might be," Lucas replied.

Mia put her hands on her hips and said, "Okay, Lukie Dukie, then what should we do about it?"

"I don't really know. Did your dad find out anything?" Lucas asked.

Mia picked up her phone and said, "Call Dad." Soon her phone started ringing and she placed it on speaker phone.

"Yes, baby girl?"

"Daddy, you're on speaker phone with Lucas and me. We were curious what you found at the address I sent you."

"I sent Deputy Troxell over there. He said there were a few guys from Copperhead, but no drone. Nothing alarming. All pretty normal stuff. What exactly did you find, Lucas?"

The sheriff's voice had an edge to it. Overworked and underpaid. For years he had been wading through the swamp in the darkness. Getting bit by deer flies. Water moccasins and alligators sliding around. Just as the sheriff did, Lucas also knew the terrain, and its perils, better than most. He'd been frog gigging, fly-fishing, bass fishing, snake hunting, and duck hunting in the wetlands where the military jet crashed. He'd ridden his bike on every trail imaginable and even created a few new ones.

"It's an orange flash drive from the cockpit," Lucas said. "For whatever reason, Copperhead was on the scene in no time, almost like they expected the jet to crash."

There was a long pause on the phone.

"Do you feel like you're in any danger?"

Mia waved her hands at Lucas and then pointed at herself, indicating for Lucas to let her speak.

"Daddy, I think we're just concerned about the national security stuff. We can hang on to it until you're done with looking for the pilot and managing the scene there," she said.

"All right, darling, but you let me know the minute something is bugging you. You have good instincts. I'll be there in a hot minute, and you know that. It's darker than a black cat's ass—well, you know what I mean. It's pitch-black and we think we know where the pilot is. So we have to find him. Feds crawling everywhere. Even some of the Copperhead guys have come out to help."

"I do, Daddy. Thank you. We won't bug you anymore unless we really need to," Mia said.

"Bye, darling. Love you," the sheriff said. "Lucas, take care of Mia. Mia, take care of Lucas."

"Love you, too, Daddy."

"Yes, sir."

Mia hung up the phone.

"Why didn't you tell him about the Copperhead guys who came in the house?"

"And make him take people off the force from looking for the pilot whose life might be in danger?" Mia said.

Lucas pursed his lips.

"Not a bad point, but might not our lives be in danger?"

"Maybe, but we ain't dangling from a tree limb by a parachute hanging over some hungry alligators either."

"Excellent point. So, we hold down the fort until my dad or your dad frees up, I guess."

"Yes, and in the meantime, we try to figure out what's on this flash drive. Remember, we're the smart ones in our families."

Lucas fired up his computer, checked the camera displays. Nothing in the driveway. Nothing in the backyard. No bad guys anywhere that he could see.

A dialogue box popped up on his display monitor and read: CppHdSkyX10#2.

"This is the drone," Lucas said. "It's still pinging my satellite connection."

"Hook it up," Mia said.

Lucas pressed the "Accept" option of the two available options. There was no way he could choose "Decline." He needed more information if they were going to figure out what made this small piece of equipment so valuable.

The drone was flying and providing imagery using a thermal and infrared camera. Lucas knew this area from Lake Mattamuskeet to the national park where the jet had crashed. As they watched, the drone performed a series of wide, circular search patterns until the field of view tightened up.

The drone camera cut through the blackness as it panned across a dense forest filled with hardwoods and pines to the east and a vast wetland of saw grass and cattails bending with the south breeze. The thermal imagery showed a whitetail deer high-stepping through the marsh and the unmistakable outline of an alligator using its tail to power through the shallows. Two small boats motored through the navigable part of the swamp while a cluster of police cars were grouped at the end of a dirt road that fed into the marsh. It might have been a rudimentary boat launch for duck hunters. The police had erected portable light stands and every car's headlights were shining brightly. Millions of bugs darted through the unfamiliar beams.

Finally, the drone slowed and hovered near a small island with a copse of seventy-foot pine trees where the pilot was hanging limply high in a tall pine in the middle of thick wetlands. The drone flipped between infrared and thermal imagery. The infrared camera detected electromagnetic radiation not visible to the naked eye. The thermal camera differentiated objects by temperature. Using both allowed the operator to rapidly scan an area with infrared and then attempt to identify an object more precisely with the thermal lens.

"That's the pilot," Lucas said.

"Can you control the drone?" Mia asked.

"Not sure I want to try," Lucas said. "Then they'll know we're in."

"Good point. I'm just wondering if he's alive."

"Looks more like a she to me," Lucas said. He pointed at the drone feed. The pilot's helmet must have come off during ejection. Her head hung limply to the right, showing a full head of hair with a braided ponytail falling across the bloodstained olive flight uniform.

"I hope she's alive," Mia said.

The Copperhead drone pivoted in the air and showed the gaggle of cop cars with police officers backing an airboat into the swamp.

"That's my dad, right there," Mia said, pointing at a large man wearing a Smokey Bear hat and sidearm over his police uniform.

Just then, the drone began vibrating as the camera view began to jump. Pocks of dirt exploded around the police officers and their cars. The cops scrambled, diving for cover as the Copperhead drone swept low into a fighter-jet-style gun run, chewing up the engine of the airboat until it burst into flames.

"That thing is shooting at the cops!" Mia screamed.

The drone pivoted again as a helicopter hovered in the darkness with an infrared light shining on the pilot that ejected from the Hyperion X Gen Six fighter jet. From above, a man rappelled down to the body, spent a few minutes untangling the pilot from her parachute cord and the tree limbs, and then secured her with a rope and snap link to his own rappel system.

"That's a Copperhead helicopter. It's the same ducted fan I saw earlier today. What the hell are they doing?"

The drone camera followed the rappeler carrying the pilot's body into the Copperhead helicopter. As soon as the doors were shut on the aircraft, it sped away.

The drone banked away and followed Route 264 back to an empty parking lot, where it landed.

Lucas looked at Mia and said, "Call your dad and make sure he's okay!"

Mia already had her phone to her ear.

CHAPTER TEN

ZARA SHERIDAN

Zara's tablet pinged with a message from Lindy Van Horn in the Charlotte air marshal's headquarters with a response to her question about Charles Lei, the passenger in first-class seat 4D.

Regarding your query about Charles Lei. We have confirmed that Charles Lei is missing but cannot confirm yet he is the dead man found in Stone Canyon Reservoir. The body had both its teeth and hands removed. No NOK notification yet. Use precaution. Not prepared to declare a threat to the flight.

It has to be the same Charles Lei. Why not declare a threat to the flight?

Still working that message. Higher ups worried about profiling still.

Of course, Zara thought. *Wouldn't want to offend anyone, would we?*

She thought about the sturdy man she had bumped into and his dead, black eyes. She remembered the Abbey Gate bomber looking over his shoulder at her directly before detonating himself into the chaotic throng at the mouth of the fence line. They had locked eyes, two predators intent on accomplishing their mission. She had encountered plenty of criminals in her life, but until that moment at Abbey Gate, she hadn't seen the impassive, soulless evil reflected in a man's blank stare that she saw that day.

And now she had seen it again, she believed. The eyes. Evil was best discerned from the eyes.

Now, today, she had been face to face with someone she suspected could be a threat. They were in the thin metal tube rocketing five hundred miles per hour across the Canadian night toward Taipei. Instead of waiting for the threat to come to her, she decided to move to the threat.

She texted Bucknell, who had been asleep less than thirty minutes ago.

No response.

She texted again.

No response.

"Damn it," she muttered.

Her dilemma was not wanting to leave her assigned side of the airplane, the port side, or the left, if you were looking to the front. She stood and began hustling to the front when she got blocked by someone opening the galley door between first and business class. Once she was through that cluster, a large man was wrestling with his carry-on luggage in the overhead compartment and was completely blocking her path.

"Excuse me, sir," Zara said.

"Hold your horses, lady," he replied. "I'm almost done."

Zara stepped up on the armrest and spun past the man as she jogged toward the cockpit. Charles Lei had beaten her there, however, just as the cockpit door opened for Prescott to hustle out and use the lavatory.

Lei was quick. Marcus Jones was moving the beverage cart into blocking position as had become Federal Aviation Administration standard after 9/11. The one vulnerability of the new locks required on all cockpit doors was the moment a pilot needed to exit. The pilot in command, Prescott, had opened the door prior to having the cart in place, leaving a gap for Lei to exploit. It was always the little things, Zara thought, that led to the biggest consequences.

Prescott was tumbling from the cockpit into the lavatory, clenching his gut, a pained grimace on his face. Marcus Jones sprang from his chair and attempted to block Lei, but he was no match for whatever blade Lei had managed to secret onto the aircraft. Jones was down and bleeding from the neck. Prescott was one step into the lavatory when he received a crushing blow to his neck, arterial spray gushing. Lei shoved him into the latrine, stepped into the cockpit, and then locked the door. Seeing all of this, Zara raced to the cockpit door as Amanda drew the curtain that separated first class from the crew area. Zara tugged on the cockpit door handle, realizing she was too late. It wouldn't budge. She heard Charles Lei speaking in a harsh voice to the copilot, Hawk Monroe.

Turning her attention to the pilot in the lavatory, she opened the door and saw him lying against the toilet, one arm splayed upward, another wedged by his side. Zara stepped over the dying pilot, whose blood was pouring onto the tile flooring, and pressed her hand against his neck.

Dead.

A gurgling noise to her rear caused her to turn her head to the forward attendant's station to her right. Marcus Jones lay next to a beverage cart he had been moving into place to block access to the flight deck. He was bleeding from the neck but not with the same arterial damage done to the pilot.

"Help," he whispered.

First-class flight attendant Amanda Gāo rushed to her side and knelt next to her boss, Marcus.

"Where's the first-aid kit?" Zara asked. She was a certified combat lifesaver yet never believed she would need those skills after leaving the army. Amanda rifled through a cabinet above them and retrieved a box the size of a lunch pail. Zara opened it and found gauze, antibiotic ointment, and other medical necessities. She poured Betadine on the oozing neck wound. Charles Lei's knife had missed the carotid artery and wedged in the neck muscle between Marcus's spine and throat.

She applied pressure to the wound with several gauze pads, tossed them, and then applied new ones and taped those into place.

"Marcus, are you with me, buddy?"

He gave a weak thumbs-up with his hand.

Amanda had the presence of mind to also draw the curtains on the starboard side so that the action in the forward flight attendant cabin was largely obscured from the sleeping travelers. It was midnight East Coast time and practically all the passengers had laid their beds out flat and were either sleeping or attempting to sleep in the pitch-black airplane.

"Let's sit him up to get the blood flow away from his neck," Zara said. They repositioned Marcus into one of the flight attendant jump seats and strapped him in facing rearward with double seat belts across the chest. She wrapped some surgical tape around his forehead and behind the padded headrest to secure his head upright.

"I can't believe this," Amanda whispered. "A hijacking?"

"What's the code to the pilot sleeping cabin upstairs?" Zara asked.

Her practice in the mockup 777 in the Charlotte training facility and review of aircraft schematics revealed the existence of two separate and little-known rest cabins above the first-class galley and business-class galley, respectively. The forward cabin was for pilot rest, particularly when a second crew was onboard. Likewise, the cubby above business class was for the alternate flight crew. Because of her late boarding, these were areas she didn't have time to visually inspect. Marcus Jones had mentioned an extra pilot, but she hadn't had a chance to meet him or her, as was customary during preflight.

Amanda stared at Zara for a moment and said, "I'll write it down for you." She took a small pad of paper from her apron pocket and clicked an ink pen as she wrote the code and handed it to her.

"What about the business galley code?" Zara asked.

Again, Amanda hesitated.

"We don't normally give that out, but let's get Marcus and the pilot upstairs and we can tackle that."

"That's bullshit," Zara said. "It's SOP. Give me the number."

Amanda narrowed her eyes and said, "First things first."

Wasting no further time on arguing, Zara pressed the dimly lit numbers of the pilot cabin above first class and opened the door when the pad blinked green. She and Amanda lifted Prescott, clearly dead, and dragged him up the steep staircase into the small hut-like sleeping quarters. A small night-light showed that there were two beds separated by a curtain and two small, padded seats at the feet of the two bunks. Pillows and blankets were stacked on one of the beds while the other bed had a man sleeping deeply with Beats headphones over his ears, a gel sleep mask over his eyes, and a CPAP mask over his mouth and nose. He looked like an alien life-form with the headphones and CPAP machine pumping.

But Zara was glad that there was someone there to help. They placed Prescott on the floor opposite the starboard bed, a small space between the bunk and the interior wall of the aircraft.

Zara said, "I'll wake up West here. Why don't you head back down and clean up. We should bring Marcus up here, too. Then we can figure out what to do."

Amanda gave her a hard stare but then nodded and climbed down the steep stairwell.

Zara hurriedly crawled over the empty bed and opened the privacy curtain, shaking the sleeping pilot. According to the manifest, this man should have been Jeremy West, another retired air force pilot and one with whom she shared some history from her brief stint with Sharpstone Global.

West's eyes opened immediately. He ripped off the CPAP mouthpiece, removed the headphones and sleep mask, reached behind his pillow, and retrieved a Glock pistol. Zara immediately swept his hand and snatched the pistol from him before he had fully secured the weapon.

"What the fuck!"

"Hold on, Jeremy," she said. "It's Zara. You're probably tripping on two Ambien."

West's short hair was askew at all different angles. His eyes were wide and stone cold, though he stared at his pistol in Zara's hand, perhaps wondering how she had so quickly maneuvered it away from him. He had obviously transitioned from deep sleep to wide awake, like a diver surfacing too quickly, but that didn't seem to compromise his memory.

"Sheridan?"

"That's me, Jeremy. We've got a situation," she said. She pointed at Prescott's body, partially hidden by the second bed.

"What's that?"

Prescott's legs were exposed, but not his face or torso.

"Logan Prescott, our pilot in command. A terrorist using the name Charles Lei gained access to the cabin as one of the flight attendants was attempting to put the service cart in front of the cockpit."

"That's Titan?" West said, shifting to a seated position and then standing to peer over the adjacent bunk. "Jesus fucking Christ." He leaned over the bed and studied Prescott's lifeless form.

"Exactly," Zara said.

"What's going on in the cockpit? Is Hawk still flying this thing?"

Zara stood and handed West's pistol back to its owner. When she did so, her sleeve drew up her forearm, revealing a small blue rhombus-shaped tattoo. West stared at it as he held the pistol. He reached over with his left hand and slid his sleeve up, revealing a similar tattoo in a similar location on the inside of his right wrist. They locked eyes and nodded at one another.

Sharpstone Global Security dated back to the French Resistance of World War II, when guides for the US Army Rangers scaling Pointe du Hoc had the Ranger Rhombus tattooed on the inner right wrist as part of the exchange of bona fides, accompanied by the French saying, "The stone is sharp." Garrett Sinclair's grandfather was one of the attacking rangers, and after the war, became close with the Resistance members of Normandy Peninsula. After his own retirement as a general, Garrett Sinclair III formed Sharpstone Global Security and hired many former Delta Force operators such as Jake Mahegan, Joe Hobart, and Randy Van Dreeves. He didn't require anyone to get the tattoo, but the peer pressure within the group of those who were the most trusted agents was insurmountable for anyone who seriously considered Sharpstone as a career option.

Zara felt comfort from having a fellow Sharpstone member and experienced pilot on the airplane.

"As far as we know. I have no idea what the situation in the cockpit is. That's why I woke you."

West ran his hand across his face, the last vestiges of sleep still showing with bags under his eyes.

"The head steward is badly wounded. We need to get him up here and do some first aid. Can you help me?"

"Of course. Where's Bucknell? Downstairs?" West was pulling on his pants and shirt.

"Not answering my texts," Zara said.

Once his shoes were on, West followed Zara down the stairs. They hooked a right, and Zara almost bumped into Amanda as she was cleaning the galley. Leaving West and Amanda to attend to Marcus, Zara shot up the starboard side of first class to find Bucknell still asleep.

She leaned over and shook his shoulder.

"Bucknell," she whispered, trying to not wake any of the passengers, almost all of whom were sleeping.

He didn't move.

"Oh, my God," she whispered to herself.

Placing her fingers against his neck, the lack of pulse confirmed what she suddenly believed. Bucknell was dead. *How?* He wasn't bleeding. She spotted the half-empty glass of Coke on his service tray, lifting it to her nose.

Cyanide. Lei's empty pod was one seat behind Bucknell. He must have known Bucknell was a marshal. Perhaps her being a last-minute replacement had spared her, she didn't know, but the "one man up" drill was in effect. Often in training, Zara and her military police unit would practice having a subordinate replace the commander or first sergeant to give them the experience of leading and having to make quick decisions that were easy to judge from the depths of the ranks, yet difficult to make and execute from the top of the chain of command.

She was now the federal air marshal in charge and the lead law enforcement officer on the plane. Along with the pilots and crew, this plane and its three hundred souls were her responsibility.

She decided to leave Bucknell where he was for the moment, as there were several more pressing actions requiring her attention. The average passenger would think he was asleep.

Returning to the galley through the closed curtains, she found West dragging Marcus Jones, who was barely awake, his eyes half-lidded and bloodshot.

"Bucknell is dead," Zara said. "Cyanide in his Coke."

"Jesus," West said. He looked over his shoulder, leaned Jones's body against his chest, and parted the curtain slightly to peer into the first-class cabin.

"I left him there. They're all sleeping," Zara said. "We can deal with him later."

"Roger, ma'am," West said. A retired colonel, West had been a Chuck Yeager–style fighter and cargo pilot in the air force, able to handle any airframe in the air force inventory. While Zara had retired as a senior enlisted master sergeant in the army, she knew that West respected her position as the air marshal in charge of the flight.

They carefully ushered Jones upstairs, laid him on the bed next to the dead pilot, and propped his head with a pillow.

"There's a phone to the cockpit here," West said, pointing at the far wall. "I'll tighten up this wound here. Good job, Zara, on bandaging this and stopping the bleeding." West reached down and grabbed a first-aid kit from beneath the bunk, opened it, and proceeded to swap out the bandages around the neck wound Charles Lei had inflicted on Jones.

Zara picked up the handset to the old-school phone with the cord riding through the cabin wall and into the cockpit. It was a direct line where the pilots would typically discuss crew changes, meals, and other minutiae with one another.

The phone rang several times before she hung up and looked at West, who was finishing his repair of Zara's hasty bandage job.

"No dice. Nothing on my FAMSCOM is working," she said.

"Nothing?"

"I'm thinking he shut off the ACARS in the cockpit somehow."

The Federal Air Marshal Service Communication System, of FAMSCOM, was a command-and-control application that ran on any tablet, computer, or phone. Zara could use it to communicate with pilots and crew or even ground command. FAMSCOM also could calculate fuel remaining and distance to nearest or farthest reachable airports. It was a fully integrated communications and situational awareness platform that Zara could rely upon, provided the satellite or radio links within the Aircraft Communications Addressing and Reporting System, or ACARS, was functional.

"He's shut down ACARS? Where are we? The controllers should be wondering about us."

"We're crossing the north slope of Alaska and about to pass within fifteen miles of Russian airspace," Zara said.

"That's not helpful," West replied.

Zara thought for a moment and asked West, "What do you know about this compartment?"

West looked at her. "What do you mean?"

"Is there any way into the cockpit from up here? Video? Anything other than this phone? Drill a hole, shoot the terrorist in the head, that kind of thing."

"Never really thought of breaching the cockpit from up here, but it's a thought. We are at least adjacent if not marginally atop the cockpit."

"I'm thinking we find a gap and get a shot on Charles Lei," Zara said.

"Better be a perfect shot," West replied.

"Is there any other kind?" Zara quipped.

West rubbed his chin. "Guess not. So how long before just one passenger starts bitching about no Internet, wants some chow, and other flight attendants start asking questions?"

A loud conversation broke out beneath them in the galley.

"Now?" Zara said as she rushed down the stairs, opened the door, and bumped into Amanda as she was arguing with Joshua Hembrick, the lead Copperhead Security contractor.

"What's going on up here?" he asked in a heated voice.

Zara opened her jacket and showed him her pistol while pushing against his formidable chest. He was a big man, well over six feet tall, muscled, and ropy.

"Back to your seat, Hembrick."

He looked at her but didn't move. His lips were pressed together. Eyes set on Zara's. She held her finger to her mouth so he would understand to keep quiet, if he wasn't going to move peacefully.

"Just one question," Hembrick said. "How did the blood get on the wall there?" He pointed past Amanda. She had missed a spot.

Zara said nothing.

"Okay, if you're not going to answer that, I'd like to know if Xiao Chen breached the cockpit."

of his home. A Tesla Cybertruck passed the house, and the video appeared to be in real time. The camera turned around and showed three men seated in an SUV who were wearing balaclavas and holding long rifles. One held up this morning's *Washington Post* showing today's date. They showed an iPhone with the date and time displayed.

"Now nod if you understand me."

Monroe nodded. "Jesus."

"The airplane Wi-Fi is off. The only way to communicate with anyone is through my device and your transponder. If we get word that air traffic control or anyone on the ground knows about what has happened here in the cockpit, your family dies. Nod if you understand."

Monroe nodded.

"I'll permit you to ask me one question for the moment."

Monroe nodded and said, "What is your mission?"

Chen smiled. "Like a true combat pilot that you are. My mission is simple. I need the TYRANT code."

"The TYRANT code?" Monroe asked, as if he knew nothing of the sort.

"You are a very bad actor, Colonel Hawk Monroe. You were once in charge of the Pentagon's Next Generation aircraft program, code named Hyperion. Why do you think I killed Prescott? He was a navy top gun pilot but is useless to me. You, on the other hand, directed the program for the most advanced avionics in the world. One that the US military is providing to Taiwan. You know the capabilities of the Hyperion command suite. The choice is yours. Lie to me, and I will kill your family before killing you, or tell me the truth and get me the code, and we all live."

After a long pause, Monroe said, "That code is Q-level classification. It's code-word-protected. I signed away all my access when I retired."

"Yes, but you still maintain your clearance because you consult for the Pentagon on the Hyperion program."

Monroe was quiet again for another long moment. The plane droned along through the night just west of the Aleutian Islands,

CHAPTER ELEVEN

XIAO CHEN

XIAO CHEN KNELT IN THE COCKPIT PRESSING THE TIP OF HIS CE-ramic knife a quarter inch behind Monroe's carotid artery. He removed the headset from the copilot and dropped it on the floor of the aircraft. The muted tone of the galley phone calling buzzed through the headset and audibly in the cockpit. He ignored it and spoke only to Monroe, his primary focus.

"Disregard the galley for now. I know every dial, button, and lever in this cockpit. Do not touch anything. Your captain is dead. I have a mission that you will help me complete, and then everyone will live. Nod if you understand me," Chen said.

Monroe nodded and muttered, "Yes."

"I didn't say talk." Chen pressed the knife into Monroe's neck, drawing blood. "Strict obedience is required. I know you have a wife and two children in Frederick. They live in your suburban home. Your teenage children go to Smyth Private School. Your son is hoping to go to the University of Virginia for a baseball scholarship. Your daughter plays the saxophone in the marching band. You moved there a year ago as you finished your assignment in the Hyperion Project. I have teams on the ground prepared to kill them. This is all very orchestrated—perfectly. Please look."

Chen showed him a small tablet that displayed a grainy image still in the NORAD zone of operations, Chen knew. The North American Air Defense Command's primary mission was to detect and destroy inbound enemy nuclear missiles or aircraft. As such, it maintained a linked network of radars and communications satellites that tracked everything that traversed the airspace above the United States and Canada all the way through the Aleutian Islands.

"I do," Monroe said. "But I don't have indiscriminate access. I always have to be in the company of another primary cleared individual to review any materials."

"This code can be transmitted wirelessly. You just need to make a phone call on my phone here and tell the person what you need. That person can transfer code to the dark web in a private room we have established. No one else will know. Your family will live. You will live. All these passengers will live. We land in Taipei and go our separate ways."

"There's no one who would do that for me or anyone else," Monroe spat.

Chen pressed the knife deeper, drawing more blood. A crimson line trickled down the white blade, sharper than a Ginsu knife.

"Rachel Fox might be able to help," Chen said.

Monroe said nothing.

Chen was certain that Monroe was calculating how much he knew about his affair with Rachel Fox and whether he was bullshitting about killing his family. It was loaded information. Major General Rachel Fox was the head of the Hyperion Next Gen Fighter Program, often called Hyperion X. A storied combat pilot, Fox had rocketed through the ranks as an F-35A pilot, commanding at every level. She had a PhD in computer science, which made her the perfect program manager for the Hyperion project.

A jet was a jet, for the most part, but the guts of the Hyperion were able to reach out and control the avionics of opposing aircraft. The hardware, software, and code were all highly classified. The weak link in the chain arose from the fact that everything had to be put in an aircraft. And aircraft had pilots and mechanics and mishaps and crews aboard aircraft carriers. So many people ultimately had access to the devices, but few, if any, could reverse engineer the hardware or code.

"I can't do that," Monroe said. "She can't do that."

"She loves you, yes? She loves her career? Her family? You love your family?"

Chen spoke his words softly, almost compassionately, though they were completely devoid of any empathy.

Monroe stared through the windscreen, obviously thinking. Chen considered that he might be willing to sacrifice himself for his family and his country's secrets.

"Should you kill yourself or us, my teams on the ground will kill your family. They are in 'go' status and will act if they do not hear from me. They need positive confirmation to *not* kill your family. They will do the same to Fox and her family as well. You will be blamed, of course. Incriminating photos will be leaked from the Ritz-Carlton in Tysons Corner, among other places."

Chen stared at Monroe, a fit man with an angular face and blond hair. His research had been thorough. Monroe was a decorated combat veteran with over three hundred combat sorties in Syria, Iraq, and Afghanistan. Monroe was on track to be promoted to general when one of his children had fallen in with a gang in his high school, become involved in heavy drugs like meth and cocaine, and was on the fast track to prison. Monroe had pivoted from his rocketing career, moved his family to the suburbs of Maryland north of Frederick near his hometown where his parents still lived, and took the Pentagon job developing the Next Generation fighter aircraft. The hours were predictable, there were no six-month combat deployments, and he could use all thirty days of his annual leave. For the air force, they lost a future general officer but gained a brilliant mind to help craft the fighter jet of the future.

But for Monroe, the stress and late nights and thoughts of what might have been must have gnawed at him. Rachel Fox was a beautiful woman and rising star herself. Chen knew that they grinded away on the Next Generation fighter and that eventually led to them grinding away in random hotels in Rockville, Maryland, and Tysons Corner, Virginia. Thirty minutes here, forty-five minutes there. It was all a wash with the unpredictable traffic and could be easily explained away to waiting spouses within that margin of error for arriving home late from work.

When Chen determined he would steal the TYRANT code from the Americans, he had deployed one of his trusted street urchins from Shanghai to Mexico, across the border, and up to Washington, DC, where he scouted and watched and even contacted Monroe's struggling drug addict son, Graham. A freebie bump here, a toke there, and Graham, who had been well into recovery, was back on the path to addiction. With this and the pictures of Monroe and Fox getting careless with their affair, Chen had enough to destroy both their lives and families.

"Your son, Colonel Monroe. Have you noticed him backsliding into drugs, alcohol? His high school baseball career suffering?"

Monroe's head snapped up, his eyes boring holes into Chen's.

"Don't you dare," Monroe said.

"My team has been slowly working him. Getting him hooked again. He's well down that path, but we can stop. We can destroy the pictures, videos, and audios we have of you and General Fox. All we need is TYRANT. We know she has a secure facility in her home thanks to the work from home culture ironically started by my country's Wuhan flu virus."

"That would be treason," Monroe said. "There's no way."

"You were prepared to sacrifice your life for your country, I understand that. But are you prepared to sacrifice your two children and wife? You've cheated on your wife, but do you want her dead? Your two kids, even though one is an addict in part because you've been absent. You're killing them all slowly, anyway, so perhaps I would be doing you a favor by killing them quickly?"

"No! Stop it!" Monroe shouted. "You can't. This can't happen. None of it."

"And we kill General Fox and her family. Of course, all anyone else will learn is that you hired an assassin to do the job and received a ten-million-dollar payment into your bank account to kill her and get the code. That will become very public. Your estranged wife, your dopehead son, your unfortunate, beautiful daughter, all dead by your hired assassin while you escape to China with your millions."

"What are you talking about?"

"This is the story that we have in place. We can make it a reality. You're welcome to come to China with me and we can pay you that money and kill your family for you. You have options."

"You're sick. Nobody would believe it because I would never do any of that."

"Just like no one would believe that you and Rachel Fox have been fucking for two years, right?"

The reality of the situation dawning on Monroe, Chen watched the pilot place his face in his hands and sob silently.

"Three options, Colonel. One, get me the code and no one knows anything. Two, don't get me the code and your family and General Fox's family die. Three, fight me here, you die, and we all die. You kill every passenger, your family, and the family of General Fox." After a pause, Chen continued, "Does the term Gǎnsǐduì mean anything to you?"

Monroe lifted his head from his hands and looked at Chen, who was still at eye level on his knees, knife pressing into Monroe's neck.

"Suicide," Monroe muttered. "Kamikaze."

"Yes, we Chinese had our own kamikaze teams. We called them Gǎnsǐduì. My family comes from a line of Gǎnsǐduì who bravely sacrificed for the party."

A final recognition seemed to register with Monroe when he nodded and said, "Okay."

Chen removed a satellite phone from his suit coat and held it so Monroe could see the dial pad.

"There are two numbers this phone can call. My ground commander, whose teams are standing by to execute your and General Fox's families, and General Fox's private line. You are to press the number one and tell general Fox these instructions. If

you say any word different than what is written on here, I will
know that is a code word or safe word indicating distress. The
families will die and we go to option three, the Gǎnsǐduì plan. Understand?"

Monroe nodded. "Yes."

Chen retrieved a folded sheet of paper with typewritten instructions to tell General Fox of the threat to her and his family
and the instructions for dumping the TYRANT platform code in
the dark web.

"Your phone, Colonel."

Monroe hesitated and then passed his cell phone to Chen.

"Look at me," Chen said. Monroe turned his head and saw his
phone open upon activation of the facial recognition passcode.

Chen opened the settings application and connected Monroe's iPhone to the satellite. He sifted through Monroe's most recent calls and smiled.

"Tell your lover good-bye *after* your wife? Tsk-tsk, Colonel."

He pressed the speed dial number. The phone rang three times
before being answered.

"I thought you were flying?" Major General Rachel Fox said.

CHAPTER TWELVE

ZARA SHERIDAN

"W HO'S XIAO CHEN?" ZARA ASKED, BUT HER SINKING STOMACH told her she already knew.

Charles Lei.

Hembrick looked over his shoulder.

"So, I'll take that as a yes," he said. "Someone is in the cockpit, and this is a pilot's blood?" He waved his hand along the galley wall above the coffeepots. He worked his jaw like he was chewing gum.

Having done little research on Hembrick or the Copperhead purpose for late boarding, she had to wonder if she could trust him. The adage "keep your friends close and your enemies closer" came to mind, however, and she decided to engage him, if only briefly. She didn't know Hembrick to be an enemy, but she knew Copperhead's loose reputation based on their performance in the wars over the last twenty years and even some of the rumors of malfeasance.

"For now, all the passengers think this flight is going as planned," Zara said to Hembrick. "We have someone on the manifest as Charles Lei who killed the pilot in command and wounded the head steward."

"Charles Lei? Can I see a picture?" Then he added, absently, "I thought I heard something in my sleep. I intentionally got first class to be ready for this kind of thing."

Zara opened her phone, found the picture of Charles Lei, and showed it to Hembrick.

"Yeah, that's Xiao Chen, one of the most brutal assassins in the world," he said. There was no hesitation in his voice. No delay. No doubt.

"How do you know him?" Zara asked.

"It's my job to know him. At Copperhead, we do protection details all over the world. He's on every list of bad guys there is. How did he get past the biometrics?"

"He came in through Burbank where they haven't fully upgraded yet," Zara said.

"Stayed airside the rest of the time. Smart. But then again, he's probably one of the top two or three notorious criminal operators in the world."

"What's his angle with us? Here?" Zara asked.

"Has he made a demand?"

"No communication with him. I assume he's speaking with the pilot and telling him what he wants done."

Hembrick chewed on his lip a minute. His gray eyes narrowed. He flexed, a fight-or-flight response. *Definitely "fight" with this guy,* Zara figured.

"Do you have a dossier on him? The last one I read was about six months ago. He was in Shanghai meeting with underworld types that are connected to senior leadership in the Chinese Communist Party. His grandfather is some failed suicide squad guy. Defected from Mao and was supposed to kill Chiang Kai-shek but got cold feet. Gănsïduì is what they call their suicide mission geniuses. Like kamikaze."

"I've got nothing more on him," Zara said. "He boarded as Charles Lei, a hotel guy from Los Angeles. We have no further information. If I could get comms with HQ, we'd have the kind of intel you're talking about. For the time being, why don't you go back to your seat and let me work through some things? Don't tell your two friends anything yet, please. Right now, no one knows this has happened. It's business as usual," she said. "Until we get a fix on what his demand is, we have no actionable information. If it's something you can help with, I'll let you know, so please just have a seat."

Zara had no idea what Hembrick's or Copperhead's motivations might be. She saw an advantage to keeping the Copperhead guys in her fold in case she needed more muscle than what she could deliver, though she was more than capable in that department. But with Bucknell out of the picture, she had no wingman.

There was also a possible downside to involving Copperhead that she couldn't quite articulate yet. It was a thrum in the back of her mind. Was Hembrick just always on alert because he was an operator, or did he have some other motivation for being interested? Could she trust him and his two other men? Would she have the luxury of sorting through that as she confronted an air marshal's worst nightmare: a hijacked airplane?

Once Hembrick reluctantly reentered his first-class pod, Zara snapped the curtains closed and turned to Amanda.

"It's the middle of the night. Most people are sleeping, but some are working. They're grumbling about the Wi-Fi, I'm sure. I'd like for you to go to every galley and tell them that we're working on the Wi-Fi and to let curious passengers know. We apologize for the inconvenience and all that."

Amanda nodded. "I'm in charge of the crew now that Marcus is incapacitated. I don't work for you, but I understand we have to work together if we're going to get through this."

Zara nodded back. "Of course. Take charge of your people. As the federal air marshal in charge of the safety of this airplane, it's my job to give you guidance on the steps we need to take to secure the three passengers onboard here. I have no interest in commanding your troops."

"As long as we're clear on that," Amanda snapped. "But first I'm going to try one more time to speak with the pilot."

She snatched the phone off the wall and pressed the button. Zara could overhear it ringing in muted tones, like a European phone. Maybe it was the pressure of the situation, but Zara didn't appreciate Amanda's defensive tone. They had to work as one team to find a path forward with an intruder in the cockpit.

"We have to find a solution together, Amanda," Zara said.

"I know. They're not answering. We can't telepathically divine what's happening if they don't talk to us."

"I'm looking for solutions here, Amanda."

"What solutions? We've seen this movie before, Marshal. If he's willing to kill the pilot and nearly kill Marcus, he's willing to kill three hundred."

"That doesn't mean we can't try to stop him."

"That door," Amanda said, pointing at the cockpit. "It's reinforced so that not even an explosive charge can buckle it. You're not getting in and doing some Rambo shit in there. He's probably using that knife on Colonel Monroe right now."

"There's been no change in altitude, speed, or direction," Zara said. "He's obviously negotiating something in there. He'll want to talk to us. He'll need to talk to us. Plus, the blowout panels provide an option if it comes to that."

Every post 9/11 cockpit door had "blowout panels" that equalized pressure if the cabin were to lose it for some reason. The panels would "blow out" and attempt to provide pressure stabilization. They were also designed to serve as emergency hatches for the pilots, should they be required.

To Zara, they presented a potential opportunity as a point of vulnerability in what was otherwise a bank vault of a door.

But to her front, Amanda was shaking, her eyes wide with fear.

"Oh, my God, I don't think I can keep my shit together. I've got a whole life to live. I can't die in a plane crash for some psycho's cause."

"You're not going to die," Zara said. "We can work together and figure this out. I know there's a fourth pilot on the aircraft, if not more. I've studied the manifest."

Amanda's eyes blinked as they retreated inward, indicating she was thinking. Perhaps she saw a path to resolution of the issue, whatever the demands might be.

"A fourth pilot? In addition to West upstairs? Where is he?"

"Yes. She's also an option."

"She? Where?"

Zara was curious why the second-in-command of the flight attendants did not know that there was a fourth pilot on the plane.
On her drive from Swan Quarter to Raleigh, Lindy Van Horn had
revealed the name of Alisha McCord, who was one of the marshal
services JPATS pilots for prisoner and alien flights. TransPac had
contracted McCord to fly backup to West on this inaugural flight,
according to Lindy. JPATS was an acronym for Justice Prisoner and
Alien Transportation System. In addition to multiple prisoner
flights, they also flew alien migrants to different locations around
the country. While the government contracted some of these
flights, the JPATS were the only government-owned airline in the
country. Lindy had briefed her on both West and McCord and
that West would be first up for a rotation into the cockpit and Mc-
Cord would be second, provided everything was moving smoothly.

That plan was obviously out the window.

Lindy mentioned to Zara that McCord had opted for a business-
class pod opposite her seat on the starboard side of the airplane
as opposed to the narrow bunk in the pilot crew rest area above
the cockpit. Additionally, boarding her as a regular passenger was
an ultimate fail-safe plan that should a need for a fourth pilot
arise, she would be hidden in plain sight.

Zara didn't want to reveal McCord's location and realized she
had given away too much by revealing the gender. The last thing
she wanted was Amanda trying to solve this herself and scaring
everyone in the process.

"She's probably in the steward cabin above business, but I'm
not in charge of the crew," Zara said. "Certainly, she's sleeping
somewhere."

Amanda locked eyes with her and nodded slowly, almost disbe-
lieving.

Zara said, "So, let's get the rest of the crew briefed up on a simple Wi-Fi outage and that we're working on it. Lots of techies onboard here. We're connecting the Research Triangle Park with
Taipei, two of the most technologically advanced regions of the
globe. Before we know it, we will have ten IT pros up here telling
us how to fix it if we don't get in front of it."

Amanda said, "No problem" as she brushed past Zara on her way to the business-class galley.

Amanda stopped and turned around. She pointed a finger at Zara and said, "There's something you're not telling me and I'm going to find out one way or another."

Before Zara could respond, Amanda breezed beyond the curtains into the passenger cabin.

CHAPTER THIRTEEN

LUCAS SHERIDAN

MIA KEPT DIALING HER FATHER UNTIL HE ANSWERED, "NOT NOW, Mia. Hot pursuit."

His breath was rapid, as if he was running. Sirens blared in the background and shouting men barked instructions.

Regardless, Mia shouted, "Dad, are you okay?"

"Not hit, but two deputies are. Gotta run."

Once she hung up with her father, Mia and Lucas stared at one another.

"Why did Copperhead shoot at your dad? Why did they shoot at me? Why did a drone follow me? Why did they come poking around my house? Why did they steal the pilot?"

Lucas rattled off the questions and ran a sweaty palm through his tangled hair, then wiped his hands on his jeans.

"There's only one reason I can think of," Mia said.

After a moment of quiet, they both turned their heads and stared at the orange, rubberized flash drive sitting on the table between Lucas's two computer monitors.

"Yeah, but what does it mean? What makes it so valuable?" Lucas asked.

"Why is any flash drive valuable?"

"Because of what's on it," Lucas said.

"Or because of what it can do, which is really the same thing," Mia replied.

"Once they talk to the pilot, if she's alive, they'll realize that she probably doesn't have what we have, unless she has some kind of backup."

"Maybe we just try to figure it out. Your dad is dealing with an emergency. My dad is neck deep in bullshit. Your mom is on an airplane flying across the world. And my mom is in the town cemetery. It's just us."

Lucas pulled at his lip, thinking. He worked the scenario in his mind several ways but kept coming to the same conclusion. The orange flash drive and missing helmet were significant. Copperhead didn't technically work for the government unless it was one of the three-letter agencies his parents always talked about, like the Central Intelligence Agency (CIA) or Federal Bureau of Investigation (FBI).

"If Copperhead is working with the CIA or FBI, we're going to have the pros from Dover coming to see us," Lucas said.

"Pros from Dover? Who are they?"

Lucas shrugged and for the first time since finding the flash drive, smiled. "I'm not sure. Something my Moms says all the time. I think it's like 'the experts,' but maybe in a sarcastic way."

"I wish you hadn't given the other half of this thing to your mom. If we had the whole thing, we might be able to figure it out."

"We don't know that. Maybe one end was just a receptacle that connected to the rest of the system. Maybe it's nothing," Lucas said.

"It's not nothing," Mia said. "We know that."

Lucas sat down at the computer and fired up several encryption and security programs, then plugged the USB drive into a portal connected to his MacBook. The screen popped to life with white letters scrolling out against a black background, then stopped.

Flashing in white letters were the words:

Pilot View Connection Missing: APVX1357.

"Maybe the system has to be connected to the pilot and that's why they took her," Lucas said absently.

"She wasn't wearing a helmet," Mia said.

Lucas stopped and looked at her. "Like in the movies. The pilot's helmet controls the plane and the weapons systems."

"Yeah, but this would have to be more than that, I think. The Hyperion X is supposed to be Next Generation, so maybe it controls more than the aircraft. Maybe it controls other stuff?"

"We should go look for the helmet," Lucas said.

"In the dark? Forget the alligators and bears. What about Copperhead?"

"I was there. That has to be part of what they were looking for."

"Would this flash drive have any kind of GPS related to the helmet?"

"Seems too easy. You'd think it would be harder to crack."

"We're not in yet. This is all surface level stuff any operator can determine. My guess is that part of the reason is that this is experimental, and part of it is that they want pilots and mechanics to be able to find all the right parts without having to do quantum computing. I'm sure the rest is compliant with the three layers of government-advanced encryption standards."

Mia nodded, looking over his shoulder.

"You know a lot about hacking government computers?"

"Know nothing about it, but you and I both know the basics here."

Lucas typed in several commands that ended in:

Find APVX1357.

After a few seconds, the black-and-white display switched to an aerial satellite image of the swamps around Swan Quarter and Lake Mattamuskeet.

"Is that what I think it is?" Mia asked.

"Has to be. The helmet is that blinking dot in between Gibbs and Richmond Baptist right off 264," Lucas said.

"Six miles. Too far for bikes," Mia said.

"Got the farm truck out back. Dad won't be home for a while. I think we can get there and back."

"A lot of risk, Lukie Dukie," Mia said.

"Did you have any other plans? Hot date? Anything like that?"

She swatted his shoulder and said, "Saddle up, cowboy."

He took a screenshot of the helmet location, then went through the process of removing the flash drive without damaging the contents.

"Gun safe?" Mia asked.

"Too obvious," Lucas said.

He walked to the bin where he kept all his athletic gear, which was a fifty-gallon drum filled with baseball bats, shoulder pads, helmets, balls, and gloves. He dug a glove from the bottom of the barrel and slid the flash drive into the pinky finger. Then he replaced the glove at the bottom of the barrel.

"You're seriously going to leave top secret info in your bat basket?" Mia scoffed.

"Yep. Let's go," he said. They jogged upstairs and Lucas snagged the truck keys from the hook, noticing that both the keys to his father's and mother's vehicles were gone, a reminder that he and Mia were alone. He activated the Ring camera system and grabbed the shotgun before entering the backyard. The truck was a twenty-year-old Chevy S-10 two-door stick shift that his father had let him drive around the ten acres of land they owned adjacent to their property.

"Don't get us killed," Mia said.

Lucas laid the shotgun at an angle, muzzle down, with the buttstock by his right shoulder and next to the stick shift. He revved the engine and popped the clutch on his first try.

"Like I said," Mia chirped.

"Chill," Lucas said. "Nervous."

On his second attempt, he rolled the truck out in second gear like his dad had taught him, looped on a gravel trail from the backyard, and hooked a right out of the driveway and then another right onto Route 264. The dim headlights cut through the black night, millions of insects swarming against the windshield.

"Careful," Mia said.

Two pickup trucks sped past them in the opposite direction.

"Those looked like Copperhead trucks," Mia said.

"Nothing we can do about it now. Check my phone," Lucas said.

Mia pulled up the Ring-style application that showed their array of cameras inside and outside the Sheridan household.

"Nothing yet," Mia said.

Lucas leaned over the steering wheel and slowed.

"Should be right in here," he said.

"Seems right," Mia said, expanding the photo on his phone. She lined it up with the mapping software. "Gravel turnout right here. Pull over and let's look."

Lucas parked the truck behind a tall row of cornfield and said, "Man, it could take forever."

They stomped around the cornfield for thirty minutes to no avail. Lucas brushed a few ticks off both of them, and they were scraped up. Returning to the truck, he said, "We were all over the dot. Gotta be there somewhere."

"Let's get back and look in the daylight," Mia said.

As Lucas was pulling the truck through the gravel turnout back onto Route 264, a semitruck blared its horn at them, high beams slicing across their windshield. Lucas turned hard to the right, the truck's wheels catching the ditch and nearly flipping them over. Mia's head crashed against the windshield, and the shotgun bounced dangerously from its loose position on top of Mia. Lucas held on to the steering wheel until he could sense the truck was settled. The engine shut off when the clutch popped again.

"You okay?" he asked Mia.

Mia looked at him. She had some blood on her hand.

"Think so," she muttered. "Can you get this shotgun off me?"

The truck was canted at a thirty-degree angle with the right front wheel in the drainage ditch, which was reasonably dry. The headlights poked into the tall grass, revealing the damp home to every type of creature living in Eastern North Carolina.

Lucas lifted the shotgun carefully and laid it behind the seats. He touched Mia's forehead and felt the blood. It was a trickle, not gushing. Her eyes seemed alert, though fixated to the front.

"Mia? Look at me," Lucas said.

She said nothing.

"Please, Mia, look at me. I want to see your eyes."

Mia remained silent. Then she lifted her hand and pointed.

"Are you okay?"

"There," she said with a raspy voice.

"Where? Where does it hurt?"

"I'm fine, you dork. Look. The helmet," Mia said.

Lucas looked where she was pointing and saw the rounded features of an aviator helmet upside down in the tall grass of the ditch.

"Oh, my God."

"Get out and get it," Mia said. "It's why we came here. Then unscrew this situation."

Lucas struggled with his door, climbed out, and jumped onto the road shoulder. Hustling into the ditch, his shoes covered in muck, he snatched the helmet, shook a few bugs out of it, and then climbed out of the ditch. He crawled back in the truck and handed it to Mia.

"Good find," he said.

"You're welcome."

"The best thing about these stick shifts is that the reverse gear has an unbelievable ratio."

He pushed in the clutch, cranked the engine, manhandled the gear shifter into reverse, looked over his shoulder, and then floored the gas pedal. The truck lurched backward and bounced onto 264.

"Holy shit!" Mia shouted.

Lucas pushed the gear shifter into second and ripped down the highway.

"Both phones? Helmet? Everything okay?"

"Check, check, and check," Mia replied.

As they rounded the corner into Lucas's driveway, two sets of truck headlights were speeding in the opposite direction. Lucas fishtailed the truck into the driveway and helped Mia out. They ran into the house through the back door and laid the helmet on the kitchen sink. Lucas took some paper towels and washed Mia's forehead while inspecting her skull. He placed a Band-Aid on the minor cut after applying some Neosporin.

"Just a bump," he said. "Should be okay. Give you some Tylenol to keep the swelling down."

As they descended the stairs into the basement, they saw the entire place had been trashed, including the upended bat barrel with equipment scattered all around the floor.

Everything except the old baseball glove with the classified flash drive, which was missing.

CHAPTER FOURTEEN

LUCAS SHERIDAN

M IA AND LUCAS SEARCHED FRANTICALLY FOR THE BASEBALL GLOVE throughout the basement, which was strewn with every type of athletic equipment he owned. All his father's tools were tossed from the workbench on the opposite side of the cellar. Both tool-boxes had been emptied, with wrenches and sockets scattered around the concrete.

"Oh, my God," Mia said.

"It was those guys in the trucks," Lucas said. He held the shot-gun in the crook of his arm and placed the helmet on his computer table. He inspected his equipment, which was disturbed but intact. Both MacBooks and terminals were locked with Kensing-ton locking stations. The monitors were flipped on the sides and the locking cables were twisted, as if someone had tried to steal the computers. Bolt cutters might have done the trick, but the intruders evidently had not come prepared. Lucas and Mia con-tinued to move around the basement, shuffling through the ankle-deep detritus that the intruders had littered the floor with.

"We should have taken it with us," Mia said.

"No. What if we'd been jumped? We can't second-guess our-selves now," Lucas said.

"How did they get in?"

"Check the cameras," Lucas said.

They spent a couple of minutes reconnecting the computer gear, and surprisingly everything powered back on. Lucas got a full screen and checked the cameras. They saw two trucks pull into the driveway. Two men dismounted the first truck and brandished long rifles, remaining outside in some type of security perimeter. Another two men stepped from the second truck, one of them an extremely large man.

"That's the guy I saw get off the helicopter," Lucas said. "Looks like the Hulk."

"He's huge. Screenshot it. Maybe my dad knows who it is."

Lucas did so, then resumed the video. The backyard cameras showed the big Hulk and his partner walk up the steps to the covered porch in the back. The partner used a crowbar to make quick work of the back door, splintering it. The indoor cameras showed them enter the basement and begin to rip everything apart, including the sports barrel. They inspected everything, obviously looking for something small. They looked in every nook and cranny. Lights reflected off the basement half windows, as if someone were pulling into the driveway. The big man was standing at the sports equipment barrel, dumping it out when he looked up at the stairwell. Someone was talking to them from the top of the stairs.

The big man dumped the barrel and kicked through the equipment. Baseballs rolled in every direction. Bats scattered like toothpicks. He grabbed three baseball gloves from the floor and put his hand in one, but it didn't fit very well. He looked back at the stairwell again and carried the gloves with him to the bottom of the stairwell. While there was no audio, it was clear he was shouting at the person at the top of the stairwell. He took the steps two at a time. The front yard cameras showed a Hyde County Sheriff's Office police car in the driveway.

"That's Deputy Cashwell. He's new," Mia said. "Like twenty-two years old or something. Big athlete around here."

The Hulk tossed the gloves aside, spoke with the deputy briefly, nodded, and pulled a pistol from his belt. The deputy ducked behind his open car door, but not before an exchange of gunfire took place. The security team scrambled into the trucks as the

Hulk walked around the open door and aimed his pistol at the prone deputy.

"Oh, my God," Mia shrieked. She placed her hand over her mouth. "They killed him."

Lucas stared at the screen. "There was nothing out front—"

The video continued to show the big man ordering two of his men to stuff the body in the back of the police cruiser and drive it away. The trucks followed to the east. Lucas ran upstairs and flew through the front door.

The glove was in the bushes. He picked it up and felt the device securely stuck all the way up the pinky finger slot.

Mia followed him, her hand still over her mouth.

"What is this thing?" she exclaimed. "That . . . that people are willing to kill for it?"

Lucas looked at her and put his hand on her shoulder.

"We're damn sure going to find out. First thing we need to do is secure this place and then call your dad in case they come back."

When they went inside, Lucas noticed the splintered back door from the kitchen to the back porch.

"Bastards," he muttered.

Mia had her phone out, but her father's phone was going directly to voice mail. She said, "Dad, call me as soon as you get this. Something terrible has happened. I need to talk to you right away."

"Help me, please, Mia." Lucas and Mia dragged a China hutch up against the door, and then he took the steps upstairs two at a time, dialed his mother's safe combination, and grabbed her combat Beretta with two magazines.

"We are going to keep these by our side as we figure out what is going on," Lucas said, handing the pistol to Mia.

"I've only shot at the range," she said. "Never at a live animal or person. I'm not sure I can."

"You saw what they did. When it comes time to shoot, think of the Hulk standing over your dad's deputy and aiming his pistol at him. That will clear your mind."

They returned to the main living area, checked all the windows, locked all the doors, and then locked the basement door behind them.

"We've got two boxes of shotgun shells and two magazines of pistol ammo. We stay here until we figure out what the hell is going on."

"I'm scared, Lucas. I mean, like, really scared."

"Together we can figure this out, Mia. The safest place for both of us right now is being right here together having each other's backs like we always have. We know the terrain. We know the house. It would make no sense to leave the turf we know and play into Copperhead's hands."

Mia nodded. "You're right."

"And honestly, I'm scared shitless right now, but we need to execute. Something's going on that maybe only we can figure out. There's a reason we've got this helmet and this flash drive."

"I'm beginning to believe that."

"But we can't be stupid. These guys will be back. They just had to deal with the police."

Mia looked at her Apple Watch and said, "Lucas, it's almost one in the morning. Are we going to work through the night or try to get some rest?"

"I don't know about you, but I'm too amped up to sleep. I've got some Monster drinks in the fridge if that'll help. Or there's a bunch of old moving blankets under the stairs over there and you can nap."

"Do you mind?" she asked.

"Of course not, Mia. I'll wake you up if there's anything going on. I'm just going to try and figure this device out."

Mia yawned, stretched her arms, and said, "Just this wave of exhaustion came over me."

"It's okay. Stress does that. It'll be good to have one of us rested. I'll probably burn out in an hour."

Mia spent a minute rearranging the thick furniture coverings that moving companies used to prevent damage. Lucas and his parents had moved several times in the military and then finally to Swan Quarter.

Lucas picked up his mother's Beretta, climbed the stairs, unlocked the door, and rummaged around the kitchen for a few minutes. He grabbed a reusable grocery bag and stuffed in it a box of Cheez-Its, four Monster Energy drinks, a butter knife, a jar of peanut butter and jelly, and a loaf of bread. He glanced intermittently outside at the eerie darkness. The only light in the kitchen was from the streetlight a hundred yards up the road. There was little ambient star or moonlight.

He heard tree branches swaying with the wind, scratching at the roof. Nocturnal animals like owls and muskrats moving about the backyard. But the sounds took on a quality he had not considered before. Were they masking something else?

He stepped into the stairwell and spun around to close and lock the door. A shadow moved across the living room window. What was it? A tree limb? A Copperhead Security contractor returning?

He dismissed his fears for the moment and locked the door behind him before descending the steps into the basement.

"Everything okay?" Mia said from beneath him.

"Think so. Go back to sleep," Lucas said. "I'll get you up if I need you."

"You always need me, Lukie Dukie." Mia smiled and then snuggled beneath the steps, swaddled in moving blankets.

Lucas set up his stash next to his terminals and popped open a Monster drink. He grabbed a fistful of Cheez-Its and stuffed them in his mouth. Dusting the crumbs from his hands, he studied the helmet and the classified flash drive. The helmet had a similar male-female port connection to it, as did the flash drive.

He first connected the flash drive to an auxiliary port by sliding the USB connection into the receptacle. Next, he slid the helmet USB connection into the receptacle next to the flash drive connection. He typed some commands into his MacBook utilities application. The screen seemed to reboot and show a heads-up display.

"Interesting," Lucas muttered to himself. He took another swig of Monster and continued to type, exploring the code within the flash drive and the helmet. After a few minutes, he put the helmet on his head. It was heavier than he anticipated, but it was manageable. He slid the visor over his eyes and saw the same imagery the monitor was displaying with the red letters:

Connect To Aircraft.

His mind buzzed for a moment. *What aircraft? The crashed jet, or any aircraft?*

His display monitor blinked and showed a new image like an air traffic control view with white airplane icons flying into Norfolk International Airport in Virginia. Other planes were transiting to the Washington DC and Raleigh-Durham areas. He used the touch pad to hover over one of the airplanes. It turned yellow and produced a dialogue box:

Friendly Squawk.

21,000 feet.

Descending.

Unarmed passenger plane.

Then separately, a blinking white box read: Control?

He hovered the cursor over the "Control?" command. The box remained grayed out, but a new box appeared, saying: Secure . . . Seeking TYRANT . . . Secure . . . Seeking TYRANT . . . Secure . . . Seeking TYRANT.

Then: Unable to pair with TYRANT.

His mind buzzed with the possibilities. Could he control another aircraft from his terminal here in the basement? Multiple aircraft? He couldn't click on the blinking cursor, but even if he could, he wouldn't, because he had no idea if anything would happen.

"Man . . ." he whispered.

"What?" Mia said. He had been so focused on the heads-up display that he hadn't noticed she was standing next to him.

"I think this classified system allows fighter pilots to control enemy fighter jets."

"What?"

"Yeah. I think that's what everyone is so freaked out about. Instead of shooting down an airplane, just control it like a video game."

"Show me," Mia asked.

"I can't. I think the other half I gave my Moms has whatever the TYRANT algorithm is that allows you to control the other plane. This seems like a cipher code because it is showing me a 'secure' and a 'seeking TYRANT' message."

Mia leaned over, no computer slouch herself, typed in some commands on the root drive, and looked at the code in the device.

"Yes, you're right as usual, Lukie Dukie. See here," she said, pointing at several lines of code that a layperson would recognize as gibberish.

"If it mates with the half I gave my mom, it allows anyone, anywhere that has this device to fly any airplane it can hack."

"Which is any airplane. That's quantum tunneling right there. Tunnels through the cybersecurity of the airplane and then takes control," Mia said.

"Oh. My. God."

CHAPTER FIFTEEN

Xiao Chen

"Y OU MUST SEND ME THE CODE IMMEDIATELY OR THIS AIRPLANE will crash into the Bering Strait between Alaska and Russia," Chen said.

"It doesn't work that way," General Fox said. Her voice was tight. Chen knew she was lying.

"I have killed one pilot. Your lover here is of no concern to me. I can fly the plane. Another delay and I kill him."

After a long pause, Fox said, "How do you want it?"

"I have a device here in my hand that will receive the code when you send it. It has created a secure link with the Yaogan satellite. You will receive a code from me once you open your classified computer terminal in your home. You click on that code, and it will connect you to the satellite. Slide the folder into the image of a satellite that will appear on your computer. Then I let your friend live."

A long pause ensued.

"Now!" Chen barked.

"Rachel," Monroe said. "You don't have to do this. Combat is combat."

"I've already started it," she whispered hoarsely.

Chen watched the handheld satellite monitor display. After a moment, a green bar spread across the surface showing 100 percent downloaded to his handheld device, but now he needed to inspect that he had received both the cyberattack algorithm and the cipher coding that worked in tandem to hack and control other aircraft.

Chen looked at Monroe and said, "You fly this plane as intended to Taiwan. You land this plane, and everyone walks off. You give off no distress signals. You don't deviate. I will inspect to ensure I have what I came for. If I have both aspects of the TYRANT platform, nothing else needs to happen. If I don't, then your families die."

Chen held his satellite receiver in his hand at eye level so that Monroe could see it.

"Except for my dead friend, Logan," Monroe said.

"A necessary casualty," Chen said. Then, to General Fox, "General, if you alert anyone, you will only kill the passengers on the plane. I am checking the code to make sure it is authentic and that you sent me both the TYRANT Control Algorithm and the TYRANT Cipher. I know that one will not fully work without the other. I will test it, and if it doesn't work as intended, Monroe will die. All the passengers will die. And I have a team outside your home at this moment ready to kill you, your husband, and your children. We start with the children. The youngest first. Then we work our way up to your teenager. Then your husband. Then we will let all that sink in before killing you."

Fox gasped audibly, and that sound was followed by a moaning wail.

"He's not bluffing, Rachel. He showed me a team outside my home in Frederick. That much is true," Monroe said.

"Good, see? I expect compliance. We are monitoring your phones, both secure and nonsecure," Chen said.

"I understand," she managed to say.

Chen said, "You will never hear from me again if you have done what I asked. Your Cyber Command and National Security Agency are being jammed as we speak. There is no way to trace this action. Your best path is to forget this happened."

In the distant background a male voice, probably General Fox's husband, said, "Rach, everything okay?"

After a brief pause, she said, "Yeah, babe. Just work. You know how it goes."

Then, "Okay, come back to bed. Rylee is scared of something. Says she sees monsters outside. She's in our bed now. Just FYI."

"Yeah, sure. Monsters. I'll be there in a few minutes."

After a minute, she came back and said, "Anything else?" Her voice was tight with anger.

"Just listen to Rylee and beware of the monsters," Chen said.

Chen hung up and looked at Monroe.

"A team in McLean, Virginia, and a team in Frederick, Maryland. They are prepared to act."

Monroe stared at him and said, "This is cruel. Kids. Spouses are off limits."

"This is war, Colonel, there are no limits."

Monroe stared at him.

"You should have a check-in with NORAD coming up. They are tracking you like any other airplane. As far as they know, nothing is wrong. I don't want to hear any special code words. The knife is against your throat. I know there are many military aircraft you could summon to your aid, but I have TYRANT now and my team will confirm it. There is no use in getting the aircraft shot down."

"I don't personally care about myself," Monroe said. "But the three hundred people onboard, I do care about. That code, though, is the key to the military fighter jet kingdom. How did you know about it?"

"We have spies everywhere," Chen said. "Literally."

"What do you intend to do with it?"

"What do you think?"

Monroe was quiet for a long time until Chen said, "Yes, exactly that."

"TransPac 1001, this is NORAD Elmendorf, confirm location and status," Chen heard faintly through the headset in the seat where Prescott had been sitting. He placed the headset on and nodded at Monroe.

After a long pause, the voice asked again, "Repeat, TransPac 1001, this is NORAD Elmendorf, confirm location and status."

Monroe cleared his throat and said, "Elmendorf, this is Trans-Pac 1001. We are currently at waypoint 11 over St. Lawrence Island at 38,000 feet, maintaining an airspeed of 480 miles per hour. No issues."

"Roger that, I'd like to send my congratulations to Captain Prescott on his retirement."

Chen's knife pressed into Monroe's throat, drawing a drop of blood.

"Captain Prescott is currently changing shift but will relay the well wishes."

After a short pause, Elmendorf Control said, "Please do. Beware of Russian MiGs patrolling over Provideniya. Routine patrol. Safe journey, TransPac 1001. Elmendorf, out."

"Roger. TransPac, out."

Provideniya was the easternmost Russia city adjacent to the Bering Strait. It was illegal for a NATO country aircraft to fly over Russian airspace, and the US-to-Taipei flight path took TransPac 1001 perilously close to the twelve-mile boundary of the international law of the sea.

"I think asking for Prescott was a code. That was not normal," Chen said.

"It was," Monroe said.

"But I gave the appropriate response."

Chen looked at his handheld satellite knowing he needed to transmit it to his trusted ground-based operative to store in a secure server. He figured it would be about thirty minutes for him to transition what uploaded to his handheld satellite device to his ground-based server using the Ku band, which he had left open on the jammer.

Chen said, "Thirty minutes, Colonel, and everyone will be okay."

CHAPTER SIXTEEN

ZARA SHERIDAN

ZARA LOOKED AT RETIRED AIR FORCE COLONEL JEREMY WEST AND said, "Nothing is happening."

"What do you mean?" West asked.

"We haven't deviated. We haven't risen or fallen in altitude. There have been no subtle shifts. Little to no turbulence."

"Depending on what the hijacker wants, he may not want any kind of deviation that would alert air traffic control or NORAD," West said.

On the bulkhead of the spare crew cabin was a monitor that could perform all the functions of the standard passenger entertainment module. Zara punched the touch screen with a slender finger and the globe spun into view. The monitor provided the effect of a zooming camera that showed the Boeing 777-300ER in cartoon fashion passing over the western tip of the Aleutians.

"We just flew over all kinds of military bases. Elmendorf, Greely, Wainwright. Air force, army, coast guard. South Korea isn't far. Whole bunch of friendlies there. Gotta be something we can do," Zara said. "Somebody we can talk to."

West pulled out a satellite phone and showed it to Zara.

"I've got one of those, too. Tried it. Doesn't work."

"You're on L band satellite?"

"Yes. Standard-issue Federal Air Marshal Service satellite phone that is supposed to work no matter what."

"Hmm," West said. "Mine's not working either."

"I've been thinking this guy put a jammer somewhere in the plane. Could jam phones without jamming the plane's GPS."

"That's a possibility."

She watched West chew on his cheek, then say, "Got to be another accomplice on the plane."

"So we have three missions. Find the accomplice. Possibly plural. Find the jammer and disable it. Then breach the cockpit door and disable the hijacker."

"All while not crashing the airplane," West said.

"Where would a jammer be most effective?" Zara asked.

"My guess is just about anywhere, but who can afford satellite phones?"

"First and business class. So somewhere in there," Zara said.

"Any guesses on who the accomplice might be? I've been sleeping," West said.

"There's always Amanda. Something's off with her. Kind of a bitch," Zara said.

"Degrees of bitchiness are my specialty when it comes to women," West quipped. "She seemed right up there near the top. But then again, she watched a pilot get murdered and her head steward throttled. So I'll cut her some slack at the beginning."

"Then there's the Copperhead crew," Zara said.

"Copperhead? The contractors? I know some of them. Some good guys. Some bad guys. Like anything."

"Three boarded late. They were last to board, in fact, along with a Blackwood Aviation engineer."

"I did some test flying for Blackwood on contract after retiring from the air force."

"Johnnie Wilson?"

"I know who Wilson is. He's an engineer, not a pilot. He pioneered drone swarming communications and some other advanced technology I can't discuss."

"Well, he's in seat 9B if you want to talk to him," Zara said. "And I have a TS/SCI clearance still."

Top Secret with Specially Compartmented Information was one of the highest classifications possible within the United States government. Zara had carried a secret clearance as a senior non-commissioned officer in the army. It was required for reading intelligence briefings in combat in preparation for developing and executing military police operations such as checkpoints or cordon and search missions.

The spare pilot cabin was eerily quiet when Zara and West weren't speaking. The thrum of the engines whined with their steady buzz.

"Well, Wilson also worked on plane-to-plane hacking and control. He calls the program Twisted Spider. TYRANT is a capability within the Twisted Spider program. There are other capabilities beyond TYRANT that I can't discuss. But this TYRANT capability is supposed to have first-generation capability to reach out to another airplane, say a fighter jet, and jam its weapons systems, reorient its GPS waypoints, or execute any number of potential software and hardware hacks. It uses free space optical technology and quantum tunneling."

"There's a word salad," Zara said.

"Roger. Most optical technology requires fiber optics. Recent advancements allow lasers to provide optical bandwidth connections without any cables. The malicious code travels to the target inside the laser-generated bandwidth and then the quantum tunneling breaches all the cybersecurity layers of the target aircraft for the hardware and software."

"In the army, we call that breach and assault," Zara said.

"Exactly," West said, pointing a finger at her.

"Why Twisted Spider?"

"Wilson had drawings that showed an airplane shooting Precision Laser Optical Bandwidth out toward other airplanes like a spider shooting its silk out to make a web or catch its prey."

Zara nodded. She could visualize what West was saying. Invisible rays of energy latching on to other airplanes in the sky, commandeering the controls, making the need to shoot it down unnecessary.

"Why shoot down the airplane when you can control it?"

"Exactly," West said.

"Where does it breach? The IFF?" Zara asked.

West pointed at her. "Exactly. The IFF ping goes out to Identify Friend or Foe, hence IFF, and when the opposing aircraft receives the signal, the quantum tunneling breaches the aircraft controls. You need a helmet, though, which provides the heads-up display of the opposing aircraft. There are two connections required to direct Precision Laser Optical Bandwidth. PLOB is the new acronym for the Hyperion. But it's mostly useless without the helmet."

"With Wilson, Xiao Chen, and Copperhead onboard, there has to be some connection to Blackwood and the Hyperion jet that crashed in North Carolina."

"When did the crash happen?" West asked, surprised.

"Directly before takeoff. My son was coming home from baseball practice and saw it happen. Checking for survivors, he found this." Zara held up the orange flash-drive-looking device with "Classified" and "Code Word" emblazoned on either side. Beneath "Code Word" was the word "TYRANT."

West took it from her outstretched hand and turned it over in his, studying it. He ran his thumb across the "TYRANT" label. "Your son found this near the crash site?"

"He said it was hanging from the cockpit dashboard or something like that."

"Instrument panel."

"Right. Any idea what it is?"

West leveled his eyes at her. His weathered face was expressionless, a feature Zara guessed he had learned from being a combat aviator who encountered many problems in the air and on the ground.

"I know exactly what this is," he said.

Zara shrugged her shoulders in a questioning gesture.

"You going to tell me?"

"It's the guts of TYRANT, or Tactical Yoke for Remote Aircraft Navigation and Targeting, but half is missing, so it's basically useless without the other piece to communicate with it, and the helmet, of course. The whole thing together is worth billions. One half does encryption so it can't be hacked, while the other half does the hacking of other aircraft."

"Which half is this?"

"Not sure. If I had to guess, I would say it's the algorithm half. The part that can control the enemy aircraft. With both together, this is the foundation of the Hyperion program. It's how you can control any other aircraft, not just enemy ones. No need to shoot them down when you can bring them down. People would kill for this. In fact, they'd hijack an airplane for this. My friend Hawk Monroe is the copilot. He worked on this program with me."

Zara studied West for a moment as a thought scratched at the back of her mind. She said, "My son Lucas has the other half."

West's eyes shot up.

"How old is he?"

"Fourteen."

"Where's your husband?"

"Working late. Might be home. Haven't been able to get in touch with him."

West looked at his phone. Still dead. Zara checked hers. Still no connection.

"We need to get into the cockpit," West said. He pulled a Leatherman tool from his backpack.

Zara didn't move. She was thinking about Lucas and what kind of trouble he might have gotten himself into. If someone was willing to hijack an airplane for this technology, what would they do to her son?

"I'm going to look for that jammer," she said.

"Watch those Copperhead guys. We're both armed, but they

might be, too. Copperhead has part of the TSA contract for augmenting screening through the Screening Partnership Program."

She thought of her confrontation with "Clark," the Copperhead screening agent through the air marshals' private screening entrance. Had Hembrick and his team been let through with weapons?

"Roger that," she said as she scrambled down the steps.

CHAPTER SEVENTEEN

ZARA SHERIDAN

Zara returned to her seat and retrieved a DefCon iProtect signals device tracker that she hoped could help her locate the satellite and Wi-Fi jammer. She also slid Lucas's homemade glasses on and stood in the aisle for a moment.

A few attendant call lights were shining yellow slivers of light onto passengers who appeared frustrated. One man was speaking in an agitated manner to one of the flight attendants standing in between business and coach class. Zara slowly approached the man, who was pointing at his seat and then holding up his phone.

"This is a sixteen-hour flight and there's no Wi-Fi?" he barked.

"Sir, we are working on the technical issue as we speak," the female attendant replied. She was Asian, maybe a head shorter than him, and had her hair pulled back in a tight bun.

"I've been trying for an hour! I'm a legit tech specialist. I have *worked* on airplane Wi-Fi. Let me look at it instead of some poser flight attendant."

"Excuse me," Zara said, stepping up to them. The lavatory door was to her right and the crew station to her left. Lucas's glasses gave her a reading of the man's attitude as "Angry," but not "Violent." "We are working on the situation as fast as we can."

"Who are you?" the man spat.

"All you need to know is that we are working on the situation as fast as we can. We apologize for the inconvenience. I'll ask you once nicely to please take your seat. You don't want me to ask a second time."

"What the fuck?" The man then looked at Zara's midsection, where her pistol bulge was noticeable. He waited a beat, let it process, and then said, "My apologies. I'll work offline. It's just I have a deadline for when we land in Taipei. It's a huge business deal. Why we took this flight."

"Good luck with your work, Mr. . . . ?"

"Randy Wellstone. I own a business in Chapel Hill, North Carolina. Like I said, this flight is a big deal for us. I'm on deadline to get this presentation done. We're straight to Hsinchu when we land."

Zara nodded. She had done her research. Hsinchu was the Science Park, much like the Research Triangle Park of North Carolina. It was located on the west coast of Taiwan about forty-five minutes south of the airport and an hour south of Taipei. Connecting the two high-technology locales was the genius behind TransPac Airline's business model. With the acceleration of artificial intelligence and ubiquity of chips, the need for secure, in-person, and face-to-face meetings became paramount. Even minor modifications in technology or code required secure communications, and many companies were finding that even their most secure cables and chips were being targeted by quantum tunneling for intercept.

In-person meetings could mitigate corporate spying, as well.

"I'm also a North Carolinian," Zara said. "Fayetteville. I understand."

"Thank you," Wellstone replied. He looked at the flight attendant before turning back to his seat.

"Oh, my God, thank you."

"Hi, I'm Zara Sheridan. You are?" Zara held out an outstretched hand.

"Julie Chang. I'm from Los Angeles but have family in the southern part of Taiwan near the port of Kao-hsiung." She pronounced it like "Cow-shung" as she pointed in the direction where Wellstone disappeared, and said, "He was beginning to become a pain in the ass."

"Glad to help," Zara said.

It occurred to her that the flight crew, other than Amanda, Monroe, and West, were oblivious to what had taken place in the cockpit. Amanda had done well communicating that the system was down and that the crew was working to resolve the issue.

"Can I help?" Julie asked. She looked worried. Furrowed brow. Downturned lips. Not the usual flight attendant expression.

"Manifest by seat number?" Zara asked. "I have one but want to confirm something."

Julie retrieved a black, rubberized tablet from the stainless-steel counter where food preparations normally took place.

"Here," she said, after tapping a few places on the touch screen.

Zara held the weighty device and scrolled until she confirmed Charles Lei's name and seat. Three rows deep in first class directly behind Agent Bucknell's first-class pod.

Charles Lei was Xiao Chen, she confirmed.

"Thank you," Zara said, and handed Julie the tablet.

"Everything okay? I'm getting a weird vibe," Julie said.

"We're good," Zara said, somewhat avoidantly. "Just need to check something."

She walked along the aisle toward the aft of the aircraft, noticing a few people were waking up and becoming frustrated they had no connectivity. Today, even on airplanes, being connected to Wi-Fi was the standard, not the exception, and people's brains had been rewired to need that dopamine hit of texts, e-mails, games, or books. A few minutes of no connectivity typically resulted in anger and frustration. Zara could see that was happening here by the mini tantrums some people were exhibiting. Punching at phones. Rebooting computers. Hitting the call buttons.

It wouldn't be long before a mutiny occurred, but she needed to find the jammer and then unlock only the satellite communications so that she could alert the headquarters, and the national command authority could then determine a response.

It was dark in all the cabins, save a few lights randomly scattered from e-book readers and phones. Over 90 percent of the passengers were sleeping, Zara guessed. As she looped through the aft galley and walked slowly through the starboard aisle, she continuously looked at her signals device tracker, hoping to get a reading on the jammer Lei had used to block the communications ports of the aircraft. So far, nothing was moving the needle.

As she passed from business to economy, Zara's handheld signal tracker remained dormant. The needle visible in the display window didn't move. She studied the passengers, mostly asleep, some who glanced up at her most likely thinking she was just another passenger headed to the restroom. She looked at the passengers laid out in business class, all asleep in the comfortable extended beds.

She transitioned through the business-class galley into first class and approached Lei's seat, where a crumpled gray blanket was wadded in the semi-reclined chair. At the foot of his pod was a briefcase. She sat on the edge of the seat in the enclosed space and opened the briefcase, even though the signal monitor needle was motionless. A MacBook with Chinese characters on the keyboard was the only discernable item of value in the black leather case. She searched the pockets on either side and found nothing but pens and paper clips. She tapped on the keyboard of the MacBook and the login screen came up. The screensaver image behind the login prompt was a black-and-white of an Asian man standing on a hill overlooking what she presumed was the Pacific Ocean. It was a profile picture, and Zara presumed this was the hijacker's father or a relative. Above his head written in block letters was the word Gǎnsǐduì.

She would have to look that word up, so she took a picture of it with her phone to document its exact spelling before closing the computer and stowing everything as it was.

Standing, she noticed in her periphery that the needle on the signals-tracking monitor twitched. Was it her motion that caused it to move or was she closing in on the jammer? She opened the overhead bin as the airplane hit some turbulence, shuddering briefly, and then continued on its smooth glide. There were two carry-on suitcases and two shopping bags above Lei's seat. She checked the name tags. One for a Benjamin Levine and another for a Wendy Levine. Zara looked at the middle two seats and saw the husband and wife team sleeping soundly. She opened the two shopping bags and saw purchases from the duty-free store with current receipts.

Would he have placed the jammer in a more hidden location or somewhere "hidden in plain sight"?

Other than the one twitch, the signals device tracker so far showed no sign of any jamming equipment. She made sure the device was working properly and walked to the first row of first class. Intuitively, she wondered if he would place the jammer near the main Wi-Fi bank, which was right here near the front of the airplane.

When she reached the forward section of first class on the starboard side of the aircraft, the tracker buzzed lightly in her hand. The indicator arrow swung wildly as she approached the second row behind the bulkhead separating first class from the galley. She moved to her right and the arrow slowed in pace. To her left, and the arrow quickened. She looked at the sleeping passengers as she opened the bin.

Hembrick, one of the Copperhead late arrivals, was reading a tablet and glanced up at her when she pulled out a black satchel the size of a bowling ball bag. It was heavy. Unzipping it, she saw lights blinking and an array of short, rubberized antennae that poked up at her like an alien sea creature. She focused on the device, noticing movement in her periphery.

"Stop right there, Marshal," Hembrick said from his seat, snapping shut his tablet.

She felt something pressing into her back as she looked over her shoulder at Hembrick's teammate, Juan Rodriguez, who must have followed her. He nodded and put his finger across his lips.

Stay silent.

What was happening?

"We want that," Hembrick said. "Just move slowly with me and hand me the jammer."

"Is it yours?" she asked from over her shoulder.

"It is now," he said.

"We know what's happening in the cockpit. We're going to take control," Hembrick said.

"Not your role," Zara replied.

"You need us to help you. Trust me. The reason we boarded late? We learned Charles Lei, better known as Xiao Chen, was on the plane. You're not equipped to deal with him. So, let's work together."

"Let's," Zara said. "You can start by removing whatever you've got poking into my back. Then I'm going to study this device and determine how best to use it while we have a . . . situation in cockpit."

"Not the way this is going to work," Hembrick said. Hembrick moved silently from his seat, through the flight attendant station, keeping Zara moving beside him via the pressure in her back.

"Let's go upstairs," Hembrick said. "And we can talk."

"Upstairs?" she said, feigning ignorance.

"Right there. Flight attendant crew rest cabin." He pointed at the galley between first and business class. "Before we wake someone."

"I don't know the door code," Zara replied. He was tugging lightly at her arm, urging him along with her.

"We do," Hembrick said.

Amanda, the flight attendant from first class, was standing by the door to the steep stairwell. When they approached, Hembrick nodded at her. Amanda looked at Zara, who nodded imperceptibly. Amanda punched in the code and opened the door so that Zara could enter first, followed by Hembrick and Rodriguez.

At the top were four bunks, much like the pilot crew rest area, but there was no one in the beds, as had been the case with Jeremy West above the cockpit.

Zara turned around and held out her pistol, aimed it directly between Hembrick's eyes as he was stacked in the stairway with Rodriguez behind him.

"Stop. Turn around. And leave."

"You're going to shoot me?"

"I will if you don't back down."

"We're trying to help you. We have a full dossier on Xiao Chen. We know why he's on this airplane. We knew there was a jammer somewhere. We followed you, which frankly was more watching you. We want to make sure you do this right."

"Not your job to manage me, Hembrick. I know the situation," Zara said.

"Are you aware that Chen is from a long line of suicide kamikaze style military men? Like I told you earlier, they're called Gǎnsǐduì in Chinese."

"Yes, and I saw it on Lei's MacBook," she said. "Gǎnsǐduì, like kamikaze. Suicide mission."

Hembrick was slowly projecting himself forward. Rodriguez had backed off a step, perhaps to give Hembrick or himself some maneuver room.

"I've got the entire dossier on the guy," Hembrick said. "You worked with General Sinclair and JSOC and Jake Mahegan and all those guys, right? Army MP to local cop to military contractor with Sharpstone to the federal air marshals. Lots of promotions in there, Sheridan."

"Get to the point," Zara said. "Because I will shoot you if I determine you're a threat to this aircraft. And if you know so much about me, then you also know I was the best pistol shot in Sharpstone. Beat Mahegan, Hobart, and Van Dreeves." Her aim never wavered. Her hand was steady. If Hembrick moved on her, she would shoot him between the eyes.

"Yes. We know this about you." He paused for a second, then continued. "Copperhead picked up the Dagger mission when your old boss Garrett Sinclair retired. We had a lead that Xiao Chen had killed Charles Lei and boarded a short hop from Burbank to Vegas, got airside, and stayed airside until he got to RDU. The president flexed us onto this flight."

"That's bullshit and you know it, Hembrick."

"It's Josh. Call me Josh, please."

His tone was gentle but firm.

"I have no updates that any Dagger team was supposed to be on this flight," she said.

Dagger team was President Kim Campbell's special mission unit that resided inside JSOC, the Joint Special Operations Command. Lieutenant General Garrett Sinclair had led JSOC and its subunit, Dagger, for his deceased wife's college roommate, who happened to be the president now. When Sinclair retired, he was building out a global private security company called Sharpstone, and it paid well.

Now, here she was going toe to toe with Sharpstone's main rival private military contractor company, Copperhead, that had a dubious reputation, at best. She couldn't envision the president asking them to execute the sensitive mission Hembrick had just described.

But what if? She had been out of communications for several hours. Charlotte HQ might have been trying to contact her. And the information about Charles Lei was late breaking.

She pressed the side of her Lucas glasses and got a reading:

Evasive. Violent.

That message wasn't reassuring, but she said, "Leave your guy down there and show me what you have on Chen."

Hembrick turned to Rodriguez, who had heard Zara. He nodded at his boss and backed away. Amanda shut the door as Zara backed up and sat in a chair facing the door. She motioned with her pistol for Hembrick to sit in the chair opposite hers.

"Talk to me," she said.

Hembrick's demeanor shifted. His pleasantness evaporated and was replaced with a stern operator's gaze. He ran his hand along his ribcage beneath his loose-fitting windbreaker. Zara could smell his sweat. His tension coiled in him like an angry viper.

Evasive. Violent.

But he didn't strike.

"This is all about the Next Generation aircraft and the cyber warfare capabilities in it. The Hyperion crash in Eastern North Carolina happened around the time you were leaving for RDU. Our guy Clark who was doing the screening told us you assaulted him and snuck a classified flash drive onto the plane," he replied.

Zara said nothing.

"And my men in Swan Quarter tell me that your son has the other half."

"Leave my son alone," Zara snapped.

"We need both halves of the platform, the algorithm, and the cipher, and everyone will be fine."

"Are you threatening me? My family?"

"No. I'm just saying that there are bad people who would kill for that cipher box. Chen is one of them. This jammer," he said, lightly kicking the bag Zara had placed on the floor next to her. "We can only open channels so that we can talk, because if word gets out that this plane is hijacked and it has the Next Gen platform onboard, we will have China, Russia, North Korea, and even our country trying to scramble this airplane to the ground. Their special forces will raid the plane and kill anyone who stops them."

"All over some software?"

"This isn't software. It's artificial intelligence that can take control of other airplanes, tanks, you name it. That's why it's a Dagger mission. My men were on the ground at the crash site and saw your son take the TYRANT harness."

"Wait a minute. Then how does Chen factor in?"

"Completely separate. Hawk Monroe up there in the cockpit? He used to be the director of the Next Generation fighter jet. He's a pilot and a computer scientist. He and General Rachel Fox were in charge. Logan retired, but Fox is still there. My money says Chen killed Prescott and has a gun to Monroe's head and they're calling Fox to do an aerial transmission of the code on a bandwidth he kept open."

Zara looked at the bag.

"This should tell us, I believe," she said.

She opened it and retrieved the shoebox-size device with twelve antennae protruding upward. She turned it toward Hembrick as they both studied the front panel.

"Battery operated. State of the art. Wi-Fi down. Satellite down. LTE down. Transponder open. Ku band open. He's transmitting on Ku band, which is big pipes."

Zara said nothing.

"If he's got the code, he's probably relayed it to a ground station. If that's the case, we're truly screwed."

"Only one way to find out," Zara said.

"You want to go toe to toe with a suicide pilot? Have him fly us into the ground? He's done his mission, if this is true. Nothing up here is useful to him anymore."

Zara listened. Something clawed at the back of her mind. Everything Hembrick was saying made sense. She remembered her military training. Sometimes the best deception was to play into the totality of the situation with only a slight deviation or hidden motive.

"What's your suggestion, Ranger?"

Hembrick smiled for the first time. Zara saw an opening to soften Hembrick and seized it.

"Did my time with First Batt, yes. But my suggestion here is that we figure out a way to let you do your job without getting us killed. We can provide backup, but it's all about getting the cockpit door open and killing Chen. Barring that, he can kill Monroe and put this puppy in a nosedive."

"Well, what I was talking about was this yellow light here. See?" Zara said. She pointed at the jammer. "If what you say is true, that Chen is stealing the Next Gen algorithms, then he hasn't passed it to his ground team yet."

"How do you know that?"

"My son is a computer genius, and he taught me a few things. Suffice it to say that this is like a sent e-mail in the outbox. It's yellow. The others are red. When the Ku band light turns green, then the data has left the control unit, but not until then."

Zara pushed the button on the control unit, shutting down the Ku band and any transmission of data.

"No!" Hembrick shouted as the airplane began to plummet.

CHAPTER EIGHTEEN

XIAO CHEN

XIAO CHEN STARED AT HAWK MONROE.

"Do you believe your lover gave me everything?"

Monroe nodded. "I'm sure she did."

Chen looked at the device in his hand that now held the cyber-attack platform known as TYRANT.

He texted his ground control operative from the Silent Fang unit in the Department of Guoanbu, the Chinese Department of State Security, that he was about to transmit the code to the ground station.

The moon is descending into the river.

As he pressed the button, the transmitter flashed green and began sending the platform.

The river is receiving the moon.

That was good news.

As the yellow lights flashed, he saw percentages of transmission moving from 5 percent to 19 percent to 32 percent.

Yellow lights flashed, and the progressing percentages slowed to a crawl until the indicator turned red. His stomach clenched. For whatever reason, the transmission from his receiver to the Silent Fang ground station was taking longer than expected. He had calculated the orbit of the satellite and the positioning of the airplane at the general window of his breach of the cockpit, but because his action was dependent upon Logan Prescott's intestinal issues, he couldn't precisely time the attack.

As the data was downloading to his team in Shanghai, the transmitter blinked from green to yellow and back to green several times. Connection with the satellite was spotty as they flew just south of the North Pole and bored through the Bering Strait between Russia and Alaska. He looked at the satellite transmitter in his hand, which had blinked from green to yellow and now . . . to red?

This can't be happening. If the data transmission from his device to his ground operator's device had stopped, it was not a good development.

He looked at Monroe, whose hands he had FlexiCuffed but were visible on the cockpit yoke. Monroe looked at him and must have noticed an expression of concern.

"What happened?"

"The code quit transmitting. Did your General Fox do something?"

"You know she didn't. She complied with your request."

"Maybe she put a malicious code in there."

"Her family's life depends on your success. She wouldn't do that."

Chen studied the satellite box in his hand. He scrolled through the touch screen window and could see that the entire file had downloaded from Fox's classified computer to his hard drive but that the transmission of the data packets on the Ku satellite band from his satellite box to his Shanghai team had been either interrupted or stopped.

"This can't be," he said in Mandarin.

His objective was to deliver the code to the ground team and then crash the airplane into a strategic target, thereby claiming his Gǎnsǐduì status in Chinese history. If the code had not fully transmitted, then he had the only copy apart from what was in the secure Pentagon servers.

He considered his options.

He could land with the airplane in Taiwan. That would not

only be a horrible idea, but he had thin backup in Taipei to off-load his bounty. Alternatively, he could troubleshoot the satellite transmitter and work through the issue, but he had deadlines to meet. The transfer of the technology was time sensitive.

"I see you thinking," Monroe said. "Maybe I can help. I don't con-done what you've done, but my mission right now is to keep every-one alive on this airplane."

"You have no control over that. I say who lives and who dies."

Monroe's eyes blinked solemnly.

"You don't believe me?" Chen snapped. Typically he was calm and collected, but not at the moment. Someone had disrupted his simple plan.

"I believe you," Monroe said.

"I don't think you do."

Chen retrieved his knife and slashed through the air, then placed the blade against Monroe's throat.

"Put us in a nosedive now," Chen said.

"What?"

"Now!"

Chen reached across and unlocked the autopilot, then pushed the throttle forward, nosing the plane over until it was in a screech-ing dive.

CHAPTER NINETEEN

LUCAS SHERIDAN

*L*UCAS PLACED THE AVIATOR HELMET ON MIA AND POINTED AT THE monitor.

"See all of the planes flying into and out of Norfolk and Raleigh?"

"Yeah," she said. "It's like one of those flight tracker apps but with perfect resolution."

Lucas and Mia had spent some time tracking airplanes and watching the systemic patterns of the aircraft and their flight routes. For a couple of nerdy kids in Eastern North Carolina, it was something fun to do.

"Whoa," Mia said. "This heads-up display is asking me to identify my target."

"Yeah, don't do that. These are commercial aircraft, and I have no idea what the algorithm does."

Mia lifted her hand and turned her head.

"I've got a drone flying at us from the lake," she said. "The heads-up is asking me to identify it."

Lucas said, "Let me see."

Mia removed the helmet, and Lucas fit it back onto his head, allowing him to immediately see the drone. The heads-up display provided information on the drone's altitude, azimuth of flight, speed, distance, communications platform, and avionics suite with a prompt at the end.

78 meters
32 degrees
14 knots
.4 miles
LTE
GPS waypoints
Acquire?

The difference this time was that the "Acquire?" prompt was not grayed out. It was flashing green.

Lucas hovered the cursor over "Acquire," and a secondary prompt appeared.

No cryptographic security.

Lucas said, "Interesting."

"What?" Mia asked. "And quit saying interesting like you're Sherlock Holmes or something. Just tell me." She smacked him playfully on the shoulder.

"For commercial airliners, the 'Acquire' prompt is disabled. It's grayed out. You can't click on it. Here, with the drone, it's enabled. I think the software in the flash drive makes a read on whether it needs to penetrate any cybersecurity. If it does, you need the other half that I gave my Moms. If the plane, or in this case, the drone, doesn't have any cyber defenses, the platform can control," Lucas said.

"So each half has a redundancy built into it?"

"Maybe. All I know is that the prompt is flashing green on the drone but it's disabled on the commercial plane."

"Try the drone," Mia said.

Lucas clicked on "Control," and the flashing green prompt switched to red. Instantly the heads-up display was showing the drone camera feed as it bore down on the Sheridan household.

"I'm seeing what the drone is seeing," Lucas said. "It's headed right at us."

Mia scrambled and found the Xbox joystick they sometimes used, plugged it into the USB port, and typed some code into MacBook.

"Not getting any connection between the joystick and the helmet," she said.

Lucas turned his head and said, "It's asking me if I want to maneuver the drone."

"Say yes!"

"Maneuver," he said.

The MacBook screen blinked a few times, and the drone imagery appeared on the monitor.

"I've got it! I've got it!" Mia shouted.

She banked the joystick, and the drone showed the terrain sweeping away. Suddenly there was a hard bank back to the path, and Mia banked it in the opposite direction.

"Either the GPS points are fighting you or there's a pilot on the other end."

"Gotta be someone on the other end. I'm in control. They can't fight me."

"Can you land it in the yard so I can grab it?" Lucas asked.

"This thing has more than a camera, I think," Mia said.

"Yeah, I see it. It's asking if I want to arm. This is wild."

Lucas was staring into the smoky heads-up display with the different commands popping up, prompting him to make decisions about opposing aircraft.

"Let's crash it and set up an ambush," Lucas said.

After a moment, Mia said, "Lukie Dukie, you're a genius. I know just the perfect spot. Talley Pond."

"Yeah, just hope old man Talley isn't out there bass fishing or something."

"At two A.M.?"

Lucas shrugged. "He's kinda crazy. 'No Trespassing' signs everywhere."

"He lets us get away with it."

"I know, but your dad's the sheriff and my mom used to be a deputy, so he kinda had to."

"Okay, here we go," Mia said.

Mia steered the drone to a remote wooded area just beyond hundreds of acres of soybean and peanut fields. Old man Talley had damned up an area where three streams converged at the south end of his property, creating a two-acre pond that he stocked with bass and bream. His kids and grandkids fished it some, and he indeed turned a blind eye when Mia and Lucas snuck out there with their fishing poles. The pond had a worn trail from the Sheridan backyard and was maybe a quarter mile to the north. Not far.

"Perfect. It will look like a mishap en route," Lucas said.

Mia steered the drone into the dam on the south end of the pond. There was a small, wooded hill about thirty meters from where she unceremoniously crashed the aircraft into some tall reeds lining the bank. The imagery made Lucas dizzy as it came buzzing into the pond as if he were the pilot.

"Good job," he said. "Now let's grab our stuff."

Their stuff included the shotgun, a box of shells, a Beretta pistol with another box of shells, their phones, two backpacks, and a turkey call.

"A turkey call?" Mia scoffed.

Lucas shrugged. "I go turkey hunting some with my dad. You never know when you might need it." He held it to his mouth and made the musical *gobble gobble* sound.

"You sound perfect for Thanksgiving," she chuckled.

They shut down all their communications gear and locked the flash drive and helmet in the gun safe this time. Lucas spun the combination before they dashed out the back door through the kitchen and back porch. They mounted their bikes and took off along the trail.

It was after midnight. The stars swirled brightly in the sky here with so little ambient big city light. Lucas led them along a well-worn trail behind some other one-acre lots with homes on them. He and Mia had ridden their bikes along this trail a million times, and they knew every bump and dip. Their wheels chattered in exactly the spots they expected them to as they arrived in less than ten minutes.

They laid their bikes in three-foot-tall grass behind the trees that would serve as their observation post. Lucas unpacked some of his backpack, including an aluminum blanket to shield their body heat from any infrared or thermal night vision goggles, which assuredly these guys would have. He mounted a directional microphone that would amplify any conversations and be recorded on his iPhone.

And they waited.

After an hour, Mia said, "Maybe it was just some kid's drone."

"At midnight? With weapons?" Lucas replied.

He felt her shrug. "Yeah. Good point. I guess I'm just tired."

"Get some sleep. I'll wake you."

"Nah. I'm your battle buddy, Lukie Dukie."

But he could hear her voice fading. She was lying next to him under the space blanket. Her body was warm and taking her to sleep. He felt her shoulders soften and noticed in his periphery when her head nestled in the crook of her bent forearm.

Twenty minutes later, a truck's brakes squeaked as it stopped near the dam. Lucas couldn't tell if it was the same truck that had entered their driveway and hauled off Deputy Cashwell, but chances were good it was a Copperhead truck.

Two men got out and slammed the doors. To Lucas, they did not seem tactically aware, which was a good sign. Lucas put one AirPod in his right ear so he could listen to their conversation through the directional microphone. He leaned over and whispered into Mia's ear, placing his hand on her back so she wouldn't startle.

"Wake up," he whispered.

She repositioned slightly, as if she were dreaming.

"Wake up, Mia. They're here."

Her eyes opened slowly, and she mumbled, "Roger that, good buddy." She placed an AirPod in her ear, too, so that she could listen in to the conversation.

Lucas lifted his binoculars to his eyes even though it was dark. He could better make out the shapes of the men, both of whom were big, muscled guys who could have been any that he interacted with throughout the day.

"I was flying the piece of shit perfectly, then it started juking around about a quarter mile from here like someone else was flying it," one man said. He had a deep voice, one Lucas wasn't certain if he had heard before. He didn't think so, but in his mind, he labeled this man "the drone pilot."

"Maybe that kid did it," the other man said.

"Nah. The DJ drones are pieces of shit. Made in China. They break every other time you fly 'em," the drone pilot said.

"Wish we could just go to the house now. We don't need to recon a kid," the second man said.

"Hembrick said to watch the kid."

Lucas believed this was the voice that was in the house previously. He made a note of the name Hembrick. He didn't know anyone by that name, but there were plenty of Copperhead contractors in the area that he didn't know personally. When his mother was a sheriff's deputy working for Mia's dad, she had a few run-ins with the Copperhead guys drinking and partying, but mostly they went up to Virginia Beach, where there were more people, especially women.

"Yeah, but Hembrick's taking orders," the drone pilot said.

"And we take orders from Hembrick. He said to watch them for now."

"Let's call him once we get the drone out of this fucking lake."

"It's a pond, dumbass, maybe one acre."

"Whatever. Snakes and shit in here," the drone pilot said.

"Well, we are Copperhead, so there's that. Maybe they'll treat you nice."

Then, after a few minutes of boots crunching through the grass and leaves, the drone pilot said, "There it is!"

"Wake up the whole neighborhood, dumbass."

"Yeah, sorry. Just excited to find it. These things go offline and sometimes you never get them back. Anyone with skills could get inside this thing and pick the SIM card clean, get all the imagery we've taken. All the missions we've flown. Where from. Where to. Lots of data in this bad boy."

The sound of splashing in water interrupted the conversation until the drone pilot said, "Damn it. Shit's muddy."

"Quit bitching. Got it?"

"Yeah, yeah, it's still intact. Almost like it wasn't a crash but a controlled landing."

More splashing, followed by, "I'm soaked."

Lucas and Mia were watching the scene unfold. So far, they had confirmed it was Copperhead private military contractors who had been flying the drone, that they were only to conduct reconnaissance on him and Mia, and that someone named Hembrick was calling the shots. Mia was tapping into the notes function on her phone, which she held beneath the space blanket.

"Got it all?" the big man asked.

"Yeah, think so. Looks intact. Just a second," the drone pilot said. He had taken a flashlight to inspect the drone.

"I'm doing a visual on this thing and there's not a scratch. Also, the comms box shows an intercept. Someone hacked into this thing."

"The kids?"

"Someone. Probably them."

"Like an ambush," the big man said. "Like intentional."

They both went silent, drew their weapons, and began scanning the area.

Lucas placed the turkey diaphragm call into his mouth and situated it between his teeth and tongue the way his father had taught him. Then he slid his shotgun from beneath the space blanket and put the buttstock against his shoulder, sighting into the moonlit darkness on the men silhouetted atop the level dam of the farm pond.

Their heads turned left and right, scanning. The drone operator slowly placed the drone on the ground and sighted his pistol with both hands as the two men went into a practiced back-to-back buddy drill. They pivoted and turned, placing night vision goggles against their eyes. They weren't wearing head harnesses. The fumbling between weapons and goggles seemed to hamper their ability to scan and detect until the drone pilot said, "Got something."

He was staring directly at the wooded area where he and Mia were camped.

"There," the other man whispered as he looked through his goggles.

Lucas could shoot either of them from this short range but didn't want to pull the trigger just yet. He was a kid, not a killer, but he was also aware of the stakes. He felt Mia's hand on his left bicep that was flexed as he nestled his left elbow into the sandy soil with his hand holding the stock of the weapon level. He understood her gesture to mean "hold your fire."

A high-pitched groaning noise emanated as if it were coming from another direction. It repeated multiple times. Mia's hand tightened on his arm.

"Fucking turkeys?" the drone pilot said.

"Sounds like they're across the pond. This guy Talley is wild. He hunts at night. Let's get the fuck out of here."

The men gathered their drone and backtracked to the pickup truck, which they mounted and drove away.

"Oh, my God," Mia whispered. "What was that noise?"

Lucas could see her big eyes looking at him as he spit out his turkey call.

"NFW."

"Yes way," he said.

"But it was coming from a hundred yards away."

"My dad taught me how to throw the call, as he calls it. You don't want the turkeys on top of you. You want them so you can shoot them."

"Ugh. I hate that you kill animals."

"Be glad, grasshopper. It might have saved our butts tonight."

"We got some intel, for sure."

They waited another thirty minutes. They saw two turkeys walking along the dam where the Copperhead henchmen had been.

"Don't you dare," Mia said.

"Wouldn't think of it with you here, my dear. Now let's book."

They decamped and rode their bikes back to the house. Retrieving the equipment from the safe, Lucas and Mia reconnected the helmet and the classified avionics to his MacBook.

"We'll keep this on as an air defense shield. You should sleep," Lucas said.

"No, I got at least an hour under the stars. You've got to be more tired."

"I could sleep," Lucas said. "But I'm nervous."

"I've got your back. Underneath the steps is a good spot if you use the moving blankets. I'll be right here."

They fist-bumped. Mia donned the aviator helmet and Lucas crawled into the wad of blankets that smelled musty from too many moves and too few washes.

He was so completely tired that his mind couldn't register what he had missed in the Copperhead drone retrieval team's conversation. There was something he believed was important, but exhaustion spiraled through his brain. With uncertainty about what he had just heard and an uneasy, paranoid feeling that they were being watched, he fell asleep within a minute not realizing his father's truck was parked out front.

CHAPTER TWENTY

ZARA SHERIDAN

*T*HE PLANE ROCKETED FROM THE SKY IN AN ALMOST VERTICAL DOWN-
ward plunge.

Zara was thrown against the bulkhead of the crew rest cabin
above the business-class seating area. She dropped her pistol when
her wrist slammed against the wall.

Because Hembrick was in the narrow stairwell, he was able to
brace himself against the opposing walls.

"Damn it!" Hembrick shouted. "He's crashing the plane because you shut down his feed! Open it back up!"

Zara braced against the G-forces that were pulling her downward like a carnival ride. She was pressed into place by the inertia,
an invisible hand holding her down and briefly reminding her of
her darkest day in the military. But she couldn't go there now.
She had tucked that incident away in a locked file cabinet in her
mind; otherwise, the trauma, the memory, the primal fear she'd
felt would trigger the most violent reaction. And while she had
never personally killed anyone in combat, she had nearly killed a
man in Fayetteville. She didn't think of him as a man or even
human. Fifteen years ago, as a young buck sergeant, an officer
had assaulted her. He wasn't in her chain of command, but he
was a well-known predator among the enlisted females. He had
picked on the wrong woman that night.

She had stood her ground and beaten the officer with several body blows, leaving his face intact. For an instant, she wanted to kill him. Felt the primal urge. Her hands went to his throat . . . and then she backed away. Reason overrode her rightful loathing of the man.

Perhaps that was what she needed now, but she had conditioned herself to tuck away emotion and think practically about every tactical situation like the good leader she had proven herself to be in combat. And now, she had a mission to complete. It was simple: save the airplane and its passengers and get home safely to her family.

Mission or men? She vowed to accomplish both.

The jammer was still in the carry bag and had slammed into the pillows stacked for flight attendant crew rest. She presumed it was still functional, even if she wasn't sure about herself.

The phone in the flight attendant crew area buzzed about the same time the airplane leveled out to a smoother ride. Passengers were screaming. There seemed to be genuine panic throughout the airplane.

Zara answered the phone as she looked for her pistol. It was wedged between one of the beds and the interior of the aircraft.

"I'll get that for you," Hembrick said before she could grasp the gun.

"No," she replied, but he already had the pistol in his hand. The look on his face was disconcerting. Eyes narrowed, brow furrowed, lips pressed together.

"We are going to have to work together," he said, flipping the pistol around and handing it to her grip first.

She nodded and said, "Hello?"

"Marshal, this is Amanda, the lead flight attendant now that Marcus is out of commission."

"Yes?"

"The hijacker just put the airplane into that nosedive to send us a warning. He says that someone has turned off the bandwidth and they have five minutes to turn it back on. I have no idea what he's talking about. I've pushed every button on this communications panel, but nothing is working."

"You're talking to him?"

"He called the flight attendant main switch!"

"Patch him through to me," Zara said.

"What?"

"Do it now," Zara said.

A long minute passed as the plane leveled out and found smooth air.

"Give me the top two bullets on Chen," Zara said to Hembrick.

He chewed his lip for a second and said, "Chen's dossier shows a grandfather who failed a suicide mission and ruined his family name. That's the big one. And if he killed Prescott but kept Monroe alive, his mission has to be to steal the TYRANT platform."

Zara nodded.

"Grandfather and TYRANT platform," she repeated. "Got it."

The line clicked and went dead for a second before a voice said, "Who is this?"

It was a male voice with a heavy Mandarin accent.

Charles Lei/Xiao Chen.

"I know you are Xiao Chen. You have hijacked this airline by murdering a pilot. I have your jammer in my possession. I'll make you a trade."

"No trade, bitch. You open the bandwidth now or I crash the plane."

"You're bluffing, Chen. You won't crash the plane until you've completed your mission. Your mission isn't complete until you pass the information you've stolen to your intended target. If you die, you fail at your mission, just like your grandfather, you're *a Shazi*."

Zara used one of the few slang Mandarin words she knew from her days operating in Afghanistan with some of the Mongol teams that were conducting humanitarian assistance. Essentially the term *Shăzĭ* was a curse word for "fool."

Chen started shouting in Mandarin, presumably at Monroe, the only pilot in the cockpit presently. She didn't know if Chen understood that Jeremy West was ten feet away from him in the pilot crew rest cabin above the cockpit. She had to find a way to get Chen out of the cockpit and restore control of the aircraft.

"You don't know about my family," Chen said. "And I am no fool!"

He paused and Zara said nothing, letting the insult sink in.

"What trade do you offer?" Chen asked.

"Whatever information you are trying to get to someone else, I'll let you do it if you come out of the cockpit and let me secure you," Zara said.

"You must think I *am* a fool," Chen replied. "This is my leverage."

"You've already used your leverage to get the information from the copilot," Zara said. "I'm the only one standing in the way of you completing your mission. So, you've got some big-time technology you've stolen for your country. It does you no good if it evaporates when we crash into the ocean."

More silence. He was thinking. Hembrick was watching her, nodding. Could she trust Hembrick or his partners? She didn't think so. Her gut told her no. But here she was, almost *having* to trust him. Were they truly a presidential Dagger mission or was it something more nefarious? In the nosedive, she'd lost Lucas's behavior detection glasses somewhere and didn't have time to think about finding them.

"I can fly the airplane," Chen said. "Your offer is of no use to me. As an appeal to your Western sensibilities, I will provide you five minutes to open the jammer so that my data can transfer. If you fail, then I kill the copilot, who has already done his part and is expendable."

Hembrick shook his head sideways, as if to indicate that Chen was bluffing, that he couldn't fly the plane.

"Mutual assured destruction here, Chen. If you fail, you're just like your grandfather. We all die, and you don't accomplish the mission. The most important thing to you is to finish your mission so you can restore you family's honor. You need *me* to do that. I have the jammer in my hand. I can solve your problem if you solve mine."

Hembrick nodded in approval, not that she cared. He was up to something. She held the pistol in her hand as Monroe came over the intercom and said to all the passengers:

"Ladies and gentlemen, your pilot from the cockpit here. Apologies about the turbulence. We had an anomaly we needed to avoid and are set for a smoother ride from here on out. The crew will be coming through to check on any injuries. If you need medical assistance, please press your call button and they will work their way to you."

Zara took this as a good sign. Monroe would only have done that if Chen had told him to, which told her the Chinese henchman wanted no internal or external interruptions to the flight until the data had been transferred to his ground station.

"What is your proposal?" Chen asked.

"You step out of the cockpit. Allow me to secure you and we sit next to the jammer and allow you to do your mission."

Chen laughed.

"Fuck you. How about this? I'll start killing passengers until you bring it to me or turn it back on."

"You don't want that either," Zara said. "You don't want anyone to know you're here until your mission is done. You want total control and the only way to do that is to keep everyone in the dark."

"Why haven't you turned the jammer off and communicated with air traffic control somewhere?" Chen asked. "Communicate distress?"

"Because I want to resolve this peacefully. I want everyone to live, including you. Even if you don't believe you deserve to live because of what your grandfather did."

"You know nothing about my family!" His voice was harsh, but he was talking.

"I know enough. It wasn't your fault. You can reclaim your name only if you complete this mission, and the mission has nothing to do with killing people. It's all about helping your country gain an advantage. I get it. Everyone every day is trying to get a leg up. You're just trying to help and I'm just trying to help you. We're all in this metal tube together."

A long period of silence elapsed. Zara thought back to her Afghanistan and Iraq days. She'd spent many hours sitting down with tribal chiefs and village elders negotiating different matters from water rights to the arrest of terrorists hiding out in the village. It was always an effort of trial and error. Probe and get rebuffed. Find a new angle of discourse and make some headway only to end up in a blind alley. Often, the most likely path was something she couldn't think of until she got into the rhythm of the conversation. Often it was with interpreters doing their best to convey the essence of the conversation to both sides while keeping pace with it. At least Chen was talking to her in respectable English.

She had no doubt that Chen was a master tactician and planner, but had he thought his way through this dilemma and could he pivot having lost control of the situation? They each had leverage. Chen had control of the airplane and Zara had control of the data flow.

That was her trade.

When the silence didn't break, Zara said, "Xiao Chen. I have fought in so many wars I don't really care who has what technology anymore, because you know why?"

She waited. She wanted him engaged.

"Yes?" he asked.

"Because it's people like you and me on the front lines doing everyone else's bidding. You think the US Army gives two shits about me or my men and women? We're all just fodder for the machine."

"I don't care," Chen said in a hoarse whisper. "You don't know me."

"I know you want your president to restore your family name, your honor, and that of your mother. I know where you come from. I came from the same place. Low-class America isn't any different from low-class China, I can promise you. Racism, bigotry, you name it. If you're rich, you've got power and influence, and if you're not, you just get shit on every day."

"I have power," Chen snapped.

Zara chuckled.

"I have your jammer. You have my pilot. We both have power."

"In Shanghai, I have power!"

"You think anyone in Shanghai gives two shits about you right now? They are praying that you send that code and then go away. And if you send the code, what happens? Your scientists take it and put it in your weapons or airplanes or whatever, then we kill a bunch of people until some scientist invents a new code or a new weapon. Your thing is temporary at best, which is why I don't care who gets it. I just want to keep people alive up here. So, let's trade. You get the bandwidth you need, and I get to keep the plane safe."

"How would it work?" he asked.

Hembrick's eyes got wide, and he shot Zara a thumbs-up before turning to go down the steps. She covered the mouthpiece and whispered, "Wait!"

He stopped at the door and looked at her, then nodded and waited.

"I'll escort you from the cockpit and into a private, secure area where I will supervise you while you transmit the code."

"No. That has me giving up leverage first. Unacceptable. I can't reasonably trust you. I have teams on the ground expecting things to happen or the families of your pilot and General Fox will be slaughtered. If you want to prevent that from happening, you will open the jammer so I can transmit the code. Once it has begun processing and downloading, I will open the cockpit door, and we will do a mutual exchange. I will give myself up as the data is nearly completely transferred. That is the only way."

"Okay, I agree to those terms. I will move to the cockpit door. You will remove the locking bar but keep the door locked. I will open the Ku band so you can transmit. When it gets to seventy-five percent, you will unlock the door. I will hold the jammer and shut it off unless you come out. I'm sure whatever this code package is, until it's complete, it's not usable, just like my MacBook updates."

"Okay, let's go. I am close to my deadline."

"I'll be there in one minute."

Zara shut off the speakerphone and hung it back on the wall.

"I'll hold the jammer," Hembrick said. "While you negotiate. I know how the jammer works."

Zara thought about all the potential deviations from what she had in her mind. She would need to be focused on Xiao Chen and not a piece of hardware.

"Can I trust you?"

"We're on the same team, aren't we?"

"You never know for sure," she said. "But I have no choice."

Before moving, she retrieved her tablet and flipped on the Wi-Fi.

"What are you doing?" Hembrick snarled. "He'll see that."

Her tablet got a Wi-Fi signal, and she texted Lindy Van Horn:

Working through comms challenges. Get cops to the homes of both pilots ASAP.

The screen started bubbling with a response from Lindy:

Don't do anything else!

Then Zara shut off the Wi-Fi. It was open maybe two minutes. Had anyone else used it? Probably not. But maybe.

"Don't tell me what to do, Hembrick."

He didn't respond. His mind was somewhere else, judging by the look in his eyes. He was processing something, that much was clear.

They climbed down the stairs and exited the flight attendant overhead crew rest area. The lights were on in the airplane and practically everyone was awake. The flight attendants were administering IVs and bandaging people who had most likely been out of their seats when Chen had put the plane into a dive.

Zara pulled up next to Amanda in first class.

"We're going to make a trade here. Block off this crew area like you do for when the pilot has to use the restroom. Close the curtains. And tell Jeremy West upstairs to get ready."

Amanda nodded, but Zara saw a disconcerted look flash across her eyes. She didn't have time to worry about Amanda now, though, as the attendant began doing as Zara instructed.

Zara handed Hembrick the jammer. He nodded at her, maintaining eye contact. As she turned toward the cockpit door and knocked, she noticed Hembrick's hand lower to his pocket and then return to the jammer. *Too late to investigate*, she thought. With the knock, she was committed.

The peephole in the cockpit door got dark as she held the crew phone to her ear.

"I'm here. Let's do this," she said.

"Open the Ku band only," Chen said.

Zara turned to Hembrick and nodded.

"Who's that?" Chen asked.

"My IT guy," Zara snapped back.

Hembrick pressed a button and one of the many red lights turned green. He nodded at Zara.

"Okay, Ku band is open. You should be able to transmit."

After a few seconds, Chen said, "It's working."

"Remember. You come out at fifty percent or we shut down at seventy-five percent."

"I remember," Chen said.

Hembrick held the jammer so that Zara could see the meter's yellow light beginning to scroll from left to right: 2 percent, then 7 percent, then 25 percent, and then quickly jump to 40 percent.

"Forty percent," Zara said.

Silence.

"Okay, fifty percent. Come out. By the time you're out it will be seventy-five."

No response.

"Sixty percent. We're shutting it down if you don't come out."

The door lock clicked. A crack appeared.

Xiao Chen stood tall and broad, but he had one hand behind the door, presumably holding a knife to Monroe's throat. Zara imperceptibly slid her foot forward, nudging a doorstop the flight attendants used when conducting logistical resupply.

"Seventy-five percent," Zara said. "Come out now or we shut off."

"If you shut off, I kill the pilot."

"We have a deal," Zara said.

"Eighty percent," Hembrick said.

"Now, Chen," Zara said.

Perhaps she had underestimated Chen's commitment to not just his data theft task, but also to his "suicide" mission, as well. Three things happened at once as they were soaring 38,000 feet above the Pacific Ocean.

Chen stabbed Monroe in the neck, severing his carotid artery.

Hembrick rushed the cockpit.

Zara shot Chen in the chest, which didn't stop him. Hembrick muscled past Zara and was atop Chen as the jammer showed the stolen data had 100 percent downloaded.

But to where? Then, she noticed the external drive connected to the tablet.

Chen croaked, "You just killed two families."

He and Hembrick wrestled in the cockpit, Monroe's lifeless body hanging limp against the interior skin of the aircraft on the starboard side.

Behind her, Amanda stepped out of the way as Hembrick's two comrades charged Zara, one pushing her up against the bulkhead while the other assisted his boss in the cockpit. Zara used a series of Israeli Krav Maga defensive moves and counterstrikes to fend off Rodriguez, the former marine infantryman, while Rogers, the former P-8 pilot, shut the cockpit door.

Miraculously, the plane continued to churn into the night with no outward disruption. Soon, the door clicked open and Hembrick dumped Xiao Chen's body on the floor. Rogers held a pistol aimed at Zara as she wrestled with Rodriguez.

Once Hembrick shut and locked the door, Rodriquez backed away and smiled.

"Copperhead is in control of this airplane, bitch."

CHAPTER TWENTY-ONE

LUCAS SHERIDAN

"*L*UCAS! LUCAS!"

Mia's voice was distant until he caromed out of sleep and into the real world, awakening to his friend's shrieking voice.

"Wha—"

"Lucas! Wake up!"

"What's going on?"

"I think Copperhead's got your dad!"

"What?"

"His truck's out front, but he's not in the house anywhere. I took your baseball bat and checked."

"My bat?" Lucas asked. He was confused, but then remembered that they were in trouble with Copperhead for some reason.

"Yes. I didn't feel comfortable with the gun."

"Bat ain't gonna do you any good against these thugs, Mia," he mumbled. Then he fully awoke and asked, "What did you say about my dad?"

"His truck is here, but he's not," Mia said.

"What time is it? Maybe he went for a run?"

Mia seemed to consider this for a moment.

"It's almost five A.M. After working all night, you think he'd go out for a run? That he wouldn't check on you, us, before going to bed?"

Lucas slid off the pile of moving blankets and stooped over until he was out from under the staircase that led from the kitchen to the basement. Standing up, he shook the cobwebs from his mind like a dog resetting for a walk.

"Yeah, that's weird," Lucas admitted. He ran his hand through his dark hair and rubbed his eyes.

"I apologize, but I fell asleep, too," Mia said. "Maybe I would have heard him otherwise."

"It's been a crazy twenty-four hours, Mia. Don't beat yourself up," Lucas said.

"I did check on you twice. You were gone," Mia said.

"Let's think this through, get organized, and then go investigate," Lucas said.

Mia nodded. "Agree."

They sat at Lucas's computer workstation. The two big monitors had gone into sleep mode. A single server rack sat in the middle, deep on the table. They faced each other in the adjacent chairs.

"First, have you heard from *your* dad?" Lucas asked.

"Oh, my gosh, I hope he's okay. I've just been pushing it out of my mind. They were literally dodging bullets. I should call him."

"Call him. I'm sure he's okay. And because he most likely is, he's got to be worried about Deputy Cashwell, who might be dead or best case is missing," Lucas said.

"If he knows. Communication is spotty out there in the swamps. Cell towers don't reach well. At least that's what I've been telling myself." Mia looked at her phone and grimaced. She pressed some numbers until the speakers emitted the soft purr of the sheriff's phone.

"Darling, we've got us a situation here," Sheriff Barlowe said. His voice was gravelly, sounding rough and tired, as if he had been in the swamp all night.

"So do we, Daddy, but I'm glad you're okay."

"Why wouldn't I be okay?"

Lucas motioned with his hand across his throat, indicating that he didn't want the sheriff to know he had again hacked into the Copperhead drone.

"You're in the swamp in the middle of the night?" she said in her best inquisitive "duh" voice.

"Baby, can you handle it or do you need me?"

She looked at Lucas, who shrugged.

"I think something might have happened to the deputy you sent out here. I'm not sure."

"Cashwell? I've been trying to reach him."

"We'll check on our end," Mia said.

After a pause, the sheriff asked, "Where's Lonnie and Zara?"

"Lucas's mom is on an airplane to Taiwan and his dad might've just got home."

"The ferry accident. That's right," he said. "If Lonnie can't help you, give me a call back, Mia. I love you."

"Love you, too, Daddy."

Lucas looked at Mia, who said, "I'm scared."

He nodded. "Me too. When I get scared, I try to focus on the things I know instead of the things I don't know. What do we know? We *know* we've got the helmet and classified flash drive here. We *know* it has some pretty awesome capabilities. And we *know* that these Copperhead guys want what we've got."

"You're right," Mia sighed. "They're so basic. I'd be *more* scared if they were more creative."

"We can keep working that to our advantage. Maybe they've already taken the *L* and moved on," Lucas said.

"No. That brings us to your dad. My gut tells me something has happened to him."

"My dad's a big dude," Lucas said. "Take more than a couple of those guys to take him out. If anything, he might have gone after *them*."

"Okay, but I still think we should check it out. I went upstairs to get some water bottles from the fridge," Mia said, pointing at the two bottles of generic Costco water sitting by the keyboard. "I noticed his truck through the living room window, so went upstairs to see if he was there. The bedroom door is still open, and the bed is still made. Nobody in any of the rooms."

"Only other wheels he has is the ATV. Did you check that?"

Lonnie Sheridan was a hunter with an array of shotguns for

geese, duck, dove, quail, and deer. After moving to Swan Quarter, he had purchased a used Yamaha Grizzly 700 all-terrain vehicle for bouncing around the Inner Banks and Lake Mattamuskeet with the local hunting club.

"Didn't think about that," Mia said. "Too scared, to be honest, Lukie."

"Everything gonna be aight," he said back to her with a wink. "Remember. Focus on what we know." After a pause he said, "And it won't hurt to grab the pistol. I've got the shotgun. Let's go check this out after we look at the cameras."

Lucas sat at the terminal and brought up the camera feed and hit replay. He let it reverse through the night until about 4:31 A.M. when the cameras on the front porch showed Lonnie Sheridan's pickup truck pull into the semicircular driveway.

"What time did you come up?" Lucas asked.

Mia shrugged. "Right before I woke you up. Maybe thirty minutes ago."

It was 5:15 A.M. Lucas found the motion alerts for 4:31 A.M. and scrolled through them, stopping when he saw one that was more than a squirrel darting across the porch.

"Here," he said. He leaned into Mia so that she could see his screen. She lowered the pistol to one hand and placed a hand on his shoulder.

"Dad's truck pulls up. Then right here you see two dudes come from behind the house or the side, like they were going to come in after us."

"Or they were waiting on him," Mia added. "What's happening to the video?"

The image on the screen became grainy and weak, making it difficult to determine what was happening.

"Jamming our cameras? Our Wi-Fi?"

"Only thing it could be. Maybe they're not so basic after all," Mia said.

"They were here. That Hembrick guy said to watch us. Maybe they are the watchers?"

"And they saw your dad come up?"

"Well, they wouldn't really be knowing when he'd get home unless someone at the ferry was watching him. Sounded like an unpredictable thing. So, yeah, they had to be here watching us and then he pulls up."

Lucas was accustomed to random incidents that caused his parents to be late and long stints of being alone when his parents were both gone at the same time. It was the life of an army brat, as the general military population affectionately referred to the children of soldiers.

"Maybe," she said.

While the image was difficult to see because his father had pulled into the driveway with his driver's side door facing away from the porch, the video showed a scuffle. Two men attacking his father. There was a flash of some type. Lucas turned on the audio and replayed the video. The flash was accompanied by a loud report. Maybe a pistol shot, maybe a head hitting the side of the truck. Because the fight occurred behind the cab of the truck, it was impossible to see who did what to whom. About the time the fight ended, the video was practically black. They couldn't see anything but black and gray lines across the screen.

"Damn," Lucas whispered.

"We've got to check it out," Mia said.

"Yeah," Lucas said. But what he was thinking was, did his father take on both men and prevail? Did they wound him? God forbid, kill him? Kidnap him? He was a big man. Strong. Athletic. A tough takedown.

"No other video?" Mia asked.

"No. It must've happened fast," Lucas said. "Usually takes a few minutes to register another motion alert. Or they were below the level of the truck, and nothing triggered. Regardless, they were definitely jamming our Wi-Fi. Let's go."

Lucas handed the small pistol to Mia, who gripped it with both her hands wrapped around the buttstock. The shotgun barrel was nestled in the crook of Lucas's right arm as he led the way up the stairs. Once they were both on the landing between the kitchen and the living room, he turned and locked the door from the interior before closing it. He patted his pocket to make sure the key was still there. He didn't want either the encryption hardware or the helmet to go missing while they were checking on his dad.

He pointed at the front door, which was closed.

"Is it safe?" Mia asked.

"Only one way to really find out," Lucas said. "I'll lead. You watch my back."

They walked slowly to the front door. It was 5:40 A.M., about a half an hour until sunrise in Eastern North Carolina. Lucas stepped onto the porch, his booted foot causing the old planks to squeak. Mia pressed into his back as he stopped and went to one knee, like a soldier in combat. Mia followed suit, staying tight behind him. He had been to many army camps at Fort Bragg, some that taught basic survival skills. He had also hunted deer with his father. The first thing he learned was to stop and listen once he was in a new environment.

The prey's environment.

In this case, Copperhead had changed his house from a home to a defensive fortification. A redoubt. But he had to venture "outside the wire," as he'd heard his mom and dad say many times when discussing combat operations overseas.

Lucas studied the entire ecosystem around his house.

The sky was a monochromatic black bleeding to gray to his left in the east, and a deep black interrupted by a lone streetlamp casting a dim yellow circle up the street to his right, the west. Across the street looking south was a wooded, swampy area that was mostly impassable to humans. It was too shallow for any normal human to traverse. "No-go terrain," as his mom called it. An uneven row of white scrub oaks lined the drainage ditch on the far side of the road.

Beyond that was swamp.

Lucas moved slowly toward his father's truck. Walking around the nose, he placed his hand on the hood, which was cool to the touch. As he rounded to the driver's side, he saw a bullet hole in the door and a large crimson stain on the gravel.

Blood.

He felt Mia's hand squeeze his shoulder, indicating that she saw it, too. The gravel driveway was disturbed in the area around the blood, signifying perhaps a fight, the beginning of which the Ring camera had shown.

Lucas knelt and felt the sticky substance and smelled it. After dressing a few deer with his father, he knew the smell of blood.

"Definitely blood," he whispered.

He stood and opened the truck door. The keys were on the floor, as was his father's carrying case for his Colt 45 Night Commander pistol. Had his dad gotten the shot off? He climbed into the cab and inspected it. Convinced everything else was in place, he collected the keys and pistol box and stepped into the driveway with a leap to avoid the blood.

He was fuming but was attempting to control his emotions. How could someone do this to his father? His family? His home?

Ignoring his building rage, he followed the disturbed gravel to a set of tire tracks that appeared fresh. Someone had driven a vehicle to the house after they had ambushed his father. The tracks went east, toward Copperhead's headquarters several miles away.

"Follow me," Lucas said.

"No worries there," Mia whispered, clutching the back of his shirt.

They rounded the back tailgate of the truck and angled toward the side yard with the open-air carport where his father kept his Yamaha ATV and Lucas kept his bike when he wasn't dumping it in the backyard before bounding up the back steps.

"ATV is still there," Mia whispered.

"Which means they took my dad," Lucas said, some ice in his voice. "They hurt him and took him. If they killed him, why wouldn't they just leave him?"

He continued to stare at the dark carport housing the ATV. Had the Copperhead guys hidden there before jumping his dad? It seemed like a decent ambush post.

"There wasn't enough blood for anyone to be dead," Mia said. Lucas noticed her slender right arm hung loosely at her side, her hand still holding the pistol.

"Knowing my dad, he got the shot off, but maybe there were too many of them. They ganged up on him."

"Like you said, your dad's a big dude," Mia added.

Lucas nodded and held up the pistol case.

"He had his pistol. Maybe he took charge of them, but then why wouldn't he check on us? Where did he go?" Lucas asked.

"Maybe he followed them. Maybe you're right."

"We have more questions than we did before we left the house."

"We're kinda exposed out here," Mia said.

"Yeah, we should go back in. I want to try to get in touch with my mom. And you should try your dad again. I think we need his help," Lucas said. The timbre of his voice had deepened in the last hour. He found himself scanning the swamp to the south as the orange hues of sunlight began to lick at the horizon.

Everything looked different in the daylight. He knew this from hunting and fishing in the early mornings. The thing you thought was a deer was just a bush with a squirrel in it, for example.

"Let's head back downstairs and try to establish communications," Lucas said.

They ascended the steps and reentered through the front door. Lucas couldn't shake the feeling that they were being watched, but the likelihood was that Copperhead was watching them. With what, he didn't know. A drone? A sniper? A satellite? He didn't know.

As they retreated into the basement, Lucas ensured all the doors were locked and modified the motion alert sensitivity on the camera network in the front and back yards.

They sat in adjacent chairs at Lucas's workstation, him feeling far more somber than he could ever remember. The idea that something had happened to his father because of something he had brought home from the accident location was weighing on him. Was this valuable technology inviting bad luck and trouble into his family?

He looked at the helmet and the flash drive.

Donning the helmet and firing up his computer system with the classified drive plugged into his server port, he scrolled through the functionality until he was able to see his mother's flight in the heads-up display on the helmet. It was a little flashing yellow light in the shape of a plane that indicated location, airspeed, and altitude, and other readings.

The altitude numbers began flashing like a slot machine, showing the airplane rapidly losing altitude from 38,000 feet above sea level to 28,000 feet in a matter of seconds.

Had he endangered both his parents?

The pressure was too much to bear, and he screamed "Mom!" into the void of the basement, causing Mia to turn away as she held the phone to her ear.

And that was when the helicopters began landing in his backyard.

CHAPTER TWENTY-TWO

ZARA SHERIDAN

XIAO CHEN'S BODY LAY BETWEEN ZARA AND RODRIGUEZ, WHO continued to aim his pistol at her.

She was nearly out of breath from the close quarters combat. Rodriguez had outdone himself with his own Tae Kwon Do skills to match her Krav Maga. Parry-thrust, parry-thrust. The butt of his pistol had scraped her cheek, drawing blood, adding a new decoration opposite her Abbey Gate shrapnel scars. The plane began dropping precipitously but leveled out quickly. Screams emanated from the passengers. No one was sleeping now.

In her periphery, she noticed that Chen moved. His eyes blinked. He was still alive. His hand moved. Something flashed as she maintained eye contact with Rodriguez.

"So, this is your Dagger mission from the president? Hijack an airplane and steal a classified Next Gen code?"

Her breathing steadied after a couple of deep exhalations. Rodriguez said nothing, just stared at her. He was the protector of the door, she determined. Hembrick and Rogers were the cockpit team. Rogers was a former navy pilot, and no doubt could fly this aircraft if he hadn't specifically trained for this mission, which she suspected he had.

Rodriguez's face flinched and his eyes went wide as he looked down at the blade sticking from his inner thigh. Chen had cut Rodriguez's femoral artery, the main source of blood to the heart. Within seconds, the man's eyes rolled up into his head and he collapsed in a heap across Chen's prone body, like an *X*. Blood seeped onto Chen and then the floor, and most of it would leak from his entire body.

Zara worked quickly to snatch the knife from Rodriguez's leg and peel him away from Chen, turning to Amanda and saying, "I need your help to clean up this blood." She was still aware that Chen was lethal, even from the prone position and even without his knife or pistol. For the second time, Amanda moved a dead body, this time Rodriguez, away from the cockpit door. She had drawn the curtains and locked the serving carts in place so that none of the now nervous and curious passengers could breach the front lavatory area next to the cockpit.

Zara removed a set of zip ties from her blazer pocket and placed a foot on Chen's neck.

"Move and I curb stomp you," she said. "Now put your hands behind your back."

Chen struggled to do so, and when Zara moved her foot to his back, she realized why. He was wearing flexible body armor, enough to stop a slug from a pistol most commonly used in tubular tactics. Tactical instructors encouraged center mass shots, which had less of a chance of missing and injuring another passenger or poking a hole in the thin skin of the aircraft.

With a knee in Chen's back, she wrenched both arms back, causing him a degree of pain evidenced by the grimace on his face and the growl he emitted when she felt his left shoulder pop.

"Fuck around and find out, asshole," she said.

Punching in the code to the above cockpit pilot rest area, she opened the door and said, "West, need some help."

"Just a sec," he replied.

She could see him at the top of the steps on his knees, fidgeting with some type of tool. In short order, he came down and helped her carry Chen up to the increasingly crowded bay.

"A dead pilot. A wounded stew. And now a prisoner. They paying you overtime, Sheridan?"

She needed the comic relief and always enjoyed West's quick wit, but came back with, "There's a dead Copperhead guy downstairs. Chen killed him."

"Damn. You don't waste any time, woman."

"No time to waste. Speaking of which, can you help grab him and stack him on top of Prescott? Oh, and the other marshal is dead, killed by this guy." She pointed at Chen. "Poison or something, but he's fine in his first-class cube, laid out like he's sleeping."

"Three dead bodies, one wounded, and one prisoner," West said, sounding somewhat in disbelief.

"I don't know about Monroe. He could be the fourth dead body. Most likely wounded, at least."

"Who's flying the plane?"

"My guess is a Copperhead guy named Rogers. He breached the cockpit when Hembrick and I agreed to the exchange. It was Hembrick's plan all along. What he's planning, I'm not sure. Claimed he's on a Dagger mission."

"Well, I know that's bullshit. Dagger missions go to Sinclair and Sharpstone. The president only trusts him . . . and us . . . to do those missions."

"I know that, but I don't think Hembrick realized I was with Sharpstone for a short period of time before this gig."

"Let me drag this dead guy up here and then I want to show you something," West said.

He was gone a minute and then working his way back up the steps with Rodriguez's bloody corpse, which he laid on the bed, rolled in a sheet, and pushed off the far side onto the similarly shrouded remains of Prescott. West took his Apple headphones and placed them on Xiao Chen to prevent him from gathering any further intelligence.

Zara waited for West to get settled and said, "Okay, whatcha got? Because I'm looking for options. We have no communications and no control of the plane. No intel at all other than what we've seen right here."

"Look," he said, pointing at the carpet between the two chairs against the bulkhead. The carpet was pulled back and the metal molding was lifted away. Some metal shaving corkscrews were askew on either side of a thin cable that was poking into the crevice between the flooring and the wall.

Zara knelt and ran her hand along the cable, ensuring not to move it from what appeared to be a precarious placement.

"Is this what I think it is?" she asked, looking over her shoulder.

West was holding a tablet and pressed the screen a few times.

"Damn straight," he replied.

She stood and looked over his shoulder. On the tablet was a fish-eye view of the cockpit in real time. Monroe's head was slumped against the starboard side, the neck gash a clear indication he was dead. Rogers was in the pilot's seat on the port side. Hembrick had placed a laptop computer on Monroe's seat edge, using Monroe's slumped body to keep the computer in place. He was tapping some keys until an image of Taiwan, the Taiwan Strait, and the east coast of China appeared.

Hembrick plugged the cable from the jammer, which had also served as a receiver to capture the code that General Fox had released to Chen, transferring it into the side of the USB port in the laptop.

After pressing a few keys, dozens of airplane icons appeared on the screen. After he pressed a few more keys, there were maybe half that, Zara thought.

He scrolled over one of the icons and a large dialogue box appeared.

Chengdu J-31B
Gyrfalcon
4 Missiles
Location 24°58′40″N 120°07′58″E
Speed 350 knots
Azimuth 97 degrees

Hembrick hovered the mouse over the icon and another box appeared, asking Hembrick a question:

Control?

The button was not functional though. Hembrick clicked it repeatedly and said a few words.

"Is he doing what I think he's doing?" Zara asked.

"If you think he's trying to get Chinese aircraft to attack Taiwan, then yes."

Then the phone above Zara's head blared with a shrill ring.

CHAPTER TWENTY-THREE

LUCAS SHERIDAN

*L*UCAS PLACED A HAND ON MIA'S SHOULDER AND STARED INTO HER wide eyes.

"Those choppers are the same kind that first landed at the crash site," Lucas said. "I looked it up. They're Eurocopters made by Dauphin. Point is, they're not official. Not cops. Not military. Copperhead."

Two civilian helicopters with rear Fenestron fan blades landed in the path that led to the farm pond where Lucas and Mia had videoed the Copperhead guys recovering their drone.

Mia moved to the basement's north pillbox window, strained upward on her toes as she looked out, and said, "Four guys getting out."

"Here," Lucas said. "You can see better."

The network of cameras they had situated throughout the back and side yards provided a clear view on his two monitors of the four men stepping off the helicopter.

"That big guy was at the crash site. Maybe two of the others also," Lucas said. He pointed at the man leading the other three whose gait and demeanor were exactly the same as the man who had debarked the helicopter at the crash site.

"Their Web site says his name is Garland Maximoff. He's in charge of Copperhead. The guy at the pond last night mentioned

Joshua Hembrick. The Web site has him as the number two guy. These guys are ex-military. Their bios show lots of combat time."

"Whatever they are, they've killed a deputy and kidnapped your father. What are they going to do to us?" Mia asked, turning away from the window and walking toward Lucas. Her hands were shaking and tears were pooling in her eyes. Lucas placed both his hands on her shoulders.

"I've got you, Mia. They can't get in here. They have to come right through that door, and I'll blast them with this shotgun. Only one way in and one way out. And they'll be leaving after the first one is dead."

Mia stepped back and looked at her friend.

"Lucas Sheridan, you're not a murderer," she said. "No matter how bad the situation . . . you . . . you can't kill someone . . . can you?"

"Nope, I'm not a murderer. But, yes, I can kill someone if it means protecting you and my family. That I can do."

"But these are trained military snipers or something," Mia countered.

"Like I said, unless they roll a flash-bang grenade in here, which they very well might do, then there's only one way in and one way out."

"I'm scared, is all I'm saying," Mia said.

"I'm scared, too. Now get under the steps and get beneath the blankets in case this turns serious."

"Why not just give them the damn cipher?" Mia said, flint in her voice.

"Because they want it too damn bad," he said. "It's important and it might involve my mother. Her plane nearly dropped from the sky. I can't communicate with her. The Wi-Fi is out. Something is going on, and maybe this can help save my mom, my dad, your dad, this town, and a planeload of people."

Mia nodded.

"Well, if you put it that way," she said. "But can you actually kill a man? A live human being?"

Lucas considered her question. He was focused on the task.

Hadn't weighed the pros and cons or his abilities. He did a quick calculation in his mind. Could he kill a man? Could he take a human life?

It was a tough question for a fourteen-year-old kid. He wasn't a violent person at all, just a normal kid who liked playing baseball and catching snakes. But what options did he have? When confronted with the binary choice of either they-kill-us-or-we-kill-them, the answer seemed pretty clear.

He could kill a man for the right reasons. Protecting Mia and himself and defending his home seemed legitimate, a good moral purpose.

"I can for the right reasons," he said. "Now go get under the blankets."

The back door crashed open. The China hutch fell over with a thud, the sound of glass shattering like a hundred cymbals clashing. Boots rumbled on the floorboards above them. Mia skittered beneath the steps. Lucas positioned a box of Remington bird shot 8 shells on the floor next to him. He had one shell in the chamber and two in the auto loading tube. While all he had handy was this bird shot, he knew the 400 BBs inside each cartridge could do some damage to a human. He knelt behind an old chest of drawers that was about thirty degrees to the right of the naked stairwell coming into the basement. He had a clear shot on the door. He aimed the shotgun at the door. Clicked off the safety. Steadied his breathing.

Someone turned the knob of the door to the basement and rattled it against its frame. Locked. Something pounded against the door. Maybe a boot, maybe a battering ram. The door didn't budge because of the dead bolts Lucas had put in place. Next, a pistol shot out the dead bolts and the doorknob, wood splintering and the door moving on its hinges.

Open.

"Let a kid fuck with you like this," a man's voice said. "I'll show you how it's done."

The big man, presumably Maximoff, took a step onto the landing. He was holding a long rifle, sweeping if from side to side. Lucas drew a bead on him, the muzzle of the shotgun steady on the edge of the bureau. Another man was on the landing behind him. Lucas took a deep breath and squeezed the trigger.

The shotgun sounded like a cannon in the confines of the basement. The bird shot struck Maximoff in the shoulder and knocked him backward onto the landing. Lucas fired another shot at the man's feet and a third shot at the man standing behind him, who spun backward into the kitchen.

All in self-defense. They shot first. That was important to him because he *wasn't* a murderer. He had a legitimate moral purpose.

He reloaded three more shells, the max the weapon could hold.

"He's hurt! Medic! Garland is hurt!"

A man was shouting from the landing, so Lucas took another shot, thought he hit him.

"I'm hit. Fuck! Get some fire on the target!"

Lucas fired two more shots, essentially blowing the door to pieces and chasing the invaders back up the steps into the kitchen.

"He needs a level two now. Artery hit," a man said. "Choppers one minute out. Let's go."

Another voice: "Get the cipher. Hembrick needs it to finish the job!"

A canister came bouncing down the steps spewing white smoke. Initially Lucas thought, *grenade*, but then thought, *smoke*, when the olive green canister started hissing. They wouldn't want to damage TYRANT.

He saw the scurry of feet at the top of the stairs. Took two more shots. Reloaded. His box had sixteen shells left in it. Plenty to do the job.

"Fuck! Hit!"

The smoke was building, and it wouldn't be too long before they would die of smoke inhalation. He thought of Mia under the steps. Worried she might be getting the worst of it with no ventilation under the steps and beneath the blankets. He fired three more times when he heard boots trying to come down the steps. Reloaded. Stuffed some shells in his pocket.

Automatic machine-gun fire raked the chest of drawers. Lucas huddled in fear behind it, the solid mahogany doing a good job of stopping the lead. When the firing stopped, he came out on the left side of the chest of drawers. Couldn't see anything. It was like he was in a cloud. He shot in the general direction of the steps. Heard movement above him. Fired twice more. Reloaded, then pulled his shirt up over his mouth.

He ran to the south side and found the window. Shot it out using one shell. Glass shattered everywhere. Smoke started sucking out of the window like escaping ghosts. He now had enough visibility to see the north side pillbox window and shot it, shattering glass. It was a smaller hole because of the distance, but it still created the cross breeze he had hoped would ventilate the basement. It helped.

He dug into his pocket and reloaded. Maybe five shells left. He was on automatic now. Conscious of his ammo load. Listening for movements amid the hissing smoke canister, which was nearly depleted. The smoke began dissipating enough for him to see a body lying on the floor of the basement, aviator helmet at the man's feet and orange flash drive in his lifeless hand.

He moved to the man, who had blood oozing from his mouth. Lucas kicked him over. He was wearing a Copperhead shirt with the dual fang logo. Felt for a pulse. Nothing. *Dead.* He had killed a man. He had a legitimate moral purpose in doing so, he kept telling himself.

He went to check on Mia, who was huddled at the bottom of the moving blankets as the sound of the helicopters landing again reverberated through the house. Were they picking up the attackers? Retreating?

She looked up at him, trembling but okay. He nodded. *I've got you.*

"Oh, my God," Mia whispered. She walked slowly through the wafting smoke toward the dead man. Lucas took a position on the steps and carefully climbed them one at a time, fully loaded shot-gun at the ready.

"Stay down and get back under the blankets," he said over his shoulder to Mia. "Let me clear the house."

Shotgun pellets had created hundreds of tiny holes in the Sheetrock, plaster blown out and now covered with blood from Maximoff and his Copperhead comrades. Lucas placed a foot on the landing separating the kitchen from the living room. The floor was slick with blood. He quickly looked right and left, then breezed through the kitchen and out the shattered back door, fol-lowing the trail of blood.

As he stepped onto the porch, one of the two helicopters peeled off from its counterpart, flying to the east, and made a low pass at Lucas's backyard. He dove just in time to avoid the bullets spitting from the side of the helicopter, sounding like a whirring burp. *Minigun*, Lucas thought. He'd been to several military family days where the equipment was on display. He remembered seeing a small helicopter demonstrate its "minigun," as it was described by the warrant officer standing in front of the bleachers at Sicily Drop Zone on Fort Bragg.

The bullets chewed at the porch. Lucas rolled to his left and slid off the porch behind some shrubs and the gas grill. He dove away from the propane tank just as a bullet pierced it. Nothing happened. No explosion. *Empty*, he guessed. He ran to the side of the house and shouted, "Mia, stay down! Under the steps!"

She didn't respond, but she had to have heard him. Probably busy with the dead guy, he didn't know.

Finally, the helicopter banked away and followed the other re-treating aircraft into the morning sun. He quickly ran around the back, dodged the blood trails, and vaulted through the nonexis-tent back door. Nearly slipping on the pool of blood, he bounded down the steps and looked at the dead man in the center of the room. Still dead.

Out of the corner of his eye, he saw Mia lying on the concrete, whispering, "Help me, Lucas."

He dashed across the floor and found his friend bleeding. She was wounded, maybe by the strafing run of the helicopter. Maybe by a ricochet. *No time to get mad*, he thought. Running upstairs, he grabbed the first-aid kit from the hall bathroom.

Back in the basement, he cut away part of Mia's pant leg and saw the bullet hole. Outside portion of the thigh. To the best of his knowledge, not the femoral artery. But still the bleeding was bad. His Boy Scout training had taught him to apply pressure to wounds. But first he used alcohol to clean it.

"Ouch!" Mia screamed.

That was a good sign. Pain was good, he thought. She was wounded but lucid.

He gently rolled her on her side. There was an exit wound, which he thought was also good. *Nothing lodged in her leg*, he figured. He wasn't sure, but just making it up as he went.

"One more coming," he said. Poured another douse of alcohol on her wound.

"Jesus," she grimaced.

He poured Betadine all over her leg and in the wound. Taking some gauze, he wadded some up and stuffed it in both sides of the wound. Mia let out a growl that sounded like a pirate.

"It's okay, Mia, I've got you."

He wrapped her leg tight. The bleeding was bad, but not terrible. He had stemmed it. *No artery*, he continued to tell himself. Tying off the flex bandage, he inspected her for other injuries. Not seeing any, he cradled her in his arms and laid her on the moving blankets, which had turned out to be their refuge.

He removed some blankets from the stack and made her a bed where she could elevate her head and leg. She was positioned beneath the stairs in case any more strafing runs came at them. She ran her hand across his cheek and said, "You're amazing, Lukie Dukie."

He hoped she wasn't going into shock. He ran back upstairs and filled a shopping bag with bottled water, brought it back down, and made her start drinking. They didn't have any IVs, so this would have to do. Not that he knew how to poke an IV, but he had watched it on some movies, so he knew that's what they needed.

He went to call 911 and saw his cell phone had no reception.

Looked at his computer. Starlink was still working. Thank God for Elon Musk. He used FaceTime over the Internet to call the local EMT.

"Need an ambulance ASAP!" he shouted.

The operator responded, "Nature of injuries?"

"Gunshot wound!"

"Is the victim still alive?"

"She was when I came upstairs!"

Mia can't die, Lucas thought. She just can't. *Still alive? Oh, my God.* He hadn't even let his mind go there, but now it was there. He was freaking out.

He provided his address. After a pause, the operator came back on the phone.

"Is the patient stable?"

"Just get here! We've been attacked!"

"We will get someone there as soon as possible. With the jet crash, all our EMTs are on location there."

"I need help!"

"We will get someone there as soon as possible."

Lucas hung up and ran back downstairs.

Mia's eyes were closed, and for a second, he wondered if she was alive.

"Mia!"

She smacked her lips, and her head lolled to the side.

"Water," she said.

He fed her another bottle, holding it as she weakly placed both hands on either side of the bottle. Gulping it down, she smacked her lips again. "Another."

He repeated the process but first gave her four Tylenol to help with the pain.

"Swallow these. Just Tylenol, but should help."

She did and drained half the bottle, then said, "Okay. I think I'm okay. God, it hurts, but I think that's a good sign."

"I've called the ambulance, but they're at the crash site. I'm all you've got right now."

She hugged him and said, "All I need, Lukie Dukie."

Tears streamed down his face, and he hugged her back. Held her for a long time until her breathing was steady, and her heartbeat was strong. He checked the bandages, which seemed to be holding and had stopped the bleeding.

He tucked her in with more blankets and then walked to the computer terminal, which was surprisingly undamaged. A bullet had come through the pillbox window and ricocheted, he figured, wounding Mia.

He thought about everything that had just happened and remembered one of the Copperhead men saying, *Get the cipher. Hembrick needs it to finish the job.*

He wondered about his mother and her flight, so he went into the dark web there amid the smoldering ruins of the basement. His fingers flew across the keyboard, sounding like a million beetles skittering across concrete.

He found his mother's flight number. Found the airplane. Found that TransPac didn't have significant security protocols. Found a way through to their manifest.

And found Joshua Hembrick listed as a passenger.

He pushed his chair back from the monitor and ran his hand through his hair.

"What is Copperhead up to? Willing to kill for? This crypto? What does it mean?" He was talking to himself, but Mia heard him and said, dreamily, "You know these warmongers, Lukie Dukie. They just want war."

He looked at her cuddled up in her blanket bed and nodded.

"*They want war,*" he whispered to himself.

CHAPTER TWENTY-FOUR

ZARA SHERIDAN

ZARA LET THE PHONE CONTINUE TO RING, LOOKED AT WEST AND instead asked, "Is this TYRANT we're seeing?"

"Yes. Next Generation cyber weapon. That's what Chen here wanted for his Chinese masters. The real question is why is Copperhead willing to kill for it?"

"No chance this is a presidentially directed Dagger mission?"

"No chance. Kim Campbell wouldn't risk something like this even if I disagree with her policies ninety-nine percent of the time. And Garrett Sinclair would have told me about it. When I'm not contracted out to fly unique missions like these, he keeps me gainfully employed with Sharpstone Security."

"Does 'Control' mean what I think it does?" Zara asked.

West sighed.

"This is all special category, Q-level classification on par with nuclear codes and all that. There have been some reports about the Wi-Fi jamming of commercial airplane avionics. All that is true but doesn't capture the real problem or threat. But yes, most likely it means what you're thinking."

"That Copperhead can control that icon, that aircraft, using the software and algorithms Chen stole from the Next Generation program via Monroe?"

"Mostly," he said. "There's typically a matching piece of cipher they need. They can see it and get most of the functionality, but to convert it to control mode they need a cipher key. Without that, all they can do is play a video game unless the target aircraft has no cyber protection like a small crop duster or a drone. Then either half of the platform can control. For the big stuff. The fighter jets and bombers and civilian airliners for that matter, the fully integrated platform must be working together as it tunnels, breaches, and executes. That's why it's called TYRANT: Tactical Yoke for Remote Aircraft Navigation and Targeting."

"Where would they find the cipher key?" she asked.

"In the cockpit of the Next Gen prototype," he said. Then paused, "Or maybe your son."

Zara sucked in a deep breath. *Lucas.*

The thought of Lucas made her heart quicken, wondering if he was okay. Assuredly, he was probably in school and then off to baseball practice again. Her mind couldn't do the mental gymnastics of figuring out what time it was back on the East Coast as they soared toward South Korea and Japan. It did bother her that she had no communications with anyone, neither her family nor her headquarters. West continued even though she was imagining her son practically defenseless while holding something so valuable.

"Like I said, there are two pieces. Each has the software that provides the transparency to see every single aircraft out there and each has a set of codes that are constantly changing, like when you're trying to get into your bank account, you have that thirty-second code that allows you to confirm its you. This is more complicated than that, but the general principle is the same. They are like two flash drives that mate together and the cipher is constantly recycling every thirty seconds to both enable quantum tunneling and hacking and so forth and prevent it from happening against you. I'm not a computer guy, but I know enough, especially about this. Bottom line, like I was saying, both halves have to be mated to have the platform work if the target aircraft has any sophistication whatsoever."

"So what would Copperhead want to do with that software from this airplane? Why here? Why now? Why this flight?" Zara asked.

"I have an idea," West said. "But I can't really confirm it."

West pulled at his lip and stared at the black-and-white video of the cockpit as Rogers played with the dials and Hembrick manipulated some buttons on the jammer. They spoke to one another but there was no audio feed with West's makeshift spy camera. Was he trying to communicate? Did he need the cipher? Did someone else have it?

"Tell me," Zara said.

"Well, the private military contractor and security business has been drying up lately. With Iraq and Afghanistan done with, and now with Kim Campbell becoming more focused on reelection and seemingly isolationist, business is hard to come by. Even Sharpstone is having to hustle to keep their investors happy. Ten percent return doesn't cut it in the private equity market. Twenty percent and higher might get you there, might keep the vultures happy. White Glacier Private Equity has a majority stake in Copperhead. I know for a fact that White Glacier has been pressuring Copperhead to increase margins and revenue or they'll find new management that can. Garland Maximoff is the founder and owner of Copperhead. He sold a big stake to White Glacier, so he's a multimillionaire, but some say he's overleveraged. Big yacht. Penthouse condos around the world. Lamborghinis. Gambling debts. The works. One theory I've been thinking about while you were cleaning up the mess downstairs is that this airplane could serve as a command-and-control aircraft while Copperhead uses the Gen Six platform and software to make Chinese, North Korean, or even Taiwanese, South Korean, and Japanese aircraft do what they most likely would never do. Provoke somebody and create demand for Copperhead services, whether those be shooters, logistics, what have you. Copperhead has done it all in Afghanistan, Iraq, Syria, and even a little bit in Ukraine. But with all those going from boil to simmer, their business opportunities are drying up. How does a private military contractor generate revenue? They go to war."

Zara processed what West had just said. It was certainly a plausible scenario when greed sadly usually ruled the day. The common Wi-Fi spoofing of airplane avionics had already been happening for years. Could this really be that different, that much of a quantum leap forward?

"But how are Xiao Chen and Copperhead connected?"

"I've been wondering the same thing. How did Copperhead know about the Chen mission to steal TYRANT?"

"Could have been tracking them. Hacked them. Hembrick seemed to know a lot about Xiao Chen. Might be at the White Glacier level, too."

"Maybe," West said, thinking.

"Anyway, we have two missions," Zara said. "Save the airplane and its passengers and stop World War Three."

West nodded and smirked. "Piece of cake."

"Taking back control of the cockpit and letting you fly would solve both missions," Zara said.

"Well, our options are limited, but there are options," West said. "The door has blowout panels in case of loss of pressurization. Maybe not big enough for someone to get through, but we can certainly get a pistol in there and shoot some people. Just don't hit the controls. If we cause a depressurization, the panels should come out, giving us an opportunity. But that's a big risk. The depressurization could in and of itself be catastrophic. Another option would be to try to talk to them and convince them of the folly of their efforts here."

"Talking seems unlikely given they've come this far, but maybe we could use what Lucas gave me as a bargaining chip," Zara said.

West's eyebrows lifted. "I'm listening."

She reached in the breast pocket of her blazer and retrieved the orange flash drive that Lucas had slipped in there before she left.

"They need this, right? If I understood you correctly."

West let out a long whistle.

"Yes. That's half of TYRANT right there. It could provide us a potential option. The system works in tandem with a cipher code, like when accessing your bank records online. The airplane carries both the attack and cipher portions. One won't work without the other except for menial tasks like controlling a low-end aircraft like a drone or jamming an aircraft's avionics. But to control the opposing aircraft, you need both halves."

"You're sure of this?" Zara asked.

"I flew the Hyperion X as a contract test pilot for the air force and navy and a bunch of other alphabet soups. I don't get in an aircraft without fully understanding the avionics beforehand. Especially a new one. What you're showing me and what you've told me leads me to believe that this thing is one half of the most advanced cyberattack weapon in the world. No way to tell at first glance which half it is, but there's a fifty-fifty shot it is what they're looking for."

"Maybe Lucas can help with the other half? I don't know. I'm just worried about him."

"What you have right here is from a separate airplane. What Chen stole and Copperhead now possesses is from the Air Force Warfighter Experimentation Laboratory, called AFWERX. Whether they got it in usable format, who knows? This came from a flying airplane. It was plugged in and ready to go until the plane crashed. My guess is it works if you can get to the other half. Who knows what gibberish Copperhead has on that box?"

"Lucas went into the crash site to help the pilot and came out with this," Zara said. Her eyes were moist.

"That's a good young man you're raising, ma'am."

"Thank you," Zara said. "Anyway, this good young man tried to get my attention before I left for RDU, but I was having a fight with his father, my husband, and then the marshals headquarters called with a data dump for me because I was a last-minute addition. Lucas was trying to get my attention, but between my fight with Lonnie and the call from HQ, I sort of ignored him."

"Happens to the best of us, Zara, go easy on yourself."

She was shaking, thinking of Lucas, and had a sudden sense of dread.

"Well, he snuck this in my pocket as a way of making me call him, not that I wouldn't have, but I did."

"Where's the other half? Did he find that, too?"

"He did," she said. "He has it."

West's eyes grew large. "Depending on what is what, Copperhead might try to get that from your son. I don't know how good he is at taking care of himself, but I'm sure your husband is there to help protect him."

Zara shook her head and said, "Lonnie had to go out on a ferry accident investigation. That's what we were fighting about."

"So, he's by himself?" West said.

Zara nodded. "He might have a friend over. Mia. They do computer stuff together. Both are kind of geeky, but Lucas is almost six feet tall at fourteen. So, he's growing. And his father may be home. I'm just not sure. I can't imagine he would be investigating the ferry accident all night long."

"Copperhead is located near you in Eastern North Carolina, Zara. We have to find a way to contact Lucas."

"I know. I'm open to ideas."

But her mind was going in the opposite direction, narrowing its focus only on Lucas and his safety. She kept reassuring herself that he was fine because he was her "little man." He was bright, resilient, and clever. He could surely smooth-talk a couple of Copperhead knuckleheads if they came knocking on the front door asking about the TYRANT flash drive.

And if he detected a threat at all, he would probably just give it to them. But she was sure his father was already home, and he was most likely bigger than any of those guys. That notion gave her comfort. Allowed her to focus on her task at hand.

The rationalization worked its magic, and she was back to thinking about the safety of the airplane and its passengers and how to maneuver Copperhead away from the cockpit so that Jeremy West could pilot the aircraft to a safe landing in Taipei.

But still. Lucas might be alone with something worth billions . . . and worth killing for.

CHAPTER TWENTY-FIVE

ZARA SHERIDAN

ZARA KNEW THAT IT WAS ONLY A MATTER OF TIME BEFORE THE PASsengers mutinied about the Wi-Fi and lack of service.

The flight attendants had been doing their best to keep the ruse going by delivering meals and beverages, but the interruptions in service that had initially led many of the passengers to believe TransPac was just experiencing growing pains as a new airline had since morphed into the sense that something was seriously wrong with the flight.

She broke away from staring at West's fiber-optic camera hack on the cockpit and said, "I need to speak with the flight attendants and assess the status of the passengers. We've had a couple of scary drops and I'm sure people are freaked."

West held his hand in the air, palm face down.

"Nothing like a little bit of smooth air to calm their nerves, but it's a good idea."

Zara nodded and said, "I'll be back in no more than fifteen minutes. Think about those blowout panels and how we might be able to get into the cockpit. These guys aren't suicide bombers. They're pawns, it seems. They want to stay alive. Doesn't mean they won't kill someone else though."

"Roger that," West replied.

She carefully threaded her way down the steps, opening the door into a cacophony of shouts and bedlam.

Amanda cornered her immediately and said, "The rumor mill has spread the word that one of the pilots is hurt. That's what they believe they know. The Wi-Fi is down, and no one can communicate outside the plane."

Zara peeked beyond the pulled curtain separating the service area from first class. Two men were shouting at each other from their pods.

"I'm telling you I heard gunshots and there are hijackers in the cockpit!" The man was tall and rangy with slicked back, gelled hair. He was wearing a blue-and-white nautical sweater, tan chinos, and Gucci loafers with no socks. Zara placed him for an executive of some major tech or defense company headed to Taiwan to close a deal or build relationships.

"Don't yell at me, fuck-stick! I've been awake the entire time and didn't hear shit. So don't cause a panic when we don't need one."

"Then why is the Wi-Fi down?"

"Ever flown Air France? Their Wi-Fi is always down on international flights. New airline. Making some mistakes. Whatever."

This man was short, balding, and thick around the waist. He was wearing an NC State hoodie sweatshirt and dungarees. He had narrow eyes and a wide mouth filled with Chiclet-like teeth.

"Gentlemen, let's calm down," Zara said, approaching them.

"Who the fuck are you?" the tall man replied, angrily.

"You actually don't want to say that to me," Zara said. She stared at the man who retreated at the sharp din of her voice.

"Air marshal," the NC State guy said.

Zara nodded at him. "Let's behave guys, okay?"

"Tell me what's going on with the plane," the tall man demanded.

"Everything is going to be okay. That much I can tell you," Zara said. It wasn't a lie. She firmly believed that they would sort it out despite the mayhem. It was reassuring to her though, that there wasn't more outcry just yet. The flight attendants were moving swiftly, conducting service of food as if everything were normal.

"Future tense," NC State man said, his first sign of concern. "Is it not okay now?"

"All okay," Zara replied, tightly. "I need you two gentlemen to calm down and go about your business."

"I need to use the restroom," the tall man said, stepping toward Zara.

"The forward restrooms are closed right now, so please use the set between first and business."

"That's suspicious as fuck," NC State guy said. "Now I'm getting worried. I was actually defending you guys a minute ago."

"No need to worry. We do routine pilot and crew changes on long flights, and when we do that, we restrict access to the forward area because the cockpit door will be opening and closing.

NC State guy studied her a moment and said, "Makes sense." He shrugged, and said to the tall man, "See, this nice lady has it all under control."

"I'm not so nice," Zara said.

She pushed past them and saw Carrie Starlight staring at her in business class. Starlight waved her down and said, "I'm freaking out here."

"Why?" Zara asked. She looked around, and the passengers, while restless, were mostly in their pods or seats and attempting to concentrate on whatever they were doing.

Nothing like a little bit of smooth air to calm the nerves.

"I'm just always right about this stuff. It's weird but true. And I told you at the beginning of the flight we have Mars conjunct Venus, which is bad for this flight. War, violence, bad intentions. There's something going on in the cockpit. Everybody is nervous. There are rumors."

"What are the rumors?"

"That we've been hijacked and we're going down like those 9/11 airplanes did. That someone is aiming this airplane at something. Maybe in Japan or Korea or Taiwan or China. I'm not the geography expert."

"That's just not true," Zara said. Again, she technically wasn't lying, because she didn't believe that the Copperhead hijackers intended to use the plane as a piloted cruise missile. Hembrick didn't seem suicidal, though Chen was a different story.

"Which part?" Starlight asked. "The hijack or the 9/11?"

She was an intelligent woman, Zara considered. Not someone to be bullshitted. And while she didn't understand, follow, or necessarily believe in astrology, in the off chance that any of that was real, she didn't want Carrie Starlight's bad karma directed at her.

"There was an incident, but now we're flying smoothly toward Taiwan. See?" She pointed at the television screen that showed the airplane route on the internal airplane network, which was evidently still functioning.

"An incident? What kind of incident?" Starlight asked.

"Now, *that* I cannot tell you, but a little bit of smooth air calms the nerves, right?"

Zara had not noticed the NC State guy had come up behind her, perhaps because he was shorter than her, but it was atypical for her not to be aware of her 360-degree surroundings.

"Wait a minute," NC State guy said. "You tell us everything is smooth and groovy, but you tell this lady, 'There's been an incident'?"

"Sir, this is not your concern," Zara said.

"The fuck it's not my concern," he replied.

"Should we be concerned?" Starlight asked.

Two or three others stood and closed in on Zara, asking questions.

"What's going on . . . ? Why is there no Wi-Fi? We almost crashed. . . . We're going to die, aren't we?" And so on.

The questions reached a crescendo when Zara said in a firm command sergeant major's voice, "Everyone go back to their seats now!"

As she said this, a tall Taiwanese man dressed in what she guessed was an Italian suit threaded through the growing throng, stood in front of her, turned around, and barked in Mandarin and then in English, "I am General John Wang, deputy commander of the Taiwanese military. Do as the woman instructs. Now."

Those who understood Mandarin quickly listened to the general and proceeded to return to their seats or pods. Even those who did not certainly understood the English version and similarly complied. Helpful to Wang's presence was a stocky younger Asian man next to him, who was also wearing a suit and carrying a briefcase. The compact man's suit was not the luxury Italian version that Wang was wearing. Rather, it was off the rack, and Zara made him for the general's aide-de-camp or personal security. He was an imposing figure, though, with cauliflower ears bent inward from fighting or wrestling. She was struck by the fact that he wasn't watching the general. Instead, he was scanning the throng of disturbed passengers, looking at their hands and eyes. Monitoring their actions. Assessing threats.

Personal security or bodyguard, she determined.

Wang, conversely, was thin and angular with a sharp chin and high cheekbones. His wispy gray hair was combed from left to right over his scalp. His almond-shaped eyes were unflinching steel marbles. A commander, Zara thought, like so many she had served with previously.

The man wearing the North Carolina State sweatshirt did not budge. "I'm not going anywhere, General. You don't command me," he said.

Zara watched as the bodyguard took a step toward the man. General Wang made a subtle move of his hand, warding off his security, and looked at Zara.

"He doesn't, but I do," Zara snapped. She turned on the man with the North Carolina State sweatshirt and retrieved a Taser X26P energy weapon, or "stun gun," from her sling bag, held it to his chin, and said, "You're returning to your seat either awake or asleep and handcuffed. Your call."

He held up his hands and backed away slowly.

"Jesus, this must be serious," he muttered.

"Return to your seat," Zara reiterated.

Wang approached Zara and said, "I need to talk to you."

"Okay, talk."

"In private."

She nodded, thinking. She didn't want to give away the fiber-optic cable that Jeremy West had drilled into the cockpit from the pilot rest cabin above first class, so she directed him toward the flight attendant crew rest area above business class. Amanda Gāo was there staring at Zara with an impassive face.

"What is going on?" Amanda asked.

"I've told you everything I know, Amanda. I need to speak with this gentleman in the flight attendant rest area," Zara said, pointing at the door behind Amanda.

"I'd like to come and listen. I'm in charge of the crew now with Marcus disabled. I need more information to help keep the aircraft and its passengers safe."

Zara turned to General Wang and said, "She has a point. Say what you've got to say in front of all of us."

Wang hesitated, then said, "It does not bother me if she listens, but I need my aide-de-camp with me. Major Li Van." Wang pointed at the younger man that Zara had made for personal security or an administrative "aide-de-camp."

Aide-de-camp my ass, Zara thought. The guy looked like he could bench press four hundred pounds.

"No problem," Zara said.

Amanda nodded, punched in the code, and they left behind the murmuring passengers, whose collective anxiety seemed to be peaking. Amanda led the way up the steep, narrow staircase emptying into the room where she and Hembrick had discussed the jammer she had found in an overhead bin. Amanda stood between the two sets of twin bunk beds, and Zara walked across the small space, turning to keep General Wang near the staircase. Major Li Van pushed past his boss and knelt in the far corner so that he had eyes on everything happening. *No slouch here*, Zara mused.

Turning her attention to Wang, she considered that Gāo and Wang might know each other or could possibly even be connected to some common purpose. Was Gāo a loyal TransPac Airlines flight attendant and crew chief? Allied with the wounded Xiao Chen being held in the pilot rest bay? Or an ally of General Wang to some unknown end state?

"State your business, General," Zara said. In her peripheral vision, she monitored Li Van's slight movements and considered them nothing more than uncomfortable adjustments of a big, powerful man in a tight space.

Chen remained two steps below the landing so that he didn't have to stoop. Zara considered that he could also send imperceptible cues to Li Van, should he desire. Wang rested a hand on the side of the wall, balancing himself as the airplane shuddered through some light turbulence. His eyes shot upward, as if calculating something.

"I know Xiao Chen is on this airplane," Wang said. "He's a very bad man and I suspect that whatever has happened here was initiated by him."

"What makes you think that?" Zara asked.

Wang's eyes briefly glanced at Major Li Van. In her periphery, she noticed a slight nod from the major.

"My aide-de-camp here got an alert from the Taiwanese National Security Council that the National Security Bureau, like your CIA, received an artificial intelligence alert on facial recognition when boarding the flight."

Zara knew that some flights had cameras at the gates, but in her rush to board, she had not noticed the typically discreet video equipment.

"Why didn't you alert anyone?" Zara asked.

"We were confirming the information when the Wi-Fi went down," General Wang said. "And there was other information we were trying to confirm. The exchanges weren't just about Xiao Chen."

Zara didn't take the bait, but Wang continued.

"All right, then, I will tell you that Taiwanese intelligence sources have detected unusually heavy logistical activity at several Chinese military air force and navy bases along the east coast.

Transports picking up missiles from ammunition storage bunkers, fighter jets and bombers taxiing into formations on ramps, refueling trucks topping off every airplane, ships replenishing all their logistical requirements, Chinese marines boarding Zubr amphibious assault vessels. Helicopters ferrying onto aircraft carriers. And so on."

Zara shrugged. "Okay, the usual, right?"

Zara had done some light study on tensions between Taiwan and China. Asian geopolitics wasn't really her wheelhouse as a noncommissioned officer in the army, a local cop in Eastern North Carolina, or a procurement specialist for Sharpstone Global Security. But once she had been assigned this flight, less than twenty-four hours ago, she did her usual mission prep to include studying the state of affairs between China and Taiwan. She had found very little unbiased information. Some painted a rosy picture while others said a Chinese invasion was imminent. She realized that many had been predicting an invasion for decades, which caused her to think through the ramifications of such an occurrence on her mission to protect this flight. She understood that Russian, Chinese, and North Korean air forces might view a direct link between the Research Triangle Park of North Carolina and Taipei, Taiwan, as threatening to their own technological advancements.

Would they shoot down an airplane to cause an international incident and stymie the TransPac daily flights? Doubtful, she had considered when studying the subject. But now, today, at this moment, the plane had been hijacked not once, but twice. And here she was talking to the deputy commander of the Taiwanese military and his bodyguard, who was leading up to some big reveal.

"No, not the usual," General Wang said. "The usual is that China flies some fighters and bombers up to the midpoint of the Taiwan Strait and turns around. But our intelligence knows that there will be no follow-through, no passing of the center line, because precisely all the preparations I just mentioned have *not* been made. To win the war in Taiwan, China must be able to breach our air and ship defenses and then sustain combat for many weeks and months across the island. A mere head fake with some jets and ships with no logistical buildup on the mainland is just that, a head fake."

"You're saying this is real? That the logistics is the tell?"

"Exactly," Wang said.

"We could be landing in Taiwan during an invasion of the country?" Amanda Gāo asked.

With her focus on General Wang and Major Li, Zara had ignored Amanda's presence as she processed the information.

"I think there is more going on than that," Wang said cryptically.

Zara asked, "Are you still getting information? Do you have communications capability?"

Zara was skeptical. There were too many conflicting purposes and motivations inside this metal tube. Her sole purpose was to get the airplane to land safely, and she found herself combating different theories about what was actually happening. Xiao Chen on a suicide mission to avenge his family's honor. Copperhead Security on a mission to start World War III just so they could up their bottom line. And now the Taiwanese military's second-in-command with his notion that China was invading today, as they landed.

A whimsical thought found its way through the density of worry: *Just another milk run.* She remembered saying this to the crew at takeoff.

General Wang interrupted her thoughts. "I don't now, but as I mentioned, I did for the first several hours of the flight. Major Li and I were receiving updates from my team. Some type of jammer is being used to block communications. I assume you know more about that than me, Marshal."

"What's your ask?" Zara said. "All this is very interesting, but I'm not sure what you're getting at."

"The severe drops in altitude. The lack of communication from the flight deck. The interrupted service of meals. No ability to communicate outside the airplane. They all add up to our conclusion that something has happened in the cockpit. In the military, we call them indicators and warnings. And I need to know exactly what is going on in the event that we get communications back, so we can actually help land us safely."

"We?"

"Yes, as I mentioned, Major Li Van here is a pilot. F-16 fighter jets, but if you need some backup in the cockpit, he could probably figure it out. Wife and two kids. He wants to live. Me? My wife died and my kids are grown. Do I want to die just yet? No." He nodded over her shoulder at the major and said, "But the major here deserves to live his life, just like everyone else onboard."

The general was articulate and thoughtful. His steely gaze softened, reflecting something closer to empathy.

Zara turned and looked at Major Li and then back at General Wang. "I'm hearing you offering your aide to pilot the airplane and some kind of ground comms link with Taiwan National Security Council if we get communications back."

"Yes. Exactly, but I need to know what has happened and what the current situation is. Otherwise, we are useless."

"I don't even know everything," Amanda added.

General Wang and Amanda looked expectantly at Zara, who nodded.

"Okay. You're correct in that Xiao Chen breached the cockpit and killed our captain, Logan Prescott. He did so to blackmail the copilot, Hawk Monroe, who was head of the air force Next Gen aircraft program. Apparently, he was successful because he got a data upload from General Rachel Fox, who was Monroe's commander."

Amanda Gāo gasped. Major Li became physically agitated. He took two steps, stopped and turned around, clenched his fists, and grimaced. General Wang took another step up on the stairwell.

"This is very bad news," Wang said. "If China has the Next Gen capability, they can control our aircraft. At least that is the theory. The prototypes have been very effective."

"How do you know so much about a highly classified US military program?"

"Like I said, we have four prototype aircraft. That's highly confidential," he said, looking at Amanda, "but I believe we are beyond worrying about classification after what you told us."

"You have four fighter jets that have the Next Gen hardware and software in them?"

"Technically, it can be any aircraft, or the software works from any ground station with sufficient satellite access as long as all the encryption and algorithms are paired properly."

Zara thought of her orange flash drive and the fact that Lucas had the other half.

Lucas. She needed to reach him if only for her own peace of mind.

"Like a drone pilot can control a drone from half a world away? The software breaches the avionics and takes control of the aircraft?"

"It's more complicated than that, but yes," General Wang said. "Is Xiao Chen still in control of this aircraft?"

"No. I need to finish telling you what has happened," Zara said. "I found the jammer, realizing that Chen had to have hidden one somewhere on the aircraft. Josh Hembrick, the second-in-command at Copperhead Security Private Military Contracting, saw me retrieve it. He offered to help, much as you seem to be doing."

She paused. Could General Wang be offering help in exchange for information that could serve some other, perhaps more nefarious purpose? She studied Gāo and Wang and wondered if they were working together or whether Gāo simply took her duties seriously and needed the best information possible to manage the crew.

"Hembrick and I came up to this room we're standing in, and we determined that Xiao Chen had left one port open for transmission of the Next Gen encryption and software code but had shut down all other channels. We choked off his data transmission until he agreed to a barter. The deal was that if he came out of the cockpit, that we would let him finish transmitting that code wherever he wanted."

"My God," Wang said. "Do you realize what you've done?"

"Relax, General. We never let the code go all the way through. The Chinese don't have it."

Wang put a hand to his chest, slender fingers splayed across his heart. Major Li shuffled his feet behind her. Amanda's stare was impassive.

"Our only opportunity to beat the Chinese is with this capability."

"Not really my job or concern presently. The rest of the story is that Hembrick and two of his Copperhead buddies reneged on the deal once Chen opened the cockpit door. They attacked him and took control of the cockpit. We believe they killed Monroe."

"What makes you believe this?" Wang asked.

"They took a Copperhead pilot into the cockpit, and we heard a gunshot. They think they have the code and they have Rogers who can fly the plane. Why do they need Monroe?"

The phone on the wall buzzed. Zara looked at Amanda.

"It can only be the cockpit or the pilot crew rest area," Amanda said.

Zara turned toward Major Li, who was standing with his feet shoulder-width apart. *A fighter's stance*, Zara thought. She lifted the phone and placed it to her ear.

"Master Sergeant Sheridan?"

Hembrick.

"Yes," she said.

"We have a mission for you," Hembrick said. His voice was not the same cocky, assured tone. The inflection carried concern, perhaps hopefulness. "Rather, it's for your son, actually."

"Lucas?"

"Yes, him. Your husband isn't giving us much, so we are about done with him and won't need him anymore."

"Lonnie?"

"Relax, everyone knows you guys weren't getting along. Regardless, we need you to talk to Lucas and tell him to give us what he found at the crash site. We'll have a nice man go over and pick it up from him, but we want you to tell him that the nice man is coming. So, we're going to open a channel on this jammer for you to communicate with him."

Zara dropped the phone, her back sliding down the wall until she was sitting on the floor with Major Li, Amanda, and General Wang staring at her.

Lucas? Lonnie?

She reached for the phone receiver, and asked, "What do you need him for?"

"He's got something we need to finish our job. Once we finish, we will land safely. It's a Dagger mission," he said.

Summoning her inner strength, she said, "I'm pretty sure this isn't a Dagger mission. In case you forgot, I worked with Sharpstone, and Garrett Sinclair is the sole recipient of those missions. Whatever you're doing is unauthorized."

"Things change. President Campbell requires alternative methods of doing things she wants done off the books."

"I'm cleared. Talk to me then. What is the mission?"

"You're not cleared for this and you're not part of the mission. You weren't even supposed to be on this flight."

"Well, I'm on it, and if you want me to talk to Lucas, you're going to have to give me more than this," Zara said.

A long pause ensued, as if Hembrick were thinking about his options.

"Or we could just raid your home in the interest of national security and let the collateral damage fall where it may," Hembrick said.

"You do that, you're a dead man, Hembrick. I love my job, but I love my family more. You touch my kid, I'll rip you to shreds."

"Tough talk, lady. We are in control of the airplane. You've failed at this job. And we have a mission. I'm not authorized to disclose it to you, but the Hyperion crash in Swan Quarter was not

an accident. It was planned. The pilot ejected. She's safe. We retrieved her. The goal was to test the survivability of the equipment
after a crash. In particular, the very specific goal was to test the
survivability of the platform. My team landed within minutes of
the crash, and we were contracted by the government to see what
we could find. Kind of like Elon Musk blows up his own rockets to
test their durability. Or carmakers crash their own cars to get
safety ratings. This crash was a planned and authorized government operation. And it was cover for what we are doing now."

The logic was certainly present in his argument, Zara thought.
But still. Something was not sitting right with her.

"Again, what do you need Lucas for?"

"I told you. He has something we need," Hembrick said.

"What is it? Maybe you can find it somewhere else."

"Fuck it," Hembrick said. "He's got the cipher key to the Next
Gen airplane. That cipher coupled with the software we have can
be used to monitor enemy aircraft. Fox only uploaded the cyberattack portion of the platform and we are expecting a Chinese attack on Taiwan, and the Dagger mission is to test this software
and see if it can disable or turn around those fighter jets and
bombers. Some call it virtual fly-by-wire. Others call it Tactical Yoke
Remote Aircraft Navigation and Targeting. So we need the cipher
that makes the cyberattack part work."

Code word: TYRANT, Zara thought. It was all about the highly
classified program that Lucas had stumbled upon.

"Okay, so how do I talk to Lucas? Not promising anything.
Don't believe he has anything that can help you," Zara said.

"We know you have half the platform, Sheridan. Our man
Clark at the TSA screening location found your flash drive and
locked it up. He told us you came back and retrieved it before he
could tell us he had it."

"Clark might still be napping," Zara said.

"Maybe. You did a number on him and his manhood. Still, he
was able to get an image of what you have and it's not the part we
need. We need the other half, and the only logical deduction is

that your son has it. It's the part that has a timer and changes every thirty seconds, like when using any of the authenticator apps to log in to e-mail or your bank account for two-factor authentication. Same principle, except this is over satellite and allows us to conduct tactical yoke remote navigation."

"TYRANT. I know what it is. You want to take control of other aircraft using something that Lucas might have?"

"Yes, and you're wasting our time," Hembrick said.

"How do I call my son if all the lines are closed?"

She was doing everything she could to stall. Though she desperately wanted to speak with Lucas, she didn't necessarily want to do so on Hembrick's terms.

"I'll open one," Hembrick said. "Shit. Two MiGs at two o'clock."

Zara looked out the window. In the distance were two fighter jets.

"Open the line, Hembrick."

"We're going into a racetrack," Hembrick said.

The plane banked left and turned toward the east as two Russian fighter jets closed in. Then, on the opposite side of the aircraft, another two fighter jets appeared. Zara knew a MiG was a Russian fighter jet, but North Korea had MiGs, too.

"Two Japanese F-35s to our port side and two Russian MiGs to our starboard. I could really use that software, Sheridan!"

"They're probably trying to talk to you. Open the channels and talk to them. We all fail if we get shot down," Zara said.

Everyone except Xiao Chen, she thought, who had been intent on dumping the airplane in the ocean, she believed.

"Shit," Hembrick muttered into the phone.

Zara exploited his frustration. "Just one channel you can talk to these fighter jets on and one channel I can talk to my son on. I don't know how any of this works, but open the line and I'll talk to my son and get whatever he has. You can keep everything else shut down."

"I don't have time to not trust you, Sheridan, even though I don't trust you."

"None of that matters, Hembrick, if we take a missile up the pipe," Zara said.

After a pause, Hembrick said, "Shit. Okay, go to TransPac Admin Wi-Fi and type in 'NextGen6' and you're live."

Then to the fighter jets, Hembrick said, "This is TransPac 1001, do you read me?"

Zara looked at her tablet and followed Hembrick's instructions. The Wi-Fi bars filled in at the top, showing she was connected to the Ku band through the airplane's antennae.

She texted Lucas's number: Lucas, this is mom. Are you there?

CHAPTER TWENTY-SIX

LUCAS SHERIDAN

"*T*HEY WANT WAR," LUCAS WHISPERED TO HIMSELF AGAIN.

Mia was sleeping soundly amid the moving blankets beneath the basement stairwell. Lucas sat at the terminal with both monitors displaying the network of cameras he and Mia had rigged together six months ago more on a lark than with any express purpose, knowing that a second burglary attempt was unlikely. He was glad they had done so.

He had dragged the dead body of the Copperhead attacker into the corner next to his dad's workbench and laid a tarp over it. *Out of sight, out of mind. Well, mostly.* The coppery smell was growing more pungent by the moment. Daylight spilled into the basement through the cracked windows Lucas had blasted with his shotgun to create a cross breeze. The acrid stench of military smoke stung his nostrils with every breath. His command module sat in the middle of the debris field from the Copperhead initial raid and their follow-up invasion. Splinters of wood and shards of glass littered the floor.

Lucas checked on Mia, who was still sleeping. The bleeding had stopped, and she seemed fine. There was color in her cheeks, and when he placed the back of his hand to her forehead, she felt slightly warmer than normal, but not feverish. Boy Scouts had taught him basic first aid, and he was thankful for the training.

He tucked the blanket up under her chin as she muttered, "Lukie Dukie," seemingly in her sleep. She smacked her lips, and Lucas held a water bottle to her mouth, which she drank from with her eyes closed. He used the corner of one of the blankets to wipe the spillage from around her chin and neck. Placing the bottle within her reach, he stepped back and nodded, reassuring himself that he had done all he could to save her and make her more comfortable and that he would continue to do so.

Returning to the console, he donned the aviator helmet and plugged in the drive. He opened the dialogue box of the digital tracer he had placed on his mother's airplane, TransPac 1001. The data indicated the aircraft was cruising at 480 knots at an altitude of thirty-eight thousand feet above ground level in a generally southwest direction. The airplane was over the Pacific Ocean in between the Kamchatka Peninsula and the northern tip of Sapporo, Japan. There were about four hours left in the flight.

"What is the endgame?" Lucas muttered aloud to himself. "What kind of war? With who?"

He saw the airplane's track alter slightly and then go into a left turn north of Sapporo, deviating from its flight path. Maybe an air traffic control tower put the pilots into a holding pattern or something else was happening.

As he watched the white airplane image on the monitor, two more appeared, identifying as JMOD F-35A. Lucas did a quick search and learned that JMOD was an acronym for the Japanese Ministry of Defense.

The F-35s were fighter jets.

In fact, the F-35 was the precursor to the technology that he had discovered at the Hyperion Next Gen crash site. Quickly, two more icons appeared on the screen. They identified as Su-57 Felon, which Lucas searched and learned were the Russian technological equivalent of the F-35.

Two more fighter jets.

Were these combat aircraft on routine training exercises or were they specifically reacting to the oval aerial racetrack that TransPac 1001 had established? Both sets of jets came close to his mom's airplane and then backed away, establishing their own or-bits. Perhaps there was a dilemma between what they should do about the commercial airliner and what they should do about each other. As far as Lucas knew, Russia and Japan weren't exactly allies, but then again, they weren't at war, were they?

Then his phone pinged.

Lucas, this is mom. Are you there?

Lucas nearly dropped his phone, which was plugged in and recharging after the events of the last twenty-four hours. He ran over to Mia and spun around when he saw she was still sound asleep. Then worry hit him that she might be dead, so he held his hand against her forehead, and she was warm but not too warm. His fingers against her neck told him that her heart was still beating. He jumped up and down for no reason at all, pumping his fists into the air as if he had just won an Olympic gold medal.

He realized in his excitement that he still had his phone in his hand and that he hadn't responded to his mom yet. Walking back to the terminal, he caught the tarp covering the dead body out of the corner of his eye and reality sunk in. He really needed his mom right now.

Mom!!!! It's me. Lucas!!!
Are you okay?
I guess so. I mean yeah. But Mia's hurt. But she's okay. I bandaged her.
Bandaged?? What is going on?? Is your dad there??
Dad not here . . . kidnapped by the same guys who attacked us.
Attacked?? Who attacked you??
Copperhead. They want the cipher key I found at the crash site. I'm so sorry, Mom.

Lucas put down his phone, dropped his head into his hands, and began to weep. It was all too much. He was glad his mom couldn't see him, because he would be embarrassed. He wouldn't be her little man; instead, he would be her little wimp.

He looked back at his phone, realizing his mom had continued the conversation.

Lucas!! You have nothing to be sorry for!
Where did you go?
Talk to me? Where is your dad? Is Mia really okay?

He picked up his phone and began typing.

Mom, I don't know where Dad is. Mia is hanging. Are you ok?
Who did this? I'm . . . in a situation. I need the other half of what you gave me
I think I've figured it out, Mom. I can see any plane and maybe control it
You gave me one. Do you have the other section?
Yes. I think they work together.
They do.
Is your plane in trouble
It is. You have the cipher key. The security part. I have the algorithm. We've been hijacked.
Hijacked?
By Copperhead.
The algorithm won't work without the cipher
That's what Copperhead is saying
Why is Copperhead hijacking the airplane
They hijacked it to steal the algorithm and the cipher and then do something
Is Hembrick one of the guys?
Yes. How did you know?
I found him in the manifest
I won't even ask how you did that
Can you plug in the device I gave you to any device that can reach the Wi-Fi?

A long pause ensued.

Yes. Done. My adaptor works and the screen has code scrolling across it now
Okay . . . good. I'm going to pair my cipher to your algorithm

Won't the Copperhead guys know?
Once I do it, they can't stop it. I think I can control your airplane
They'll shut my Wi-Fi off. They're controlling all the communications.

Another long pause ensued.

That's a problem
Can you see the fighter jets off our wings?
Yes. Russian and Japanese. I can see their messages
What are they saying?
Just a second
Not much time. Hembrick calling me on the cockpit phone.

He wished Mia were helping him now, because he was having to translate every message from Russian or Japanese to English. He cut and pasted the text that was scrolling from each of the fighter jets back to their commands. He noticed a blinking light in the periphery of the heads-up display that read:
Translate?
Yes, please, he thought. He clicked on that prompt and immediately artificial intelligence began translating the various communications to English. Much better.

Mom, the Japanese are talking about the commercial airliner and why it went into orbit
And the Russians?
The Russians want to shoot down your airplane
They've gone behind us
I can see them. They've got approval to engage
Copperhead is calling me!
Hang on, Mom! Trying something.

Lucas placed his cursor on the Russian Su-57 Felon that was lined up behind TransPac 1001. He had a positive connection with his mom's algorithm flash drive in her tablet. When he toggled over the Russian jet, the word "Control" flashed green, as if inviting him. It hadn't done this before when he was using just his half of the platform. He had seen the word but was not able to take control.

He clicked the blinking cursor. The aviator helmet heads-up display showed him a range of new cockpit controls, all in Russian, but a blinking cursor asked him if he wanted to translate. He clicked on English and the artificial intelligence immediately translated all of the cockpit controls into English.

There was a button for missiles, which blinked with a yellow "Armed" warning. He hovered over the flashing "Armed" button and toggled it in the opposite direction, hoping he wasn't firing a missile.

Disarmed.

The light quickly went back to "Armed," and Lucas flipped it back just as fast. Knowing he couldn't keep playing this game, he hovered the cursor over the "Joystick" image, trying to figure out what to do. He and Mia had played several video games that included airplanes and jets. Would this be the same? It would make sense that the video game makers would attempt to create as much realism as possible. Plus, Lucas thought, the pilots that flew combat drones overseas did so from air force bases in the United States. Why couldn't he fly these airplanes? Control them?

"Whacha doin'?" Mia asked. She leaned on him to take pressure off her wounded leg.

Lucas jumped. He had been so focused on the inside of the cockpit that he hadn't noticed her rise from the moving blanket bed and lean over his shoulder. "Geez, Mia!"

"Sorry," she said. "Didn't mean to scare you."

"It's okay. Lots happening. My mom has contacted me. They're in trouble and I'm flying a Russian jet."

"A Russian jet?"

"Can you help me understand this cockpit?" He pointed at the monitor where all the cockpit information was displayed as if they were sitting in a cockpit themselves.

Mia pulled out her phone and began using translate. She pointed at an instruction on the monitor.

212 ANTHONY J. TATA

"That's something called HOTAS, or Hands on Throttle and Stick."

"Shit. It's armed again."

"Where are they aiming?"

"At my mom's airplane!"

"Try turning the aircraft. Like a video game. Move the joystick right or left."

He hit "Disarm" again and then did a hard yank on the joystick yoke function. The airplane banked steeply to the right and downward. The image appeared to collide with the other Felon aircraft.

The icons began dropping in altitude fast. He immediately received a text from his mother.

Lucas! The Russian jets crashed! Did you do that?
Maybe. IDK.
Giant fireball behind us.
Sorry?
Don't be. You might have saved us.
I'm checking the Japanese planes now.
Copperhead wants the TYRANT cipher. Can you send it?
You've got it now, but I have an idea.

As soon as he sent the text, the heads-up display appeared with a new prompt: What is your objective?

CHAPTER TWENTY-SEVEN

ZARA SHERIDAN

ZARA STARED AT HER TABLET AND READ THE MESSAGE FROM LUCAS: You've got it now.

She had the complete TYRANT platform, evidently, but she didn't want to tell Hembrick. Instead, she found herself shaking with rage.

She was sitting in one of the two comfort chairs in the crew rest area above the business-class galley. General Wang was sitting on one of the beds with his elbows propped on his knees. Amanda had climbed the stairwell and was straining to see what was on Zara's tablet. Zara shifted to the other seat to keep her back to the wall of the airplane and eyes on Amanda and the stairwell. She was getting a strange vibe from Amanda's nosiness, but perhaps the attendant was just trying to stay informed so she could do her job.

It finally sank in for her. Copperhead had somehow coordinated an attack on her family. Her home. Her husband.

Her *son*!

All because he had happened upon a crashed jet and taken a piece of the airplane for safekeeping. She knew Lucas would want to do the right thing, and now the wrong thing was happening to him. Where was the justice in this world when such bad things happened to such good people? And Lonnie, no matter their marital discord and differences, she loved him. Loved the way he held her with his massive chest and arms wrapped around her. Loved the way he pitched to Lucas until the sun went down and even after that. "If you can hit a ball in the dark, it will be easier in the daylight," he would say. And she loved the feeling of family. The three of them scratching out a life in North Carolina's Inner Banks. She wanted that back. She wanted Lonnie back.

But what was his fate? Was he even still alive or was he being held as some kind of bargaining chip? Was he removed so that Copperhead could get to Lucas?

She hadn't even thought to ask about Mia's father, who was the sheriff of the county and had been her first boss out of the military. She imagined that the jet crash had consumed some resources but shouldn't have diverted the entire lot of them. Surely someone could help the sheriff's daughter and her son and husband, couldn't they?

She looked at her tablet, which pinged with a message from Lucas: I have an idea.

The phone rang, not giving her a chance to respond, but she was concerned that Hembrick had intercepted Lucas's message.

"Sheridan," she said.

"Hembrick. Any luck? You've had five minutes. Better not be doing anything stupid."

"I want my husband back and for you to leave my son alone! What have you done?"

"It will get worse before it gets better if you don't get me that cipher. We're fortunate those two Russian jets collided. Rogers up here put the engines at full thrust to create some backwash. The Russian pilots must have been caught in the backwash. We got lucky. Maybe they were just trying to scare us, but maybe they wanted to shoot us down. We have the Dagger mission to complete, and we will complete it."

So Hembrick wasn't aware that she had the other half of TYRANT, nor could he monitor her communications with Lucas. He evidently had no idea that by matching the two halves of the hardware Lucas had found that she had the entire platform on her tablet. Likewise, Lucas now had the entire platform on his power-ful array of computers in their basement. As long as one of them had Wi-Fi access, they would be able to operate the technology.

Nor did Hembrick understand that her son had saved them by using TYRANT to maneuver the Russian jets into one another. As Lucas's mother, she was both proud of Lucas and fearful for him. It probably hadn't dawned on him yet, but his actions had killed two human beings. He would have to confront that at some point but she believed that Lucas was focused only on saving her and her airplane.

She could deal with Lucas's psychological ramifications later, she knew. Now, she needed to tell Hembrick something to buy some time to develop a plan to protect the airplane and protect her son, husband, and Mia. And if Lucas had an idea, it was better than what she had right now.

"He needs time to get his Wi-Fi reconnected, you asshole. Your 'nice man' seems to have been not so nice."

"I have plenty more nice men that I can send over to help him, and I think I'll do just that," Hembrick said.

"Well, thanks for confirming this isn't an official Dagger mis-sion authorized by the president," Zara said.

"You don't know what you're talking about."

"If it was, President Campbell would be leveraging General Sin-clair and his team to help. You'd have backup. Seems like they're not involved. That you're rogue. Maybe some grand scheme to start a war."

The phone line remained silent for longer than Zara was com-fortable, but she said nothing.

Then he unleashed something he had to know would knock her off balance.

"Our man Clark at the TSA checkpoint told us you attempted to sneak a nefarious code onto this airplane. You attacked him when he tried to stop you. You're the only one who has any ill in-tent on this airplane. You're stacking bodies up trying to kill everyone involved. No one has seen you do anything but attempt to take over the plane. Once we land, you'll be arrested for international terrorism and attempting to hijack an airliner. Your psychological dysfunction after failing to stop the Abbey Gate attack, which was your mission, has caused you to be suicidal. You have a well-known distaste for flying and airplanes in general, but the files that will be found on your tablet will reflect months of planning to go down in a blaze of glory as an apology for the thirteen men and women killed at Abbey Gate. Instead of being one of the twenty-two suicides servicemen and women commit every day, you wanted something more profound, that would stand out from what has sadly been forgotten. The suicide note that will also be found in your Dropbox will talk about your marital problems with Lonnie, his cheating, his abuse. You'll admit that Lucas has hacked into government databases and sells the information on Discord. He'll be found with classified documents regarding the China-Taiwan conflict that is imminent. He will have leaked those to senior members of the Chinese Communist Party. The payment money will be found in your bank account. He'll be arrested, of course, as will his girlfriend. Everything you care about will be ruined and destroyed."

Zara gasped. The scenario that Hembrick painted was entirely plausible. She had throttled Clark, the contract TSA agent. Lucas had hacked into the flight manifest to locate Hembrick's name. She was on record as detesting flying but had come around to tolerating it. She did believe that Lonnie had been unfaithful to her and she bore the weight of the Abbey Gate thirteen on her shoulders every day. But she was not and had never been suicidal. She knew that anyone with cyber capabilities could create the documents and digital trails to reflect everything that Hembrick had just laid out.

He could in fact destroy everything she cared about.

"Do I have your attention?"

"You do," she croaked.

"Now, Amanda Gāo should be directly in front of you. Do as she says."

Zara looked up. She had been so consumed by the harrowing picture that Hembrick was painting that she noticed too late

Amanda's quick draw of a Beretta 9mm pistol, which was now aimed at her. In her periphery, Major Li Van also drew a weapon, which seemed to be aimed at Amanda.

"I know you have the platform," Amanda said. "Now, let's get the transfer done."

CHAPTER TWENTY-EIGHT

LUCAS SHERIDAN

WHAT IS YOUR OBJECTIVE?

"What is your objective?" Mia asked, staring at the monitor and seeing the same thing Lucas was seeing on the heads-up display.

"Yeah," Lucas mumbled. He was distraught having "chatted" with his mother over text. She was in trouble, and so were he and his father. He couldn't throw the TYRANT platform "back into the ocean" as Kino had done with the pearl, because it seemed too important to saving his mother, her airplane, and her charges. Besides, he hadn't known the TYRANT platform hanging in the mangled cockpit was valuable, per se. He knew it was important information to protect. He was trying to do the right thing, not the greedy thing.

Was there a difference? *Maybe*, he thought. His intentions were pure, not the least bit motivated by personal gain. It seemed though that everyone else was after this valuable platform.

"Earth to Lucas," Mia said.

"Yeah," he repeated. "I think that's actually artificial intelligence. I didn't see that coming. This platform is high speed. It not only can control other aircraft, but it looks like it might be able to help you achieve your goals, like kill all the bad guys or protect the good guys."

"Like that old-time movie where the kid talks to the computer?"

"*War Games*. Yeah. Like that. What if the AI wants to do its own thing? Artificial intelligence is only as good as the people who program it. Blackwood Aviation made this. Like you were saying, all these people want war, right? It helps them make money. So is this thing trying to trick us by asking us what our objective is?"

"It's hard to imagine something this powerful is in our control at this moment. We can take any airplane and do anything we want to it. How is this possible? Who can invent something like this?"

Lucas shrugged. "Isn't it inevitable? Is there a difference between the good guys and the bad guys when the supposed good guys make this kind of software? I mean, I just killed two people who weren't a threat to me. Those Russian pilots."

Mia placed her hand on Lucas's back. "You protected your mother and all those innocent people. The pilots had the order to blow up the plane. Your mom would have died. You did what you had to do just like you did earlier this morning when Copperhead came after us. You saved my life, Lucas. Just understand that."

His nerves were frayed. He objectively understood everything that Mia was saying. The weight of the responsibility was overwhelming to him. He had shot and killed at least one person in his basement, wounding several others. But like Mia said, they were attacking him and Mia. Invading his home. No holds barred. These were bad people doing bad things.

Mia's hand was making circles between his shoulder blades. He knew she should be resting to recover from the shrapnel or bullet wounds, but here she was consoling and helping him. He removed the helmet and put his head into his hands. He wept for a minute. Choked. Coughed. All the worry bubbling up, releasing itself so he could process it.

"Part of me thinks we should just toss everything in the swamp," Lucas said. "Like Kino did with the pearl. But I know we need it to help my moms."

"We use it for good. The pearl brought out the worst in people. If anything, this device has brought out the best in you, Lucas. You've been a hero."

"I'm no hero, Mia. I'm just . . . we're just . . . making it up as we go."

"So, let's keep going, Lukie Dukie." She rested her chin on his shoulder and hugged him from behind. "You and me. We're a team. A force for good in the face of bad."

"You make it sound like superheroes or something."

"Is that so bad?"

"I guess not."

He straightened up and thought about the request: *What is your objective?*

"What is our objective? What should we tell the platform?"

"Practically speaking, our objective is to save TransPac Flight 1001," Mia said.

"That's right. So, if we type in something like 'Protect TransPac Flight 1001,' then maybe the platform will automatically take actions to do so."

"Maybe. How does it tell if a friendly Japanese fighter jet is trying to be friendly? Or if it wants to shoot it down like our military was going to do on 9/11? Does it automatically assume a Chinese jet is a bad guy? And what does it do about it?"

"There are no fighter jet type weapons like machine guns or bombs on the TransPac flight, so it can only fly. Let's assume the software will look for other fighter aircraft that might arm themselves and then maybe it does something like I did with the Russian jets."

"That sounds right. We're programmers and developers. The ability to harness external assets to achieve a common purpose is the kind of functionality we would want in an artificial intelligence platform," Mia said.

"Okay, let's do it. For the record, I don't trust Blackwood Aviation, and we know we can't trust Copperhead."

"Noted."

Lucas slid the helmet over his head. The heads-up display continued to ask him his objective. He clicked on the prompt, which led to a dialogue box. He typed: Protect TransPac Flight 1001.

The monitor and heads-up display both showed a digital image of TransPac Flight 1001 and its positioning over the Pacific Ocean near northern Japan. A red box appeared around the airplane image and another prompt appeared:

Correct Aircraft?

Lucas clicked, "Yes."

Code scrolled across the screen and quickly highlighted four airplanes, two over North Korea and two in Northeast China:

Possible threat. Monitoring.

"That sounds good, right?" Mia asked.

"So far."

Mia's phone pinged with a text.

"My dad!" she exclaimed.

"Is he okay?"

"He's asking us to meet him at Hyde County Airport."

"What? That doesn't make sense. That's thirty minutes by car and forever by bicycle."

"Well, it just says 'Hyde County Airport.' I'm assuming he wants us there or he's telling me that's where he is, but something's off."

"You sure it's him?"

"Actually, no. You know how he calls me baby girl and all that embarrassing stuff? None of that here."

"Call him," Lucas said.

Mia said, "Call Dad" into her phone, which began ringing on speakerphone. It rang six times until the voice mail function kicked in, saying, "I'm sorry, this mailbox is full."

"Either he's not texting, or he can't answer."

"Neither of which is good," Mia said.

"What's up with Hyde County Airport? It's kind of remote and close to the bombing range up there," Lucas said. He removed the helmet and looked at Mia, who was now sitting on the table with the computers and keeping her leg elevated on it.

She had a faraway look in her eyes as she stared at the shattered window to the south of the basement.

"You've got that look like when you're about to write a new line of code," Lucas said.

She remained silent for a few more seconds.

"It's a clue. Remember when we were kids—"

"We are kids," Lucas interrupted.

"Well, younger kids, then. And Copperhead had hidden all those ghost prisoners from Afghanistan in the tunnels beneath the bombing range? It was connected to Hyde County Airport."

"I didn't live here then. My parents were in Afghanistan or Syria, one of those luxurious vacation spots. We got here four years ago, so this is new to me."

Lucas pulled up a search engine on his computer and typed in "Copperhead Security Hyde County Bombing Range Ghost Prisoners."

Only a few articles appeared, but there were enough to confirm that there had been such an incident ten years ago when Mia and Lucas had been four years old.

"This one," Mia said. It was an article written by a local Dare County reporter that went into detail about how Copperhead Security had smuggled prisoners from Afghanistan to northeastern North Carolina and used them to clear old bombs from the bombing range. They kept them in a prison beneath the airfield."

"Where my dad might be?"

"And maybe even my dad," Mia added.

Lucas looked at the image of his mother's airplane with the green box around it. Four red boxes highlighted the two North Korean and the two Chinese jets that were inching closer to Trans-Pac 1001. The two Japanese jets were orbiting to the east and for whatever reason the platform AI had chosen not to highlight those jets yet.

"The truck?" Mia asked.

"Let's recon first using a drone," Lucas said.

"Long way for a drone," Mia said. "Thirty miles, give or take."

"We can't leave here just yet," Lucas said. "I've got to stay in contact with my moms."

"What's the worst thing that happens if we do leave?"

"I don't know. Those guys are evil. They're trying to kill a couple of kids, you know—us."

"They'll start a war," Mia said.

"I think we both believe that. Think of all the kids like us who will die because some simps want to start a war. Bombs everywhere."

"What about intercepting a Copperhead drone? Their last one seemed to have sick range," Mia said.

"That's fire. I've got the program locked onto Mom's airplane. Do you think it can multitask?"

"No need. We hacked the last one ourselves. I wouldn't mess with the TYRANT thing."

They both stared at his mother's airplane, TransPac Flight 1001, moving slowly on the monitor.

"Actually, let's try this," Lucas said.

He removed his DJI drone and laid it on the ground outside the shattered north window. Returning to his console, he powered it up and steered the drone so that it flew north and east for about fifteen minutes along Route 264. He found Copperhead's makeshift headquarters where they had followed the previous Copperhead drone. Hovering for about five minutes, the drone showed two men exiting the trailer and getting into a pickup truck while both were shouting into their phones. Something was happening.

Lucas flew the drone low and landed it in the bed of the pickup truck as the men got in the truck and slammed their doors. The truck spun out from the dirt lot and turned north on Route 264, toward Hyde County Airport. He put the battery into low power mode as they piggybacked a ride from the Copperhead employees. After twenty minutes of racing at eighty miles an hour down Route 264, the truck slowed.

"Tracking the drone GPS, it shows us maybe a half mile now from the airport," Mia said.

"Yeah, once they slow down, I'll lift it out."

The truck made a hard, bouncy turn, hit a pothole that bounced the drone up in the air. The camera showed it was tilted so that only two of its rotors could spin.

"That's a problem," Lucas said.

The truck continued to bounce along what must have been a dirt road, because the camera jiggled and jittered the entire time. He tried powering the blades, but the two resting on the truck bed wouldn't turn.

"Keep trying, Lukie," Mia said.

"Yeah, I don't want to burn up the motor though. I'm already beyond max radio frequency range, Mia. One in a million shot here, but it's mostly soybean fields, so there's a chance."

"Gotta try," Mia said.

Lucas held the remote with both hands. The truck came to a stop and suddenly the drone was lifted, as if by hand. A quick glimpse of a bearded face and Copperhead double-fanged hat indicated that someone had found their drone.

The DJI audio function transmitted a voice saying, "Is this ours?"

Lucas gave it full throttle, all four blades spinning at full RPMs while toggling to the left. The maneuver worked. The man said, "What the fuck?" and the drone slipped from his hands. Lucas lifted the drone high and sped it west toward the end of the hangar, where they had parked. The gimbal spun back and aimed the camera at the two men, holding their hands over their eyes to watch the drone.

On one monitor, they watched his mother's airplane track across the Pacific Ocean, while on the other, they watched the camera focus on a Copperhead operation of some type. He took the DJI out to Route 264 so that they would lose sight of it and he could get his bearings. The road asphalt was framed by a deep drainage ditch on either side. Peanut and soybean fields scattered as far as the eye could see. The leaves were broad and green, growing through the mild spring. The runway was basic, ending about a football field from the road. Lucas's connection with the drone was weak but present.

He toggled the drone to the northwest and followed the fence line. There were a few warehouses including one at the far end of the runway, which backed up to more crop fields. He hovered the drone just above a row of broad soybean leaves and aimed the camera at the hangar opening where the truck had parked.

"This is what I was talking about," Mia said. "That hangar and the airfield. There was a big fight there in the tunnels. A local guy named Mohican or Mahegan had sort of saved the day."

Lucas opened Grok Ai on his phone and read to Mia, "Ten years ago, a former Delta Force operative named Jake Mahegan had uncovered Copperhead's elaborate plan to ship ghost prisoners from Afghanistan to the United States in containers. They were unaccounted for in Afghanistan and literal "ghosts" in the United States. No one knew they existed until Mahegan had disrupted their plan to escape Copperhead captivity and attack Norfolk naval base in Virginia."

"Sounds right," she said.

"Gotta be something in there and only one way to find out," Lucas said. He watched two Copperhead employees through the drone camera. When they appeared bored, he maneuvered the drone straight up to about two hundred meters above ground level, then exactly perpendicular to their would-be line of sight if they were still watching. He brought the drone down center mass of the rooftop and then flew it on the airfield side of the hangar until he found an opening in the opposite hangar doors.

Inside the hangar was an airplane with the Copperhead double-fanged logo on it. Two more Copperhead pickup trucks were parked inside the hangar. They looked just like the trucks that had taken away Deputy Cashwell and maybe even his dad. There were also two ducted fan helicopters in the large hangar. These were the ones that had landed at the crash site and had raided his home. The ones that had wounded Mia with their miniguns.

Anger boiled inside Lucas, but he suppressed it . . . for now.

He risked pushing the drone farther inside the hangar, keeping it high. He zoomed the camera on a group of men huddled around something on the floor. The camera showed a large square hole with a ladder.

Two men emerged carrying another man, dumping him on the floor like a sack of flour.

"That's my dad," Lucas said. He recognized his father's broad shoulders, thick biceps and forearms, and knotty black hair. His eyes were closed, or seemed that way from the brief glimpse he was able to get. His dad was still wearing his Swan Quarter NCDOT Ferry coveralls. Lonnie Sheridan appeared to have been doing exactly what he said he was doing, working through the night with his employees to fix a ferry. The commuters from the Inner Banks to the military bases across the river relied upon his dad's ferries to get to work and earn their livings. Swan Quarter wasn't a wealthy part of North Carolina, but the selflessness of people like his dad provided opportunity to people who might not otherwise have it.

Then they dumped another man on the floor next to Lonnie Sheridan.

"That's *my* dad!" Mia said.

Both men remained motionless, perhaps unconscious, as the group huddled around them.

Lucas stared at the monitor, wishing he had one of those drones that could fire bullets or drop bombs.

Two Copperhead thugs lifted Lonnie Sheridan and held him up against the wall. He did not open his eyes but was able to stand, which meant he was still alive. They wrapped a chain around his wrists and cranked a pulley high enough to brace his dad's hands above his head, arms outstretched, shoulders at full extension.

They performed a similar maneuver with Sheriff Barlowe, who was equally passive as they lifted the big man and shackled him.

"They're drugged," Mia said.

"But alive," Lucas replied.

"Battery indicator is low," Mia said, pointing at the red line approaching 5 percent power on the drone display.

Lucas reluctantly backed the drone out of the hangar and flew it south into a soybean field, where he landed it and shut it down. He switched on the GPS beacon so they could retrieve it.

"It's just us against them," Lucas said. "Copperhead has my mom *and* dad and your dad. We have to save our parents and then destroy this thing."

Just then the artificial intelligence tracking TransPac Flight 1001 pinged with an alert:

Threat detected.

CHAPTER TWENTY-NINE

ZARA SHERIDAN

Zara's instinctive distrust of Amanda Gāo had come to fruition.

Gāo held a Beretta pistol level at Zara's face. General Wang remained motionless, watching. Major Li Van aimed a firearm at Amanda, she believed, but he was off her left shoulder in the tight confines of the stew crew rest area.

Li Van barked something in Mandarin at Amanda, who replied harshly in the same language, waving her pistol at him and General Wang. Zara's interpretation was that Li Van was protecting his general but didn't want to shoot Amanda without a direct threat to the man.

Amanda turned her attention to Zara, who was the center point between the three of them.

"I'm going to show you something," Amanda said. She retrieved a tablet from her smock pocket and lifted it so that Zara could see it.

"We know how to use Wi-Fi, too, Sheridan. Tell me what you see here, please."

Zara studied the image a few feet away from her face. It was a live or recorded video of her husband being chained to a corrugated metal wall in a warehouse or airplane hangar. Next to him was Sheriff Barlowe, who was similarly restrained. Their bare feet were barely touching the cement floor. A slow breath escaped her mouth, more of a quick exhalation that typically preceded lifting weights or some other strenuous physical activity. The stress had been too much, but wasn't comparable to what she saw next.

Amanda hit a button on the touch screen, and she saw helicopters flying around her backyard spitting minigun bullets at her home. For a moment, Lucas was visible carrying a shotgun as he ran behind the grill into the west-side yard of the house. The door to their home had been demolished, and she wondered if Lucas was still alive. Her face gave the first clues of fear and worry as her eyes narrowed and then widened at the destruction of her home.

"Oh, my God," she whispered.

"Got your attention?" Amanda barked.

"Is my son still alive?"

"It's an evolving situation. The little shit has proven tougher to crack than we gave him credit for," Amanda said.

"I'll take that as a yes. Why else would you kidnap Lonnie? The sheriff?"

"We will do what is necessary to get the full platform, which I believe you have right there on your tablet. So let me have that and we can do what we need to do. Then we will release your family and focus on our mission."

"What *is* your mission?" General Wang asked of Amanda.

Amanda snapped her head in his direction.

"Just remember, General, you're not in charge up here. We are," Amanda said. She looked over Zara's shoulder at Li Van. "Major, like I told you, this is not your concern."

"Who is 'we'?" Wang said.

"We are on a presidential mission to stop the Chinese from invading Taiwan. You should be happy about this, General and Major. This software platform can do that. It's your country, and mine, after all."

"That can't be true, though," Zara said. "The US government would gladly employ technology to stop a war between China and Taiwan. It seems that you want to start one."

Amanda shrugged. "Start. Stop. Sometimes I get confused. Semantics. Now hand me your tablet, which I believe has the entire TYRANT platform uploaded."

Zara's body sagged, knowing that she had lost the initiative by not outmaneuvering Amanda earlier, but there were so many double crossers that she was having a difficult time triaging them.

"Let Lonnie and Sheriff Barlowe go, and I'll happily hand you the tablet. And keep your thugs away from my home and my son." She didn't mention Mia because she wasn't sure if Mia was involved with Lucas. She suspected she might be, but didn't want to give away free information, namely that the sheriff had a daughter, to Amanda or the Copperhead ground team.

"Works the other way around. We get the tablet. If it has the right information on it, then we release everyone and back off."

In her periphery, Zara noticed Li Van take a step to his left to gain a better site picture on Amanda. General Wang's hand was moving slowly inside his suit coat pocket. Whatever he had planned would add a new variable. One that could hurt her husband and son or possibly help. That was her dilemma. Everything was an unknown outcome from this point forward. Every one of the people in this compartment with her had different motivations from her.

The army had trained Zara in multiple stressful decision-making environments, and she had employed those in combat. Likewise, the Federal Air Marshal Service training had similarly put her through a series of simulated fight-or-flight responses, Zara's usual being to fight.

There was the adage, however, to live to fight another day, or hour, or minute. With her family at risk, Zara weighed the threat to national security that the TYRANT platform presented in the hands of Copperhead against the safety of her family.

She raised her hand in the direction of General Wang while keeping eye contact with Amanda.

"Okay. I just need assurance that you'll leave my family and Sheriff Barlowe alone. That you'll let them all go free. Copperhead has exposed itself here and I have very little trust right now that you'll do anything in my favor. More likely, you'll try to cover your tracks. Kill my husband. Kill my kid. Kill the sheriff."

"We will move them to a secure location. We just need the platform now. Hembrick needs what you have. I have no issue with anyone in this room. I just need what you've got," Amanda explained.

Thus far, the top of Amanda's head had been below the stairwell landing and not in the line of site of General Wang or Major Li Van. Wang's subtle movements had gone undetected by Amanda, as far as she could determine, because he was now holding a Taiwanese T75K3 standard officer's sidearm in his hand. The pistol was a knockoff of the Beretta 9mm sidearm and was aimed directly above the railing where Amanda's head would appear if she were to take another step. Li Van continued to aim whatever weapon he held in his hand, but Zara didn't believe either Wang or Li Van had a shot on Amanda, who was concealed in the steep stairwell leading up from the main cabin area.

She thought of Lucas, but in a hopeful way. His last words to her were, "I have an idea." She needed to delete the text thread from her tablet before she handed it to Amanda.

"I'll open it for you and then hand it to you. But first I'll lock the screen so that it doesn't close out on you."

General Wang said to Amanda, "If your intentions are to save Taiwan, then we should all be in agreement."

"Those are my intentions," Amanda said.

Major Li Van said, "But what does that mean? Save Taiwan? Reunification or separation?"

As they were debating Amanda's purpose, Zara's fingers were moving swiftly on the tablet. She had the text application up and she swiped the text thread with Lucas to the right, hit the red delete prompt, and scanned the rest of the texts. She deleted her dialogue with Lindy Van Horn and all the research reports that had been delivered to her. She checked her delete bin and double-deleted everything until it was all completely gone, as far as she could tell. Last, she clicked on the TYRANT application icon, which came to life on her screen.

"What are you doing?" Amanda snapped.

"Handing you the platform," Zara said. "Here you go."

Amanda said, "Hand it to me."

"I am. Meet me halfway. That's not so much to ask, is it?"

Amanda cocked her head and said, "Sure. I can already see the major has a weapon. Do you really want to start a gun fight on a plane, Major?"

She placed one foot on the next step, then dropped low and spun onto the landing like a skilled operator, snapping off two silenced rounds from her Beretta. General Wang shook as both rounds impacted into his body. He fell backward onto one of the two beds in the crew rest area. Li Van rushed to his boss instead of fighting back against Amanda. Most likely he had no shot.

Zara dropped her tablet and retrieved her compact Sig Sauer as Amanda Gāo, apparently not only a flight attendant, performed a martial arts sweep of Zara's leg, which Zara anticipated. Leaping in the air as Amanda kicked out, Zara rolled toward the bed that General Wang now lay upon.

Her tablet skittered across the floor within arm's reach of Amanda, who snatched the device where it spun like a top at the landing of the steps. She raced down the steps, pistol aimed over her shoulder as Zara rolled toward the landing opening only to see the door closing. Did she follow in pursuit of an armed assassin carrying lethal technology or did she tend to General Wang? She looked at Major Li Van hunched over General Wang, removing his suit coat and shirt, and decided to pursue.

She flew down the steps and through the door, moving swiftly in Amanda's vortex. She had tucked the pistol and looked like a flight attendant moving along with a distinct purpose. Perhaps a passenger in need of medical attention or an urgent call from the cockpit? The already nervous passengers craned their heads as they watched Amanda blow along the port side aisle toward the cockpit. Zara moved swiftly in her wake, attempting to cast the same confident yet urgent façade to not further incite the passengers' worry.

Amanda knocked on the cockpit door with two raps and then

three. Hembrick opened the door slightly, most likely staring through the fish-eye peephole to confirm it was an ally, Amanda, and not his pursuer, Zara.

Amanda slid the tablet with Lucas's TYRANT flash drive connected to it through the opening. Hembrick snatched the device. Zara shouldered into Amanda, pushing them both into the cockpit but only marginally.

Hembrick pushed back, leaning his shoulder into the cockpit door. Zara leveraged her height and toned body into Amanda, using her hand to push up on Amanda's chin and wedge her head in the door that Hembrick was trying to close.

Jeremy West came from the pilot rest area where he had presumably been watching through his makeshift spy camera into the cockpit. West pushed into Zara, like a lineman trying to get the quarterback over the goal line. Competing vectors of force caused a stalemate at the door. Passengers in the first-class cabin began to shout.

"What's going on up there?"

"We're being hijacked!"

And so on. Shouts and screams began to surge through the large airplane like a wildfire on dry grass. The pandemonium Zara had hoped to avoid was upon them.

Suddenly the plane shot upward, like a fighter jet hitting max gravitational force. The unexpected move caused Amanda, Zara, and West to tumble backward.

Hembrick closed and locked the cockpit door.

Zara put an MMA-level scissor lock on Amanda and used her forearm to wrench Amanda's head backward, immobilizing her. West took the FlexiCuffs from Zara's exposed belt and zip tied Amanda's hands behind her back.

"Upstairs," Zara said.

They walked Amanda up the steps, West leading. They dumped her in between the two small beds. West pulled a strip of tape across her mouth and a pillowcase over her head, then tied her ankles using another pillowcase.

Zara stared into West's makeshift cockpit cam.

Hembrick had the tablet. Somehow Amanda must have pre-vented the screen from locking because he had connected it to his receiver and seemed satisfied with the result. She assumed that he was continuing to operate on the Ku satellite band, and if that was the case, she might have an option.

She looked at Amanda Gāo writhing on the floor and resisted the urge to pummel her. Jeremy West caught her eyes.

"Don't do it, Zara," he said.

"I would never, but if I were ever to, now would be the time for me to unload on this psycho."

"Well put, but we've got a problem to solve."

She looked around the room. Three dead bodies. A wounded Marcus Jones. Two detainees in Rodriguez and now Gāo.

"The passengers are going into a frenzy," she said. "I should say something on the intercom. Something like, 'Some warmonger-ing assholes have hijacked this airplane so they can start World War Three, but don't worry, there's no plan to crash the airplane that we know of, so everyone should be okay. Your flight atten-dants will be bringing the next scheduled meal out in a few min-utes."

West nodded, grimaced, and smiled.

"And here I thought I was in charge of comedy," he said.

"Fucking Greek tragedy right here," Zara said.

"What's your plan, Marshal?"

She took a deep breath, sighed, and straightened her posture.

"Thank you, Jeremy. I needed that moment, but I do have an idea."

She retrieved her Federal Air Marshal Service issued satellite phone and found that Copperhead had opened the Ku satellite band. Most passengers would not be able to access this discreet satellite connection. She texted Lucas: Lucas. We need to talk.

As she texted her son, she looked through the cockpit cam and saw that two jets with Russia icons had appeared on the starboard side while two jets with Chinese flag icons flanked them on the port side. The Japanese jets, she presumed had pulled away to monitor and avoid conflict.

No response from Lucas, which worried her.

"Come on, son," she whispered.

Hembrick was talking into a headset and maneuvering icons on the tablet. The TransPac airplane broke out of the racetrack pattern it had been flying and set a course for Taipei.

"Is Hembrick controlling these fighter jets?" Zara asked.

She moved to the side so that West could make his own assessment.

"Either that or they are escorting us somewhere, or both."

A text from Lucas appeared: Mom! I found Dad and Sheriff Barlowe. They're in trouble but still alive! Plus, there's a bunch of Chinese airplanes headed straight for Taiwan! Right where you're going! All of them have programmed targets to different parts of Taiwan! Be careful!

Zara's heart skipped a beat. Lucas had found Lonnie and the sheriff. What the hell was going on?

West read her phone and said, "Hell of a kid right there."

"Yeah, but this is crazy. Bombers headed right for Taipei Semiconductor. General Wang talked about all the logistical preparation, meaning this is no head fake."

"Well, you have to wonder what would happen if the largest manufacturer of semiconductors in the world was destroyed."

"It would bring the entire world economy to a screeching halt. Like shutting off oil flow from the Persian Gulf."

"Is Hembrick trying to stop that attack? Or facilitate it?"

The phone rang.

It was Hembrick.

"If you want your husband and son to live, you will do nothing to interrupt our Dagger mission."

"Stop with the bullshit, Hembrick. There is no Dagger mission. You're a lone wolf on some wild escapade. If we survive this, your ass is going to jail."

"Like I told you. We have the video of you disabling our TSA augmentee Clark and sneaking this software onto the plane. If anyone has committed a crime, it's you. We are communicating with authorities across a range of countries for clearance to land as scheduled despite your efforts to interrupt and divert the flight for nefarious purposes. Authorities will be waiting on *you*, not me, Sheridan."

"You don't even make sense when you're telling the truth, much less when you're lying like this."

"Trust me. Don't contact your son."

Hembrick hung up. Zara looked at West, who said, "We have to try."

Zara nodded. "Yes, we do."

CHAPTER THIRTY

LUCAS SHERIDAN

"**M**Y MOM'S TABLET IS IN THE COCKPIT," LUCAS SAID.

He pointed at the screen of his monitor, which showed a blinking red dot inside the digital image of the 777-300ER airplane that the TYRANT algorithm produced.

"Is your mom in the cockpit?"

"Her phone location is showing just behind the cockpit, so I'm guessing she's not," Lucas said. "But it's impossible to tell which device she's with, if she's with either. But the good news is, I checked before I made those behavior prediction glasses for her and both devices have satellite Ku band SIM cards. So, we have comms as long as the hijackers keep the Ku band open. They've shut off the Wi-Fi again and all the radios." Lucas and his mother shared their locations in the Find My Friends application on their phones. He was able to integrate her smartphone location into the fully functional TYRANT platform on his computer, giving him close to full situational awareness.

"Look at that," Mia said. She pointed at the Russian and Chinese jets flanking the 777-300ER passenger plane. "Is that because you told the program to protect your mom's plane? Or are they doing something for the Copperhead guys in the cockpit?"

"The mission in the software is still to protect the plane, but I'm assuming that Copperhead has something up their sleeve."

Lucas's fingers flew across the keyboard. He was simultane-ously exploring TYRANT's top-secret code while also monitoring the situation. Gone from his immediate thoughts were any dangers that he and Mia might be in. The predicament that his father and the sheriff were in was important, but in choosing where to put his efforts, he chose the airplane flying at forty thousand feet above sea level in the Pacific Ocean.

"Got any more Tylenol?" Mia asked.

Lucas looked at his friend's face. She was grimacing from the pain medication wearing off. He stopped what he was doing and pulled out the bottle of Tylenol, handed her a few tablets and a water bottle, and then inspected the bandage.

"My Boy Scout training says it's okay. I called 911. They know we have an emergency, but something tells me that Copperhead has taken control of everything. There is no coming back from kidnapping your dad."

"I know," Mia said. She swallowed the pills and drank half the bottle of water.

"Drink more," Lucas said.

Mia took another swig and then finished the bottle off.

"Feeling a little light-headed," she said.

"Which is why I'm going to make you lie down again."

He slid his arm around her waist as she put her arm over his shoulder. He lifted her into a cradle in his arms and walked slowly to the moving blankets where he laid her gently in the middle. He lifted one of the loose blankets and covered her as if he was tucking her into bed.

"I've got you," he said.

"You've got me," she repeated.

"Now get some rest."

Lucas returned to the command console, studied the screens, and then decided to follow an instinct.

His understanding of world affairs was limited in part to discussions his parents had at the dinner table and the unique view he got from the global gaming and developer network. He belonged to a few Discord channels that traded information about computer science, artificial intelligence, and quantum tunneling.

Invariably, politics would filter into the conversation with a light touch, such as, "Macron's bad for cryptocurrency algos . . . El Sal going full bore Bitcoin is boss . . . Xi and China cornering the market on quantum . . . and so on."

Lucas dismissed much of the chatter as random conversation with the occasional thought that a "bad actor" might be in the chat trying to persuade, as in any information operation. Most importantly, though, he formed most of his understanding of international relations from his mom, who made sure Lucas understood why she and her father had joined the army and why they had gone to war.

"Bad people are doing bad things to good people," his mother had once said when he was younger. Those general statements had led to more specific details about China, North Korea, Iran, and Russia forming an alliance to weaken the United States' power and economy. Lucas certainly understood this from a computer scientist's point of view. He knew the legions of hackers that all four of those countries employed to try to steal trade secrets, top secret information, and private personal data.

"But everything begins and ends with money, Lucas," she had said. "We go to war over oil and power, which is all about money and control. Your dad and I, we believe in a better future for you, which is why we serve, but make no mistake. At the end of the day, we are all just pawns in someone else's chess match. The key is that we need to keep the bad guys off-balance so that our freedoms stay protected."

Lucas replayed the conversation in his mind. He was maybe ten years old then, right before his parents had retired and moved to Swan Quarter.

Everything begins and ends with money.

On that thought, he began researching Copperhead Security, which was largely controlled by White Glacier Private Equity. He spent a few minutes researching White Glacier and saw that they had several former White House, Defense Department, and State Department senior political appointees in their executive leadership and on their board of directors.

After fifteen minutes, he was inside White Glacier's root drive, bypassing their faulty cybersecurity software. There, he found an interesting series of communications between the current secretary of defense and the former secretary of defense, who was the chairman of the White Glacier board.

> Need to chat about TYRANT to Taiwan
> Not here
> Today. Pentagon City Ritz. 7 P.M.
> Roger.

Then, the following day, internal communications between the board chairman and the White Glacier chief operations officer revealed:

> Green light on Taiwan reconstruction should there be a need
> Good news!
> Need Copperhead to execute CONPLAN TYRANT
> Big guy okay with that?
> More than okay. Chip plants are done and ready.
> Roger that
> Phu Shen and CL are onboard with plan, too
> Backup or primary
> Leave the details to them.

Lucas pushed away from his computer station, stood up, and began pacing.

"This means that Copperhead is just a pawn," he said to himself. "The big money is in rebuilding Taiwan. Billions of dollars. But what has to happen to rebuild? The country must need to be rebuilt. Why would they need rebuilding? They would need to be destroyed. And what are the chip plants?"

He stopped pacing and sat down again, something gnawing at his brain.

Phu Shen. CL. He wondered about those names. He spent another ten minutes searching White Glacier's Slack application database and found communication between Stanley Stanhope and Phu Shen, the founder and CEO of Clouded Leopard private equity based in Taipei, Taiwan.

"They are teaming up on this?" he muttered to himself. He stood again, running his hands through his hair, slick with sweat and dirt from the last day, which included baseball practice, finding the TYRANT platform, and warding off Copperhead assassins, as he thought of them.

He stopped pacing and looked at Mia, who was curled up in the blankets and muttering something. He walked closer to her and heard her say, "They want war, Lukie. It's about the money."

"I know, Mia. What do you think it means when they say the chip plants are ready?"

"Taiwan. Taipei Semiconductor is the biggest in the world."

"They're going to destroy the chip factory so that everyone will have to use the White Glacier chips?"

"You're a genius, Lukie Dukie."

"But why would White Glacier and Clouded Leopard team up to do that?"

"It's all about the Benjamins," Mia said. Her voice was weak and fading.

Lucas placed the back of his hand to Mia's forehead, which was warm to the touch. She was running a mild fever. Had he done everything right? He cleaned the wound. Rinsed it out good. And then did the best he could bandaging her up. Maybe she was going into shock. It was a big deal to be shot, Lucas considered.

"How do you feel, Mia?"

"I'm okay, Lucas Sheridan. I'll be ready to go in a few minutes. Just need to rest my eyes."

"Okay. Rest up, Mia Barlowe. I've got you."

"You've got me."

He stood and started pacing again as he spoke.

"Just FYI, those jets are protecting Mom's plane because China and Russia know it has TYRANT onboard. This was planned out."

"Planned," Mia repeated weakly.

He stared through the shattered north-facing window.

"Copperhead is going to use TYRANT to make it so that the Taiwanese Air Force can't respond."

"Sounds right," Mia whispered.

He stood and returned to his console, a million thoughts running through his mind.

He texted his mother: There?

After a minute:

Yes. Phone tho.
What I thought. They have your tablet with the TYRANT platform?
Yes. How did you know?
Not important. This is all controlled by White Glacier Private Equity
Know v little about them
I got into their internal Slack account
I'm not going to ask
No need. Copperhead is using TYRANT to hold back the Taiwanese Air Force.
Why?
Because White Glacier and Clouded Leopard have the contract to rebuild Taiwan
What??
Yes. And they've built chip plants to replace Taipei Semiconductor
Is that the target?
Probably the main one. idk
Keep digging into White Glacier and Clouded Leopard. I'm going to try something
Ok
And Lucas . . .

About a minute passed without a follow-up. Lucas fidgeted, worrying about his mother: Moms?

I love you so very much.

CHAPTER THIRTY-ONE

ZARA SHERIDAN

I LOVE YOU SO VERY MUCH.

Zara stared at the words on her screen. Tears formed in the back of her eyes, but she held them at bay.

She couldn't let go of the fact that Copperhead commandos had attacked her home—*her home!*—hell-bent on getting the cipher platform that Lucas had found and secured from scavengers. *No good deed goes unpunished.*

The additional information about White Glacier, one of the largest private equity companies in the world, was unnerving. Were they teamed with something called Clouded Leopard? Nothing good ever came from greed being vested in war.

At the same time, Lucas's information gave her a sense of focus. The airplane was throttling through the sky like any other passenger jet, but now she understood that big money wanted to make bigger money, so they co-opted some low-level Copperhead operatives to do their bidding. In no way did she believe this was a Dagger mission as Hembrick continued to say, which would be an official, sanctioned government operation authorized by the president.

Something clawed at the back of her mind, perhaps a name she had missed. She had so far interacted with every person of interest on her initial list, except for Johnnie Wilson with Blackwood Aviation. Maybe it was time to talk to Wilson.

She looked at West and said, "Keep an eye on these guys. I'm going to go down and try to impart some calm and bring a Blackwood Aviation engineer up here."

"Who's the engineer?"

"Johnnie Wilson," Zara said.

"I know him. Smart guy. He developed the TYRANT platform."

"You think he can help us?"

"Can't hurt. What did your son have to say?"

Zara looked away, then back at West.

"This whole thing is controlled by White Glacier Private Equity. They own Copperhead."

West let out a long, low whistle.

"Both have a huge stake in Blackwood Aviation and about a million other companies. They will profit immensely from the Hyperion program being fully adopted into a formal acquisition with the Department of Defense, much less sales to all our allies and partners."

"Lucas said that the TYRANT platform appears programmed to block the Taiwanese Air Force from responding to a Chinese attack," Zara said.

"Did he have any rationale for that?"

"He . . . was able to view some communications from White Glacier's server. They own the contract to reconstruct Taiwan in the event of a Chinese attack. And they also have just completed a very large semiconductor manufacturing plant."

West's forehead crinkled and his eyes narrowed.

"Those bastards are going for a pick-six," West said. "Like in football. The defense intercepts the ball and scores a touchdown on the same play. White Glacier gets the Chinese to knock out Taipei Semiconductor and they get to rebuild that and the surrounding countryside while their chip plant picks up the slack in global demand for chips."

"Always comes down to the almighty dollar," Zara said. "Let me go calm the troops down and drag Wilson up here."

"Might want to just make an announcement," West said.

"Great minds think alike. That's exactly what I'm going to do if that too isn't shut off."

"Shouldn't be. Their jammer can't impact the hard-wired internal communications."

Zara nodded and walked downstairs. She had retrieved her pistol after the scuffle with Amanda and patted it for reassurance that it was still there tucked in her holster. She opened the door to complete pandemonium with Julie Chang, the flight attendant managing business class, standing with her back against the door, hands up in a fighter's pose, feet spread wide for balance.

To her front were four big men with a beverage cart. Their apparent intent was to ram the cockpit door like Todd Beamer and his 9/11 hijack colleagues on United Airlines Flight 93.

"Back off!" Zara said, retrieving her pistol. "Federal air marshal. Back. The. Fuck. Off."

One of the big men next to her attempted to body slam her, but she stepped to the side and landed an uppercut on the man's chin and a knee to the groin. He doubled over and she brought the pistol down on his head, using both hands balled into a fist. The man rolled onto the floor. She put her foot on his back and looked at the other men holding the cart.

"Who's next, bitches?" she said.

"Who's in the cockpit?" one of the men shouted.

"To your left!" Julie screamed.

Zara spun with a high kick just in time to thwart an attacker descending on her position from the starboard side of the plane. She finished the lanky, bespectacled man with two straight kicks to the throat. He grabbed his neck and went to his knees before crawling backward.

"Keep it coming. Easier this way," Zara said.

She was breathing steady and completely in her zone. Flashbacks of Abbey Gate hung on the fringes of her mind. Instead of pursuing, here she was in one place defending, using her best skills. Talking, fighting, and shooting. She could do any of them or all of them at once, but she would accomplish this mission of getting the plane under control.

"You want some of this?" she said to the three men.

"We want to know what's going on."

"Sit back down and I'll tell you. I was going to make an announcement, but you assholes got in the way. Don't try to be heroes. Not today."

"What's going on?"

The question reverberated throughout the cabin until it became like a political chant.

"What's going on?" "What's going on?"

Zara grabbed the intercom and asked Julie, "How do I work this thing?"

Julie pressed some buttons on a panel and said, "Should work now."

"Thanks. Get me Johnnie Wilson please. Seat 11B. Have him bring his briefcase."

Julie looked at the throng of people doubtfully, then back at Zara.

"You can do it," Zara whispered. "Go." She nodded her head in the direction of the first-class cabin. Then to the three-man crew remaining on the beverage cart, she said, "Back up for our flight attendant. Now."

The men stepped away as Julie removed the beverage cart and placed it next to Zara.

Zara held the intercom in her hand and said in a loud voice, "Quiet!"

After a few more tries, the three hundred raucous passengers lowered their voices so that they could hear Zara's announcement.

"Thank you. I am the air marshal assigned to this flight," Zara said into the intercom, which played in every speaker throughout the airplane. "We've had a change of crew, who is now flying the airplane. There are some international tensions coming into play, which may be why you see Russian and Chinese fighter jets off our wings. The activity in the cockpit area has been intense, but we have a former US Navy pilot flying the airplane. Our destination remains the same. I have had to neutralize a threat to the cockpit and was successful in doing so. A man named Xiao Chen breached the cockpit door and he is now in captivity. As you can see, the flight is smooth now that we have another pilot in the cockpit. While there may be more developments, my expectation is that the flight will proceed mostly as scheduled. I will keep you updated. Some rules: Do not try to do anything to put the plane or your fellow passengers in danger. Do not come near the cockpit. Do not block the aisles. If you have questions, hit your call button and one of the flight attendants will visit you at their first opportunity. Thank you."

She hung up the intercom phone.

Julie reappeared with an African American man wearing a brown corduroy blazer and carrying a briefcase.

"Johnnie Wilson?" Zara asked.

He looked at her through thick John Lennon glasses.

"Yes, ma'am."

"This way," Zara said.

She led Wilson to the flight attendant crew rest area where she had left General Wang and Major Li Van. Given the sensitivity of the camera portal that West had established and the fact there were several detainees and dead bodies in the pilot rest area above first class, she wanted to talk to Wilson in as much privacy as possible. She was also concerned about General Wang and whether he needed medical attention.

With all passenger eyes tracking her, she walked with Wilson to the business-class galley, had Julie punch in the code to the door, and then climbed the steep stairwell into the room where she had just fought off Amanda Gāo. To her right, General Wang was sitting on the bed holding a CAT Covert Armored T-shirt in his hands. Two bruises showed on his chest and abdomen. He would surely be dead or severely wounded without the protective layer of clothing. His white shirt and blue suit jacket were laid neatly on the opposite bed.

Major Li Van sat on the opposing bed with an open medical bag. He and his boss were speaking quietly in their native language.

"Glad to see you're okay," Zara said.

"I'm anything but okay if Agent Gāo has the TYRANT platform."

"Agent Gāo?"

"Amanda Gāo is a well-known Chinese intelligence operative. We have a full dossier on her. Initially, I wasn't sure it was her, but it's rather obvious now. She changes her name and appearance quite often. Major Li here showed me her dossier. She's called 'Sharp Lotus' in the Chinese Ministry of State Security. She's a member of the Silent Fang team of assassins."

"Well, we've got her hog-tied in another room like this one," she said.

Li Van's eyes grew wide. "She's a master escape artist. I hope she's under guard," he said.

"She is," Zara said.

"Does this mean you retrieved the tablet with the platform back from her?" Li Van asked.

"No. She got it to the pilots in the cockpit."

"That's not good news," Wang said.

Wilson appeared at the top of the steps.

"General Wang," Wilson said. "Major Van."

"Mr. Wilson," Wang replied. Li Van nodded.

"You three know each other?"

"Yes. Mr. Wilson was coming to Taipei to help us fully integrate TYRANT into our fighter jets and bombers," Wang said.

"I'm an engineer with Blackwood Aviation, the defense company that makes the Hyperion Next Generation fighter jet."

"I've read your bio. You created the TYRANT program," Zara said. "Right now it's in the cockpit on a handheld tablet and most likely plugged into the avionics of this airplane."

"It has the capability, yes," Blackwood said.

"My son believes that White Glacier is doing this to allow the Chinese Air Force to destroy Taiwanese infrastructure to include Taipei Semiconductor," Zara said.

"Your son?" Wilson and Wang said in unison.

"Yes. He found the TYRANT harness in the jet that crashed in Eastern North Carolina."

Wilson and Wang exchanged glances.

"What exactly did he find and what did he do with the 'harness,' as you call it?" Wilson asked.

"Well, if I could see the display but not maneuver the commands, I could tell you what is happening."

"And if there were another TYRANT system at your control, one that you couldn't see but one which you could relay commands to, would that be beneficial to our situation?"

Wilson shifted uncomfortably.

"Perhaps. I'm an engineer, not a visionary, so I'm trying to understand what you are cryptically describing."

"Imagine that you can see the TYRANT screen here in this plane that they have in the cockpit. Now imagine that you can talk to someone who has an independent TYRANT platform halfway around the world. Could that independent platform be helpful to this airplane? To Taiwan? To preventing World War Three?"

After a long pause, Wilson said, "I imagine it could."

"Two rubberized orange flash drives mated together, each with the words 'Classified, Code Word. TYRANT' on them," Zara said.

Wilson's eyes got big.

"I'm sorry?" he asked incredulously.

"I can't describe it any better than that. We've got precious little time here. He's got internal text messages between White Glacier senior leadership that confirm what I just told you about their intentions in Taiwan."

General Wang said, "That part makes sense, Johnnie. They will freeze our air force using the TYRANT platform, but that doesn't mean we can't take a chunk out of their ass with our air defense systems."

"True," Wilson said. "But without the layer of offensive aviation, the air defenses are just that—defenses. They're static and targetable with redundancy."

"Is there any way to circumvent your TYRANT platform?" Zara asked.

Wilson looked away and said, "Not really, no. If someone has the satellite connection and the algorithms coupled with the cybersecurity cryptology codes, then they can pretty much hack into any airplane using the quantum tunneling and then take control of the automatic pilot and fly-by-wire. There are some versions of remote fly-by-wire right now. It's not a new concept. TYRANT has a lethal combination of quantum tunneling, hypersecure cryptology, and precise algorithms driven by artificial intelligence. Once TYRANT has control of the airplane's avionics, all you have to do is tell it what you want done and it will do it. For example, if you want to highlight the entire F-16 fleet in the Taiwanese 443rd Tactical Fighter Wing, you could override their ability to fly, countering their self-determination. Or disarm them or make them fly into each other. But I would think that something on this scale, the Chinese would likely try to keep as many aircraft on the ground as possible."

"What about aircraft that already have TYRANT uploaded? TYRANT versus TYRANT, so to speak."

Again, Wilson and Wang exchanged glances. Li Van sat silently

250 ANTHONY J. TATA

on the opposite bed, listening. He performed the duties of aide-de-camp and advisor well.

"That is an area beyond classification of this airplane."

"You don't want to piss me off, Wilson. We've got maybe two hours to save this airplane, prevent World War Three, and save my family."

"Your family?"

"Yes. All your Copperhead buddies have been attacking my kid, and they're holding my husband captive."

Wilson's face fell.

"I told Stanhope not to do this," he muttered.

"Who's Stanhope?" Zara asked.

"General Michael 'Stanley' Stanhope is the chairman of White Glacier Private Equity. He's a former air force four-star general and secretary of defense. Since he came onboard, he has significantly altered the course of White Glacier's investments into defense-related stocks and companies such as Blackwood and Copperhead. So far, the effort has been profitable, but the outlook was growing bleak with the wars drying up. That's when he called me in to work on TYRANT. He pulled me over from DARPA. Paid me a big salary. I have to tell you, I'm uncomfortable with where we are today."

"You know they've teamed with Phu Shen and Clouded Leopard, too, right?"

"What?" Wang snapped. "Phu Shen is not a friend to Taiwan."

Zara looked at her watch. Time was passing too quickly. The plane was boring a hole though the morning sky in the Western Pacific. "We can debate this bullshit another day," she said. "We have to do something about this plane."

Wilson continued. "Context is important before we decide what to do. This could explain Phu Shen working with Stanhope. Blackwood Aviation has the generation six platform, but what good was it if there were no wars to test the concept? It is cutting edge. Cyber warfare has reached a point where cyber hackers can spoof airplane transponders and Wi-Fi systems. If they can do that, how long until someone can develop the technology to con-

trol the avionics of the airplane? That day has come. In
had been coming for years. It all began with my researc
Defense Advanced Research Projects Agency, modeling s
drones and learning how aircraft could talk to one and
same way schools of fish do in a bait ball, or the way flock
all know to swoop or dive or juke in one direction or
That modeling led to plane-to-plane mimicking, which
tually to rudimentary control."

"Engineers always over explain," Zara said. "We need

"With artificial intelligence and machines learning
millions of tasks in fractions of a second, the breachin
curity system and the control of the airplane became
put this capability in a fighter jet or bomber would be
being allowed to tie his opponent's hands behind h
then pummel him or prance around him all match lo
finished.

"Yeah, I get the picture. So, is there any way to ne
thing so Taiwan can defend itself?"

"Not unless another aircraft has TYRANT. That's t

"My air force will be decimated," General Wang sa

"Your country will be destroyed," Zara shot back. "/
will go to war."

"In many ways," Wilson said. "This was my fear. Th
was a horrific but necessary invention. The reas
fought Reagan so hard on Star Wars was because it
nukes useless. TYRANT does the same thing for
fighter jet in your enemy's inventory. And this is j
bility. Think of the way this could be applied t
tillery. Everything uses satellite or LTE connectio

"If you could see the TYRANT display, is the
could tell us?"

Wang and Wilson exchanged glances again
spoke.

"What exactly are you saying?"

"You're a computer genius. You know what
answer my question."

CHAPTER THIRTY-TWO

ZARA SHERIDAN

ZARA CALLED WEST FROM THE PHONE IN THE CREW REST COMPART-ment while Wang and Wilson listened.

"Jeremy, we need to move some bodies and ... people," she said. She was about to say "prisoners" but didn't know how Wang and Wilson would interpret that.

"I'll need some muscle," West said.

Zara looked at General Wang and Major Li Van. Li Van nodded that he was up to the task.

"I've got some for you," Zara said. " I've also got the guy who invented the TYRANT platform and the Taiwanese number-two defense guy with me. I'm thinking the general's aide can help you carry the dead and wounded up to the flight attendant crew rest cabin above business. It will get them out of our way and let the four of us figure out a way to reclaim the airplane and prevent whatever they're trying to do. For the record, my son thinks Copperhead's parent company, White Glacier, is trying to destroy the chip factory in Taipei and a sizeable portion of the country because they make an ass-load of money if that happens."

"I'm not going to ask, but I'll take your son's word for it," West said. "Sounds as reasonable as anything else I've heard."

"Okay, we're out of time. I'm coming to you with three people. The general, his aide, and the computer scientist. We'll swap them out with the people in there now."

"Roger that," West said. They hung up, and Zara turned to Wang and Wilson.

"Major Van, escort your general and follow me. Mr. Wilson, you come, too."

They descended the steps and stepped into an eerily silent airplane. The engines churned with a steady thrum. The sky was bright blue with a few wispy clouds in the distance. The fighter jets winked in the morning sunlight.

Carrie Starlight tried to reach out to Zara, but she kept her eyes focused ahead as she walked briskly through first class.

"Please!" Starlight said. "Listen to me! The transit is happening now!"

Having no idea what Starlight was talking about, Zara punched in the code to the pilot crew door."

"For your son!" Starlight shouted from the aisle.

Zara stopped and looked at the woman with long blond hair dressed in comfortable yoga pants and a hoodie with Nike sneakers.

"My son? What do you know about my son?"

"He's in trouble. Aries is ascendant to his midpoint. You asked me to do his chart. He needs you. He's at war with someone or something."

That tracked with everything she knew to be true and shot up the steps.

"I'll keep that in mind."

But all she could really think about as she ascended the stairwell into the pilot crew rest area was, *Holy shit, how does she know?*

"Any news?" she asked West, shaking off Starlight's comments.

"Nothing I can say in front of these people," he replied.

"I have a plan for this," she said. "You and Major Li here have some work to do."

Major Li was just under six feet tall and muscled, like a gymnast. He was wearing a suit, like his boss, and took the jacket off, rolled up his sleeves, and said, "Who first?"

"Dead bodies first. They're starting to smell," Zara said. "Wrap them in sheets and carry them to the flight attendant area. Passengers will freak out, but we have no option. Then come back and get Xiao Chen and Amanda Gāo, who have worked separately to hijack the airplane."

Li and West wrapped Prescott in a sheet and hauled him down the steps. Zara held the door and watched as they dragged him through the aisle to the gasps of the passengers on both sides. Some were praying while others simply stared. They returned and carried Rodriguez in the same fashion. After that, they came and carried Amanda Gāo, wrapped in sheets as if she were a dead body, into the crew rest area. Lastly, they carried Xiao Chen, terrorist zero, as Zara thought of him. The one who set all this in motion. He didn't go so quietly, however, and began trying to escape from his sheeted confines.

"He's alive!" one of the passengers shouted. "Let him go! He's alive!" Other passengers craned their necks and watched, but Zara patrolled the aisle behind them with her pistol cupped in her hands.

"We have the airplane under control," Zara said. "Now stay in your seats!"

Zara followed West and Li into the flight attendant rest cabin and watched as they dumped Xiao Chen's body on the floor. The two dead bodies were next on the far bed. Amanda Gāo was on the near bunk and Xiao Chen was in between them on the floor.

"You have a pistol, correct?"

"I do," Li said.

"I need you to guard these two prisoners. Shoot them if they give you reason to."

Li Van smiled with his yellowed and crooked teeth.

"I would gladly shoot both of them now if you prefer."

Zara grimaced and said, "Use your best judgment, Major. I'm sure you've had military training on the rules of engagement in warfare?"

"Yes, ma'am," he replied.

"Then don't do anything stupid. Think of the intelligence value of a guy like Xiao Chen to your general. Your country. Guard him right and good things will happen."

"Like a promotion, you think?" he asked eagerly.

"Beats a firing squad," she said before heading down the stairs with West.

"Little hard on the major, weren't you?"

"All you air force guys go easy," Zara said.

They climbed the steps into the pilot crew area amid the shouts and tugs of worried passengers.

"What's happening? Who's in the cockpit? Why can't I call out? Where's the Wi-Fi?"

Back in front of the cockpit camera that West had set up, Zara said to General Wang, "I've got your guy guarding Xiao Chen and Amanda Gāo. Is he trustworthy?"

"Yes. Olympic wrestler for Taiwan. They call us Chinese Taipei, but he competed in freestyle. He's loyal and powerful. That's a problem you don't have to worry about."

"Okay, good. Now, Mr. Wilson. Can you take a look at this, please?"

Wilson sat in one of the two chairs and looked at the tablet hardwired into the fiber-optic camera that West had inserted. West, Zara, and Wang leaned over his shoulder as the engineer studied Hembrick's display the best he could. After a few minutes, he looked up at the three of them.

"It appears that he is using the cursor to select an entire group of fighter jets that are on the apron of military airfields closest to Taipei. Here, he's selected Hsinchu Air Base and its fifty-plus Mirage fighter jets. Those are easily penetrated by TYRANT because they are older and do not have the same cybersecurity capabilities of newer airplanes. I can't tell what he's commanding them to do, but my guess is that he is either disarming them so that they can't fire when engaging the Chinese airplanes or jamming their flight controls so that they can't take off."

Wilson pointed at a map of Taiwan he opened on his tablet.

"Here is where the Mirage jets are," he said, pointing just south of Taipei.

"Where are we right now?" Zara asked.

"You can see our 777-300ER to the north of Taipei about three hundred miles, no less than an hour out from landing, if that's what they intend to do."

"Where's Taipei Semiconductor's main plant?"

"Here," he said, pointing due south of Taipei.

"Where are the rest of the fighter jets? The F-16s? The Hyperions?"

"Over here," General Wang said, pointing at the east coast of Taiwan. "Hualien Airport. Outside the range of most Chinese rockets."

"How many Hyperions do you have?" Zara asked.

"Only four. They are protected by bunkers."

"If I'm making a target list for kinetic operations," Zara said, "it includes those four Hyperions and Taipei Semiconductor. Those would be my priorities. And maybe the seat of government to decapitate decision-making."

General Wang stared at her.

"You were a sergeant in the military police. You investigate crimes. Now you're a strategic war planner?"

"No, just someone who understands how to fight a war, General. It's common sense, not computer science."

"That's where you're wrong, Sergeant," Wilson said. "*This* is computer science. This is new technology that is applied to the battlefield."

"Doesn't change the objectives, Mr. Wilson. Only the methods. They will use your new tech to their advantage and try to disable Taiwan in the manner I identified."

West chimed in: "Geopolitical bullshit aside, to the Taiwanese equivalent of Joe Sixpack, this airplane is just another flight coming into Taipei. Very few people understand that it has the TYRANT platform capable of conducting massive cyber warfare on the Taiwanese Air Force. No one will ever know that those guys in the cockpit shut down the Taiwanese Air Force. Do I have that right?"

"Us in here, the two prisoners, and the Copperhead and White Glacier guys know. That's it," Zara said.

"And they're all sworn to secrecy with nondisclosure agreements," West said. "If this airplane crashes, it takes care of a lot of loose ends for White Glacier in particular."

Zara looked at West's face, creased with worry. The normally relaxed and confident pilot used to pushing the envelope understood that there had to be a catch in the plan that took their airplane into the ocean or a Taiwanese mountainside. Zara nodded, agreeing that to White Glacier, there was no other option. Get the war started and then destroy the evidence. "Wouldn't surprise me if they started taking out the Copperhead guys in North Carolina, too. A few of them know."

Zara seized up, so focused in the moment of doing her job, she had tucked Lucas's predicament into a neatly compartmentalized filing cabinet in her mind as she had done on so many combat deployments.

"What?" West said.

"Lucas," she muttered.

"They've enabled TYRANT," Wilson said. His statement was a mix between concern and joy. "The entire Mirage wing appears disabled in some way. They're taxiing, but some of the icons have disappeared into the ocean after taking off. The screen is showing twelve Chinese Mighty Dragon J-20 fighter aircraft taking off from Longtian Air Base, which is about one hundred thirty-five miles from Taipei."

"Closer than we are," Zara said.

"And they can fly Mach two for eleven hundred miles," Wilson said.

"My country," General Wang muttered.

"My software," Wilson said, looking away.

"My God," West said.

"My son," Zara said, pointing at the screen in Wilson's lap.

CHAPTER THIRTY-THREE

LUCAS SHERIDAN

*L*UCAS STARED AT HIS MOTHER'S LAST TEXT: I love you so very much.

With the helmet on and both monitors displaying the TYRANT platform imaging, Lucas watched his mother's airplane fly directly toward Taipei on a collision course with twelve icons that flashed with "J-20 Mighty Dragon" labels. The jets divided into three groups of four, with one group continuing toward Taipei while the second group flew to the south reaching Mach 2 speeds, according to the data display for each icon. The third group of aircraft pivoted to the north toward the Boeing 777-300ER.

As he was watching, Mia limped over again and pulled up another chair that had a missing wheel. The chair tilted, causing her to subconsciously use her wounded leg to balance herself, and she winced.

Lucas jumped up and reached out to hold her until she steadied herself in the chair.

"I'm worried about you, Mia," Lucas said.

Mia fidgeted until she was comfortable.

"Don't. I'm the one who is worried about you, Lucas," Mia said earnestly.

After a pause, he said, "Yeah, me too." His eyes darted between Mia and the monitors. "Look," he said. "China is attacking Taiwan."

The icons of four jets traveling at Mach 2 moved south of Taiwan and flew north along the east coast headed directly toward a location on the map called Hualien Airport.

"Why are they going there?" Mia asked, pointing.

"My guess is that these are the lead airplanes of an attack, and they want to destroy the most important things first."

He zoomed in on Hualien Airport and saw four icons that were labeled "Hyperion X" and another two dozen or so labeled "F-16."

"This TYRANT thing gives you total view of everything," Lucas said.

As the Chinese J-20 Mighty Dragons descended upon Hualien Airport, the screen lit up with explosions billowing into the sky, blocking the real-time video feed. The Mighty Dragons circled and dodged air defense rockets as they unleashed another salvo of missiles on the stymied airplanes.

"Someone used TYRANT on those airplanes. They can't take off. The ones that did get in the air have been shot down," Lucas said.

"I'm watching the icons of the Chinese J-20 jets, and they've made three passes at the airfield. All four of the jets are out of missiles but have thirty mm, whatever that is."

"Thirty mike mike, is what my moms called it. Millimeters. It's a type of machine-gun ammunition."

"These jets have machine guns?"

"Yes, mostly for aerial combat, but can be used against ground forces, too."

"I'm seeing that. They're making runs along the airfield."

"Chewing it up so that no airplanes can take off," Lucas said.

"They're about out of ammo," Mia said.

"Okay, I guess that's good. Four we don't have to worry about."

"What's happening here?" Mia asked. She tapped the monitor, showing the four airplanes headed to Taipei. They were closing in on the Taipei Semiconductor manufacturing plant south of Taipei as they dodged air defense missiles.

"Same thing. These airplanes here in Taipei can't respond. TYRANT has them grounded or useless."

"Does our system work? Can we fight them?" Mia asked.

"Yeah, that's what I'm thinking. When we synced with my

mom's tablet, we provided her the cipher code, and she provided us the cyberattack algorithms. So, it should fully work because we have the entire system. Only one way to find out."

Lucas looked through the heads-up display of his helmet and used his touch pad to draw a box around the four Mighty Dragon J-20 aircraft flying toward the semiconductor plant. They were highlighted on his screen and a prompt appeared.

Control?

Lucas clicked "Yes" and proceeded to maneuver these aircraft as he had done with the two Russian fighter jets.

"Like we're air force drone pilots or something," Mia said under her breath.

"Yeah, but controlling the bad guy's airplanes," Lucas replied. "On that thought, see if you can take these two," Lucas said, pointing to the two jets nearest the bottom of the screen. "Turn them away using the joystick. I'll use the touch pad."

The icons on the screen separated and moved wildly in opposite directions, like a starburst.

"Oh, shit," Mia said, slapping the joystick back and forth. "They might have crashed."

Lucas was maneuvering his two Mighty Dragon J-20 jet icons away from Taipei and toward China. He maneuvered them north toward the Chinese border but perilously close to his mother's inbound 777-300ER. The two Russian jets escorting the 777-300ER pulled away and flew north, lining up behind the passenger airplane.

"What's going on?" Mia asked.

"Can you grab those two Russian jets and try to control them?"

"I can try," she said.

Mia did some maneuvers with the joystick and said, "I've turned them and I'm firing their missiles into the ocean." After a minute, she said, "I think I've disarmed them."

"Don't forget the machine guns like we saw on the others on the other side of the island."

"Says here 'thirty mm autocannon,'" Mia replied, looking at the icon data prompt.

"Empty that," Lucas said.

"They're trying to turn back toward the airplane."

"Get rid of their ammo," Lucas said. "That's what I'm doing with the Chinese jets."

Both Mia and Lucas focused on moving icons and protecting the 777-300ER inbound to Taipei.

"We put my mom's airplane on 'Protect' mode. I'm not sure what that's doing," Lucas said.

"Maybe that's why nobody has shot it down yet?"

"Maybe. I don't want to take any chances, though."

With the threat to Taipei diminished for the moment, Lucas focused on the two Chinese aircraft that were now the sole escorts of his mother's airplane. Should he try to empty their weapons, as they had done with the other four? Or did they have good intentions?

"Nobody up there has good intentions," he muttered.

"True, though it sounds like you're talking to yourself," Mia said.

"Just trying to figure out what to do about these two Chinese airplanes escorting Mom's plane."

"Let's try to empty all their ammo. That's our best option," Mia said.

So focused were they on the aerial combat surrounding Taiwan that they didn't hear the men rushing into the house until it was too late.

CHAPTER THIRTY-FOUR

XIAO CHEN

*T*HE NIGHT VIPER LOOKED DOWN THE STAIRWELL OF THE FLIGHT attendant crew rest area and turned to Xiao Chen's writhing body. He removed Chen's shroud and asked, "Are you okay, *zhànyǒu?*"

Zhànyǒu was a common moniker for Chinese combat soldiers to address one another. It meant "comrade in arms" or "battle buddy."

"I'm hurt, but can fight, Night Viper," Chen said. He only knew Major Li Van as the Night Viper, the man who had offered him the deal a year ago to save his family name. Night Viper was a trained assassin with the Silent Fang enforcement unit.

"What about her?" He looked at Amanda Gāo, whose head was not fully covered by the sheet the Americans had used to transport her.

"She's okay. She knows the door codes and can get us in for our Gǎnsīduì mission. We're almost there."

"What about TYRANT?"

"Copperhead has the platform in the cockpit. We can breach the cockpit and transmit the algorithm and cipher to our ground teams prior to doing our duty."

Chen stood with the assistance of the Night Viper.

* * *

The two men had been introduced a year ago when Chen had been arrested by the Chinese Ministry of State Security for operating his Shanghai cartel running drugs, prostitutes, and stolen US intellectual property. After a few nights in a basic cell in the Tilanqiao facility, Major Li Van had appeared alone.

He had opened the cell door with a skeleton key and sat on the steel bed next to Chen. He said, "You will only know me as Night Viper. My grandfather was with your grandfather's Gǎnsǐduì mission to kill Chiang Kai-shek. While your grandfather was weak and decided to escape, mine was killed attempting to assassinate Chiang Kai-shek. Some believe your grandfather revealed the mission to Chiang Kai-shek during his Great Retreat."

"That is not true!" Chen spat. "He failed, yes, but he would never reveal the mission."

"I have my grandfather's diary and Mao's official CCP intelligence reports," the Night Viper said. "I have been assigned to your case."

"My case?"

"Your criminal enterprise in Shanghai is commendable, but your family was one of the few that was not eliminated by Mao. Was it an oversight or simply that other priorities took over? I don't know, but what I do know, Xiao Chen, is that you have a mission to intercept the avionics in the new American fighter jet called the Hyperion X. China, your motherland, needs you to do this. We know that at the heart of your operation is a cryptocurrency theft operation reaching over one billion dollars."

Chen began to protest but Night Viper silenced him with a wave of his hand and continued.

"When presented with this information, the minister of state security, my boss, asked me to speak with you. You have built this empire of illegal and illicit goods and services, which is not all that bothersome. However, we are interested in your team's computer science skills. Our government is good, but the Americans are tracking everything we do. You? You're off the radar in the dark web moving stolen cryptocurrency and ransomware. We need that skill set and that capability. The Americans will continue to watch our government while you and your teams do what we ask."

"What do you need me to do?" Chen asked.

Night Viper tapped the key to the cell on his leg. The man was muscled and fit. His broad shoulders filled out the black long sleeve T-shirt he wore. Trapezoids flared like striking cobras and his biceps seemed to be ripping at the material. The key bounced off the quadricep that was flexing against the olive cargo pants. He was dressed like an operator with closely cropped black hair shorn to the skin above his ears and a thick tuft on top. His ears were deformed in a way that Chen had not seen before. The Night Viper's teeth were yellowed and crooked, but not excessively so. His face was flat and hard, eyes narrow and black as night.

"You can restore your family name by helping the party, Xiao Chen. You can make up for your grandfather's transgressions. We need you to threaten to crash an airplane into the Taipei Semiconductor manufacturing facility on Taiwan in exchange for the TYRANT platform that America has developed. This platform renders all airplanes useless. We must own it."

"And if they don't give me the code?"

"Then you will fly the airplane into the factory and destroy Taiwan's ability to make semiconductors."

Chen looked at the Night Viper and saw that he was serious. It was important that he not show fear. Saving face was everything.

"But I'm not a pilot," Chen said.

"And I'm not a Taiwanese citizen, even if I've lived there under cover for twenty years. I was raised there. I wrestled on the Olympic team as a Taiwanese army officer. I reported to the party on a weekly basis. The island is ready for reunification. We must secure this platform prior to doing so."

"But still, I don't know how to fly an airplane."

"In the next six months, we will train you. The first flight of a new airline is scheduled for next May. You will be ready."

Chen nodded. "I want to develop the plan to acquire the platform."

"It cannot be breached or stolen remotely for the time being. It requires two authenticating personnel, like the nuclear codes. This is the only way."

"I will use teams on the ground to threaten the pilots and the authenticators. My teams will kill their families if they don't comply. I can figure out a way to breach the cockpit and do it. Leave it to me. I will get the platform you seek. And in return?"

"In return, your family name is restored. You come back to run your enterprise and perhaps do some business with the government," the Night Viper said. "If you are successful."

"I will be successful."

That conversation over six months ago came rushing back to Xiao Chen as the Night Viper, Major Li Van, cut the zip ties that the air marshal had used to secure him. When Chen stood up, he was slightly taller than Li Van but in no way compared to the former wrestler's width.

"This is your last opportunity to acquire the TYRANT code. You know the alternative, Xiao Chen," Li Van said.

"What about her?" Chen said, nudging Amanda Gāo's foot.

Li Van knelt and removed the sheet and ties from Amanda. She ran her hand across her face through a dried trickle of blood. She stood slowly, looked at Li Van, and said, "Son, I am proud of you. My Night Viper."

"This is your mother?" Xiao Chen asked.

"Only in Taiwan. She raised me as a spy and trained me in my craft. Her legend is Sharp Lotus." He looked at Amanda. "Phu-Shen of Clouded Leopard Private Equity has funded our entire existence. We are here now, on the brink of victory. And the first rule of spy craft is to never let emotions interrupt the mission."

"Correct," Amanda said. She reached into the small compartment under the bed and retrieved three Taiwanese T75 pistols that looked very much like Beretta 9mm handguns.

"Now we take the airplane back and secure the platform. Be ruthless," Li Van said.

They began moving down the steps, the Night Viper in the lead, followed by Xiao Chen, with Sharp Lotus in trail.

CHAPTER THIRTY-FIVE

ZARA SHERIDAN

ZARA POINTED AT THE SCREEN AND SAID, "MY SON," BECAUSE SHE noticed some of the icons moving in opposite directions, and to her knowledge, Lucas was the only one who could be doing that.

"Your son has the TYRANT platform loaded?" Wilson asked with an incredulous tone.

"Yes, I already mentioned that he found it on the Hyperion jet that crashed in the marshes of Eastern North Carolina."

"That was a mechanical failure, not an issue with the TYRANT avionics," Wilson said defensively.

Zara cocked her head and asked, "So it wasn't on purpose, like a crash test dummy kind of thing?"

"What are you talking about? You don't just go out and crash a one-billion-dollar airplane," Wilson said.

"He's right," West said. "Though I've crashed a few, it was never on purpose."

"You're still walking," Zara said.

"By the grace of God," West replied.

"Why did you ask?" Wilson said.

"These guys," Zara said, pointing at the tablet. "These guys told me that the crash was intentional. To see how it fared. In particular, how the TYRANT software survived. Their analogy was to the car industry and how they crash cars to test survivability."

Wilson smiled briefly. "That's not how this works. We have put the platform and avionics through simulated crashes in test facilities. There's no need to test crash a jet."

"China is attacking my country," General Wang said. "Why are my airplanes not responding?"

Wilson looked at him and pointed at the tablet sitting in his lap that was relaying the video feed from West's fiber-optic camera.

"It's hard to see, but the icons for the aircraft are moving in three flights of four airplanes. One to the east. One to the north and one to the heart of Taipei. I can't tell what kinds of airplanes these are because the camera isn't good enough, but my guess would be the J-20."

"Mighty Dragon," West added. "Most capable jet in the Chinese inventory."

They watched as the icons maneuvered around the screen. Hembrick became visibly excited as the four aircraft in the eastern part of the country near Hualien Air Force Base destroyed all the Taiwanese aircraft and runway there. Hembrick zoomed in, affording Wilson and Zara a view of the destruction.

"They just leveled Hualien," Wilson said.

"That's where we keep our Hyperion jets."

"Not anymore," Zara said. "They lit that place up."

"Four headed to Taipei and four headed south, most likely to the port of Kaohsiung where the biggest navy base is. Destroy the F-16s and Hyperion jets. Destroy the navy."

"Why is my air force not responding?" General Wang shouted.

"TYRANT," Wilson said. "I can see they've locked down all the flight controls of your Mirage and F-16 aircraft at your major bases. They can't take off and the ones that have seem to have been shot down. Probably disabled the weapons controls."

"Your son did this?" Wang fumed.

"My son is the only thing keeping this airplane in the air, General. You can bet your sweet ass on that. Those assholes are the ones doing this. This was their sole purpose. To act as a command platform to disable the air force and attack."

"To what end?" Wang asked.

"White Glacier wants the semiconductor manufacturing plant destroyed so that their new one can seize market share," Zara said.

"I still can't actually believe that," Wang said.

"Believe it," Wilson said, looking up. "There are four jets headed not to Taipei but to Taipei Semiconductor. They're armed and on final approach."

"This can't be happening," Wang said.

"The whole point was to have this happen with no one knowing about it. We could land in Taipei and this thing could be over and everything could be normal except a few attacks that will soon move out of the news cycle," Zara said. "Lucas wasn't supposed to find the TYRANT platform, but he did for a reason."

"Can he shut down those jets?" Wang asked.

"He's already maneuvered something," Wilson said. "From the looks of it, Hembrick is not happy."

Zara looked at the screen and noticed Hembrick gesticulating wildly with his hands. Shouting at Rogers. Standing and sitting down again. He expanded the screen that showed the four Mighty Dragon fighter jets bearing down on Taipei Semiconductor manufacturing plants. He seemed to breathe easier. Pushed at the air with open palms while the tablet rested on his lap, as if he were telling himself to calm down.

Without warning, the Boeing 700-ER dove and tilted from its smooth glide path. Zara heard the screams from the cabin below. She fumbled with her phone but caught it as she was tossed into the stairwell. *Status?*, she texted Lucas. And then:

Can you stop the four jets headed to the Taipei chip plant?

As she awaited his response, gunshots rang out below her.

CHAPTER THIRTY-SIX

LUCAS SHERIDAN

"W HAT'S THAT?" MIA SHOUTED.

Three men poured down the stairwell, rifles at the ready, as if they were an infantry fire team entering a room to clear it.

Lucas had just seen his mother's text.

Can you stop the four jets headed to the Taipei chip plant?

"Stop what you're doing!" one man shouted. He was dressed in black tactical clothing, wearing a helmet cut above the ears, and pointing a rifle at him. He had a name tag stuck with Velcro across his body armor: *Smith.*

Lucas stood and raised his hands, moving Mia behind him. He had the helmet on and realized that wherever he looked on the screen, his eyes functioned like a cursor. Lucas knew about Windows Eye Control and OptiKey software programs that helped students with disabilities better access computer information. It appeared that the TYRANT program embedded optical tracking capability in the pilot's heads-up display.

"Back away from the computer terminal," Smith said. His two partners moved to the opposing corners of the basement, looking for others, Lucas suspected.

"Here's Donnie," one man said, lifting the sheet from the dead man at the south end of the basement. "Little fucker killed him." The man had a name tag that read: *Jones.*

Smith, the evident team leader, seemed to consider this, and said, "Call up and have the rest of the team come down. Might as well make this a family affair."

Two similarly dressed men dragged Lonnie Sheridan and Sheriff Barlowe down the steps, hands cuffed to their fronts.

"Dad!" Mia shouted.

Even though every ounce of his being wanted to do the same, Lucas remained focused on the heads-up display. His eye movement created a box around the four J-35A War Thunder fighter jets. These were different than the Mighty Dragons, and it was a few seconds' delay before he received the "Control?" prompt.

Control?

Lucas used his eye movement to check the box, and again it was a few seconds before the next prompt appeared.

"What's he doing?" Jones said, approaching Lucas.

"Looks like that guy that sees dead people," someone named Johnson said. "Like a freak show Stephen King novel kid."

Lucas ignored them. He had one chance to save his mom.

"Lucas!" his father growled. "Do what these men ask."

He remained focused on his mission. The data for each of the four selected aircraft appeared in dialogue boxes below. A new prompt appeared:

6th Generation Fighter. Disable all weapons systems?

His eye moved to the "Yes" prompt as he was tackled by Jones. His head hit the concrete, the pilot helmet absorbing most of the blow. Another Copperhead commando ripped the helmet off his head. A third began to pull the wires and smash the display terminals until the team leader shouted, "Stop! We need that!"

"Stay away from my son!" Lonnie Sheridan shouted.

"Mia!" Sheriff Barlowe screamed.

"Everybody, shut the fuck up!" the Copperhead team leader said.

A man lifted Lucas to his feet. Lucas couldn't see the monitor, or whether he had completed the task his mother had asked him to do, which was to disable the fighter jets bearing down on Taipei Semiconductor manufacturing plant.

For the first time, Lucas snapped out of his fog, like a ship breaking through the mist. A large man was holding him by the shoulders and pulling him toward the computer station. Another man dressed in Copperhead black commando attire swung his long rifle to his back and sat in Lucas's chair. Another man held Mia. Lucas could see two men were restraining his and Mia's already shackled fathers. He shook his head as if shaking off a long sleep. He had been so deeply enmeshed in diverting the Chinese J-35 fighter jets that the reality of his predicament just came into view.

"Dad, are you okay?" Lucas asked. "Sheriff Barlowe?" Where he had been confident and serene before, he was now exactly the opposite. His voice was shaky, and he was scared.

Lucas's father suddenly broke free, his hands cuffed in front of him, and landed two powerful blows to each of his abductors with his bound hands. He swung his arms like a sledgehammer in a lumbering arc. The man holding Sheriff Barlowe took the hit but was able to retrieve a yellow-and-black Guerilla Defense Tactical Taser Pulse 2. He shot the electric hooks into Lonnie Sheridan, who buckled and jerked to the ground looking like a *World War Z* zombie until he flopped on the cement. His muscled frame bulged and flexed. His face contorted and his mouth was wide open in a silent scream with fifty thousand volts of electricity running through his massive frame.

As his father fell and writhed on the concrete floor, Lucas noticed something odd about his father's wrists. He looked at him and shouted, "Dad!" He tried to run to his father, but the man holding him put him in a hammer lock so that he couldn't move. Mia began crying and shouted, "Daddy, I love you!"

"What do you need?" Lucas shouted. "What do you need me to do? I'll do it!"

"That's more like it," the team leader said.

"Tell me," Lucas reiterated. "I said I'll do it."

"Stand here and tell him how to make it so those jets can attack that building," the team leader said, pointing at the Copperhead man sitting at Lucas's command console.

So, he *was* successful at using his eyes to lock up those Next Generation fighter aircraft. He looked at the screen and saw that the four J-35A fighter jets were circling in orbit showing a red flashing icon.

Weapons controls disabled.

"How do I fix that?" the man asked.

Lucas looked at Mia, sobbing softly to his right. Then he looked at his father and Sheriff Barlowe.

"I know how," Lucas said.

"Then tell me!" the seated man shouted. "We're out of time."

"But I know why you want to do this. White Glacier is blackmailing you or promising you a big payday. I saw e-mails that said they aren't going to pay you." His words tumbled over one another. He hadn't really seen that exact language, but it was the best he could surmise from what he *had* seen.

"The fuck you talking about, boy? Just get in there and fix it so they can shoot," the team leader said. The man behind him holding his shoulders squeezed them hard and whispered, "Better get to work, boy."

Lucas didn't move. "The e-mails said that someone named 'Hembrick' was getting the money. That he was on the TransPac plane and had cut a side deal with White Glacier and Clouded Leopard. That all of you were expendable. Dead once this is over."

The entire basement was silent for a moment.

"How the hell do you know any of this?"

"Because I hacked into White Glacier's server system. If I can shut down Chinese fighter jets on the other side of the world, how hard do you think it is for me to get into some hedge fund's Slack messages?"

The men were silent again.

"Ain't doing this shit for free, boss," one man said from across the room.

"He's mind-fucking us. Show me," the team leader said.

"I stored everything in an encrypted file and sent it to a friend who knows the password. If they don't hear from me, they'll expose everything," the commando said.

"We're pretty much fucked any way," another man said. "We've got the sheriff in cuffs."

Sheriff Barlowe said, "If you leave right now and leave us all alone, I can promise you there will be no charges. I just want my family and the Sheridans to be okay."

"You're crazy, Sheriff, if you think we believe that."

"Nobody has to know," he said. "You can all go and deploy overseas or do whatever it is you do. Just don't hurt us. Leave us alone."

"I'm just a kid," Lucas said. "I wouldn't know how to mind-fuck anyone. I'm just telling you what I got from the White Glacier Private Equity text message account."

"You really know how to do that?"

"I did it," Lucas said. "I also controlled your drone and crashed it in the pond."

"Little fucker," a voice from across the room said. "I scraped my ass up getting that thing out of there."

"Hembrick's taking the money once he lands in Taiwan," Lucas said.

The team leader looked at him and smiled. Lucas immediately knew he had said too much.

"Hembrick ain't landing in Taiwan, smart-ass," the team leader said. "You're making all this shit up."

"I'm not! I swear!"

"Nice try, though. Sammie, take the team out back with the two men and the girl. Me and Jonesy here will deal with the kid once he finishes the job. For every minute we don't have control of the Chinese fighter jets, shoot one of them. I don't care which order. Might be good to start with the girl."

"No!" Lucas said.

"Please, mister. We have no beef with you," Sheriff Barlowe sobbed. "Please. You can take me but not my girl. She lost her mama a while back and it's just the two of us. Take me, not her."

"Great story. Sammie, do as I instruct. Understand?"

The man the team leader called "Sammie" nodded and spit some tobacco on the concrete. He didn't look to Lucas like he would have any issues murdering three people. He felt a dam begin to break in him. He wanted to cry. He wanted to hug his father. He wanted to hold and protect Mia.

But he stood strong.

"You already wounded Mia with your helicopter," Lucas said.

"You're wasting my time boy. Sammie, go," the team leader said.

Of the five Copperhead men in the basement, three of them escorted the sheriff, Mia, and Lucas's father up the steps. They struggled lifting Lonnie Sheridan off the floor but steadied him as he stumbled up the stairwell. Mia looked over her shoulder at Lucas, tears streaming down her face.

"I love you, Lucas. There's no better friend than you," she managed to say.

As the commandos and the people he loved disappeared into the kitchen above them, Lucas shouted, "Please!"

But what he was really thinking about was the ties around his father's wrists. He knew knots from Boy Scouts, and something was wrong with the half-hitch wrapped around his wrists.

"Get us into those jets, boy, and everything's cool as a cucumber," the team leader said.

Lucas regained focus and thought of his dilemma. Was he killing his mom? His dad? Both of them? His best friend and her father? What could he do to save them all? He stepped toward the man in the seat, realizing that it was just the three of them in the basement: the team leader, the computer guy, and him.

"Okay. You must put on the helmet. The helmet has a heads-up display. You find the jet icons and highlight them. You get a prompt asking you to control the airplanes. You say yes. Then you have full access."

"Slow down, kid," the computer guy said.

"You have one minute, starting now. Sammie, do I have you?" the team leader said into a handheld portable radio.

"Roger, boss. Got 'em lined up. Starting with the girl, as directed."

Lucas heard Mia's scream through the shattered north window.

"I can do it!" Lucas said.

"Then do it," the man said, standing up and giving him the helmet.

"Forty-five seconds," the team leader said.

Lucas's fingers flew across the keyboard and manipulated the mouse. He highlighted the four aircraft with the cursor. He got the prompts.

"See these prompts? I'm in," he said.

"Thirty seconds," the team leader said.

Control?

Lucas clicked on the "Control?" box and the weapons systems functions were grayed out. He highlighted those and clicked to activate them.

"I'm activating their weapons systems," Lucas said.

"Fifteen seconds," the team leader said.

He watched as the TYRANT system gave him a "spinning rainbow" as it had before. It would make sense that the new J-35 fighter jets had better encryption than an older airplane. The result would be that the quantum tunneling of the TYRANT platform would take longer to hack the J-35 avionics. He had to rehack the jets to turn their weapons systems back on.

"These are new airplanes. It takes longer!" he shouted, knowing he was out of time.

"That's it. Kill the girl," the team leader said.

Lucas shouted, "NO!"

Shouts outside canceled one another out as Mia's higher-pitched voice broke through the cacophony with a piercing shriek.

The boom from the gunshot echoed loudly through the basement, like a sonic wave. Lucas shook violently as he did his best to save his best friend, but he was too late.

He was a failure. Like *The Pearl*'s Kino, he had brought death and destruction to his community with the TYRANT cyberattack platform. No good deed went unpunished, and he was being punished in the most unforgiving way.

The ringing in his ears became too loud. The pressure of the situation finally overcame his fourteen-year-old sensibilities, and he fainted right there in the chair.

His last conscious thoughts were about Mia.

Images hurtled through his mind. They were hunting frogs and snakes in creeks and streams; playing baseball and soccer in their school green-and-gold uniforms; and they were racing their bikes along the chattering trails of the Inner Banks.

He fell to the floor, slapped his head on the concrete, and then there was nothing.

CHAPTER THIRTY-SEVEN

XIAO CHEN

Xiao Chen followed Night Viper through the starboard aisle of the 777-300ER with Sharp Lotus—Amanda Gāo—following him.

They openly carried pistols and aimed them at any passenger who might try to get in their way. The airplane was descending, breaking away from its cruising altitude. It went from a smooth glide to a shuddering descent. The pitch of the aircraft became steeper, and the passengers appeared confused and afraid. Some screamed, yet most were silent for fear of getting shot. Were these people a rescue team raiding the cockpit to save the day, or were they something more nefarious?

Chen watched Sharp Lotus move to the starboard aisle of the aircraft and approach a woman who was standing. She had brown hair bobbed at collar-length and was wearing practical slacks and a button-down shirt. She retrieved her credentials and held them up to Sharp Lotus, saying, "I'm Alisha McCord, the backup pilot. I can help."

"You can," Sharp Lotus said. "Thank you for confirming. Come with us."

The group of four moved in parallel along the two aisles until they reached the first-class galley where beverage carts were stacked against the drawn curtain. Night Viper used his considerable heft to lean a shoulder into the fortification and was able to budge it from its locked position. Two more shoves and he had it canted at a forty-five-degree angle.

They poured through the gap in the forward galley and drew the curtain again as Sharp Lotus rearranged the beverage carts into a better fortified position. She handled the carts with ease, having trained as a flight attendant specifically for this job. Her résumé had been completely fabricated by the Ministry of State Security.

Sharp Lotus pulled Alisha McCord to the starboard side of the galley and told her, "Stay here until we tell you."

"Who are you?" McCord asked.

Chen watched as Night Viper walked over to the two women and leaned into McCord, getting very close to her ear, whispering something. Night Viper's ceramic knife was quickly upon McCord's neck, as he covered her mouth and bled her out, lowering her to the ground, dead.

Sharp Lotus and Night Viper nodded at one another. They returned to Chen at the cockpit door as Chen was recalling the plan as explained by Night Viper a week ago.

The first effort was to steal the TYRANT platform by blackmailing pilot Hawk Monroe and his lover General Rachel Fox. That had almost been successful until the air marshal and Copperhead had interrupted their efforts.

The second effort if Xiao Chen failed was to execute this backup plan, which was to overtake the cockpit and for Night Viper and Sharp Lotus to do what Xiao Chen could not do. They had ultimately wanted Chen to sacrifice himself, because he was expendable and remained so. They had not planned on an armed security force being on the airplane, but they did have contingency weapons that Sharp Lotus had smuggled onboard. When Sharp Lotus had entered security with Copperhead's part-time TSA agent, Clark, she had done so as Amanda Gāo. Flirting with Clark, keeping him engaged in titillating conversation, made him focus more on her than the disassembled pistols scattered throughout her luggage. She had also strategically placed a few loose rounds and a small block of C-4 explosives in a medical kit bag that was filled with scissors, scalpels, ointments, tweezers, gauze, and other medical supplies.

Now, they each had four 9mm bullets in their QSZ92-9 pistols. They were blocky-looking handguns that mimicked the Beretta pistol. They lined up outside the cockpit door with Night Viper placing some chewing gum over the camera lens facing into the galley from the cockpit.

"C-4 on the top blowout panel," Night Viper said to Sharp Lotus.

Amanda Gāo, operating as Sharp Lotus, stood, placed the sticky explosive substance in the corner of the top panel, which was maybe eighteen inches wide by twenty-four inches tall. The purpose of the blowout panel was to rapidly equalize pressure in the cockpit in case of a depressurization event in the cabin, such as a breach of the integrity of the aircraft.

The panels were the one weakness of the post 9/11 cockpit policies. While necessary, they provided a point of attack, which Night Viper intended to exploit.

"Now," Night Viper said.

Sharp Lotus inserted the detonator and pulled the time fuse, which was set for thirty seconds. The C-4 ignited and the door buckled and jolted, but the blowout panel did not come completely out. A small curve of metal gave Night Viper a view into the main pilot's seat. He aimed his pistol in while reaching down to unlock the door. He could see a man moving from the seat quickly and felt a sharp pain on his wrist.

But the cockpit door flew open as he withdrew his arm.

Xiao Chen was at the ready with his pistol, firing into the face of the Copperhead leader named Hembrick, who tried to fight back, but he fell against the controls and the plane dipped wildly to the right and began plummeting.

The passengers began screaming, but Xiao Chen was focused on accomplishing his mission.

His two Silent Fang handlers let him place his pistol to the head of the pilot as he took Hembrick's tablet, which had dropped on the floor. Sharp Lotus dragged Hembrick's body into the galley.

As she did so, the pilot crew rest door opened, and she was staring into the determined face of Zara Sheridan.

CHAPTER THIRTY-EIGHT

ZARA SHERIDAN

*F*ACE-TO-FACE WITH AMANDA GĀO, ZARA SHERIDAN RAISED HER PIS-
tol as Gāo raised hers.

Instead of pulling the trigger, Zara used her size advantage to
barrel into Amanda and brace her against the lavatory door. Two
butt strikes with her pistol grip to Amanda's face had the ersatz
flight attendant stumbling backward.

Zara used her left hand to place a vise grip around Amanda's
pistol-controlling wrist, aiming it upward. Two shots fired
through the ceiling of the galley, most likely burrowing into the
pilot crew rest area, perhaps a bed and hopefully not Jeremy
West. She would need West shortly, she surmised.

There was the potential the bullets could breach the integrity
of the aircraft by punching through the very top, but the manner
in which lead flattened and spalled upon impact made that an
unlikely outcome. Regardless, two little holes in the plane most
likely wouldn't cause a depressurization event.

The shouts and screams from the passengers were at a fever
pitch. The plane was rocketing toward the ground, nearly out of
control.

Zara slammed Gāo's wrist against the lavatory door, which
opened. She used that opportunity to wedge Amanda's arm in

the gap and repeatedly slam the door on her wrist bones until she heard a crack, and the pistol fell to the floor.

Still, Amanda was not without fight, pushing against Zara with her one arm hanging limply. She flayed with her left arm, which Zara parried with ease. She then put her left hand around Gāo's throat, choking her and holding her in place when she put the pistol to Amanda's forehead and pulled the trigger.

Blood and brain matter splattered everywhere, but one assailant was dead, and Zara didn't even know what else she had to deal with.

Next, she felt a deafening blow to the right side of her head and saw Major Li Van in a fighter's stance. His foot arced up quickly and knocked her pistol from her hand. It skittered to the opposite side of the galley. Zara took a step back and noticed that Li Van was not holding a weapon, though his big hands and forearms could be debatably considered lethal. Behind him, Xiao Chen was trying to crawl through the ajar cockpit door.

The plane continued to shudder and shriek against its max limitations. Metal grinding against metal. Wings vibrating through the descent. Passengers hanging on for dear life.

Obvious to Zara was that Li Van's job was to let Xiao Chen get back in the cockpit to do his thing, whatever that might be. Her guess was to get the godforsaken TYRANT platform under control and allow China to finish its attack on Taiwan to destroy the semiconductor plant that Lucas had warned her about.

White Glacier was in control of all of this. No matter what happened, they would come out smelling like a rose. And if the airplane bore a hole into the ground or vanished into the ocean, 90 percent of the world would see it as just another unfortunate plane crash, none the wiser as to what had transpired. And yet, White Glacier would deploy its military contractors and weapons to Taiwan for increased security. Maybe their chip plant in the USA would get new business. The president of the United States and White Glacier's CEO would ensure the contents of the airplane's black box was forever concealed for "national security" purposes.

As she prepared to fight an Olympic wrestling champion, she determined her only path to victory was to retreat. So, she did.

She backed up until she was against the beverage carts. Li Van moved like the *Shifu* he was, carefully, one foot over the next. *Shifu*, or martial arts master, was akin to the Japanese ninja. Li Van, or Night Viper, was a lethal and skilled assassin. He rested his hand against the galley walls to steady himself as the airplane shook violently and continued its free fall. He passed the door to the pilot crew rest area, eyes focused on Zara, who raised her fists, prepared to defend herself.

Li Van removed a ceramic knife from his pocket. Like Xiao Chen, he was wearing a thin bulletproof vest. Li Van was backup or the handler, Zara surmised. Amanda Gāo was the insider. It was a team of three. One was dead. She needed to neutralize this threat to get to Xiao Chen, who appeared stuck between the cockpit and the galley. The gap wasn't big enough.

"Your general will be so disappointed in you, Major," Zara said, taunting Li Van.

"He's not my general, Air Marshal. You, a lowly military police sergeant, against me, a martial arts expert and Olympic wrestler? I'll make it quick and painless for you," Li Van said.

"I had an officer say that to me once at Fort Bragg. It didn't end well for him," Zara said.

Li Van cocked his head and smiled.

"Yes, you would be a nice prize, but my mission is more important than my desires," Li Van said. He was maybe three feet from her and two feet beyond the pilot crew rest door. Shouts from the cabin continued at a frenzy. The plane was diving at forty-five degrees toward the ocean.

Li Van lunged toward Zara as she parried his knife-hand thrust with her left arm and landed two uppercuts on his concrete chin.

The door to the pilot crew rest area opened and Jeremy West pushed his way inside the cockpit, wrapping a garrote around Li Van's neck, and pulled his arms in both directions to cut off the major's oxygen and sever the carotid arteries. But Li Van was strong and wasn't going down without a fight. He stabbed at West furiously with his knife, but Zara was quick to immobilize the wrestler's thick forearm. He flailed and thrashed. West was a lanky man with a height advantage over Li Van.

The garrote was biting into Li Van's powerful neck. Zara slammed her knee into Li Van's groin, causing him to gasp doubly for air. His arm pushed against her grip, bringing the knife perilously close to her neck. She felt West give an extra hitch of the garrote around Li Van's bulging neck muscles. Blood began pouring down his flexed trapezoids. The force of his forearm weakened in Zara's grip as the plane tilted even further toward whatever lay beneath them.

Li Van's eyes rolled up into his head and his body went slack against West as he released the garrote.

Zara stepped over Li Van and Xiao Chen's bodies and pushed against the door. Who was flying the plane, if anyone?

"The door is like it's welded shut," Zara said, doing her best to reach inside.

"No one alive in there?" West asked.

"No one responding."

West looked at Zara and said, "Strap in." He pointed at the flight attendant seat. Zara sat down, stumbling into the pull-down retractable seat. West retrieved a twenty-foot rope from the stairwell of the pilot crew rest area. Zara had seen his go bag sitting at the base of the bed when she'd first gone into the crew rest area. West's reputation was that of a combat-oriented jack-of-all-trades, which seemed to be the case here. A garrote? Twenty feet of rope?

He tied a quick bowline knot around his waist and around an anchor bolt in the floor of the galley.

"We're close to the ground! Maybe fifteen-thousand feet!" he shouted. "That's a good thing!"

Normally at high altitudes, the pressure against an airplane door would make it an immovable object, sealed tightly against the frame of the aircraft barring a mishap. But once the aircraft broke through pressurization altitudes below ten thousand feet above ground level, the door could be opened. The middle ground, around fifteen thousand feet, and the plane was still pressurized, but less so.

West struggled and muttered, "These Boeing doors usually fall off by themselves." He eventually broke the seal and managed to create the depressurization event he desired. A large whooshing sound whistled inside the airplane. Unsecured napkins and snacks flew out the door. Importantly, the pressurization differential caused the cockpit blowout panels to explode off their hinges and land in the middle of the galley.

West momentarily got sucked to the gaping opening as the plane was screaming toward the mountains around Taipei, making him look like a jumpmaster conducting a door check. His bowline knot held in both locations, and he pulled against the rope with both hands. Zara reached out and clasped his forearm and pulled him in while remaining buckled in her seat. She continued to use her height and strength as leverage to counterlever the gravitational force pulling in the opposite direction. As she focused on saving West, it registered that both Li Van and Xiao Chen were not where they had been. Had they been sucked out of the door that West opened? She didn't recall seeing any bodies fly out, but it was certainly possible.

West climbed through the blowout panel hole in the cockpit and tossed his rope to Zara, who slid the tied loop around her waist and unbuckled the seat belt. The air rushing through the airplane was deafening.

Next, Zara followed West and also climbed through the blowout panel opening. Rogers was sufficiently wounded that they were immobile. Hawk Monroe, the pilot with access to TYRANT, had been dead for some time, his dried blood now caking on the controls in front of him.

West managed to sit in the pilot seat while Zara moved Monroe out of the copilot position. She stacked bodies behind them. The ground was rushing at them quickly. West played with dials and began maneuvering the throttle. She didn't have time to consider what had happened to Li Van and Xiao Chen.

Pulling the plane from a nosedive, West was able to bank it

away from a looming mountaintop. Zara knew that Taipei was surrounded by high hills or low mountains topping out around thirty-five hundred feet. They were so close to burning in. Could they avoid the next series of hilltops coming directly at them?

West said, "Hang on," and banked the lumbering jet as hard as possible to the right, the belly of the airplane narrowly missing the tree-lined top of the ridgeline. He powered up and pulled up, the plane ascending into the sky.

"Check to make sure we don't have any heroes coming to take over the cockpit," West said.

"Roger that," Zara replied.

As the plane leveled over the Taiwan Strait west of Taiwan, Zara stood at the ready with her reacquired pistol to stop any heroics.

West had saved the flight with his quick thinking.

"Oh, shit," West said.

Zara turned around and said, "What now?"

"I've got a lone wolf Chinese J-35 squawking me for friend or foe. I'm sure these clowns had some kind of code worked out."

"Fifty-fifty shot," Zara said.

West put the headset on and began talking to Taipei air traffic control. On his radar was the lone J-35 lurking menacingly out of sight.

"I'm squawking friend," West said.

"Okay," Zara said.

"Oh, shit. He just said, 'wrong answer,'" West said.

Zara stared at Hembrick's tablet on the floor. Whatever software that was on it was not functional, as the device was shattered and bent.

"He's lining up," West said.

"Do some pilot shit," Zara said.

"You got it," West replied.

He nosed the airplane over until it was screaming toward a high mountain range jutting out of the ocean.

Zara thought of Lucas and Lonnie and how much she loved her family and how that was all that ever mattered.

CHAPTER THIRTY-NINE

LUCAS SHERIDAN

*L*UCAS HEARD VOICES THAT SEEMED DISASSOCIATED FROM HIS reality.

He was lying on his side, staring at the concrete floor of his basement. Tactical boots were shuffling around him. Shards of glass were scattered across the cement. A rectangle of light shined on the wall across from him.

He heard more shots. His body jerked with each blast.

Mia, his father, Sheriff Barlowe.

What had he done? He had killed them all. That was what he had done.

Since he'd found the TYRANT box in the plane crash, trying to do a good deed, he had seen nothing but violence and destruction. If he could do it all over again, he would have left everything where it was and just come home. Maybe he could have broken up the fight between his mom and dad. Maybe Mia would still be alive. Maybe, maybe, maybe kept circling in his foggy mind like a gerbil in a wheel.

A bit of clarity seeped into his mind, though, as he remembered that he did help his mother by colliding the two Russian jets that were going to shoot her down. Maybe there was a purpose to his discovery. Maybe the bad things would have happened to the airplane even if he hadn't found the TYRANT platform. And unlike Kino, he didn't get greedy. He didn't try to sell the platform. He was simply trying to protect it from evildoers, which he discovered there were plenty of.

Regardless, he was vaguely aware that his father, best friend, and best friend's father were most likely dead by the gunshots he had just registered, and that he was most likely next. He didn't have time to be scared or do any big processing of the impending doom. Nothing flashed before his eyes. No big "Oh-my-God-my-life-is-over" moment. He was just a scared kid doing his best.

He felt hands tugging at him saying, "You have to finish this!"

It was the team leader and the IT guy, as Lucas had come to think of him. They were both on their knees trying to lift him up, slapping him in the face, and even pouring one of the water bottles he had brought down from the kitchen for him and Mia.

As they were down below Lucas's command center, footsteps thundered down the stairwell. Lucas knew his time was coming and that while he wasn't okay with it, he didn't have much choice in the matter and frankly deserved what he had coming.

"Sammie, give us a hand here with the kid," the team leader said.

Lucas's heart skipped a beat when he heard his father's voice say, "I'm not Sammie and you're not living."

A thunderous boom exploded in the basement. The team leader grabbed at his neck and rolled to his right, trying to decide whether to stop the bleeding that was obviously not going to stop or to grab his weapon. In the end, it didn't matter. The team leader bled out next to him.

The IT guy stood with his hands up and for a moment he thought his father was going to shoot him, too.

"Keep your hands up," Lonnie Sheridan said. "Lucas, get away from him."

Lucas did his best to crawl over the dying team leader and move to the north side of the basement.

"Move and you're a dead man. All your friends are dead or

dying up there. The sheriff has them under his control. He's call-ing in reinforcements."

Lucas watched the IT guy, who was staring at the computer monitors as he had been doing when Copperhead had come down the steps earlier.

"Dad! He's trying to crash Mom's airplane!"

"What?"

The IT guy looked at him and smiled.

"Smart kid," he said. He made a move for the pistol he had laid on the table, but Lonnie Sheridan's shotgun blew him back against the wall. The man was hit in the shoulder, but not dead. Lucas ripped the helmet off his head, blood dripping down the side. He placed the helmet on and returned to the monitors, say-ing, "Dad, make sure he doesn't get up."

He knew he sounded like a stone-cold killer giving his father an order to execute the man, but that wasn't entirely what he had meant. *Whatever*, he thought. He had to protect his mother.

He saw the plane plummeting but maneuvering. When he got a lock on the icon on the screen, the dialogue box read:

Manual Control.

Was that a good thing? That an actual pilot was flying the air-plane? If so, the pilot seemed to be doing some crazy stuff, be-cause he was flying directly toward the tallest mountain near Taipei.

Then Lucas realized what was happening.

A Chinese J-35 jet was maneuvering across the Taiwan Strait in the direction of the 777-300ER. He moved the cursor over the J-35 icon. The dropdown box showed that while the 777-300ER had signaled "Friend" to the J-35, the J-35 had instead armed all its weapon systems.

"He's trying to get behind the mountain," Lucas muttered to himself.

In his periphery, Lucas was aware of his father holding a gun to the IT guy's head.

"Lay flat on your stomach. Arms spread wide on the floor," his father said. "Lucas, do what you need to do. I trust you."

"Roger that, Dad," Lucas replied.

His father put a knee in the IT guy's back and used the man's own zip ties to lock him down before standing and walking over to Lucas. He put a large hand on his son's shoulder and didn't say a word.

It was comforting knowing his father trusted him to do whatever he needed to help save his mother.

"Save her," his father whispered. "Save them all."

The J-35 fired a missile, which the TYRANT program was tracking. It moved at Mach 2, giving his mom's airplane little time to do much in defense. There was no match between a sixth-generation Chinese fighter jet and a Boeing passenger airplane or a PL-10 short-range missile, as the TYRANT program was indicating.

The Boeing 777-300ER flew so close to the mountain that Lucas was certain it would crash. He clicked an icon that read "4D," which he used his eyes and heads-up display to highlight and activate.

The 4D image on the panel was a high-resolution portrayal of the terrain, like the metaverse. Rugged hills were covered in lush green trees and foliage. Deep ravines cut Vs into towering cliffs. The 777-300ER tilted and spun through a valley so narrow Lucas pushed his chair away from the table, expecting the plane to crash.

"No!" he shouted.

"What's going on?" his father barked.

But the plane was still flying according to the TYRANT imagery. Lucas used the cursor to pull an outline over the Chinese J-35 until the "Control?" prompt popped up. He focused on the spinning rainbow as TYRANT used brute cyber force to take control of the aircraft's weapons control systems.

The hack took longer than usual. He watched as the Boeing passenger plane flew low across the Taipei skyline, narrowly missing skyscrapers. Whoever was flying that plane, Lucas thought, was either going to crash it or was attempting to put buildings and mountains in between it and the J-35.

The 777-300ER flew over the massive roof of one building that read: TAIPEI SEMICONDUCTOR.

The plane banked hard, tilting on its wings, and flew toward Taipei-Taoyuan Airport, the big commercial airfield that handled all the international and domestic airline traffic. It was also a low-lying area within range of the J-35.

The race was for the airplane to land before the J-35 could shoot it down.

But what if the J-35 still had the mission to destroy Taipei Semiconductor, too?

He looked at the icon and the spinning rainbow had stopped. The status of the weapons showed that one DL-10 missile had been fired and that there were two PL-12 long-range missiles prepared to launch. Since these were guided missiles, Lucas guessed that one was for the airplane, and one was for the chip manufacturing plant.

Lucas thought that because the mission from the 777-300ER seemed to be failing, White Glacier most likely had given the go-ahead to China to do a straightforward attack.

Before Lucas could stop the J-35 jet from firing its missiles, they launched from the aircraft's weapons rack. Still, he hit "Disable" on the drop-down box and shut down any further missiles from the J-35.

He switched his attention to those that were launched and were seconds from impact. One was smoking a Mach 2 trail toward his mom's airplane and the other was headed directly to the manufacturing plant.

The only thing he really cared about was saving his mother. He couldn't care less about a big hedge fund and its profit and loss statements and some chip plant. He had to save his mother, but he didn't know how he could or what to do.

As the missiles flew on distinct paths, he moved the cursor over their path. He whispered to himself, "Yes," when dialogue boxes appeared over each one:

Control?

Could he control the flight of the missiles? It made sense because the missiles were programmed and monitored by the J-35.

He clicked "Yes" on both missiles and saw that the information in his helmet heads-up display changed. In the 4D metaverse imagery, the missile heads-up display now followed *his* eyes, not the eyes of the J-35 pilot. He saw the missile turn when he looked to the right and then back at his mother's airplane. He quit looking at the 777-300ER and focused solely on the J-35, like a child possessed, which perhaps he was. The technology followed his eyes and so he concentrated on the Chinese fighter jet.

The PL-12 missile turned and began to veer toward the J-35, whose pilot saw what was happening. The J-35 turned and sped away, conducting a variety of high-speed maneuvers. It spit chaff, shooting flaming aluminum and fiberglass into twirling arcs.

It was all to no avail. The PL-12 impacted with the J-35, which exploded in a bright fireball.

He quickly turned his attention to the next PL-12 missile, but with the destruction of the J-35, he lost all visibility of the rocket. He was now in wide field of view with multiple icons moving about the airspace. He watched as the missile spun wildly, slamming into a mountainside, having lost its guidance control mechanism.

Searching for his mother's airplane, he was helpless as he watched the icon rapidly descend toward the ground.

Then his entire command monitor blacked out, as if some Department of Defense cyber chief intentionally shut him down. Everything was black.

He pushed away from the table and said, "Oh, my God."

"What's going on?" his father asked.

"I'm not sure. Everything just blacked out."

"Is Zara okay?"

"I don't know, Dad. I don't know," he said in hurried voice. "I have to get out of here."

The weight of the last twenty-five hours descended upon him like a crashing wave. He looked at his father, then at his dad's knee in the IT guy's back. He glanced at the corpse of the man he had killed and found it hard to breathe.

So much death and destruction. Over what? A flash drive?

He ran upstairs and through the back kitchen door, where he saw three Copperhead men lying motionless on the ground. Sheriff Barlowe stood watch over them with his pistol and was talking on the phone, trying to call in an ambulance. Far in the backyard, Mia was on her knees, crying and hugging herself beneath the giant oak tree.

Lucas kept running, sprinting to her and then skidding to a stop. He asked, "Are you okay, Mia?"

His voice broke as he tried to talk. She was sobbing. Her body was heaving with soundless gasps. Hyperventilating.

Lucas hugged her from behind, but she turned and hugged him hard, placing her wet face on his shoulder.

"I thought you were going to die," she whispered through choked gasps. "I really thought so."

"I thought I had killed you," Lucas said. Now he was crying. Tears were running down his face.

Mia pulled away and looked at him.

"Killed me? Oh, my God, Lucas. You saved me. Us. Your mom. Everyone."

Lucas looked at her and saw Mia as the friend she was. Her eyes were wide and wet. Her flawless cheeks were red. Her hair was tangled and still somehow perfect.

Lucas looked away.

"I still don't know about Mom," he said.

"We need to find out," Mia replied. "Let's go."

Mia placed her arm over Lucas's shoulder as they limped into the kitchen through the splintered remains of the broken back door. Bullet holes riddled the back of his home. The helicopter had done a number on the wood and bricks. He sat Mia down in the sofa and propped her wounded leg on a pillow. Then turned on the television to find a news channel that might be carrying the 777-300ER in distress story. He scrolled through a dozen channels carrying talking heads discussing President Kim Camp-bell's reelection bid and her likely opponent. Politics bored Lucas. On YouTube TV, he found what he was looking for.

The television camera was focused on the Taipei airport and all they could see was flames.

"Oh, my God," they both said in unison.

CHAPTER FORTY

ZARA SHERIDAN

ZARA WATCHED AS RETIRED AIR FORCE COLONEL JEREMY WEST MA-
neuvered the lumbering commercial airplane through the steep
ravines north of Taipei as if he were jockeying a Next Generation
fighter jet.

"We're almost out of fuel," he said.

The fuel status was absolutely the last thing on Zara's mind.
The green valleys below and rising mountains above them
seemed so close that they might sheer off the wingtips. West tilted
the plane until it was canted at a forty-five-degree angle blowing
out of the valley onto the cityscape of Taipei.

They soared past high-rise office buildings and banked hard in
the opposite direction. Indicator lights were flashing like they'd
just won the slot machine jackpot. Oxygen masks dangled from
the ceiling like taunting puppets. The shouts from the main
cabin had become a cacophony. Zara looked through the mangled cockpit door and saw that some were praying, others screaming at them.

"What's the plan?" she asked West.

"Shit," he said.

"I mean besides that," she replied.

"No gas. No gas. No gas," he said. "Shit."

Through the cockpit window, they noticed a giant explosion in the distance over the ocean.

"I always hated flying," Zara said. Then, "Can you do a Sully?"

"About the only option we've got," West said.

He tried restarting the engines to no avail. He started talking to Zara as if she were a copilot.

"Turning on APU," he said.

The auxiliary power unit in the rear of the airplane could provide power to the flight controls. Zara listened and repeated the command to assure West that she was with him. Zara understood that this method was his training and he needed to do exactly as he had trained and perhaps even executed in "real life" previously. His eyes were focused on the horizon one moment and the controls the next.

"Turning on APU," she repeated.

He nodded.

"Throttles to idle," he said.

"Idle throttles," she repeated.

"Flaps two," he said. "Minimize drag."

"Minimize drag," Zara echoed.

West placed his headset microphone to his mouth and said, "Taipei Tower, this is TransPac 1001 calling for emergency services in the Tamsui River north of Luzhou."

"State nature of emergency," the tower controller replied.

"Complete failure of both engines. On glide path for river landing."

"Understand. Will clear the airspace. Move to channel 7755. We will coordinate emergency response."

"Roger, out," West said.

West spun the communications dial and changed the channel as directed.

"TransPac 1001 here. Assuming pitch angle of thirteen degrees, which should have us landing just north of Taipei Metro depot."

"This is the director of Taipei emergency services. Confirm no fuel."

"No fuel. Glider landing."

"Roger. Do you need any assistance in the air?"

"Keep airspace clear. Have boats in the water for my people."

After a moment of silence, the emergency services director said, "Reports of terrorist activity and Chinese attack. There are two United States F-35 jets that will monitor your landing."

"No," Zara said to West. "That's White Glacier telling the military what to do."

"Where are they?" West asked the director.

The plane was carving quietly through the sky, aiming directly at a bridge connecting old Taipei and New Taipei cities.

"We have given clearance for two US naval jets from the Ronald Reagan Carrier Strike Group to escort you," the director said.

"We decline the escort. We are crash landing in the river and do not need escort," West said. He maneuvered some dials to adjust the glide path.

"You're doing your pilot stuff, but to an army MP, it looks like we're going to hit that big bridge," Zara said.

"Possible," West remarked.

She snapped her head in his direction, a slight smirk on his face.

Ice water in his veins, Zara thought.

"They are approaching Taiwanese airspace at Mach two and have been given clearance," the director replied.

"Again, we do not need their support," West said.

"The bridge," Zara said, pushing back in her seat, bracing for impact. The suspension bridge towers loomed large, as did the cables angling upward to the peaks of the saddles housing them.

"Should be okay," West whispered. Less sure this time. He spun a dial and adjusted a flap.

"Should be," Zara repeated.

"American jet support on station," the director said. "You are up on comms with them."

Two F-35s buzzed close to the Boeing 777-300ER. The wake from the wing foil caused turbulence that was unnecessary and not helpful.

"Told you," Zara said.

West nodded.

The plane passed over the bridge between the two towers, wings narrowly missing the U shape of the cables.

"Obstacle number one down," West said. "Glide path confirmed."

They were less than ten thousand feet above the river now, flanked by steep mountains on one side and skyscrapers on the other.

"TransPac 1001, this is Reaper 20, state your intentions."

The voice was most likely the US pilot lead of the two F-35 Joint Strike Fighters.

"Reaper 20, this is TransPac 1001," West said. "Intentions are to land with no engines in the river in about twenty seconds."

"Say again, you're breaking up," the voice said.

West repeated himself.

"Still cannot understand. Breaking up. Must declare you hostile."

"Jesus, after all this, we're going to be shot down by the United States Navy?" Zara said.

"This was a DoD operation all along?" West said. "What? The president needs a poll boost, so she starts a war?"

He was fuming, but it was the best explanation Zara had heard yet.

"The good news is we have no fuel to cause a secondary explosion when the missiles hit."

"Don't give me the bad news," Zara said.

"I'll be quiet then."

Zara found herself in that continuous bracing for impact posture, wondering when the missiles might strike. West adjusted some dials and tilted the nose up to increase pitch.

"Fly-by-wire pitch at nine and a half degrees."

"Nine and a half degrees," Zara said.

The first missile inexplicably missed the TransPac plane and slammed into the bridge, destroying one of the supports and dumping cars into the river. The second missile flew wildly into the mountainside, exploding in a small hamlet.

"Flaring aircraft and putting airplane in ditch mode."

"Flare and ditch," Zara repeated.

In her periphery, she noticed movement. Instinctively springing from her seat, she delivered a high kick to Major Li Van's bloody throat. She couldn't understand how he had lived. Perhaps he had faked his death. He was a wrestler and martial arts expert.

Her foot landed under his chin and snapped his neck upward. The laceration from West's garrote was deep but evidently had not severed the jugular vein or carotid artery. Perhaps the bulging muscles in his neck had protected those vital conduits.

His face was a demonic mask as he stumbled backward into the galley. Zara tried to shut the cockpit door, but it was too damaged and wouldn't budge. Wasting no time, she pursued Li Van with a series of high kicks to the wounded neck. More blood flowed. She drew her pistol, but Li Van was quick, lunging with a double-leg takedown. Zara parried the thrust, but ultimately did not escape his tight grip on her right leg. He lifted her toward the open starboard door that was wide open, filling with air screaming into the cockpit.

Li Van hugged her leg tight, making maneuvering impossible. She bounced on her left leg, which opened her femoral artery to Xiao Chen's arcing knife. He appeared from behind the curtain separating the galley from the first-class cabin. Rudimentary first-aid bandages patched his neck and head. Li Van had saved him if for no other reason than to change the battlefield geometry of the tubular tactics inside the aircraft. At the last moment, she spun hard, twirling in the air like a gymnast, eluding Li Van's grip and narrowly missing Xiao Chen's slicing knife.

The aerial maneuver, however, landed her next to the open door. The plane was well below five thousand feet, negating any pressurization that might have resulted in being sucked out of the plane. Still, the door was open, and, judging by the bared teeth and severe facial contortions, her two descending attackers were filled with rage. She presumed they had abandoned their plan and now were just intent on creating havoc and killing her for disrupting their efforts.

Her hair was blowing in the breeze outside the open service door. Her head was inches from the lip of the opening. On her back, the bowline knot and rope that West had used fluttered within arm's reach.

"I am the Night Viper of Silent Fang," Li Van spat. "You don't win!"

The plane was still a few thousand feet above the river. She could see the mountains to the north as Li Van raised his boot to stomp her face. She spun and slipped the bowline knot around Li Van's ankle, tripped him, and used his momentum to push him through the opening, like a hung static line jumper.

Xiao Chen was wounded and moved slowly toward her, like a man about to die. She landed a flurry of rabbit punches to his bruised and battered face, then flipped him over her shoulder onto the floor. With an unceremonious shove of her foot, she rolled his weakened body through the gap into the terrain below.

She grabbed both sides of the door frame and risked a look. She caught the sight of Chen's body tumbling over large boulders and into the river. Li Van was dangling head down, all the blood rushing to his lacerated neck. Still, he had a knife that was sawing away at the rope, which gave way directly prior to the plane hitting the water.

She rushed back into the cockpit and belted into the copilot's seat as best she could.

"Everything okay?" West asked, focused on his task at hand.

"No issues," Zara replied. "Now land this puppy."

"Doing that, but who or what are Night Viper and Silent Fang?"

"Dead in the river, I hope. All of whatever that is."

West nodded.

The nose of the airplane lifted as the tail began skimming the river surface. Ditch mode on an airplane sealed all the vents and openings to make it more survivable in a water landing. The screaming from the cabin was out of control, but West focused on the task at hand.

As he brought the nose down, the airplane slowed to 140 knots, just above stall speed. When the back third of the fuselage impacted with the water, the aircraft's velocity slowed considerably. West bled off the speed by gently dragging the tail and then the back third of the aircraft in the murky river.

When he was approaching one hundred miles per hour, he had to lower the engines into the river, keeping them angled as much as possible, but they ultimately served as brakes when the open turbine faces sucked in the water. The aircraft slowed, then stopped with a suddenness that pulled Zara forward against her seat belt harness with significant gravitational force.

She looked at West, who was staring ahead, and not even Zara could believe they were still alive.

For now.

Soon, the head flight attendant, Susan, was on the intercom walking the passengers through the emergency evacuation process. The wing doors were opened and inflated safety ramps deployed.

Zara and West moved quickly through the aisles helping every passenger. Taiwanese helicopters began circling overhead and safety boats rushed to the rescue.

As she was the second to last person exiting ahead of West, Zara realized she held the tablet that Hembrick of Copperhead had been using. She stepped on the gunwale of the rubber raft and let the Taiwanese security team guide her onto the boat. West was next. She looked at the tablet, which blinked to life, and saw the image of the 777-300ER in the water with a red "Protect" box flashing around it.

With sudden clarity, she realized that Lucas had used the TYRANT program to somehow keep her airplane safe. With the sunlight shining in her eyes, she held on to the center console as the rescue boat bobbed in the water. Four Taiwanese SWAT members came out and shouted, "All clear!"

They carried Xiao Chen's body and dumped it in the boat at Zara's feet. General Wang and Johnnie Wilson were in their wake, Wang evidently commanding a modicum of respect from the military team.

"Found floating in the river about a half mile back," one of the paramedics said as he nudged Chen's body with his foot.

"Should be another body," Zara said.

"Nothing so far," he replied.

Zara looked at Xiao Chen, the instigator. His face was badly bruised from the impact in the water while the plane was traveling one hundred miles per hour. He was nearly lifeless when she had encountered him one final time.

"My apologies for the actions of my aide," General Wang said. He bowed his head and stepped away as two military members escorted him. Johnnie Wilson followed in his wake.

Indeed, Li Van was a different story, Zara thought. Her instinct that he was no aide-de-camp had been a solid call. Seemingly indestructible, Li Van had continued to pursue her. She would not sleep well until the Taiwanese found his body and confirmed his death. Then she thought of Hembrick and Copperhead and the utter violence they had imposed on her and her family as well as the passengers.

"There's plenty more in there. Copperhead guys. The second hijack team. They'll fill another boat," Zara said.

The patrolman understood and nodded at the captain of the boat, who revved the engine and sped to the ferry landing.

Finally, she turned to West and said, "Good job."

West looked over his shoulder at the airplane and said, "One of my smoother landings."

Zara smiled. "Can't believe it's still floating."

"No gas in the tanks. It will be up there for a while."

They climbed the ladder to the asphalt parking lot and turned to take one last look. The massive airplane sat idle in the brown river. On the far bank, a hulking man was clawing his way out of the river over large rocks and through a mucky inclined bank. He stumbled and looked over his shoulder, locking eyes momentarily with Zara before climbing into the dense green forest.

"Li Van?" Zara asked.

"You had a better look at him than me, but with names like Night Viper and Silent Fang, it wouldn't surprise me that he slithered away."

She placed a hand to her side, instinctively reaching for her pistol that wasn't there. All the rescue personnel were busy tending to the passengers they had ferried off the wings of the airplane. The police helicopters continued circling the airplane, and local cops were directing traffic. There was no one who could go after the escaping Olympic wrestler, who had found a path to survival.

She looked at the throng of passengers huddled in the parking lot. She locked eyes with Carrie Starlight, the astrologer who had warned her about Mars or Venus or something going on with the stars. They nodded at each other as Starlight mouthed "thank you" from across the distance.

A black Suburban stopped behind them. The passenger window buzzed down. A man in sunglasses, suit coat, and tie called out, "Sheridan!"

Zara and West walked to the Suburban while the Taiwanese police sorted through the teeming crowd of rescued passengers.

"Who's asking?" Zara said. She stood an arm's length from the Suburban.

"General Garrett Sinclair," the man said.

Zara looked at the man's exposed arm purposefully propped on the passenger door. The underside of his wrist sported a two-inch-wide blue rhombus-shaped tattoo with the letters *SGS*. She knew this was the mark of a Sharpstone Global Security agent.

She turned her wrist outward to him, as did West, and they all exchanged bona fides.

Zara and West slid into the backseat of the SUV. The agent

handed her a phone in the process of a FaceTime call with General Garrett Sinclair, the founder of Sharpstone Global Security. His steely eyes, gray hair, and prominent jawline filled the screen.

"Jeremy, I thought you were a better pilot than that," Sinclair said.

"Still learning, boss."

"Back to remedial training for you," Sinclair joked. "Zara. Hell of a job."

"Night Viper got away, General. You know this guy?"

"We've been tracking both Xiao Chen, Night Viper, and other Silent Fang assassins for a couple years. We've got teams on the ground now to track him down north of Taiwan. Not your mission."

"Roger that," Zara said.

"Besides, you almost single-handedly stopped World War Three."

"Almost? Single-handedly?" Zara replied.

Sinclair withdrew his face from the iPhone, and instead of his chiseled features, she was looking at the oak tree in her backyard.

"You've got a hell of a son," Sinclair said. "Future Sharpstone commando right here."

Lucas popped into view. He had Mia's arm draped around him. His lip started trembling, but he held it together.

"I'm so sorry, Mom. It was all my fault."

"Lucas, you and Mia saved the Free World with a little bit of help from your mom," Sinclair said.

"Baby, listen to the general. What you did by finding the TYRANT platform was critical," Zara said.

Her own lips trembled some. There was her son and his best friend standing with her former boss, who had probably helicoptered in from somewhere to protect them. The phone spun a bit and her husband, Lonnie, was standing in the background speaking with Sheriff Barlowe.

Lonnie saw the conversation and walked next to General Sinclair, placing his arm around Lucas. Sheriff Barlowe appeared next to Mia, and it was all too much for Zara. She broke, not even knowing half of what Lucas and Mia had been through. But if the sheriff and General Sinclair were there, it had to have been bad.

"Zara, everything's going to be okay, baby," Lonnie said. "And I mean everything."

CHAPTER FORTY-ONE

PRESIDENT KIM CAMPBELL

"STANLEY, IS THAT ATTACK ENOUGH?" PRESIDENT KIM CAMPBELL asked from behind the Resolute Desk in the Oval Office. "I mean, I thought White Glacier and Clouded Leopard had this thing covered."

Seated in front of her was White Glacier Private Equity chairman and CEO, General Michael "Stanley" Stanhope. His black hair was gelled and slicked back. He was thick through the middle and his white shirt pushed through the open lapels of his navy Italian suit. His pink tie fell from his neck and rose again as it lay across his belly. His right leg appeared to be uncomfortably crossed over his left, showing off two-thousand-dollar Italian loafers and black silk socks.

"I talked to Phu-Shen last night," Stanhope said.

The president gave him a blank stare.

"She owns Clouded Leopard Private Equity," he said.

"Oh, right," Campbell said.

"Night Viper and Sharp Lotus handled Xiao Chen, who, like his grandfather, failed at his mission."

"No kidding," Campbell said. "They created a giant clusterfuck."

"They never found Major Li Van, known as Night Viper. Marshal Sheridan reported him running into the woods north of the river where the plane landed. Your friend Garrett Sinclair has a

Sharpstone Global Security team on the ground trying to find him.

"I couldn't give two rats' asses about some Chinese operative that failed his mission. I want to know if I have enough to spank China. And leave Garrett out of this for now."

"Kim, that bastard Jeremy West made a spectacle by landing in the river. If he had just landed at the airport, we could have stuck with the plan. Once I got the report the mission was going sideways, I told the SecDef to get a couple of jets up there to knock it down as a threat, but, and this never happens, the missiles missed."

"TYRANT?"

"TYRANT does have a protect feature we've been exploring where the protected entity, in this case the airplane, emits a signal that scrambles the waypoints and guidance systems of any GPS-guided missiles coming at it. It's a hell of a cyberattack and counterattack platform. May be what happened here. Not sure. But Sinclair will have the tablet with the platform, and that's a problem. And Sheridan's kid has it on his hard drive."

"Because this Zara Sheridan person will give the TYRANT platform to Garrett?"

"She and West have already linked up with the Sharpstone team. I'm sure that's part of the plan. If they give it back to DoD, then we're good. I've got the SecDef in my pocket. Twenty-million-a-year salary guaranteed once he finishes."

"Should I call Garrett?"

"That's your call, Madam President," Stanhope said.

Kim Campbell and Sinclair's deceased wife Melissa had been college roommates in Raleigh, North Carolina. Sinclair had led President Campbell's special mission unit, called Dagger. The relationship was a complicated one in which Campbell trusted Sinclair completely because of his ethos and dedication to the country. Meanwhile, she knew that the matter was more complicated for Sinclair. He wanted to trust her, she suspected, but didn't completely believe her all the time. There was always that suspicion that she might have her own agenda.

And of course, he was right.

"Let me think about it."

Stanhope held out his hand as if to say, "Your prerogative."

"So, the entire fleet of advanced Taiwanese fighters was destroyed. A US commercial plane is in the river. And we can't fight back."

"We can. Maybe we should. But it's not as clean as it could have been. And China issued a statement that Taiwan provoked it and seeks no further conflict with their own people. Kind of a hard statement to beat back. Kind of like Iran launching two hundred missiles at Israel and saying, 'We're done. Peace out.'"

"So, China is walking it back and we can't attack?"

"Well, you're the president. You can do anything you want."

"But you promised me stealth. To shut down the Taiwanese Air Force. Controlled attacks by Chinese fighter jets. All of that."

"And I delivered most of it. That kid and his mom got in the way. Dirtied it up. It was almost flawless."

"If a kid and his mom can beat the most advanced technology in the world, how advanced can it be?"

Stanhope looked away.

"He's a smart kid. She's a good operator," he said. "And like I said, he still has TYRANT."

"I don't want to hear that bullshit," Campbell said. "Let me think about my options. Don't harm Garrett, but you can do whatever you want to this Sheridan lady. And West needs to be punished, as well."

"The kid?" Stanhope asked. "We need to get TYRANT from his hard drive."

"Do what you need to do to protect our state secrets," Campbell said. She stared at him for a long moment and then turned away.

Stanhope brushed off his pants legs, planted his feet, stood, and said, "Roger that. Pleasure to see you, Madam President."

He left the office as Campbell spun around in her chair and closed her eyes. How had she become such a craven member of the Washington, DC, game? With flagging poll numbers and re-election looming, all she needed was a tidy little war where she could exert her leadership and show the world what a tough bitch she was.

Instead, she had just put out a hit on a mom and a kid.

She looked through the Oval Office window. The cherry trees were budding. *New life and all that happy horseshit,* she thought.

An airplane followed the Potomac River as it lowered toward Ronald Reagan Washington National Airport. Its silvery wings cut against the blue sky and the Arlington skyline. The National Mall was teeming with happy high schoolers on spring break trips.

No, she thought, Washington, DC, politics was the dirtiest game of them all, and she concluded that she was no better than a mob boss erasing people who could do her harm. Despite the blossoming white and pink flowers, in Kim Campbell's dark mind, there was no new life—there was only the life you could hang on to until it was taken from you.

She had tasked certain individuals and teams to kill before and she would continue to do so until she was reelected. Then maybe she would reconsider.

But she doubted it.

GLOSSARY

Swan Quarter

Zara Sheridan, air marshal
Lucas Sheridan, son
Lonnie Sheridan, husband and ferry maintenance
Lincoln White, CSM (R), Zara's father
Sheriff Barlowe, Swan Quarter sheriff
Mia Barlowe, Lucas's best friend
Sandy Acton, Mia and Lucas's teacher and tutor
Deputy Cashwell

777-300ER Pilots

Logan "Titan" Prescott, chief pilot
Richard "Hawk" Monroe, colonel and copilot
Jeremy West, backup pilot
Alisha McCord, fourth pilot

777-300ER Crew

Marcus Jones, head flight attendant from Grifton, North
Carolina
Amanda Gāo, second-in-command of flight crew
Julie Chang, flight attendant
Priscilla, flight attendant
Agent Lloyd Bucknell, head marshal

Copperhead Security

Joshua Hembrick, Army Green Beret communications specialist
Terrance Rogers, former navy P-8 pilot
Juan Rodriguez, former marine infantryman
Garland Maximoff, Copperhead CEO
Clark, TSA agent

Taiwanese Military

General John Wang, deputy commander of the Taiwanese Air
Force
Major Li Van, aide-de-camp (also Night Viper)

TYRANT Platform

Johnnie Wilson, aerospace engineer with Blackwood Aviation,
owned by White Glacier
Rachel Fox, major general and Hyperion X director

China

Xiao Chen
Silent Fang
Night Viper
Sharp Lotus

Notable Passengers

Carrie Starlight, astrologer and yoga instructor
North Carolina State sweatshirt guy
Nautical preppie tall guy

Private Equity

Michael "Stanley" Stanhope, White Glacier chairman
Phu Shen, Clouded Leopard CEO

ACKNOWLEDGMENTS

Thank you to the entire team at Trident Meida Group who surrounded Scott Miller's authors with care and compassion upon his passing. All of us are heartbroken and thinking of his family. Mark Gottlieb is filling Scott's large shoes in stride, and I appreciate his and Trident's guidance and commitment to this book and the others to come. Thank you to Kristen Bertoloni, as well, Scott's last assistant, who steadfastly served as a conduit as Scott bravely battled his illness.

Gary Austin was by my side every step of the way since we were Little League baseball players. He was there every time I returned from West Point for the brief summer breaks and every time I returned from a deployment. He and his family, Susie, Wes, Reed, and Parker, were and are the epitome of friendship. Gary attended every Virginia Beach book signing for all 16 books and typically brought a crowd of friends. When I made Gary a cameo character in one of my first novels, *Rogue Threat*, he most likely sold more copies at our local Barnes & Noble than anywhere else in the country. I miss him daily.

Thank you to the great team at Kensington Books, including my former editor Gary Goldstein, now retired from the business, who had the high concept for this novel, "Hijack but different." And to my new editor James Abbate, whose consistent support and expert feedback has already made me a better author. Thanks to Kensington production editor Robin Cook for her patience and flexibility. Lastly, I appreciate Steven Zacharius welcoming me back into the Kensington family. Working with the old team today reminds me why I loved Kensington from the very beginning. It's good to be back.

Thanks to Kaitlin Murphy Knudsen, my writing coach, who uses good humor and a ruler to knuckles to make me a better author.

Life has moved at a quickening pace recently, and I'd like to thank my two children, Brooke and Zach, their spouses, Peter and

Lindsey, and my grandchildren, Allison Kate, Leonardo Anthony, and Maddox James for reminding me daily what life is all about.

The past year has included some professional milestones that would not have been achievable without the encouragement of hundreds of friends, colleagues, and family around the country, and I thank everyone for their support.

Lastly, thanks to my wife Laura and our two little guys, Snowy and Bandit, for standing by and loving me in the good times and tough times. Having your constant love and support makes it all worthwhile.